DEFTI

PAULINE MANDERS

Published in 2024 by Ottobeast Publishing
ottobeastpublishing@gmail.com

Cover design by Pika Creative Ltd.
www.pika-creative.com

ISBN 9781912861200

A CIP catalogue record for this title is available from the
British Library.

This novel is written using English (British / UK) with
some light swearing. International spelling, terms, and
phrases may slip in from time to time.

To Paul, Fiona, Alastair, Karen, Andrew, Katie and Mathew

MONDAY

Pember Quinn sat at his desk, bowed his head, and massaged his forehead. *How much longer will this meeting last?* When would the dark-haired woman who sat facing him leave*?*

'So, you'll investigate it for me?' she ended. He reckoned she must be about thirty-five-years old. And assertive. She'd done most of the talking so far. In fact, she'd talked solidly for the past twenty minutes, her soft Canadian accent sounding so out of place in rural Suffolk that it could have been mistaken for an affectation.

He didn't answer. He couldn't.

She waited a moment, as if for his agreement, and then stood up, pushing the no-frills, standard, conference chair backwards. 'Good.' Her voice sharpened, now businesslike. When she spoke, she rolled her Rs low in her mouth, 'It's with the coroner. I want everything investigated before the inquest. I've left you a copy of the post-mortem report. Get back to me once you're done with it. Give it priority, eh? No stones left unturned.'

He sat, feeling her eyes on him, but he didn't look up. He was consumed by the squealing in his right ear. *God, it's happening again.* The pressure in it rose, ready to explode.

He took a deep breath and raised his head, but no one was there. The office door was partly open. She must have left already, not even waiting to hear him out.

'I'll be in touch, Mrs Alconbury,' he said to the vacated chair.

He caught the clicks of her heels on the laminate floor at

the head of the stairs. The harsh, snappy sounds felt like a trigger. The pressure inside his ear dispersed. His world launched into sudden rotation. Faster and faster the room spun around him. He closed his eyes, but the movement didn't stop despite his self-imposed darkness. Nausea gripped his stomach.

He slumped onto his desk, but the flat surface couldn't slow the rotations. He slithered further, collapsing onto the office floor. He grabbed the wastepaper bin and vomited into it.

Time had no meaning for the next couple of hours – the slightest movement triggering the spinning sensation. *Why do I have to suffer these bouts of vertigo?* He resented it with every ounce of his stocky frame. It was like a captive demon buried deep in his inner ear. The doctors called it Ménière's Disease, but he called it Flossy after an army counsellor had suggested he find his own name for it.

'It'll make the Ménière's seem less threatening, Staff Sergeant Quinn. Give it a harmless, silly tag and it'll be cut down to size. Stop it controlling you and your mind,' the counsellor had explained.

'Then I'll call it Flossy, sir.'

'Flossy?'

'Yes, Flossy – the Alaska pet rabbit I had as a kid, sir.'

'But that's an excellent name. Soft. Fluffy.'

'Yes, sir.'

He'd failed to tell the counsellor that Flossy, like all rabbits, needed to keep gnawing. Even the name Alaska was a misnomer. Her luxurious fur harked back to her origins in Germany where she'd been bred to make her coat resemble an Alaska fox. But Flossy wasn't exotic or rarely seen; she was as firmly present as her foxy disguise and constantly nibbled.

And so, it had become his private joke – and despite the innocent rabbit's ever-growing teeth and misleading name, the irony always raised an inner smile. So maybe, the army counsellor had been of some help after all.

Pember knew the routine. If he stayed still, the spinning would stop, and he could sink into an exhausted, drifting sleep. The hissing in his right ear was almost soothing. The blocked feeling was just more damage to his hearing. Good ol' Flossy.

***

Clive Merry climbed the narrow staircase. The sign at the entrance door to the building read THE HATTER STREET PRIVATE INVESTIGATION AGENCY 2ND FLOOR.

The stairs creaked under Clive's tread, the old wood complaining. Like many of the buildings in the ancient heart of Bury St Edmunds in Suffolk, it was several hundred years old. Clive's curiosity grew as he climbed, distancing himself from the shoppers flowing along the busy Abbeygate Street nearby. The text message he'd received had been brief. *I'm in Bury St Edmunds. Look me up – Hatter Street PIA.* And the sender ID? *P Quinn.*

So why had Pember set up as a private investigator here? A stab of excitement stoked Clive's curiosity. *Will I recognise my old friend?* A man could change in eighteen years.

The second flight of stairs turned sharply and ended on a landing. A wormed beam spanned the open ceiling, the space stretching up through exposed attic to the sloping roof above. A skylight shed watery April sunshine onto the landing and stairwell. It felt old world but touched by modern times, and an architect. The trick of the light and the laminate flooring made it seem almost spacious.

There were two doors onto the landing. One was partly open, and Clive strode towards it, not even breathless from the climb. He knocked on the door.

'Hello? Anyone there?' he asked and stepped into the room. A quick glance told him it was an office, with a desk, a couple of conference chairs, and a faux leather office chair completing the décor. It was a swatch card of neutral shades, apart from the brightly coloured Toby jugs. They stood proud, an announcement on the row of three-drawer filing cabinets set against one wall. The sight of them jolted Clive back to his childhood. For a moment he was transfixed by them, but a sweet, slightly acid smell hung in the air. The odour drew him back to the office.

'What the hell?' Clive breathed as something else caught his eye.

The lower half of a man's body lay motionless on the sisal matting. He was on his back, the rest of him hidden by the desk. Two strides and Clive crouched beside him. The man's eyes were closed, his head to one side and an arm around a wastepaper bin. *Is he dead?* He looked pale enough, despite the unshaven, five o'clock shadow. Clive touched his hand. The skin felt warm.

'Is it you, Pember? Hey, wake up!' He gave the man's shoulder a gentle prod. There was no response.

Clive felt for a pulse and watched for the rise and fall of the chest. He knelt to get his ear closer to the man's parted lips. He felt, more than heard, the soft warmth of an exhaled breath.

'Right, I'll call an ambulance.'

'No-o-o,' the man moaned and stirred, turning his head.

4

'Aargh.' He put a hand to his eyes. 'Shouldn't have moved so fast.'

'Pember!' Clive would have recognised his old friend's voice anywhere. Appearances might change, but voices less so. This time he looked for more than signs of life as he studied the man. He caught the traces of a young Pember in the weathered face beneath the stubble. *Yes – there's even the tell-tale scar under his chin.* The man was stockier than he remembered, and the brown hair thinner and shorter. 'My God, Pember. What the hell's happened?'

The man uncovered his eyes and squinted, seemingly searching Clive's face, but making no attempt to speak, just the hint of a smile.

'You look bloody awful. Are you sure you don't need an ambulance?'

'No. I'm better now – just need to rest here a bit longer. Good to see you, Clive.'

'If this is "better", what the hell were you like before?' Clive scanned the room again. There were no obvious signs of a break-in or fight, but the state of the wastebin told a tale. 'You've thrown up. What's wrong? A sick bug? Hung over? What?'

'Huh. The great detective, Clive Merry.'

'You always were a sarcastic bastard, Pember,' Clive chuckled.

'Yeah. You got my text.' He spoke slowly, as if the effort of talking was exhausting, 'I wondered how long it'd take you to visit.'

'Not soon enough, judging by the state of you!' Clive cast another glance around the room, 'This office doesn't seem like you, Pember.'

'It's complicated. Hey, my tablets are in the desk. Top

drawer, righthand side. Get them for me, will you?'

Straightening up, Clive raised a questioning eyebrow. *Was his friend into drugs now?* He bit his lip but didn't voice his fear.

'If I'd taken my bloody meds…'

'You're on meds? Regular meds?' *Thank God I didn't ask about drugs.* Clive might be retired now, but the thirty-five years spent working as a police officer were ingrained. Perhaps he shouldn't have suspected his friend of a drug habit, but in his own defence, Clive knew Pember had always been impulsive. Drugs and alcohol weren't an unreasonable assumption. Clive rummaged through the drawer. The names on the packs of medicines were either Serc or Stemetil. He was none the wiser. He racked his brains. *Was his childhood friend seriously ill?*

'The last I heard, Pember, you were still in the army. A red cap heading out to Iraq.'

'Yeah, that will've been 2006.' He paused, 'You know they discharged me to pension a year early?'

'Hah! Let me guess. You messed up, broke too many rules?' Clive grinned, happily slipping into banter.

'Nah, it was my health. 2009. I never got to make twenty-two years.'

'Ah, I'm sorry. You should've got in touch.'

'I did. I texted you last week.'

'No, I meant years ago. After you were discharged.'

Pember sighed. 'Are you going to give me those tablets?'

'Yes, of course. Which ones?'

'Both.'

Thirty minutes had passed and Pember rested on the partly reclined office chair, his eyes half-closed and its tall back supporting his head.

Clive had made himself comfortable on one of the conference chairs. He felt at ease in Pember's company. An initial awkwardness was predictable, but the chemistry had always been there, even from the start of their primary school days, just as it was today. He'd spent the time looking through the open file on Pember's desk. It drew him, grabbing his attention in a way nothing else had since his retirement.

He'd opted for the police minimum pension age of 55. It was still early days, in fact barely a couple of months since he'd cleared his desk and handed in his police ID card. But his retirement-age and pension choices came with smaller payouts. He'd expected it to bite financially but he was surprised; he had never imagined it would be a post-mortem report that could make him pine for his police-working days.

He knew he'd miss the camaraderie of a police team, with its shared purpose and pooling of information. He'd always relished bouncing ideas off other professionals, and he enjoyed the challenge of solving a case. It was as essential to him as breathing air. It was his lifeblood. He glanced at Pember.

'You're a better colour now,' Clive said and smiled.

'Yeah, the meds have kicked in.'

'Good. I've been looking through this file…Mrs Alconbury. There isn't much here. I've read the post-mortem report. What's her angle?'

'Hah, that could be a problem.'

'Why?'

'Because Flossy grabbed my attention when Mrs Alconbury dropped by this morning.'

Clive frowned. 'Flossy?' He wasn't going to make the mistake of asking about a drug habit.

'I've got Ménière's Disease. I've been good for a while but moving here and setting up, well I guess it's set it off again.'

Something clicked into place in Clive's brain, 'Good for a while? Is that why you were discharged to pension early?'

'Yeah, I was about to hit forty, and then Flossy hit me.'

'And Flossy's…your name for, what did you call it? Anywhere's Disease?'

'Ménière's Disease.'

Memories came flooding back. 'Didn't you have a rabbit called Flossy?'

Pember sighed. 'Yeah, I did.'

'That's dark, even for you, Pember.'

'Nah. It's irony.'

'Like your old man's Toby jugs up there?' Clive inclined his head, as if pointing to Aramis, Porthos and Athos, the three musketeer characters on the jugs on the filing cabinets.

Neither man spoke for a few minutes.

'My Ménière's struck again this morning,' Pember said, breaking the silence. 'I've had warnings, pressure building in my ear, and tinnitus. But I didn't want to believe it.'

'Thought you'd ride it out?'

'Yeah, well you know me.' He paused as if pulling his thoughts together, 'It's my inner ear, deep in the bone. Balance and hearing. I'm okay for ages, and then *wham!* I'm dizzy again.'

'Like this morning?'

'Hmm.' Pember tapped his right ear, 'At the moment I'm a bit deaf in there.'

Clive wasn't entirely sure he understood this Ménière's thing, but Pember had always been tough; a knock-me-down-and-I'll-get-straight-back-up kind of guy. Nor had he been one to dwell on illness. Clive changed track, 'So what does Mrs Alconbury want?'

'I didn't catch all she said.'

'Yes, but you know if she's Morton Alconbury's wife or mother?'

'Wife.'

'And you know something about diving?'

'Nah.' Pember shrugged. 'Up to her if she wants to waste her money.'

'Okay. Well according to this,' he picked up the open file, 'Morton Alconbury died about five weeks ago while SCUBA diving in a disused chalk or lime quarry. The pathologist's report sums up with *no obvious underlying cardiac, cardiovascular, or pulmonary disease to primarily cause the,*' Clive read more slowly from the report, '*fatal Immersion Pulmonary Oedema. The condition was brought on by the dive.*'

'So, it was a diving accident?'

'I don't know. It looks like they did a whole body MDCT scan, whatever that is. But there's no report here, just the pathologist saying *Morton Alconbury's multi-detector CT scan* - of course, the MDCT - *was reported as too delayed to confidently interpret the distribution of gases and establish those from the dive and those from natural post mortem decomposition. The CT appearances of the lungs and chest are reported as compatible with immer-*

9

sion pulmonary oedema. There's no coroner's report.'

'Mrs Alconbury said the inquest is coming up.'

'So, are there any investigators' reports? No doubt the police handed it over to Health & Safety, or dive investigators.'

'Dive investigators?'

'You know, dive specialists. They mostly work for insurance companies. But Health & Safety may have commissioned one.'

'Yeah, but–'

'I know, they'll report back to the insurers. It'll be about liability. The does-the-insurer-have-to-pay-a-negligence-or-a-life-insurance-claim kind of thing. But the coroner will have legal access to the report. So, does Mrs Alconbury think you're a specialist diving investigator? And, what's her angle? How did she leave it with you?'

Pember closed his eyes and almost imperceptibly, shook his head.

'You're not sure? Hell Pem! Right, okay. It shouldn't be a problem finding out who Morton Alconbury was diving with. Then we can talk to them. And we've got the date and location of the fatal dive. So, do you want me to start scratching around for you?'

Clive couldn't believe what he'd just offered to do.

***

'Yeah, I'm going to need help,' Pember muttered to the office, the Doulton character jugs on the filing cabinets, anyone who'd listen.

At least his brain fog had lifted after sitting quietly. But what of his balance? It was fine while resting on his office chair, but could he ride his Yamaha Tracer 900? No. The motorbike would have to wait until the medications had stabilised his ear again. Added to that, Mrs Alconbury had come across as demanding. She'd be breathing down his neck, wanting results.

'Of course you'll need help. That's why I said I can start scratching around the Alconbury case for you.' Clive still sat opposite him, the pale-wood desk separating them. He exuded an air of calm.

But hadn't it always been like this with Clive? Pember the one muscling into situations, and Clive, the taller, more articulate one talking them out of the mess? Back at school in Norwich, Clive would have been…well, frankly boring if Pember hadn't got them both into scrapes. And Pember, for his part, would likely have been excluded from school if it hadn't been for Clive's steadying influence. It was why Clive joined the police force, but Pember signed up to the army and joined the Military Police, because of course Pember wanted to see the world as well.

And hadn't it just happened again? Another tight spot; another rescue by Clive? A sense of inevitability coursed through him. Except, now forty years on, it was coupled with feeling a failure because, despite all his experience, he was still the one needing help.

'There isn't any money if you work on the Alconbury case,' Pember said, surprising even himself with his peevishness.

'No problem. We aren't specialist dive investigators, but if I turn up something we can charge for, then we can talk about payment. Relax, it's a bit of fun for me. I hadn't set out to do any PI work, but why not give it a try while I've still got police contacts?'

'Jeeez, protect me from over-keen rookies. I don't have

time to hold your hand, you'll be on your own. It's not a game, Clive.' A sense of guilt seeped into his soul. He hadn't put all his cards on the table... *Hell, Clive's well able to take care of himself.*

Clive pulled a face. 'But I want to do it and this way we both win. Consider your options, Pember.'

They'd left the office door ajar, and Clive had opened the old window to get some ventilation through the room. The sound of footsteps travelled up the stairwell.

'Are you expecting another client?'

Pember closed his eyes for a second. The tread was too heavy for Dove, the cleaner. 'Oh no, it'll be Mr Smith.'

'Smith? Seriously? His real name?'

'People use false names...at least at first.' Pember could have added that it reflected the discreet nature of client requests or mirrored their embarrassment. But he didn't. He'd let Clive work out the differences between PI and police work. Wanting to remain anonymous didn't automatically imply guilt in the PIA world.

'Hmm, well we have to get the waste bin out of here.' Clive stood up. 'It's hardly–'

'Then take it next door. Here...' Pember pulled a small bunch of keys from the open desk drawer, 'Quick!'

Without another word, Clive grabbed the waste bin and the proffered keys. A couple of strides and he'd left the office, a faint smell of vomit trailing behind.

Pember waited. There was no point in being tetchy because age had been kinder to Clive than to him. It was fair enough it had spared Clive's ears. *But did it have to keep him looking fit and slim as well?* 'Bloody Flossy, you've a lot to answer for,' he muttered.

Knock knock! The office door reverberated like a sounding board.

'Come in.' Pember kept his head steady, no sudden turns and his eyes straight ahead.

'Mr Quinn?'

'Yes. Mr Smith, isn't it? Please sit down.' Pember indicated a conference chair and took in the slight man, his greyhound build, and the surprisingly thick head of dark hair. Was it a wig?

'You phoned yesterday to say you wanted our surveillance services.' Pember spoke slowly, keeping his tone even.

'Yeah; I want a tracker on her car.'

'I explained about tracking devices. Discreet surveillance might work better and stay inside the law.'

'Yeah, yeah. But it's my car. She drives it. You said I can track my own property.'

'Yes, we can track your car but not your wife, and not without her consent.'

'I just want to know where she goes.'

'Have you asked her, Mr Smith?'

'If I ask, she'll know I'm on to her!'

Pember sighed. He'd had this type of conversation with so many clients over the years.

'Where do you think she goes? Is she having an affair, Mr Smith?'

'I don't know. Something's up. I want to know what.'

'And you can't ask her?' The tinnitus changed pitch in Pember's right ear. 'Can you at least give me some idea of her weekly routine; if she works, visits the gym, collects kids from school...that kind of thing? And if anyone else drives the car?'

Mr Smith shifted in his seat.

This was going nowhere fast and Pember needed to end it before he became irritable with the client. He made a flash decision.

'Okay, I'll need the car's particulars. Remember we can check the name of the owner with the DVLA through the car's reg details, so we want your full name and address, the address where the car is kept and your wife's name, or should I say, the name of the person who is the focus of the surveillance. Oh yes, and a photo of her, please.'

'Yeah, yeah and I want the package deal – two weeks of surveillance and a result.'

'Yes, Mr Smith. Two payments, one upfront and the second at the end of the two weeks. There's a lot of paper-work to read through and sign first.'

'Yeah?'

'Yes, so let's get started on it.'

***

Clive felt drained after visiting Pember; if not physically, then certainly emotionally.

It took him about twenty minutes to drive back from Bury St Edmunds to his home in Woolpit, a small Suffolk village with a name more to do with wolves than wool, and its existence dating back further than twelve hundred years. He'd deliberately avoided the busy A14. He wanted to connect with the gently rolling countryside and vista of fields, green with shoots of wheat and barley, and yellow with patches of flowering rapeseed. It stretched as far as his eyes could see, loosely latticed with hedgerows and patches of woodland. The view helped him to relax while he drove and cleared his mind of extraneous noise. It was time to start processing his meeting with Pember.

Firstly, he asked himself how he felt about Pember. Hmm…the friendship was still there, but time had taken its toll. They were both older, and life had bowled different balls at them. Clive had survived a failed marriage and divorce, which was scarring enough, but what of Pember? He hadn't said much about himself apart from his ear. Even leaving Norwich had been précised into one word: *complicated*. What the hell was *complicated* supposed to mean?

And another question niggled Clive. Would he have committed so quickly to the private investigator's work if he hadn't found Pember collapsed on the floor? It was just like Pember to trigger the softer side of his nature and push him into a flash decision to help. Hadn't it always been so?

He'd always believed he should try to do the right thing. But it had soured Clive's faith in the police, turned him into a cynic, and finally triggered his retirement. He'd uncovered, too late for the defendant, a wrongful conviction based on "lost" evidence. He'd tried to right the wrong, but he'd been swimming against a tide, and it was time to leave the police.

Clive had known he'd have to supplement his pension when he retired at fifty-five. It had placed him early at one of life's crossroads. A sign pointed to training as a teacher. Another suggested a start-up business such as a walking guide for designer trekking holidays. But why not take an easy option, one with a flavour of semi-police work? It would feel natural to step into the security-advisor business or, as he'd just demonstrated, become a private investigator, however temporary.

But what would Chrissie think? He figured his long-term girlfriend would have an opinion about him joining a private investigation agency. She was a trusted sounding board for his ideas but if he mentioned PI work, there'd be an avalanche of questions from her. He wasn't sure if he was ready to answer them yet. No, he'd tell her about this obliquely. The small matter of Pember's bad ear could wait.

He smiled. It would be good to exercise the DI skills he'd honed during his years in the police force.

He parked his black hybrid Lexus NX300 in the lane outside a row of three terraced, Suffolk-brick cottages. A stone plaque on the central one read *Albert Cottages 1897*. He shared No. 3 with Chrissie, and since his retirement he was starting to find the rooms a little claustrophobic.

'Hi, I'm home,' he called as he closed the front door and dropped his keys on a narrow table. The hallway was cramped and the staircase steep, its first few treads near enough to air kiss the front door when it opened. The late afternoon light was fading, and the space had become a shaded corridor. He strode through to the kitchen.

He found Chrissie sitting with her laptop and a mug of tea, the modest kitchen table strewn with papers and balance sheets. The white porcelain butler sink was empty, the drainer and counter clean and tidy.

'Hi,' she said, looking up and smiling. 'Good visit?'

He bent and kissed her lightly, catching a flowery fragrance. 'Hmm,' he murmured searching his memory for the image of her new hair conditioner. 'Is it…honeysuckle and lavender?' He hoped he'd remembered correctly.

'That's very clever of you.' She smiled and then wrinkled her brow, 'Except you've never been good at identifying different flower scents, let alone picking out what's in a mix. You must've…'

'No, but I saw it in the shower and–'

She laughed. 'And you read the label. Always the detective. So, how was Pember? Did you have a good time?'

'Well...'

'Come on, you've spent most of the day with him. How is he? Has he changed much from how you remember him?' Her grey-blue eyes fixed him with a wide expression, and he knew she was focused on him and him alone. He guessed there'd be no fridge audit and dinner plans, at least not until he'd answered her questions. He waited, a little mischievous and ready to tease.

'So, if you can't say how he is, what's his office like? Where does he live? His family – a wife?'

'Woah, slow down.' He smiled, amused by her predictability. She looked energized and young, or rather younger than her fifty-plus years. Perhaps it was down to her trim figure and short blonde hair.

'Okay then, where does Pember live?' she repeated.

'Ah, now that was a bit odd. I don't think he'd 've told me, but a client suddenly arrived, and we had to lose the...er...over-full waste bin in a hurry. He gave me the keys to his next-door office.'

'And how's that odd?'

'It was more of a storeroom. Boxes and piles of files. And someone had been sleeping there.'

'You mean Pember?'

'Maybe. Or someone else. There was an inflatable mattress.'

She frowned. 'Are you describing something redlight-sleazy or is he camping out for a few days before moving into a flat?'

'Maybe.'

'Which? Sleazy or waiting for a flat?'

'I had to move the mattress to get to the basin and there

was a gun, as if he'd been sleeping with it close.'

'What? You mean like he was expecting trouble?'

Clive shrugged. He didn't want to say what he really thought, didn't want to freak Chrissie out. He was banking on her getting more engrossed in other aspects of the tale.

'Well,' she reasoned, 'all the farmers round here have shotguns and air rifles. It's common. And Pember's ex-army, so it kind of follows he might own a gun.'

'Yes, that's what I thought too. It's a SIG Sauer P226. I figure he probably kept it after Iraq. Got hold of it somehow and didn't hand it in. He said he was over there in 2006.'

'There, what did I say?'

'Exactly.'

'Is a Sig-whatever a kind of rifle?'

'More of a semi-automatic pistol.'

'What? Was it loaded?'

'I didn't check. I only went in there with a waste bin. I wasn't doing a search, and I certainly wasn't going to risk leaving my prints on a gun.'

She fell silent for a few seconds. 'Did he talk about his time in Iraq?' she finally asked.

'No.'

'So, you don't know if he has a post-traumatic stress disorder. Like flashbacks and nightmares? The pistol could be to make him feel safe. You know, so he can protect himself inside his nightmares? Or when he wakes from his terrors, at least he's got his gun. Mind you, if that's the case, I'd expect him to keep it unloaded.'

Chrissie had a point. He should have checked the SIG Sauer. Except the Pember he used to know had been an expert at compartmentalising the bad things in his mind. He'd always avoided talking about painful memories. It was his way of coping, and Clive couldn't imagine Pember having disabling flashbacks or letting an ear problem take over. He reckoned it was more likely that Pember kept the gun to protect himself from the living.

'Okay, so if in true blokey fashion you didn't touch on the personal or emotional, you must have talked about his private investigation agency,' Chrissie said, interrupting Clive's train of thought.

'Ah, now that was fascinating.'

'Great. So, tell me about it. What did he say?'

'He's got an interesting coroner's inquest coming up. It's a local SCUBA diving death. The relatives want it investigated by Pember's PI agency. Except Pember isn't a specialist dive investigator and until I've, I mean he's asked them what exactly they want from us...' He ignored her frown and ploughed on, 'we won't know why they don't trust the police and dive investigation experts. It looks interesting so I-I've offered to help him.'

'Hmm, do they suspect something shady about the death and no one else does?'

'I don't know. It could be the other way round, Chrissie. Everybody else may think there's something dodgy and they don't.'

'Wow. Like the relatives are trying to swing an insurance fraud? Hey if it's local, it will've been in the news. What's the name?'

'Alconbury. Morton Alconbury.'

She seemed to focus into the middle distance. He knew the look. It meant she'd heard the name before and was sieving her memory. He watched and smiled. It had just got a whole lot easier for him to justify taking on some private investigator work. After all, she was already curious about the case. Her urge to know would soon override her misgivings about him teaming up with a gunslinging partner prone to occasional bouts of dizziness. He was sure of it.

'I can tell from your face. You know the name from somewhere.'

She tilted her head, by way of an answer. 'I know the surname, but it wasn't a *Morton* Alconbury. It was a Gillaine or Gillian Alconbury. I'd be able to look it up if I was in the Ipswich office, but…' She let the word drift. 'I'm there tomorrow. I'll check then.'

'It'd be helpful…anything you've got.'

'Right, but…'

'I know. It's confidential, I understand. I thought you were at the Barn Workshop all day today?' he said, now able to relax.

'I was, but my wood delivery's been delayed, and Jason's at the sale rooms. I thought for once I'd take advantage of being the boss, so I slipped away early. The rolltop writing desk can wait an extra day for repair while I catch up on this.' She vaguely indicated the papers and her laptop on the table.

'It doesn't seem very long ago you were worried your forensic accounting wouldn't take off, and now you're so busy with it, you've barely time for furniture restoration.' He laughed, happy for her success.

'And I'm still getting my head round you leaving this morning a retired DI, and returning as a what exactly? A specialist dive investigator?'

'No. A PI. But I haven't signed anything yet. It's just a trial run.'

'Really? So, you're a temp but you're already talking

guns. I hope you know what you're doing. Will you be based in Pember's office?'

'The locked office? Hell, I hadn't thought about that.' In truth, he'd forgotten about the overfull waste bin and stacks of boxes and files.

'Well, at least you look happy,' Chrissie said.

'Yes, I feel...well I feel almost excited about it. You know, I think I'll go in early tomorrow and get a head start.'

TUESDAY

'Hey Pember? Are you there? Open the door. It's me; Clive!'

The words broke into Pember's awareness. At first the sound had been faint and ethereal, drifting without meaning through his blank, undreaming sleep. Then, like strands of a cobweb it had laced into a familiar pattern. He rolled onto his side and remembered he'd gone to sleep on the inflatable mattress in the second office.

'Pember! Open the door. It's me. Clive.'

'Okay,' he groaned as meaning registered and he recognised the voice, 'Yeah, right.' He fumbled for the sleeping bag zip and eased himself out, each movement stiff and awkward. He listened for the sound of hissing in his right ear and squinted at his wristwatch. 8:30am. He registered the time, saw his trusty SIG Sauer out of the corner of his eye, and slipped it under the mattress.

'Come on, Pember. What's taking you so long? I know you're camping in there. Just open the door, will you?'

'Right.' He gave up the pretence and opened the door.

'What the hell, Pember? At least put some clothes on.'

'Huh.' His lethargy surprised him. But then he hadn't had his morning shot of coffee, and the memory of yesterday still rang in his right ear. 'Prude,' Pember muttered under his breath.

'And how's today going to go?'

Pember didn't bother to dignify Clive's question with an answer. Instead, he looked heavenwards. 'Here...' He shuffled to his pile of folded clothes. 'The key to my office.' He tossed the keys to Clive. 'Mine's an espresso.'

'And the coffee maker?'

'Top drawer, filing cabinet nearest the desk.' He waited until the door closed before collecting his thoughts. It'd take a few minutes to get his joints moving, and army training dictated he'd feel more secure with a plan. 'So, make a plan,' he muttered.

He focused. First, a quick flannel-wash at the sink and forget the shave, facial hair was a useful disguise. Second, a fresh set of clothes. Third, remember the Serc and Stemetil alongside the espresso. Fourth & fifth, Clive could start on the Alconbury case while he concentrated on Mrs Smith. Oh…and sixth…lighten up. Clive might be a couple of months younger than him, didn't have sun-damaged skin, and clearly had better joints, but heck he was his oldest friend. 'I need all the friends I can get,' he muttered, and swallowed the staleness left in his mouth by the night.

It didn't take Pember long before he'd washed and dressed, slipped the latch on his make-do sleeping quarters, stepped out onto the landing, and slammed the door shut.

'What's this?' he asked as he stepped around a 12-inch-square cardboard box outside the door to his functioning office.

'What's what?' Clive stood near a filing cabinet, a mug in one hand and the top drawer pulled fully open. The smell of rich nutty coffee wafted from his general direction.

'This box.'

'Isn't it more of your unpacking?'

'No.' Pember bent closer to read the label, 'My name and address. No sender ID. I haven't ordered anything.'

'One of your impulse buys? Like that oversized-print shirt you bought for your fifteenth birthday?'

'Don't remind me! So, how long's it been sitting there?'

'Since I got here.'

They both stood staring at it, the hair on Pember's neck starting to bristle. Clive finally broke the silence and said, a wry smile on his face, 'I don't know the last time a parcel bomb was delivered to anyone in Suffolk.'

'What? D'you think it's an explosive device?'

'No. It was a joke, Pem. Are there people out there who might send you one?'

Pember shrugged. This was crazy. His guts twisted but he steadied as he automatically went through the check list, 'It doesn't have a sender or return address and no stamps, so…' He knelt to get closer, 'it's been delivered by hand. There isn't excessive tape sealing it, no staining or leakage.' He bent to sniff and listen, 'No smell of nitroglycerin or trinitrotoluene, and no perfumes to disguise it. Nothing ticking. And the size and shape look ordinary and unremarkable.' He gently lifted the box to test the weight. 'It's not unduly heavy.' He tilted it, 'And nothing moves around inside. Also, there's no visible wire, or hole left from a safety wire.'

'I thought you were in the military police, not bomb disposal.'

Pember caught the respect mixed with concern in Clive's voice. Emboldened, he continued, 'Dead right, but RMPs were trained to recognise explosive devices. Key facts: a parcel bomb isn't meant to go off in transit, only when the target opens it. It'll be excessively taped, well-sealed, and secure for the journey. Warning: there'll be a place on it which looks the obvious point to open it. Don't. It's a trick to tempt the victim to open it at the trigger point.'

'Thanks for the tutorial. So, after factoring in you're in

Suffolk, not Iraq, Afghanistan, or Northern Ireland, do you think it's a bomb addressed to you?'

'The odds are at least two hundred to one.'

'Good. Ready for a coffee now?'

'Yeah.' Pember bit back the mix of relief and embarrassment. It was all very well making light of the false alert, but how'd Clive react if he knew there'd been parcel bombs delivered to his army barracks, or seen car bombs devastate marketplaces and landmines explode?

'Single or double shot espresso?' Clive asked and grinned.

'Double.' Pember sucked air and steeled his nerves. He peeled back the sticky tape and opened the box. 'Wow,' he breathed, as with a surge of excitement and relief, he recognised the shape inside the bubble wrap.

'What is it?' Clive asked as he loaded a coffee pod into the machine.

'It's…it's another…' Reverently, he lifted the contents out of the box and unrolled the bubble wrap, 'It's D'Artagnan.' He couldn't keep the awe from his voice.

'What?'

'It's Royal Doulton, 1982,' Pember whispered, as he turned the character jug this way and that.

'You mean another Toby jug like your dad's?'

'Yeah; Dad's set was made in 1956. Doulton only added D'Artagnan in 1982. I'd 've been twelve at the time.'

'And you're sure you didn't order it?'

'I've already bloody said, haven't I? But…'

'But what?'

'I've always wanted one.'

'So, who sent it? Is there a note with it?'

Pember looked inside the box and checked through the

wrapping again. 'Nothing.'

'It's got to be someone who knows you'd want it.'

'No one knows.'

'Except you've got Athos, Porthos, and Aramis up on the filing cabinets for any visitor to see. It could be anyone's lucky guess. Does this place have a cleaner?'

'Yeah, Dove. She does the main foyer and stairs. I told her I don't want her in my rooms. She won't have seen the jugs.' He ignored Clive's frown.

'And security? Any CCTV in the building?'

'Ha! It's supposed to be front and back entrances.' His irritation rose. 'I checked and found the cameras are dummy. Gave the agent a piece of my mind.' He took a long breath and pictured his SIG Sauer. It would be okay. He had security.

'Here, your double espresso. You look as if you need it.' Clive put a coffee cup on the desk. 'If I'd still been with the police, we could've asked for the CCTV recordings up and down Hatter and Abbeygate Street.'

'You still can; just charm your way rather than flash a card.'

'But won't we have to shell out a sweetener?'

'Maybe.'

Pember placed the D'Artagnan character jug with great care on the desk before settling on his office chair. He pulled the double espresso closer. 'Thanks,' he said and downed the concentrated brew in a couple of gulps. 'Good.' He opened a desk drawer and took his medicines.

He thought back to his RMP training. *What Motivates an Informant to Inform*? The lecture, part of the interrogation module, was still as fresh in his mind as the day it was delivered back in Chichester in 1988...or was it 1989?

'A deep thought is crossing between your ears. I can tell,' Clive murmured.

'Don't underestimate the power of charm.'

'Whose? Yours or mine?'

'I can be Mr Charming when the job demands. And sweeteners for information? We offer our services at special rates. Favours to call in later. But it's cash if it can go on a client's pre-agreed expenses slate.' He watched Clive nod.

'Well, Pember, I reckon it's down to you to decide which deals you're offering as sweeteners. I'm going to start on the Alconbury case.'

'Yeah, makes sense. I'll tell Mrs Alconbury I've assigned you. Hey, ask her what she wants from us. I should know, but...' He tapped his ear. And then remembering the lecture, he flashed some charm. 'It's good to have you on board, Clive.' The line could have come out of a film. He grinned at his lack of originality.

***

Out on the pavement, Pember blended into the crowd - easy if you're of average height, average weight and have averagely-thinning brown hair. He had a photo of the cardboard box on his phone, Hatter Street Private Investigation Agency business cards in his breast pocket, and his Association of British Investigators (ABI) membership card in his wallet. He'd called in at the jewellers, clothes stores, gift shops, restaurants, and food outlets in the streets around his office, but he'd drawn a blank. It required a manager to access CCTV recordings.

'Leave your business card,' the sales assistants had said, 'the manager will be in later. Maybe call back then?' Pember's mood had darkened.

The task had been busy for his eyes as he searched for CCTV warning notices and sales assistants. The modern shopwindows replaced most of the street-level front walls of the buildings and masked the true antiquity of the wooden-frame and Suffolk-brick buildings behind. And once inside, Pember couldn't help but notice how the old shop spaces had been enlarged by knocking through into back parlours and side rooms. He was so focused on looking up and around for cameras that the shallow internal steps almost tripped him where floor levels changed by as much as six or eight inches and the old street sloped down to the Abbey Gardens.

But despite the shoppers milling around, Pember's balance had passed the test. At moments, the bustle had transported him back to the hectic Iraqi markets, somewhere he didn't care to revisit. But the old memories and a current sense of threat were playing on his mind. He needed security. He'd install his own CCTV cameras, and he'd do it this afternoon.

He cast over his shoulder as he made his way back. If the D'Artagnan jug was meant to spook him, then it had done its job. It had also taken him away from his office, and he needed to return. He quickened his pace along Hatter Street.

A rapid check didn't show any signs of an intruder or unexpected deliveries during his absence. Reassured, he sat at his desk, and made a start on the *Mr Smith tracking Mrs Smith* case. He opened his laptop and using his ABI membership, logged into the DVLA site. Mr Smith had told him the previous afternoon that the car to be tracked was a ten-year-old white Fiat Panda Hatchback. He'd also fessed up to his real name being Idris Brafman.

Pember entered the car registration number into the DVLA site and waited. 'Hah,' he sighed as the site gave Idris Brafman as the registered keeper of the car, 'So, the address matches the one given by Idris. Better confirm that our Mr Smith is Idris Brafman.'

It was time to move up a gear. Pember opened a photo on his phone. It was the face shot he'd taken of an unsuspecting Mr Smith the previous day when he signed the paperwork. It only took a few seconds to transfer the image to his laptop and blow it up to full-screen size. The impression he'd got of the man on first meeting had been of a greyhound. The thick wig had distracted from the face but the thin legs and lean torso, his general attitude and stance, had shouted *greyhound*. And now, focusing on his enlarged screen-face, Pember homed in on the fine bone structure. The chisel-straight nose with its narrow bridge seemed to bring the eyes close together. *Sharp* was another label that came to mind.

'Right, let's see who you really are.' Pember signed into his secure Virtual Private Network and loaded the photo onto *Pipl*, a specialised people identification site. It was a search engine for the deep web but configured to report back through regular web browsers. Something he felt safe with. A kind of halfway house between the visible and invisible web.

Pipl took its time. It found some partial matches. But they were weak likenesses, nothing certain. He was none the wiser.

'Okay, then let's turn this around a bit. Let's see what Idris Brafman looks like.' Pember didn't have a photo of Idris, but he reckoned *Pipl* might find a facial image for the name and address. And he was in luck.

'Well, there's a surprise. Idris Brafman doesn't look like Paul Smith.' It was just as he'd suspected. Paul Smith wasn't Idris Brafman. He read on through the profile details.

'What? Idris Brafman is dead?'

It felt spooky. So, when did he die? The answer came fast. He'd died about four months earlier, in January 2022, at the age of seventy-six.

'So, who the hell is the man who calls himself Paul Smith?' It was time to play dirty.

'To the dark web!' It felt like a battle cry.

Pember turned his computer off and inserted his USB stick with the bootable copy of *Tor* that he used to anonymously browse and access dark net sites. He then switched the computer back on, but this time rebooted from the USB, and again using a Virtual Private Network, opened *Tor*. It was a trick he'd been taught to protect his laptop's operating system when accessing sites on the dark web.

It was a slow process, but his attention was gripped when a dark net site finally matched the photo of Paul Smith, the man who'd signed the papers in his office the previous afternoon.

'Four different names? And all strong matches,' Pember breathed. What was this man? A serial bigamist? A con man? An intelligence officer? A killer?'

He wrote down the four names: Paul Smith, Dave Jones (a name that had been a weak match on *Pipl*), John Williams, and James Brown.

Pember took notes and compiled a spread sheet, trying to make sense of what he was finding. An hour later, he needed a break and stopped to make himself another espresso. So, what had he got so far?

Paul Smith could be traced back about two years but prior to this, the trail went cold. The man had traded as a travelling salesman or businessman, but it wasn't entirely clear what he'd been selling nor the nature of his business. And as for his lookalikes? Pember picked up a chronological line that became sketchier as he looked further back in time. Each lookalike appeared as if from nowhere and then vanished after a couple of years, or less.

One thing was certain; the names Paul Smith, Dave Jones, John Williams, and James Brown had to be aliases. All the first and last names were on the top one hundred list of the commonest first or last names in the UK. It couldn't be down to pure chance. It had to be a deliberate ploy to make the identities difficult to trace.

Pember downed his espresso and turned his attention to the woman he'd been contracted to follow, Mrs Veronica Smith. He studied the photo her husband had given him. She looked about thirty years old, with dark, curly, shoulder-length hair. It wasn't a straight, full-on, face view. She'd half turned her head as she'd gazed at the camera with a coy smile. No, perhaps not coy; it was more of a self-conscious look, as if she hadn't enjoyed posing for the photo.

'I hope to God she's who he says she is because this is getting complicated,' Pember murmured. A thought struck him. Paul Smith wasn't Idris Brafman and therefore didn't own the car he wanted tracked. So, following the letter of the law, Pember shouldn't put a tracker on it. But if he refused, Paul Smith might guess why. Instinct warned him it might be dangerous to show Paul Smith he'd broken his cover. He needed a compromise plan.

'I'll take my own photo of Mrs Smith to identify on the facial recognition sites, and in the meantime I've an address to visit and a tracker to put on a Fiat Panda.'

Dark-web searching, and information trawling were inherently risky. The threat from hackers and malware was real. He needed an expert to trawl the dark web for him. But he wasn't too sure who he could trust.

***

After leaving Pember's office, Clive planned to begin investigating Morton Alconbury's death by first driving to see the dive location. He then intended to visit Mrs Alconbury. He was working on the question, what had happened? He knew he should keep an open mind. But diving incidents were the territory of specialists and he needed somewhere to peg his initial thoughts. Also, by starting the morning with his trip to the scene of the fatality, it allowed time for Pember to contact Mrs Alconbury. This was assuming he'd recovered enough from the D'Artagnan distraction.

Clive joined the A14 at Bury St Edmunds and cruised down the dual carriageway towards Ipswich, his black Lexus hybrid silently eating the miles before leaving the A14 at the Great Blakenham junction. Quietness suited him, and he relished the lack of interruption from a police mobile and radio. It was the one thing he hadn't missed since retiring from the police.

Alone with his thoughts, he took in the slim flues pointing heavenwards above the treetops; evidence of a huge incinerator where electricity was generated from waste. It struck him as futuristic. Technology on a massive scale.

'And now I've got to get my head around diving equipment. It'll be about valves and gas pressures, I guess.'

A few turns, and he was away from the industrial land-scape and onto small lanes. To one side the flat landscape stretched into the distance, and on the other side low hills were covered in rough pastures, sprouting crops, and clumps of trees. It felt secluded, the views measured in hundreds of yards rather than miles, as the lanes twisted and curved along the sides of hills. He headed towards Nettle-stead. It was the postcode location of the diving accident, but he soon discovered Nettlestead was a hamlet of scat-tered farms and dwellings, the heart of the village barely more than a handful of houses on a quiet street.

He drove along a track and parked the Lexus before walking the last few hundred yards to gaze over a fence. A notice warned KEEP OUT – OLD CHALK PIT. Below him, the uneven ground sloped steeply into a grassy bowl cut into the side of the hillside. Shrubs and small trees had taken root. It was a natural wilderness in the making. The horse chestnuts, silver birches, ash, and elm growing further down the slope had created a canopy and hid what lay be-neath. He stood and leaned on the fence, wondering if he could climb over and down the slope.

'The ground'll slip away unless you're a goat.' An el-derly man with a small rough-coat terrier walked towards him.

'Is there a footpath around the side of this?' Clive asked.

'Nah. It follows the ridge. Takes you back to the vil-lage.'

'So how do I…?'

'Back that way. A farm turnin' to your right.' The man didn't seem inclined to talk further and walked on by.

Clive strode back to the Lexus and retraced his route at

low speed, keeping an eye out for the farm turning. *Access must have been a nightmare for the rescue services*, he thought as he eventually turned onto a concrete entrance drive.

The farmhouse was long and rambling, part lath and plaster, and part brick, as if it had been added to and extended during times of prosperity. It looked old, hundreds of years old, and he figured the thatched-roof section was likely to have been the original dwelling. He parked and headed to the front door. The metal knocker seemed too feeble to raise a response from inside, but he clanked it against its plate and hoped he looked unthreatening, a genuine visitor.

He heard a window being opened above him and stepped back to look upwards and along the front of the farmhouse.

'Yes?' A middle-aged woman frowned down at him from inside.

'Good morning. I wonder if you can help me. I'm from the Hatter Street Agency in Bury St Edmunds.'

'If you're sellin', make an appointment with my husband.' She made as if to close the window.

'No please; I'm not selling anything.'

She paused.

'You see, I don't know who to ask. Perhaps you can tell me?' He knew he'd caught her interest by the way she looked at him for a few seconds, as if sizing him up again, but this time more carefully.

'What you want to know?'

'I've been asked…as an independent, to give my findings on how inaccessible the old chalk quarry-pit is to the public. So far, I've seen the fence and notice up at the top of the hill.'

'And?'

'I'm impressed. A good fence and a clear notice.' He smiled and she seemed to visibly relax. 'But you could add *No Swimming*.'

'My husband asked a diver to check it. See how deep, what's at the bottom?'

'Very sensible. What did they say?'

'There's an old van at the bottom. Nothin' of interest. That was last September. But we've always wondered if there's more. When one of them divers came back wantin' another look, we were pleased. And then…'

'There was the diving accident?'

She nodded.

Clive decided a lie would be less threatening. 'I heard it was because he had a weak heart. My interest is simply in the perimeter and public access. I don't suppose you've got a moment to walk me round?'

He watched her hesitate and smiled at her reassuringly. She shrugged ample shoulders and nodded.

'I'll come down.' She closed the window.

'Tell me about the pit,' he said when she joined him in the courtyard, 'your memories of it, when it was last in use. That kind of thing. I'd like to get a feel about it.' He realised he was speaking genuinely, no subversion or trickery, this time just curiosity.

She seemed to sense his sincerity and smiled. He fell into step with her as they followed a track out of the courtyard.

'Have you lived here long?' he asked.

'Since I married, thirty years or more. Before that we used to play here as kids. I don't remember the pit ever bein' active.'

'Has it changed much?'

'The trees have grown and more sprung up.'

The track sloped downwards with a gentle incline and curved into the hillside. A line of fencing cut across in front of them. The only way through was to follow the track, but a gate blocked their path.

'Same fencing as up on the top of the hill and top track,' Clive said with approval.

She nodded. 'We keep this padlocked.' She produced a key and released the chain holding the gate closed.

'Good, and a notice on the gate - DANGER PRIVATE KEEP OUT.' A few moments later and beyond the gate he murmured, 'It's like an enchanted glade.' They walked between the trees, some in early leaf and some still in bud. The ground sloped, but it felt as if they were close to the base of a giant natural bowl.

'It's a bit flatter here,' she said.

He saw ruts where tyres had cut through turf and gravel to the pale chalk beneath. The tracks looked recent, and he supposed they'd been left by the rescue vehicles. She walked on another twenty yards and stood at the edge of the water. He trailed behind.

'When we were kids we thought fairies lived here.'

'It's magical enough,' he said, and standing next to her, gazed down at the water. It felt ominous, the surface like glass but dark below.

'There's treasure at the bottom.'

'Really?'

'It's what we were told as kids. And that there was a monster. Turns out it's an old van.'

'So, all folklore. Or is there a grain of truth in the tale of treasure?'

She didn't answer but instead said, 'We were told *don't swim in it.*'

'But you did, of course. You were kids.'

'Yes. But it was always cold. Even in a summer heat-wave.'

'So, is this where the divers went in?' He bent and dipped a finger into the chilly water.

'I think so. It's the obvious place.'

'If anyone was down here, would you be able to hear them if they got into trouble?'

'No. But they'd have had to cross our courtyard first.'

'So, you'd know they were here?'

'Yes.'

'But you wouldn't be able to see them from the farm or the track unless you came through the gate. It's hidden by the trees.'

'Yes, it's a secret place.'

'Have you thought of keeping a buoyancy life-ring here? For an emergency?' he said remembering his cover.

'It's on the list since the accident.'

'Ah, the accident. What happened?'

'It's…I wasn't down here; no one was, except them divers. There should have been three of them, but on the day, only two turned up.'

He waited, sensing she was working through it in her mind.

'I keep wonderin'; would it have happened if there'd been three of them?'

'How do you mean?'

'There'd 've been more people to raise the alarm.'

'How was the alarm raised?'

'The one who survived got his companion out, phoned for help and tried to…what's it called?'

'Do CPR? So, there's good signal here is there?' Clive pulled his mobile from his pocket. The signal gauge indicated it was weak.

She watched him for a moment. 'It's stronger near the gate.'

'Right.' He was building a picture. Two divers, not three; an isolated location, and cold water. Hmm, and poor phone signal. It felt like an accident waiting to happen. 'Well thank you Mrs…?'

'Call me Ann.'

'Well thank you Ann. You've been most helpful.' He took a few photos of the location under the guise of checking for phone signal and together they walked up the track to the farm courtyard.

Back in his car he drove towards Great Blakenham, pulling off the road when his mobile indicated a strong signal. He wanted to phone Mrs Alconbury and collect his thoughts, but more importantly, he wanted to relish his elation. It was a couple of months since he'd questioned a member of the public, and back then, following protocol, he'd first have flashed his police ID or introduced himself as a detective inspector. But talking to Ann as an undercover PI had been liberating. And it was nice not to be met by a wall of silence or outright hostility frequently reserved for the police.

'PI work might just turn out to be okay,' he murmured and located Mrs Alconbury's number in his notebook before tapping it into his mobile.

'Hello, is that Mrs Alconbury?'

A soft voice answered, breathy and Canadian, 'Hi. Who

wants to know?'

'This is Clive Merry from Hatter Street PIA. I believe Mr Quinn has let you know I'll be working on your case?'

'He has, but I don't see why?'

'For my field skills. I've just visited the chalk pit so I'm between Nettlestead and Great Blakenham. Can I call by and see you?'

'Well, I…'

'Yes, I know you won't have been expecting me, but it's important I get facts straight, right from the start.'

'Can't we do this on the phone, huh?' Her voice sounded stronger, more as if taking control.

'We can but talking face to face is more secure. No third-party listening. Less chance of misunderstandings. You're the client. I assumed you'd insist on meeting me.'

'I do.'

'Good. I've got your address. Great Bricett, right? In twenty minutes?'

'Make it thirty.'

'Thirty it is, then.' He ended the call and smiled. *So, she was the type who had to have the last word and be in control.* He'd met a lot of people like her. He keyed the address into his satnav. 'Hah, less than nine miles.'

It wasn't going to take Clive long to drive there, and he didn't want to be seen waiting near her house, so before setting off, he filled in the time thinking through the questions he wanted to ask. Quiet, solitary moments like these had been gifts in the midst of his busy job, and he'd learned to grab them when he could.

***

Mrs Alconbury's house was a newbuild, possibly twenty-years-old, with four or five bedrooms. From certain angles and by straining his neck, it was just about possible for Clive to get a distant view of Great Bricett's ancient church tower. He rather liked the sense of history it portrayed, however remote. He rang the doorbell and waited.

He listened to the tread of someone approaching and the door latch being turned.

'Hello, I'm Clive Merry from Hatter Street PIA,' he said, and smiled at an attractive woman with luxuriant, shoulder-length, dark hair.

'I expected a younger guy.' She frowned and then added, 'I'm sorry. That sounded kinda rude. You'd better come in.'

He followed her through a squarish hallway into a lounge. Large French windows looked onto a weathered, stone sea creature standing close to water spouting into an ornamental pool, surrounded by patio decking. A beautifully maintained lawn stretched beyond and was edged by small shrubs. It struck Clive as shorter than it appeared, a trick with small-scale landscaping and designed to deceive the eye.

'The decking's my little touch of Canada.' She sat down in one of the wood and leather armchairs and looked at him. He took it as a what-do-you-want-to-know and a get-on-with-your-questions-because-I-don't-want-to-waste-time kind of look.

'Okay, then,' he said and pulled a notebook from his pocket before sitting on the sofa. 'Your husband's tragic death, please accept my condolences.'

She inclined her head.

'Yesterday you left a copy of the post-mortem report with us. I've read the pathologist's findings, and it says your husband didn't have an underlying health issue to cause him to die.'

'Yeah, I guess that's right.'

'So, what would you like the Hatter Street PIA to investigate for you?'

'I want to know why Morton died.'

'You understand that all your husband's diving equipment will have been seized by the police, and I assume handed over for specialist investigation, probably by the insurer's experts? And the incident has likely been referred to the Health and Safety Executive for their investigation. All their findings will be sent on to the coroner. We must wait for the coroner's verdict.'

He was rewarded with a blank stare.

'Do you have a reason not to trust the police or the specialist dive investigators?'

'No.' She rolled the sound low on her tongue.

'Do you believe your husband's death was an accident?'

'No. He'd been threatened…calls to his mobile late at night…nothing was said but the silence was kinda threatening. And then there was the dead hare left on his windscreen.'

'Really? When?'

'A couple of weeks before he died.'

'Did you tell the police?'

'Not at the time. My husband didn't want to. It didn't seem important…but the accident got me thinking. So, then I told them.'

'And?'

She shrugged her shoulders. 'So, now they know.'

'Did you keep the dead hare?'

She pulled a face and shook her head.

'And his mobile? Did the police take it to check the anonymous, late-night calls?

'No.' Again she rolled the sound low on her tongue.

'But you have his mobile?'

'Yeah.'

'So, do you want me to investigate who may have made those calls?'

She didn't answer.

'Ah…I see.'

'What do you see?'

'I don't mean to be insensitive but was your husband having an affair?' He let the question hang in the air, watching her face for any tell-tale flicker of her eyelids, some hardening of her expression, or even a flash of anger. But there was nothing.

He soldiered on, 'Did your husband have any enemies? Had he upset anyone recently?'

'Not that I recall.'

'What was your husband's line of business?

'Morton was…an entrepreneur. He had several start-ups.'

Clive waited for her to say more but she simply gazed at the floor. He felt as if he was missing something. *Was it her way of controlling the interview?* Let the PI make all the moves and lay his cards on the table? This wasn't meant to be a confrontation. He was on her side, if for no better reason than she was the client. Pember hadn't said anything about her being reluctant to talk, but then Pember hadn't been particularly forthcoming himself.

'So, am I to investigate anything that could be construed as a threat to your husband's life?' He tried to keep the frustration out of his voice.

She nodded.

'Okay, well I'm going to need a list of names: friends, family, business partners, that kind of thing. And his mobile.'

'Yeah, sure. But…maybe you should know. Morton's first wife died ten years ago. A car crash in Canada. That's how I came to meet Morton. One thing led to another, and we married.'

'So, there was a previous Mrs Alconbury?'

'Yeah.'

He nodded. It explained her being Canadian and about twenty years younger than her husband. 'Can I have a photograph of him?'

Her expression softened for a moment before the mask-like composure returned. He guessed he must have scratched a surface. But what exactly was running behind her cool exterior?

'Do you SCUBA dive, Mrs Alconbury?'

'No.'

'Was your husband an experienced SCUBA diver?'

'He'd been diving for years. He said it was another world.' She fell silent, and Clive guessed fragments of the past jostled in her memory. He waited to see what she'd say without prompting.

'It was our joke, finding fragments of the past, like fossils on the beach, or clay pipes on mudlarking expeditions along the Thames estuary. It was our treasure. He said one day he'd find real treasure like a pot of gold from a shipwreck.'

'Clay pipes?'

'Garbage from the 1580s to the early 1900s. Tobacco was expensive, Mr Merry. Clay pipes were like cigarette butts.' Her wistfulness had gone. She was back in control.

He glanced around the room.

'No point looking, Mr Merry. Our little finds are where they belong.' She indicated the ornamental pool in the garden.

It was time to change track. 'Who was your husband diving with at the quarry pit?'

'You mean his diving buddy? Phil Barner.'

'Yes. Can you tell me what you know about him?'

'He's one of my husband's diving friends. At least twenty years younger than Morton. And crazy about diving. Even owns a diving air compressor to fill his tanks. It used to be on the family yacht, or rather his parents' yacht.'

'So, diving since a kid? And wealth somewhere in the family?'

She nodded. 'American, but most of his accent's rubbed off.'

'Whose idea was it to dive in the quarry pit?'

'Phil's. He said he'd dived it last year but hadn't had time to explore a van they found at the bottom. He wondered if Morton was interested.'

'And of course, he was interested.'

'You bet.'

'You said *they* hadn't had time to explore the van last year. Any idea who might have been diving with Phil last year?'

'No. But Phil said he'd moved away.'

'And the fatal dive? Was there a third diver meant to be joining them on the dive?'

'Sorry, I don't know anything about that. Look, about those names you want; friends and family. I'll email them to you, and his photo. Leave me your card and details.' She stood up and led him to the door. 'Now, goodbye Mr Merry.'

Clive was intrigued. 'Yes, of course. Goodbye, Mrs Alconbury, and thank you.' He handed her one of Pember's Hatter Street PIA cards.

***

Pember sat in his office and downed a shot of espresso. It was a reward. He'd completed his internet searches, or more accurately, as much as he could cope with in one sitting. His thoughts drifted to Clive, and he wondered how he was getting on with the Alconbury investigation. The question jabbed his conscience. It was a tough first case to have given Clive. But he hadn't. Clive had volunteered.

'Shite, I bet he's buggered it up.'

Mrs Alconbury might be a difficult client, but Pember sensed she had money. He figured a large bank balance boosted her air of confidence and entitlement. 'I reckon she can pay her bill if she's a mind to. Let's hope Clive hasn't brassed her off.' And with that foremost in his mind, he sent Clive a text: *Hi - check in tomorrow first thing re the Alconbury case. Pem.*

With his conscience temporarily soothed and his ear feeling stable, he set his mind to his own security and the car tracker. He found what he was looking for in a couple of the storage boxes in his office-cum-storeroom and began checking and charging the equipment. *D'Artagnan was a warning, right? What if next time they don't stop at leaving a box on the landing? What if they force their way in? Take my gun? Steal my files?* His prints would be all over the SIG Sauer. He could be framed for something he hadn't done. His stomach flipped.

45

Forty minutes later he'd set up his CCTV cameras: one covering the top of the stairs and landing, and two further cameras catching different views of his office doors. The app on his phone meant he could view the images stored on the monitor when he was elsewhere.

Feeling slightly more secure, he wiped his SIG Sauer and locked it away before changing into motorcycle trousers and black leather jacket. He checked the tracker gear a final time... *Yeah, it's working okay.* It reminded him of kitting up before his Royal Military Police patrols and missions, routines laced with adrenalin. The thought triggered a mix of excitement and heightened awareness, while his tinnitus hissed in the background. It was time to load his backpack, lock his offices and visit the address Mr Smith had given him.

His trusty Yamaha Tracer 900 GT was parked where he'd left it, padlocked to a parking bolt nearby, round the back of Hatter Street. Seeing it gave him a rush of pleasure. The bike was charcoal grey, nothing flashy, a sports/tourer with outstanding performance. 'A bit like me,' he muttered and then laughed. The bike's designers had probably had a younger body in mind, not Pember's. The tours of duty in Ireland, Bosnia, Kosovo, Afghanistan, and Iraq had taken their toll. But he'd softened the ride with genuine Yamaha comfort seats, adjusted the suspension and upgraded the tyres. No one would guess.

He started the 847cc engine. It burbled gently as he cut through the old Bury streets, many with one-way systems, and headed for Westgate. The ride was effortless, and the bike gave him poise. He filtered past stationary traffic and caught the wind on his helmet as he sped down a hill to the outskirts of Bury. The address took him to a housing estate constructed in the late seventies. The modest, pale Suffolk-brick houses had been built in a style typical of the era, and the layout gave a sense of space with quiet cul-de-sacs, mature trees, and wide grassy verges.

He made a circuit, riding past the address and then stopping about fifty yards beyond it where a tree sheltered him from view. The white Fiat Panda was parked on a driveway in front of closed garage doors. He pushed up his visor and pulled his phone from his pocket to check the numberplate.

'Are you lost?'

'What?' Startled, he twisted to get a view of the owner of the querulous voice.

'I said, are you lost?'

He looked into the pale eyes of an elderly gentleman. *Hell, what if it'd been Mrs Smith?* His cover would have been blown.

'I didn't catch what you said.' Pember tapped his helmet and glanced back to see if there were other pedestrians afoot. This was all he needed.

'Are you looking for somewhere? Nice bike, by the way. I had a Norton, and then Hondas.' The man's eyes drifted from the bike to the phone in Pember's hand.

'I'm trying to find...perhaps you might know a Mr Brafman? Idris Brafman? He lives somewhere round here.'

'Iddy Brafman? He died in January.'

'What?' Pember gasped, and hoped he hadn't over-hammed it.

'Yes. His great-niece and her husband live there now. It's that one over there where the white hatchback's parked. Number 17.' He pointed.

Pember nodded.

'They came for Christmas and stayed on.'

'What happened? I mean why did he…?'

'I-I heard it was COVID. They brought it with them. They'd had the jabs, but he was an antivaxxer.'

'That's…tough.' Pember turned his attention back to the Fiat Panda. The front door of Number 17 opened and a woman stepped out. *Mrs Smith? Yeah.* She looked like the photo Mr Smith had given him.

Peep! The Panda's lights flashed as the remote door lock released. She slipped into the car.

'Sorry, my phone…I've had a message. I've got to leave,' he said and pulled his visor down in an abrupt this-conversation-is-over kind of way.

He started the bike, pulled a U-turn and slowly eased into the road. He kept the Panda in sight, following it as Mrs Smith drove away. He hung back as she turned onto the road into central Bury and then loosely tailed her into one of the short-stay car parks on the site of the old Cattle Market. It was perfect for him, an extensive ground-level parking area, open to the sky and with a steady flow of pedestrians walking through. Once he'd taken his helmet off, he was just another shopper hurrying into the town centre.

He walked between the cars, the pillbox-sized tracker ready and activated in his hand. He ducked down alongside the Fiat Panda. The powerful magnet attached under the car to the chassis with a *clonk!* He straightened up and strolled on. The tracker was in a good position. Ideal to pick up the GPS signals reflected off road surfaces. No one gave him a second glance.

Back at his bike, he checked the tracker app on his phone. A small dot blinked at him on a map. 'Signal's working okay,' he murmured and flipped to his CCTV app. Thumbnail views from Camera 1, 2 and 3 showed the head of his stairs, and office doors. The small images sat together and filled half his screen, a veritable security collage.

Something moved on Camera 1's thumbnail. 'What the…?' He tapped the image and it expanded to fill most of his screen. A head and shoulders, fuzzy with movement, froze for a couple of seconds before the next image relayed. Pember's guts twisted. He hadn't been expecting clients, *so who the hell…? Dove the cleaner?*

He needed to get back to his office fast. Getting his own photo of Mrs Smith's face would have to wait.

He kicked the bike's side-stand up and swung his leg over the saddle. The 847cc engine leapt into life. Torque and low gearing pulled him away sharply. A hard left onto Parkway, straight over a mini roundabout, then traffic lights, Westgate Street, College Street, and the one-way system weaving to, Hatter Street and his offices.

'Use your brain,' he told himself. *Don't rush in; check the intel.* The words burned into his memory from his tour in Northern Ireland, his first ever tour.

He pulled out his mobile, but before he could re-check the CCTV images, the ringtone burst into life. The banner announced, *Caller ID – Clive.* He killed the sound with a swipe. 'Yes?' he hissed.

'Where are you, Pem?'

'I'm outside in the bloody street. Where the hell are you?'

'Sitting on your stairs.'

'What?'

'Maybe if you gave me a key, I could wait in your office?'

'Jeeez be careful; someone could be in there. I'm coming up now.' He ended the call. No point in explanations.

Clive's a professional. He must have spotted the security cameras; he must know they weren't there this morning and worked out the subtext.

Pember took the first flight of stairs two steps at a time, then crept up the second flight. He saw Clive's shoes and his steel-coloured chinos bent at the knee. *Clive was still bloody sitting on the top of the stairs.* Pember shot him his didn't-you-get-what-I-just-told-you look.

'The doors haven't been forced, and I haven't heard any sounds from your offices. At least not since I've been here,' Clive said.

Pember scowled and checked the CCTV app on his mobile. The thumbnails told him what he'd begun to suspect. It had been Clive's head and shoulders all along. Embarrassment chased his relief, and now he looked a fool in front of Clive.

'I thought I texted to say we'd meet tomorrow morning. How the hell was I supposed to guess it was you?' he snapped.

He stared down at his mobile, but he knew Clive would be studying him, ready to catch his briefest facial expression. Over the years Pember had developed a thick shell, but at his core he was still the old Pember. The one Clive had known in those pre-military days. He reckoned Clive sensed it and would be trying to read him like a book.

'So, are you going to open your office and tell me what the hell's going on, or are we staying out here on the landing?' Clive's tone was measured, his body language calm as he stood up. 'I know you've got a gun. And the speed you've put up these CCTV cameras after D'Artagnan was delivered tells me you're in trouble.'

'How'd you know about the gun? Have you been bloody

snooping?'

'No.'

'And why've you come back now when I said tomorrow?' Pember asked as he unlocked his office door.

'I hoped you'd be here. After all, you're camping here. You never used to be this suspicious and secretive.'

'It's a temporary arrangement.' Pember glanced around his office before stepping across the threshold. Nothing had been disturbed. He relaxed, but he was still careful. Clive had always known when he was lying. *So, no out-and-out lies. Stick to part-truths*, he decided. 'Come in then. Take a seat. It's more comfortable than the stairs,' he said.

He waited for Clive to sit down before claiming his leadership position, the office chair behind the desk. 'Well?'

'Well, what?'

'How'd it go with Mrs Alconbury?'

'She's controlling and...I'd say attractive. Morton Alconbury's second shot at marriage. The young Canadian wife. The first one died in Canada, ten years ago.'

Pember was intrigued. 'Do we know how?'

'A car crash. I checked out the quarry site on my way to see her. Turns out Morton was interested in...how did she put it? Finding treasure. I haven't worked out if it was a shared interest or one she acquired when she married him. But that's why he dived the quarry.'

'So, what does she want from us?'

'He'd received threats for a couple of weeks before the accident. She wants us to check it out because apparently the police weren't interested.'

'One mystery solved, then.'

'Yes, but there's something else.'

'Oh yeah?'

'It's the Data Protection stuff. How do I record what I find out? I'm used to a system, case files, paper and digital. I can't just keep it all in my head. And what's the arrangement when I need to look up past records, data, intel, etcetera? Which sites do you use? How do I access them?'

'Yeah, yeah; I get it. You want a door key and a password for the encrypted files?'

'Yes.'

'You're used to a team of IT helpers running around assisting the police, right?'

'Yes.'

'Well, it's just me and you.' It sounded, even to his own ears, like a line worthy of a Raymond Chandler novel. He caught Clive's raised eyebrows and reverted to norm. 'Actually, I use the dark net, or sites pulling information from the dark net and...'

'Is that why you get surprise deliveries? Why you camp in your second office? Oh yes, and why you carry a gun?'

'Woah, you're making me sound like a dealer.'

'You said it first. So, are you?'

'No.' He held Clive's scrutiny without glancing away. 'But life would be simpler if I had an IT expert I can trust. I mean really trust.' He watched Clive frown.

'The way you said it Pem, makes me wonder...is there someone out there you *shouldn't* have trusted?'

'Yeah.'

'Just one? Several? Are they a threat?'

'I don't know. Threats can come from where you least bloody expect.'

'What kind of an answer is that? A mantra from a self-help book?'

'No. My first tour of active service.'

Clive coughed and frowned. 'I had time to think about things while I sat on the stairs, and I reckon there's plenty of online searching in this job. And you're right. I'm not your man to surf and drill the net. I used to have a department to do it for me.'

'Hmm, do you know of someone?'

'Yes, a computer geek I've worked with before. Takes you literally and sees things as black or white. Shades of grey confuse him. But he's loyal, one hundred percent.'

'Name?'

'Matt Finch.'

'Age?'

'Just about hitting thirty, I guess.'

'And you trust him?'

'Yes.'

'So, I should trust him too?'

'Yes.'

'Was he one of your police researchers?'

'More of an occasional consultant.'

'Where's he based?'

'Bury St Edmunds and Stowmarket.'

'Okay, arrange a meeting.' Pember slipped out of staff-sergeant mode and into logistics mode as he wondered where Matt Finch would have space to work.

'If you tidied up next door, put in another desk and a couple of chairs…that'd help.' Clive said, as if reading his thoughts.

'But–'

'But what about all your stuff? You could lose it behind a couple of screens.'

'But–'

'But you don't want him in another room. You want him where you can keep an eye on him, right?'

'Yeah. But I don't want him listening when I interview clients. I must be able to use this room.'

'Were you thinking of employing him full time, then?'

'No, but...' Pember's irritation almost exploded. And just as he was about to snap, *stop best-guessing what I'm going to say*, Clive's phone burst into life.

'Hi, Chrissie,' Clive said, and Pember noticed how his friend's face softened. How he nodded and said, 'Yes, I'll ask him. Are you sure?'

'Is Chrissie your...?' Pember asked when Clive ended the call and then felt foolish for asking.

'Yes, eleven years or so. She said to invite you back to our place. It's Italian Night at the White Hart this evening. Do you still like Italian food?'

Pember grinned and allowed the gesture of friendship to penetrate his protective shell.

***

Clive felt young again, as if liberated and out for a bit of fun with a good mate. He drove, and Pember followed on his Yamaha Tracer 900.

'Make sure you hang back, Pem. I want to see how good you are at discreet, live tracking,' Clive had laughed.

Who, other than Pember, could he have challenged for enjoyment like this? Certainly, no one while still a DI. There'd be too much red tape, risk assessments, equal opportunities, and fending off possible accusations of intimidation or bullying if he'd won the challenge. But if this exhilaration and excitement was a taste of what retirement could be like, then he wanted more of it.

They were both heading to Woolpit and Number 3 Albert Cottages, to meet up with Chrissie, and then an Italian themed menu at the White Hart.

'But you already know I'm following on a motorbike,' Pember had replied.

'True. But I haven't seen your bike yet. So, if you keep enough distance, I won't be able spot your bike's make, model and reg number. I want enough info to find the bike's registered owner.' He'd watched as Pember smiled. He'd caught a flash of the younger Pember with the jaunty adolescent nod and competitive squaring of his shoulders.

'Yeah, okay, Clive. But you'll fail. I'll win and the drinks will be on you.'

'Oh, yes? Hey, and keep your rear out of view.'

'Why only my butt?'

'Motorbikes have rear-facing reg plates. Don't make it any easier for me than it's going to be.'

They had both laughed.

'I drive a black, hybrid Lexus NX 300. So, this is the deal. I walk to my car, then drive down Hatter Street. The rest is up to you.'

And that's how it started.

Clive figured he knew the central Bury one-way system better than Pember did. Old childhood rivalries resurfaced as he drove down Hatter Street and threaded his way to the Green King brewery and through the entrance to the grounds of a small private hospital. He leapt out of his car, his mobile at the ready and crouched out of sight. Sure enough, a few moments later a Yamaha Tracer burbled past the entrance, grey-black, unremarkable. Clive recognised the rider's black leather jacket. He focused his mobile phone on the bike, and took a series of photos, time and dated. 'Got you, Pem; make, model and reg plate.'

The rest was simple. Clive got back into his car, manoeuvred, zipped back into the one-way system, and headed for the A14. He sped east on the dual carriageway and each time he checked his rear-view mirror, he saw the dark speck of a motorbike cruising behind in the distance. *What about the old exit trick? The one where you leave the carriageway fast and then tuck yourself out of sight as your pursuer comes down the exit slipway?*

'No way. Pem will be expecting it.' Clive took the Woolpit exit slowly, aware that behind him Pember had accelerated to catch up at the junction. A bridge carried Clive over the A14, and he meandered past the village cricket pitch with its leafy perimeter and modest clubhouse. A glance in his mirror told him the motorbike was gaining ground. 'Okay, time to lead you home. Let's see if I can tempt you closer.' But Pember kept his bike at sufficient distance to make identification difficult beyond colour.

Finally, Clive slowed to park in the lane outside the end-of-terrace cottage he shared with Chrissie. It had been fun, more fun than he cared to admit, and he grinned as he relived his trick pulling through the entrance to the private hospital grounds. The adrenalin rush still fizzed in his brain. But Pember had always pushed him into spur-of-the-moment pranks. And for once, Pember hadn't initiated this dare. It felt great. Invigorated, he got out of his car.

'I win,' Pember shouted, his visor raised as he coasted in on his Yamaha Tracer.

'You think?' Clive shouted back, and gripping his mobile, waved it in the air.

'But that's cheating,' Pember boomed.

Number 3's front door opened, and Chrissie emerged into the handkerchief-sized front garden. 'What's going on? I heard raised voices. Is everything all right?'

If words could frown, Chrissie had puckered them up and laced them with angst. She directed her gaze at Clive.

'Hi, we're home.' Happy, he cast her a smile, his well-honed reassuring one, but his exuberance bubbled through, and he added more loudly, 'We wouldn't need to shout if Pember turned his motorbike off.'

The three-cylinder engine fell silent.

'Ah, you must be Pember. It's nice to meet you at last. Why all the excitement? You both look...have you been racing each other?'

'I wouldn't call that a race. Good to meet you, Chrissie.'

'So, why all the excitement?'

'A contest...except Clive changed the bloody rules partway through.'

Clive knew to step in before Pember skewed the facts and cast him as villain. It was one of Pem's old tricks guaranteed to blur the intel.

'No way! I just happened to be out of your view when you rode past the Green King Brewery. Anyway, how's playing by street rules, cheating? I bet your Mr Smith didn't worry about using a false name. And I reckon you didn't call *him* a cheat because he plays street rules.'

'What do you know about Mr Smith?' Pember's bantering tone vanished.

'I don't know anything about him, Pem. But remember, I guessed Smith might not be his real name. That's all.' He was surprised by the way his friend had switched so quickly from playful joshing. The DI in him registered an alert. He felt Chrissie's eyes on him, knew she sensed it as well. That's all he needed; her curiosity would be unstoppable.

'I think it's about time we walked to the White Hart. I don't know about you two, but I think walking will clear my head,' he said.

'Good idea,' Chrissie murmured.

***

The White Hart was in the centre of the village and within spitting distance of its small but ancient, triangular-shaped market square and old water pump. The building was set back several feet from the pavement. Wooden barrels had been placed outside and planted with a mix of lilac and purple wall flowers, and pale pink peonies in a sugar rush of colour.

Chrissie led the way through the main entrance into the bar. Wormed-oak ceiling beams hinted at the age of the building and a warm aroma of cooked cheese, herbs and tomatoes hung in the air. Clive inhaled deeply, felt a pang of hunger, and checked his wristwatch.

No wonder, it's seven o'clock. Apart from his breakfast and the ham roll he'd wolfed down while he'd waited on the stairs for Pember, he hadn't eaten anything else all day. He turned his attention to the Italian selection on the menu board hanging on the old chimney breast. He barely listened while Pember ordered a couple of pints of the draft beer on tap, along with a glass of pinot grigio for Chrissie. He supposed it was Pember's way of acknowledging he'd lost the challenge, but Clive knew from the past that thanking him for the drinks would be as welcome as rubbing salt into a split lip. A toast to street rules would likely be taken in better spirit.

'I booked a table after I rang you,' Chrissie whispered in his ear.

'Oh good,' he murmured.

They carried their drinks past the lounge bar's vintage, treadle-base tables, the old sewing machines long since removed, and headed for the quiet, more secluded side room where scrubbed pine tables were laid out for dining.

The noise of drinkers talking and laughing ebbed and flowed as it filtered through to the side room. The space had a less old-world feel to it than the lounge bar, but it was more private. Clive saw immediately why Chrissie had chosen it. *Uh oh, she wants to talk work, but not her antique-rolltop-writing-desk-repair kind of work. No this was going to be Hatter-Street-investigation-agency themed. Oh yes, and some deep and penetrating questions into Pember's private life, no doubt.* He hoped Pember didn't react badly and get defensive.

While they sipped their drinks and waited for their food, Clive launched into a goodhearted explanatory analysis of the challenge he'd set for Pember. It was mainly for Chrissie's benefit. He hoped it would distract her from whatever her agenda might be and make her feel included.

'I wanted to know how good Pem is at discreet tracking,' he said, winding it up.

'I try to blend in.'

'Is that why you chose a grey-black bike?' Chrissie asked.

'Careful, Pem. I expect you noticed Chrissie's yellow TR7?'

'Parked in front of the cottages?'

Chrissie nodded.

'So, you like old bangers,' Pember said, raising one eyebrow and casting a glance at Clive before gulping his beer.

They all laughed.

Once the food had arrived, the conversation ran broadly as Clive had anticipated. It limped between Chrissie's bland questions and Pember's economical answers, all the while punctuated by Chrissie nibbling a mushroom-and-cheese-topped pizza, Clive eating mouthfuls of fettuccine and pork in a sour cream and caraway sauce, and Pember tucking into a generous serving of lasagne al forno.

How do you like Bury St Edmunds, Pember? was met with *it's okay.*

How does it compare to Norwich? was batted away with a shrug and another mouthful of lasagne.

Have you found anywhere nice to live yet? was answered with raised eyebrows, a glug of beer and finally *I'm still looking* addressed to his dinner.

Harmony was maintained and any awkwardness sidestepped as they focused on their food. But when Chrissie pushed her empty plate away, rested her elbows on the table and cupped her glass of wine in both hands, Clive knew the signs and braced himself. *Please don't ask Pember if he has a significant current lover or problems with post-traumatic stress. He's like a clam with grit inside. It'll get awkward.*

'Has Clive told you I work part time as a forensic accountant?' she said.

Pember lowered his fork.

Clive silently thanked the gods of discretion for, as yet, no probing questions.

'No? Well, I guessed he probably wouldn't of mentioned it.'

'But I haven't had a chance, Chrissie. It's still my first day. Hey, a toast to *street rules*.' He laughed and raised his glass. Pember winked at him.

'Do you work for the police, Chrissie?' Pember sounded serious.

'I work in a firm of accountants in Ipswich. We cover most things, but my area is forensic accounting. So, I *do* some work for the police, but I don't–'

'Work *for* the police?' Pember finished.

'Exactly. Their funding and the bureaucracy are a nightmare. Private investigators and solicitors pay us better. And of course, if one of my colleagues in our firm suspects fraud when they're auditing a client's end-of-year accounts, then they ask me to take a look.'

'Are you touting for work?'

'From you? No, of course not.' Her face flushed.

'Ah,' Clive breathed. *Was she fishing or did she have something to tell?* Today was her Ipswich day and she'd promised to check why the name Alconbury had sounded familiar. He kept quiet and waited.

Pember seemed to be following his own thread, 'Clive suggested one of his cronies take on my IT. Are you angling to join my PI agency as well, Chrissie?'

'What me? No, I've just said.' She looked at Clive. He could see she was plainly confused by Pember.

'Are you two trying to take over my PI agency?'

'Hey, cut the paranoia, Pem. This isn't Iraq. I'm your oldest friend. I know something's up. I get there's a threat to you, but not from us. I said Matt was someone you could trust with your IT. Chrissie is completely professional and someone I trust with my life.'

'Has Matt left Balcon and Mora?' Chrissie chipped in.

'Not that I've heard. Now look, Pem. I told Chrissie I had an interesting SCUBA diving accident to investigate. It's not a secret, it's in the public domain. And I know from

61

looking at her that she's got some nugget of information. But if it's to do with her forensic accounting work, then she'll be bound by client confidentiality.'

He shot a glance at Chrissie and caught the faintest of nods. He was on the right track.

'Okay, okay, Clive. But you two, on the same day? It's a red flag.'

'Well, stop being so suspicious. You're not in a war zone.'

Chrissie's face gave nothing away. She stared at her plate. 'I-I'm sorry, Pember. I didn't mean to upset you. I wasn't looking for work or trying to take over anything.'

'Yeah, sure.'

'I-I just wanted to say that when Morton Alconbury died five or six weeks ago, there's...well a process was set in motion. The executors of his will must apply to the probate service for probate to be granted before they can administer his will and wind up his estate, or rather, what his wife doesn't also own.'

Clive guessed she was hiding her embarrassment behind the legal jargon.

'So?' Pember grunted.

'It means Morton Alconbury's accountants are preparing his accounts, ready to send to HM Revenue & Customs, who report to the probate service. It's about income tax, death duties, and inheritance tax.

'Do you manage his accounts?'

'No. Another accountant in the firm deals with it.'

'And your point?'

'The will has already been presented and lodged with the Probate Registry. It's now a public document.'

'So...we can get to see it, already?'

'Yes, Pember. But they charge for a copy.' She smiled faintly.

'Just so I've got it clear,' Clive asked slowly, 'has one of your colleagues asked you to–'

'Take a look because the accounts don't add up?'

'Yeah. Well, have they?' Pember pitched in.

'They're about to ask. But my point is, if you employ Matt for your IT, then get him to look more deeply into both Morton and Gillaine, his wife.' She stared at her plate again, as if to discourage further questions.

'I guess the coroner's verdict will decide whether she gets life insurance payouts. There could be a lot of money at stake.' It was obvious, but Clive felt it needed to be said.

'What's she like?' Chrissie asked.

Her change of focus threw him for a moment. 'When I saw her today, she was prickly, impatient, angry, Canadian…still a grieving widow. I couldn't ask about life insurance.'

'Not the right moment. And the house?'

'Ha,' Clive laughed. 'Trust you to want to know. Actually, Chrissie, it was nice. Nothing flashy. I'll be surprised if there are death duties to pay. Anyway, won't it all go to his wife?'

'It depends on his will.' And, as if it was an afterthought, she murmured, 'It was renamed inheritance tax, but it's funny how everyone still thinks of it as death duties.'

Clive smiled at her. 'I'd say it's an unsuccessful example of HMRC legalese used as spin.'

'Their version of street rules,' Pember murmured.

WEDNESDAY

Pember sat at his desk and focused on a blue dot displayed on his computer's monitor. It was the tracker signal from the white Fiat Panda, and it was being recorded and displayed in real time. The programme was satisfyingly versatile, and the recording could be replayed at slow or accelerated speed, even backwards. He could zoom in and out, enlarging the scale of the map for greater detail. But for now, he was content just to watch the dot move slowly along the A14 towards Newmarket.

He was pleased the tracker was transmitting well. He'd already checked it on his phone app, but he preferred the larger picture a bigger screen gave. Out of the corner of his eye he caught a flicker of movement on the CCTV monitor. His stomach twisted.

A fleeting image showed a shoulder and the top of a head, the hair short and dark auburn. His mind raced through the sequence. *Who the hell's on the landing?*

'Jeeez. Stop doing this to me,' he muttered as Clive opened the office door.

'Good morning,' Clive said, seemingly unaware of the anxiety he'd just sparked. 'I'm in to see if Gillaine Alconbury has emailed a list of her husband's friends and family yet.'

'You could have called me.'

'Yes, but you serve such excellent coffee. Anyway, Matt Finch is going to drop by.'

'Drop by? When?'

'Shortly.'

'What? How the hell d'you know if I'd even be here?'

'Woah, it's why, along with the pull of your espresso machine, I came this morning…in case you weren't here.'

Pember knew Clive's smile repertoire, and this one, the one that held you, spread from his eyes to harness his face. It was genuine. And then a sudden frown wiped it away.

'Are you okay, Pem?'

'No. I'm not bloody used to working with another PI. Sorry. I'll get used to it.'

'Good. I'm not here to cramp your style, but I want Matt's services too. So, once I've spoken to him then I'm out of your hair. I'm going to call in at Raingate and have a word with one of my old colleagues.'

'Raingate?'

'The police station on Raingate Street.'

'Okay, but what about?' He tried not to bristle.

'Their take on the SCUBA diving accident? Why else?'

Pember closed his eyes and counted as he breathed slowly. It was the bloody rollercoaster again. This time it was called Clive, but it could have been Flossy. He forced himself to detach as he relived what had just happened. *One*; he'd spiked anxiety. *Two*; he'd spiralled irritation. *Three*; he'd soared with anger. *Four*; he was deaccelerating into the docking bay of reason. *Five*; his ear hissed gently, reassuringly. This wasn't about Flossy. *Six*; what was happening to him? He'd joined the army; he was used to being organised. He liked it. So, why rail against being organised by Clive? *Seven*; he must keep his anger in check. But anger was his most difficult emotion to suppress. *Eight*; empty the mind. *Nine*; drain away emotion. *Ten*; float in a vacuum.

'Are you sure you're okay Pem? Are you still taking your meds?'

'Yeah, sure. I…it's just I seem to have a short fuse these days.'

'These days? It's always been short. Remember when some punk rode off on your bicycle? What age were we, ten or eleven?'

It was something Pember preferred to forget. He'd raced like a sprinter after the taunting teenager. He'd lunged at the bike. The punk fell off and the bike crashed into a tree. It should have been enough, but when the young Pember saw the buckled front wheel, something flared in his head. He threw a punch. It missed. The punk laughed and legged it. The mocking jeer was the flame. Pember had exploded in uncontrolled rage and punched the tree. Bust his hand.

'Espresso, Pem? I'm having one.'

While Clive made coffee for them both, Pember split his screen and checked his emails again.

'There's a new one from Gillaine Alconbury,' he said and opened the curt email. 'I'll forward it. You can work your way down her list.'

On the other half of his screen the blue dot had moved off the A14 and was heading into Newmarket. Pember zoomed in, 'Now that's interesting, she's going to the July Racecourse…or is it the National Stud next door?'

'Is that the tracker on Smith's car?' Clive put a double shot of espresso on the desk for Pember, and cupping his own single shot, positioned himself behind the desk to view the monitor. 'It's a good signal, Pem.'

'Yeah, and I reckon it's getting more interesting.'

'Why? And why did you get shirty with me about Smith yesterday?'

Paul Smith, both as a person and client, made Pember feel deeply uncomfortable. Something he didn't want to dwell on for too long. But with Clive standing behind him and watching the monitor with him, it felt like old times playing computer games when they were kids. 'It's like playing River Raid,' he murmured.

'River Raid? That takes me back. So, you're a fighter jet and Smith's what, an enemy tank?'

'Smith's a mystery. That's why I need your friend's help.'

'What's Smith's real name?'

'I don't bloody know. It keeps changing.'

'Are you holding back on me?'

'No, but I reckon our Mr Smith's tech savvy.' He waited, wondering if Clive would tumble to what he already feared.

'Are you saying he could track his car himself?'

'Yeah. Or someone close to him could. His name change is a professional job.'

Clive frowned. 'So…why…?'

'Spit it out.'

'Why involve you?'

'Yeah, that's what I was wondering. Why the hell does he need me?'

It was a relief. Finally, he'd put words to what had been niggling him. It had been easier than he'd expected. But Clive had always been good at reading him. In fact, he didn't really understand why he'd kept it close at all. Except it raised other questions, and Clive was bound to be thinking them. Questions like why leave Norwich? Why the anonymous delivery of D'Artagnan? And there were other blanks to fill, secrets in his past.

Movement flickered on the CCTV monitor. Clive had seen it too. Pember stiffened and stared. The top of a head,

67

the hair…dark…sandy-coloured. The shoulders…a rounded torso. Slow steps laboured along the landing. The man gazed up into the camera. A scrappy, sandy beard.

'It's Matt.'

'What? Already?'

A knock sounded on the door.

Pember hadn't known what to expect, but Matt was still a surprise.

'Hi, I'm Matt Finch.' He sounded breathless, his accent soft Suffolk. He glanced around pointedly for a chair and at Clive, as if seeking reassurance.

'I'm Pember Quinn and the director of the Hatter Street PIA. I've been expecting you. Tell me about yourself.' Pember almost barked the words, adopting his punchy, staff-sergeant tone. He'd met plenty of tech assistants during his army days and he wasn't going to let this paunchy, unfit specimen question who was boss.

'You've been expectin' me?'

'It's okay, Matt. I told Pember. Take a seat.'

Pember shot Clive a look. A don't-molly-coddle-him, I'm-asserting-who's-boss kind of a look.

'Ta.' Matt sat heavily on one of the conference chairs. He was dressed casually in a biker's jacket, sweatshirt, jeans, and trainers, his eyes darting between Pember's face and the monitor on the desk.

'Okay, so tell me about yourself.'

Matt frowned.

'He means your CV. He wants to know about your computing background, work, and experience.'

'Ah, got it. Yeah well, I done the Computin' & IT course at Utterly Academy, back in 2011 'til 2013. I started workin' at Balcon & Mora part time in 2012. I'm still part time with Damon.'

'Balcon & Mora? Who's Damon? Explain?'

'He's Damon Mora of Balcon & Mora. It's in Bury, just off the Buttermarket. Most of the work is contact tracin' for credit card companies. Oh yeah, and there's no Mr Balcon. He's just a pretence to make the outfit look bigger.'

'Really? What else? That's when you're not contact tracing for card companies?'

'I help out and do some teachin' in the Academy's computin' & IT department.' He lifted his plump hand and scratched his scrappy beard.

'Which academy? Where?'

'Utterly Academy, Stowmarket.'

'And that's it?'

'I do commissions...see I can work from home. Me mum died a couple of years ago, so I got space now for me computers an' monitors.'

'Where's home?'

'Stowmarket. You want me address?'

'Not now. Do you work for the police?'

'I-I...' He glanced at Clive.

'It's okay, you can tell Pember.'

'I done some consultancy work for Clive. But he's retired now.'

'So, you've signed non-disclosures? You understand about keeping information safe.'

'Yeah, have I got the job?'

'What?' Pember almost exploded. Matt was too blunt, too transparent, too literal. He was almost without trappings and Pember was singularly unimpressed with the CV. He closed his eyes, forced himself to breathe slowly and counted under his breath.

'You okay?' Matt asked.

He opened his eyes and glared at Matt. *What age is he? Barely thirty?* He watched transfixed, as under his gaze Matt scratched his beard again. *Jeeez, he's even giving away when he's nervous.*

An idea shaped in Pember's mind. This was exactly the type of person he wanted: blunt, transparent, literal, and easy to read. Someone who didn't have the skills to double cross without showing it. *But is he good at his job?*

'Let's start with this. Show me what you can make of it.' Pember took a memory stick from his desk and handed it to Matt. 'I've listed several names and loaded some photos; some are mine and some provided by a client called Paul Smith. He's using an assumed name and I believe he's had several names over the past ten years. I want you to find out all you can, past and present.'

'What here? Now? How long I got?'

'No, not here. Not now.'

'Good, coz it don't look like you've much tech here. I'll be faster usin' me own computers. How long I got?'

'24 hours. I want all you find. Keep me updated. Meet me here, same time tomorrow.'

'Hey, and Matt,' Clive added, 'I've got some names for you as well. I'll email the list, okay?'

'Yeah, Clive. Cool. Frag an' burn, I've got the job!'

Pember waited until Matt had left the office, downed the dregs of his cold double espresso and grimaced. '*Frag and burn*? Where did you find him?'

'Through Chrissie. They were on the same carpentry course at the Academy for a while. He's good and he's not driven by money. And *fragment and burn* is computer-game language!'

But Pember was only half listening. Something was wrong.

'Hell, the blue dot's dead.'

'What?'

'The tracker's stopped transmitting.' Pember moved the curser back along the time bar and clicked play. They both watched the blue dot, motionless in Newmarket's National Stud carpark. He ran the recording forward at double speed. The blue dot was visible…visible…gone.

'Now back and slowly over when it disappears,' Clive said. 'There. It vanishes at 09:42:20. Ten minutes ago.'

'Yeah. Accurate to the last 20 seconds.'

'It was stationary when it disappeared, so what do you reckon? More likely discovered and removed than fallen off?'

'Yeah. Bugger!' Pember cursed under his breath.

'What'll you do?'

'Ride to Newmarket. Check the carpark. And I'll take another tracker with me…just in case.'

***

Pember kept a selection of different motorbike gear. This time, instead of his black leathers and backpack, he chose his blue backpack and a jacket with high-vis yellow panels on the shoulders. He'd found drivers rarely recognised or remembered the make and model of a bike, but the colours of the rider's helmet, jacket or backpack were more likely to stick in their minds. So, he liked to mix and match his gear. He called it the *art* of discreet tracking and his various outfits were his civilian camouflage.

He gunned along the A14, wind buffeting him as the road cut across swathes of flat and gently rolling country.

To the sides of the dual carriageway, rough grassy banks and verges stretched towards hedgerows of windbreaking trees and bushes. And beyond, fields were filled with the fresh green of young wheat and barley, and the shock of yellow, flowering rapeseed. The Yamaha Tracer ate the fifteen miles effortlessly, cruising at 70 mph. He took the slip road exit and sped past paddocks and rides close to the straight road into the centre of Newmarket. He negotiated a busy, cramped junction and then he was out of the central scrum and turning into the grassy calm of the racecourse grounds.

It was a maze of small tree-lined roads, notices, and directions, designed for race-day traffic. On a Wednesday at 10:20am it was quiet and almost deserted. Directions to VIP and grandstand parking didn't apply to him. He pictured the map on the tracker app and navigated to the National Stud car park.

He spotted the Fiat Panda immediately. A lone, white hatchback, impossible to miss because no other cars were parked close by.

'Odd,' he murmured, the hackles prickling on his neck. It looked staged, as if the Panda had been positioned for maximum visibility. The car appeared to be empty. *Jeeez, is a sniper waiting for a clear shot if I approach it?* A spike of adrenaline fired through his veins. He coasted, hyper-alert and in low gear around the parking area and scanned for trouble. It seemed safe. He turned his attention back to the Panda.

Someone was sitting in the driver's seat. 'Where the hell's she come from? Shite.' He recognised the woman immediately; the dark, shoulder-length, curly hair was unmistakable. *It's Veronica Smith.*

She looked straight at him.

'Hell.' He manoeuvred to ride away.

She got out of the car. 'Help me! Please,' she called and waved at him.

He paused.

'Please, I need your help.' She stood glancing over her shoulder, a mix of fear and urgency in her voice.

He eased the bike forwards, ready to accelerate away in a split second. *Is it a trap?*

She put a finger to her lips and closed the car door. 'Please, I took the tracker off to get you to come. What took you so long?'

'What took me so long?' Now he was cross. No, not cross, more a rush of humiliation for allowing himself to be tricked. He pushed up his visor. 'Have you been hiding in your car? What the hell's going on?'

She didn't answer, but instead walked over to a tree and stood waiting for him to follow.

He glanced through the car windows. There was no one hiding inside under a blanket, ready to pounce. *Good.* Intrigued he rode slowly to where she stood.

'Please, I haven't much time. You took longer than I expected. My husband is trying to kill me.'

'What?'

'I didn't want to talk about it near the car in case he's got it bugged.'

'Bugged?'

'I guessed he'd have me tracked. I-I thought you might come out to where the signal stopped. Here…' She handed him the tracker. 'Now you can say you came out and found it lying here. I'll tell him I had a flat tyre and fitted the skeleton spare. He'll believe it came off when I used the jack.

He'll think I drove over it.'

'So, you changed your wheel? Don't you carry an inflater / sealant kit?'

'No, Uncle Iddy had a skeleton wheel. Look, when you still hadn't come, I thought I'd misjudged you.'

'Misjudged me? You took a bloody gamble. It was pure chance I checked the monitor ten minutes after the tracker stopped transmitting.'

'I bet on the horses. I'm used to weighing the odds.'

'And that makes it all right?'

'There's less luck needed if you do your homework.'

He shook his head. 'What's your plan?'

'I hoped you could help me.'

'Oh yeah? How?'

'Like a bodyguard. Stay close.'

'What?'

***

Clive told himself to stop mulling it over. If he'd really thought he should have gone to Newmarket with Pember, then it was too late. Pember had already changed into his motorbike gear and thundered down the stairs. The best use of time now was to concentrate on the Alconbury case.

He opened Gillaine Alconbury's forwarded email, but his thoughts strayed from the contents. *Why had the tracker's signal died.? Was it a trap?* He shook his head.

'I should have gone. She's never seen me or my car,' he sighed. *But this older Pember will simply accuse me of trying to steal his case. Where the hell's his paranoia come from?* 'Hmm, It's best if I stay focused on the Alconbury case.'

The walk from Hatter Street to the Raingate Police Station sloped gently along old pavements and cobbles and past historic buildings. The fresh air helped to clear his mind, and the mid-morning sun brightened the sky. If it hadn't been for the modern traffic and steady flow of pedestrians, he could have imagined himself in an earlier age. His pace was frustrated as he wove between cars parked in the old Chequer Square. He crossed to Crown Street and glanced back at the south facing walls of the Norman Tower and the Cathedral's Millennial Tower. They were bathed in sunshine. The sight warmed his heart and lightened his step, but he didn't need more distractions. He wanted to catch DS McLaren, and he lengthened his stride along Crown Street and then Honey Hill to link with Raingate Street.

The main body of the police station was two storeys high and built with pale-coloured brick. It stretched in front of him like an army barracks with old-style sash windows on the first floor and arched-top, half-length, tilt-opening windows on the ground floor. He imagined Pember feeling at home in the building and headed for the main entrance. It was singularly unimposing. A pair of traditional, dark-blue-glass lamps hung from the front wall either side of the door. The police station may have been built in the early 1960s, but he reckoned the architect had designed it with heritage in mind. The outward nod to the twenty-first century was the steel-railed wheelchair ramp and a security camera.

He strode up the ramp, took a deep breath, and pressed the door-entry buzzer.

'Hello, sir. Back to join us already.'

It was a greeting not a question, and Clive smiled at the duty uniform behind the main desk. He didn't stop to chat but walked through the reception area and took the stairs two at a time.

The office he wanted was on the first floor. He knocked on the partially open door and poked his head into the room. 'Hi Chakra.'

Chakra McLaren looked up from his desk. He was in his late twenties with short dark hair, a long face and skin tones suggesting his mixed heritage.

'Good to see you, sir.' His smile was genuine, warm.

'Don't call me sir. I'm Clive, please.'

'So, how's retirement treating you?'

'Retirement? It's okay.' He glanced round office. It was a long oblong shape. IT assistants worked at computer stations at the far end. 'And you? There'll have been some changes, I guess.'

'A few. But you know how it goes. I'm still a DS under a tonne of shi–'

'Forms and bureaucracy?'

'Yeah. You left just at the right time. Before Russia invaded Ukraine. Now there'll be Ukrainian refugees as well as the Afghans to settle. Why do people make baseless accusations of theft? It's got so sensitive. Translators, victims, politics...it's a minefield.'

Clive nodded in sympathy. 'Not so easy to give a case number and then close the case, ey?'

'Something like that. And now we're finally officially out of Europe, customs checks are taking so long that people-smuggling through Felixstowe and Harwich...well, they're either suffocating, freezing, or overheating. They're becoming murder investigations.'

'Seems I left just in time. And by chance, before one of your other cases...which is why I came in.'

'Oh yeah?' Chakra's body language changed. He

straightened his back and regarded Clive with an air of expectancy.

To Clive it felt like old times, as if he was giving a case briefing at the start of an investigation.

'On Monday March 21st, a fifty-two-year-old man called Morton Alconbury died in a SCUBA diving accident while exploring a chalk pit near Nettlestead.'

'Nettlestead?'

'It's near Somersham. The pathologist reported...' Clive pulled up a chair and read from his notebook, '*fatal Immersion Pulmonary Oedema.*'

'So, was it a drowning accident?'

'I don't know. The report didn't use the word drowning, and the coroner's hearing is a few weeks away, yet.'

'So how come you're involved?'

'Morton Alconbury's wife says he'd received threats in the weeks leading to the fatal incident. She says she told the police after he died, but they weren't interested. So, she engaged a private investigation agency to check it out.'

Chakra frowned and typed a name on his computer keyboard. He waited a few moments and then clicked to open a file.

'There's a statement from his diving buddy.'

Clive checked on his phone for the email from Veronica Alconbury. 'Phil Barner?'

'Yes. A Mr Phillip Barner, aged 30 years. In his statement he says it was a 25 metres, no-stop dive. The water was cold, and visibility was poor. He and his diving buddy, Morton Alconbury, took about 15 minutes to find the van at 25 metres depth leaving them about 10 minutes to explore the van. Morton Alconbury seemed to become distressed after another 8 minutes and signalled to end the dive. Mr

77

Barner pulled him out of the van, cut the rope that snagged both of their tanks on the way out and took him up to the surface, giving him breaths of air from his own tank on the ascent. He hauled him onto the bank, gave him more air from his emergency supply on his belt, phoned 999 for emergency services and attempted CPR. There was no suspicion of foul play, so we handed it over to the accident investigators.'

'Any mention of the alleged threats?'

'No. DC Paulton filed the forms and…there's the post-mortem report. I'll ask him if he remembers the wife saying anything about threats. What kind of threats?'

'She says text messages and a dead animal left on his windscreen.'

'A dead animal?'

'I believe she said a dead hare.'

'You mean like it'd been…?'

'She said it looked okay. I mean it was dead, but I guess poisoned.'

Chakra looked at his screen. 'No poisons on the pathologist's tox report. Do you believe her?'

'Why would she lie?'

'Does she still have her husband's phone?'

'She said she had.'

'Hmm…I'll send someone to pick it up. We'll get it unlocked.'

'Does this mean you're reopening the file?'

'Better see what's on his phone first. And I'll speak to Paulton and see if he remembers her saying anything.'

'And run it past the new DI.'

'Yeah, of course. DI Cedar. But Paulton? Why the hell didn't he…?' He shook his head. 'So, are you working for a

PIA now?'

'I don't know, I'm still deciding. Let's just say I'm helping an old friend.'

'Mrs Alconbury?'

'No, my old friend is the PI she asked to investigate it.'

'Do we know him?'

Clive wasn't sure how much to say. Pember hadn't confided in him for a reason. *If he's in trouble with the police, then wouldn't he have said to keep his name out of it when I visited the station?*

'We still keep tabs on the local PIs. The new DI hasn't changed that.'

'It's the Hatter Street PIA on Hatter Street, and Pember Quinn is the PI.'

Chakra typed the name into his keyboard. 'Quinn with one or two Ns?'

'Two.'

Silence sat heavily on Clive while Chakra waited for the computer to respond.

'Ah, now this looks interesting,' Chakra frowned, put an elbow on the desk, and rested his chin in his hand. 'Hmm…' He rubbed his upper lip with his forefinger. 'Would you like a coffee? White no sugar?' He stood up, 'I'm having one. We've a new hot drinks dispenser.'

'Okay, thanks.'

With Chakra out of the room, Clive shifted his chair slightly to get an oblique view of the screen. It showed a members' page on the Association of British Investigators website. And there, listed under the Qs was *Pember Quinn*, and his location, *Norwich*. He glanced around the office. None of the far-end IT assistants seemed to be taking any noticed of him. *Huh; it's one of Chakra's tricks to see if*

I've peeked at the screen. He shifted his chair back and decided to play him along.

'No sugar,' Chakra said as he walked back into the office and handed Clive a paper cup of scalding coffee held in a cardboard guard.

'Thanks. What's so interesting about Pember Quinn? He moved from Norwich recently. I expect he hasn't had time to notify the ABI... Or it hasn't filtered onto their website yet.'

Chakra laughed. 'I knew you'd take a look, sir.'

'Please call me Clive. I knew you were setting me up! You touch your lip when you lie.'

***

Veronica Smith turned on her heel and walked back to her Fiat Panda.

Pember watched, his mind trying to make sense of what she'd just said. Her husband was trying to kill her. She'd given no reason why, or even how. *Was she crazy? If her husband really was trying to kill her, why pay a PI to put a tracker on her car? Unless...unless by tracking her for a few weeks and getting to know her routines, her husband would know where and when to kill her.*

Pember couldn't risk that her fears were unfounded. Already she was back in her car and about to drive away. He made a snap decision to follow her.

'Don't overthink it, just go with your guts,' he muttered and suppressed the tiny voice in his head saying *trap. It could be a trap.* He flipped down his visor and drew away smoothly.

This was going to be easy. Following someone without having to stay hidden from view was fun and a primary school-level skill for him. He hung back a little, and out of habit kept other cars between them. He even felt relaxed enough to let his thoughts flow around what she'd said. A thought dawned. *Jeeez! Am I the sitting target?*

The idea was so twisted and cunning, it had to be true. Paranoia took control. His guts cramped and the gentle hiss in his right ear notched up a level. He was the one sitting high on a bike, his ride taller than the average car-driver's seat. He was in clear view, unprotected by car door panels. His bike's front windshield was low, and it wasn't bullet-proof. *Of course, I'm the target, not Veronica Smith.*

It threw his mind back to his tours of duty in Iraq, the period before his discharge to pension in 2009. It was the time of the counterinsurgency, and one of his roles in the Royal Military Police had been to provide advisory training for Iraqi police recruits. But the insurgents in Iraq weren't always obvious, just like today's assassin in Newmarket waiting for a clear shot at him. Killers looked like everyone else in a crowd. It was why the recruits had needed to watch each other's back while patrolling Iraqi marketplaces.

'Stick close together. Don't get isolated. Don't let a kid grab your hand and lead you away. Next thing, you'll be lost in the crowd with a knife between your ribs, or a bullet through your brain,' he'd barked at the recruits, like every good staff sergeant before him.

And here he was, the last in the line with no one to watch his back. He was exposed and sitting up tall, like the bloody Eiffel Tower. *Do they think I'm stupid? Well, staff sergeant Quinn's going to show 'em.*

He dropped his speed and a couple of gears. Grit steeled him. He shifted his weight and heaved the handlebars sharp right. He leaned into the U turn and crossed the on-coming lane. He was lucky; it was a wide stretch, and both he and his bike were perfectly balanced.

'Bugger you!' he shouted to the inside of his helmet and accelerated away in the opposite direction to the Fiat Panda.

He could have been flying, with the wind buffeting his chest, his body weightless, and the bike an extension of his form. The forward motion was so smooth he felt disconnected from the ground. And just as his body sensed it, so his mind let go. He left Iraq, the heat, the dust, the fear, and the anger. They belonged somewhere else in a world of landmines and with the snipers he'd escaped. He flew and flew before he glanced down at his speedometer…shite!

He slowed and pulled onto the verge of the B1506. He was already out of Newmarket and a few hundred yards before the slip road onto the A14. Calmer and once again focused on the here and now, and present-day issues, he dragged his mobile from his pocket and called Clive.

'Hi. Did you find the tracker?' Clive's voice sounded pleasant, relaxed.

Pember tried to keep it light. 'Yeah, but it's complicated. Veronica Smith says her husband wants to kill her.'

'What? You've spoken to her?'

'Yeah. She tricked me. She disconnected the tracker. Hid in the car 'til I arrived.'

'But–'

'And like a bloody lemming I walked straight into her trap.'

'Are you okay?'

'Yeah, but she got it bloody wrong if she thinks I'm her knight in shining armour. She'll play more tricks. I know it.'

'So, we walk away? Drop the case?'

Pember heard the *we* and was surprised he liked it. 'I don't know. I need the intel on Paul Smith, ASAP.'

'But Matt won't be back 'til tomorrow morning, some time after nine. You told him yourself. Remember?'

'I…we need it sooner.' If they'd been speaking face to face, he'd have given his old friend the get-me-out-of-this-scrape look and then got irritated with himself. But they weren't. So, he waited and tried to stay calm, counting slowly in his head.'

'Pember, are you still there?'

'Yeah. Poor signal.'

'Right. I was worried something might have happened to you. How about I call Matt? He'll probably start our job this evening after he's finished work. It will mean going to Stowmarket tonight to get the intel from him hot off the press.'

'It's good with me.' He knew he had to fit a new tracker to the Fiat and depending on the intel, he might do it differently this time. So, the cover of darkness after he'd visited Stowmarket would suit him fine. 'Yeah, set it up with Matt. Let me know the time and address.' He ended the call and counted out ten long breaths.

He was back in control and a step closer to making a definitive plan. *Hell! I forgot to ask Clive what he discovered from the Raingate Station visit. Well…it'll have to wait until this evening.* In the meantime, Pember needed to get back to Hatter Street and his office.

***

Pember parked his bike and hurried through Hatter Street, and into his office building's unmanned reception. The oak-beamed ceiling would have made it gloomy had it not been for the glass door panels. They shed natural light onto the dominant feature, a directory board. It listed the offices on each of the three floors; ground, first, and of course, the Hatter Street PIA on the second floor. He ignored the door on one side of the staircase sporting PRIVATE in bold letters, and the corridor with more offices heading towards the rear of the building. Instead, he frowned at the double doors with *Meeting Room* on the lintel and the *vacant /occupied* slider sign. He'd been told he could use it to see clients unable or reluctant to climb the stairs to his office.

The slider sign indicated *vacant*. But his sixth sense, the intuition that helped him survive his active RMP service, made him uneasy. He needed to take a closer look. He opened one of the double doors.

A gasp and sudden movement startled him. A woman dressed in slim-cut trousers under a knee-length pinafore-style overall stared at him for a couple of seconds. Her brown eyes widened before she glanced down and resumed polishing the conference table.

'Sorry. I didn't expect anyone to be in here. It said *vacant* on the door,' he murmured and cast a glance around the room, appraising it for danger. The polished conference table and chairs were low threat. The carry box of cleaning materials, a greater threat.

'No, no. The room is here to use if you need it.' Her face was framed in a grey-blue headscarf which loosely swathed her head and neck and draped around her shoulders.

'Are you...are you Dove, the cleaner?'

She straightened up. A slight nod. 'Yes. But my name is Amina.' She spoke precisely, her manner serious and with a trace of American to her accent.

Pember frowned. He guessed she hadn't reached middle

age, and she certainly wasn't a youngster. Somewhere between twenty-five and thirty-five-years old?

'Amina? Amina Dove?'

'Amina Abdul. People find *Dove* easier. You must be Mr Quinn, the two offices on the top floor?'

'How the hell d'you know who I am?'

'I clean here. Naturally, I have a list of the offices and when they are to be cleaned.' She spoke calmly, her quiet poise almost unnerving.

'Were you in this building early yesterday morning?'

'Tuesday morning?'

'Yes. Someone delivered a package, a cardboard box. It was left outside my office.'

'I come at six in the morning. I didn't see anyone.'

'You have a key?'

'Yes. The entrance door stays locked 'til eight o'clock. I have four offices to clean early morning. They work late days. The rest I clean in the evenings. It's the same every day.'

'So, whoever delivered the parcel would've needed a key to get in?'

'Yes, from six at night 'til eight in the morning.'

'Unless someone let them in, or they were already inside,' he said, thinking aloud. 'Is this room kept locked?'

'Yes. Every office has a key to the meeting room.'

'But you're in here cleaning it now…why not on your evening or early morning roster?'

She frowned. 'Sometimes I come to spend quiet time here. But I'm Dove, so I polish the table while I'm here. You want the room now?' She moved to put her duster and spray can of beeswax and lavender polish back into her carry box.

'No, it's okay. Look, I don't want you cleaning my offices.' He caught a flash of hurt in her eyes as she dropped her gaze. He relented, 'At least, not yet. I'm still unpacking.'

'If you put your garbage out for me, I'll collect it in the mornings.'

'Thanks.' He smiled and left, his mind working overtime. *Is she harmless or a threat? Dove's a clever name, neutral, nationless...peaceful.* And the name had done what he guessed it was meant to do. It had reassured him. *Jeeez, was she anything to do with my tours in Iraq?* He didn't know, but he suspected she might be a refugee. *Afghanistan? Could she simply be part of a scheme to encourage companies and bosses to employ refugees?* He reckoned a call to his landlady would tell him.

***

Early that evening Pember rode slowly through a cramped Stowmarket housing estate. The Yamaha's headlights came on automatically with the ignition, and although it wasn't dark enough to need the main beam to see the way, he was glad of its bright LED lights. They shafted a warning to anyone who cared to look. 'I may be a stranger round here but don't mess with me,' they seemed to say, as he cruised deeper into the maze.

Perhaps it was the fading daylight, or maybe the dropping temperature, but the utilitarian and tired 1970s houses looked unwelcoming. Front room, plate-glass windows looked on with wide, unblinking eyes. Several youths hung around near the council waste bins. Clive had referred to the place by its nickname, The Flower Estate, the words conjuring images of floral tubs and hanging baskets fit for a

Britain in Bloom award. There was barely a leaf in sight.

He coasted into Tumble Weed Drive. There weren't any flowers here, nor, he suspected, had there ever been. Just discarded paper cartons and sweet wrappers blown into gutters. *Ha – the moniker was satire.* It almost made him warm to the place.

Tumble Weed Drive was silent. Several dozen 1970s semi-detached bungalows edged the pavements and grass verges on both sides of the road. It was isolated, a dead end. And beyond the edge of the estate, fields stretched into a distance made bleak by the fading light.

He spotted Clive's black Lexus parked directly outside one of the bungalows and headed to it. A motor scooter was tucked in the gloom close against the brickwork. *Of course - Matt was wearing a biker jacket when he dropped by the PIA office. This must be the right place.* Two factor verification was reassuring: both Clive's car and the motor scooter were parked outside. Automatically he noted the make and model, a Vespa GTS 300 Super Tech, the colour of mercury and with custom yellow and black paint on the trims. *So, Matt either has Italian blood or a taste for iconic bikes.*

Pember secured his motorbike in front of the Vespa. He glanced up, spotted a security camera set under the overhang of the eaves, and smiled.

'Hiya,' Matt said, opening the bungalow's front door before Pember had time to knock.

'Oh hi, Matt.'

'Cool bike.'

'Thanks.' Pember felt uncomfortable. On any scale, this place and Matt were strange. *Hadn't Clive said something about the mum dying and Matt staying on in her bungalow?*

He peered past Matt into the dreariness of the hallway.

'How long've you been here?' he asked, wondering if a freshen up with a lick of paint might have been in order.

'Coupla hours,' Matt said, his Suffolk tones broadening.

'I meant how long have you lived here?'

'Dunno. Most o' me life I s'pose. Why?'

'I wondered how long it took to get used to this place.'

'How'd you mean?'

'I mean...'

All the troubles of the day came to a flashpoint in Pember's head. He breathed slowly and counted.

'Are you okay, mate?' Matt asked.

'Is that you, Pember?' Clive's voice carried from a room further back along the hallway. 'Did you have trouble finding here?'

'Yeah.' Pember felt his tensions defuse. 'It's not what I expected.'

'Nothing here is ever what you expect, Pem. Run with it.'

Matt nodded. 'Come in, an' close the door. Don't know about runnin', but there ain't no point lettin' people peer in.'

Pember followed Matt into the hallway and through a doorway into the living room on the right. Two large computer monitors, and a couple of computer keyboards dominated a long trestle desk set against the far wall. Hard drives were stacked close by on the floor. A plush sofa dwarfed the rest of the space. A colour card of brushed-velvet greys, it sat like a beached whale that had died in the centre of the living room. Clive stood at the desk, his back to the door and his attention seemingly on one of the monitors.

Matt squeezed past the sofa.

'I said it were too big. But Mais insisted. She said it were like a comfort present after me mum died. That an' me Vespa 300 Super.'

'Mais?' Pember asked.

'Yeah, Maisie. She's out with her mates. She's me longstandin'.'

'Partner?'

'Yeah, girlfriend.'

'Is she good with computers too?'

'What Mais? Nah. You're jokin', right?'

Pember smiled. 'Just wondering about the security here.' He noted the heavy blind at the window and muted lighting. 'So, what've you got for me so far?'

'Got?' Matt looked at him for a second or two, scratched his scrappy beard, and mumbled, 'Yeah, Clive said about Paul Smith wantin' to kill Veronica, his missus. So, I'm searchin' with facial recognition for previous. It's bein' slow.'

'Dark web?'

'Yeah, for this kinda stuff. But it's snail pace.'

'Hey, something's come up, Matt,' Clive said, his eyes on the screen. 'There's a match for Paul Smith's face on the criminal records search. Seems he breached a restraining order,' Clive paused and read out, '*section: 5(5) PHA 1997.*'

'Are you using the photo I took of him? The one on the stick?'

'Yeah.' Matt sat down and edged his office chair closer. He stared at the screen. 'What the bloggin' hell's a PHA 1997?'

'The Protection from Harassment Act of 1997.'

'Scammin' spam. S'pose you know that from bein' a DI.'

'A retired DI.'

'Seems he were usin' the name Dave Jones when he breached the restrainin' order in 2018.'

'Hah! Dave Jones is one of Paul's previous personas. It's on the stick I gave you this morning.'

'Yeah, ta, Mr Quinn.'

'He also went by the names John Williams and James Brown. It's on the stick.' Pember wasn't going to let himself look like an amateur in front of Matt. 'Who was the victim?' he added.

Clive sighed. 'That could be difficult. It may mean going back to the original conviction when the restraining order was first made.'

'And who's to say he wasn't bloody intimidating a witness as well as the victim?'

'Exactly, Pem. Hey Matt, try drilling deeper into his 2018 conviction. The public can request transcripts of hearings and trials, but witness names or addresses may be withheld.'

'Then bloody try the dark net.'

'Yeah okay, but no botnettin' promises.' Matt's plump fingers moved across a keyboard.

Pember voiced his thoughts, 'So, he breaks a restraining order in 2018. Now Veronica Smith says he's threatening her. The bastard's got history. Hell! I should've believed her. I should have followed her today.' His stomach lurched.

'Yes, Pem. He's got previous. But what do you know about Veronica Smith?' Clive asked softly.

'Not a lot. She's Idris Brafman's great-niece and Paul's

wife.'

'Have you searched 'bout her already? Coz, see there weren't no more on the stick than a name.'

'No, Matt. I thought I'd leave something for you to do.' He bit back his irritation. 'But what I've got so far doesn't bloody stack up. Paul told me his real name was Idris Brafman, the name the DVLA have as the registered keeper of the car I'm tracking.'

'Fraggin' hell, you sayin' Veronica married her great-uncle?'

'No, Matt. Idris Brafman died of COVID in January. Paul's a liar. He said he was Idris Brafman, so I'd think he owned the car.'

'Blog almighty.'

'Yeah, Paul gave me a photo of Veronica. It's the one you'll find on the stick. But I'll need to take my own one of her.'

'Why, Pem?'

'He may've rigged the one he gave me.' Pember felt sharp. It was like briefing military police recruits.

'You realise she may be complicit in this.'

'Yeah, Clive. She may be as rotten as Paul. But maybe she had no choice.'

'Okay, while we're waitin' for them deep n'dark search-es, I'll start on Veronica Smith with a facial recognition.' Matt reached for the second keyboard.

'You like her. She's got to you, hasn't she, Pem?'

Pember shrugged. 'I don't know her. But I don't bloody like Paul, so if I'm taking sides, it'll be hers.' He watched Clive frown.

'Pem, you're being paid for discreet tracking of a car, not protection work. You signed a contract with Paul. You don't have a contract with her. She can always go to the police if she needs protection.'

'What? You're bloody joking. What would the police do? Log her call, give her a unique reference number and then ignore it? Mix with hoods, and the police don't protect you...unless you're an informant. And even then...' He let his words drift as he remembered the mess he'd left in Norwich.

'They'd ask her for evidence, which is more than you've done.'

Clive was right, and Pember didn't like hearing it. He counted slowly.

'Spammin' hack! Veronica's face is matchin' with...a Josephine Evans, a forty-year-old cyclist ridin' round the Welsh coast.'

'What?' The hissing in Pember's right ear screamed and distorted. 'Paul must've altered the image or used a shot of a similar looking woman. It's to throw me off track.'

'It follows. Calm down, Pem. He's a serial liar. Anything on searching her name. Matt?'

'There's forty Veronica Smiths in her age range. That's only usin' her name an' no facial. See, I ain't got no middle name or year of birth to narrow me search. It'll take a while checkin' each one.'

Pember waited, forcing himself to take measured breaths. 'Well?'

'Spammin' hell. I said it'll take a while. I'm workin' on it.'

'Okay, then how about Idris Brafman? He'll be easier for you. You've got his address on the stick. He was seventy-six when he died. I found that out yesterday when I searched. And his photo online certainly wasn't anything like Paul Smith.'

'Yes, good idea, Pember. Someone amongst this lot has got to be the person they say they are. Get his family tree, Matt. Everything you can on him. Yes, and the land register. Find out who owns the house now. Idris could be the one thread of truth through all of this.'

Pember fizzed with pent-up frustration. If he didn't do something, he'd explode. 'Okay, this time I'll put several bloody trackers on Veronica's car. If she pokes around, at least one'll get past her.' He dropped his voice, muttering as his thoughts romped ahead, 'And how about I get a tracker on Paul's car? Except there was only the Fiat Panda parked outside the house. Yeah, I must talk to her. Find out more.'

'Keep up your guard, Pem. Paul Smith's a nasty piece of work.'

'Yeah, I've got that. How much longer to get more on Paul, Matt?'

'Hours.'

'Then I'll bloody well split. I've got trackers to fit. See you tomorrow morning, eight-thirty sharp in the office.'

***

Clive watched Pember leave. He seemed to walk with a stocky roll to his gait, something Clive had seen him perfect into a swagger when he was a youth. But now the swagger had gone and only the stocky roll remained. How his friend had changed over the years, and if Clive dropped his loyalty for a moment, he'd have to say the changes weren't necessarily for the better. Okay, Pember had always run on a short, impulsive fuse, but now there was a vein of anger and irritability replacing the cheeky fun. It unsettled Clive.

The front door slammed and a few minutes later, a throaty, three-cylinder engine burst into life directly outside.

Matt, his attention still focused on the screen, had appeared unaware of Pember's departure until the Yamaha's engine roared. 'He gone then?' he muttered.

'Yes. I'm worried about him.'

The words were out. Clive had barely acknowledged his concern to himself, let alone condensed it into worry. Now he'd verbalised a gut fear.

Matt didn't respond, so Clive let his thoughts flow on and shape into sentences.

'Something's up. Why won't he say what happened in Norwich? And the D'Artagnan Toby jug? His reaction...everything was so odd about it. He never used to be so secretive. You'd imagine a slimy crook like Paul Smith could easily put his own tracker on a car...or get someone from his seedy, underbelly of a life to do it for him. Is Pember just unlucky to have Paul as a client, or what?'

'What you say, Clive? I were concentratin' on me searches.'

'I'm worried about Pember.'

'Oh yeah?'

'Yes, I'm...very worried about him. I think we need to find out why he left Norwich.'

'When'd he leave, then?'

'Two, maybe three weeks ago.'

'You want more searchin'?'

'Yes, in fact this takes priority. Hold the searches on my list of names for the SCUBA diving investigation.'

'What?'

'Check out what happened to Pember in Norwich first.'

'I get paid, right?'

'Yes. I reckon Pember's in some kind of trouble. The people for the SCUBA diving case can wait a few days. Besides, I'm still fixing times to interview them. It could take days to get round them all.'

'But what 'bout Paul and Veronica Smith?'

'They're a priority too.'

'Spammin' hell. How many priorities you got? Half an hour ago it were Idris Brafman.'

'You need to focus on him as well.'

'Blog almighty!'

'And don't tell Pember about the Norwich search. It's between you and me.'

He watched Matt redden, or rather the skin on his plump face and neck beyond his scrappy beard.

'Are you okay with that, Matt? It's Paul, Veronica, Idris and Pember first.'

'Yeah, an'…it's mega cool. It's like when you were workin' as a DI.'

'Good. Then I'll leave you to get on with it. See you in the office tomorrow, first thing.'

'Hatter Street?'

'Yes, and Pember'll be there so, if you find anything urgent about him, give me a call first.'

Matt nodded and turned his attention back to his screens.

THURSDAY

Clive noticed there was something odd about the top floor landing as he climbed the last few steps to the Hatter Street PIA offices. Pember's nearest office door was closed, but the far door stood wide open. The stillness felt ominous.

'Pember?' Clive spoke softly, then repeated more loudly, 'Pember?'

Silence.

This was unusual at eight fifteen in the morning, or for that matter, at any hour of the day. Pember was far too security conscious and secretive to leave his filing cabinets and computer unattended in an open room. He wouldn't have just vacated his office, unless...*oh no, is he flat out on the floor with his ear problem again?*

'Pember?' he shouted, 'are you here?'

Clive hammered on the locked door to Pember's spare office-cum-storeroom.

'Pember? I don't care if you've been up half the night fitting trackers, we've work to do. Matt'll be here soon. Get up!'

He listened for a moment. There was no sound from behind the closed door. He was wasting precious time He covered the landing in a couple of strides and burst through the open doorway into the main office.

'What the hell?' It took him a few seconds to take in the mess. 'Pem, why the hell didn't you answer me just now? I-I thought you might be ill again.'

'Don't nanny me. I'm taking my meds.' Pember stood, leaning against the desk, his face ashen, a sheaf of papers in one hand.

'Did you do this?' Clive swept his arm around, indicating the room.

'What? You think–'

'I don't know what to think anymore, Pem.' The filling cabinet drawers had been wrenched open; the contents ransacked. Sheets of paper and folders littered the floor. Documents were strewn on the desk. It was chaos, something Clive had seen many times before in his professional career. Plainly, if Pember hadn't done it in a fit of rage, then there'd been a break in. Someone had searched violently, frenziedly. 'Did they get what they were looking for?'

Pember shrugged. It was a defeated gesture. 'I don't know.'

'Hey, your Toby jugs have gone!' Something else dawned on Clive. 'You're wearing the same clothes as yesterday...and your backpack. Have you even been to bed? No, don't tell me, let me guess. You've been out all night fitting trackers and walking the streets, and you've only just discovered this, right?'

'Yeah.' Pember hung his head and then added, 'and they're character jugs.'

Clive was lost for words. Exasperated, he pulled his mobile from his pocket, ready to press the automatic dial for DS Chakra McLaren.

'What the hell are you doing, Clive?'

'I'm reporting the break in. No, don't argue. If you won't tell me what's going on, then I reserve the right to protect myself...no, both of us, in the way I know best.'

'Don't be so pompous. And don't you dare involve the police!'

'Settle down. I'm calling my old DS. No. Shut up and listen. Think. This way we get fingerprints and forensics. I

97

reckon someone out there is after you, and until you start sharing, this is how I'm going to play it.'

'No! Who the hell's agency d'you think this is?'

'Yours, Pem. But at this rate, one of us is going to get hurt. Now go and check your SIG Sauer hasn't been taken and then get it out of here. If the police check for drugs, their sniffer dogs may pick up on gun oil, gun cleaners… guns. Lose the SIG Sauer while I make the call.'

Pember grunted and picked his way across the littered floor. His shoulders seemed to sag, as if his rucksack was full of lead weights. Clive waited until Pember's key grated in the lock to the next-door office. He held his breath, expecting a shout of outrage, but all was silent. *Phew! They haven't broken into there, then.* He pressed the automatic dial for his old DS.

The call was short and to the point. Chakra ended it with a curt, 'Don't touch anything, sir.'

'What a mess,' Clive breathed and bent to pick up a handful of papers, soggy from the water reservoir in the upended coffee maker.

Brrring! His phone burst into life, its ringtone a lightning strike through the tension. *Caller ID – Matt.*

'Yes?' Clive snapped.

'I'm goin' to be late,' Matt said in a hushed voice. 'Can you tell Pember?'

'He won't like it. It's not a good moment. Have you got anything for me…or Pem?'

'Not exactly. See when Mais got back last night…she don't like me workin' late and–'

'You stopped searching? Overslept?' Clive snapped.

'Yeah, and see I'm teachin' them computin' students at ten. No time to get to Hatter Street n'back now. Can you clear it with Pember? I'll drop in after?'

'Damn it, Matt. You should have told us today was your Utterly Academy day.'

'Yeah, but see I can work on your stuff after.'

'We were relying on you. Just…just call me when you're done with the students. We've had a development here.' Irritated and frustrated, Clive ended the call. *Hell, is Pember's grouchiness catching? Are my reactions turning into knee-jerkers as well?* He needed to get a grip on his emotions before firing off became a habit. He gazed at the papers littering the floor.

'Okay?' Clive asked when Pember returned five minutes later from checking the spare office-cum-storeroom. At least he'd left his backpack in there, even freshened up a little. But one look at his face told Clive it wasn't the moment to mention Matt's phone call.

'Yeah, no one's been in there.' He sounded subdued.

'Good. And the gun?'

'Outside the window. Better get started on this lot.'

Clive bit back *but we shouldn't touch anything* and sighed.

They spent the next twenty minutes sorting through some of the papers. All they achieved were chaotic heaps across the floor. Clive had expected client files, but there were none, most of the paperwork related to training, qualifications, and professional insurance. More of a surprise were the photos and sales receipts related to porcelain, stoneware, and earthenware.

Chakra arrived within half an hour of the call, smart in dark chinos and grey jacket. He was accompanied by a DC, more colourful in brown brushed-cotton trousers and rust jacket. For Clive, it was a new experience to be on the receiving end of his old DS's investigation and he didn't bother to hide his embarrassment.

'Good morning, sir,' Chakra said, his tone measured as he shot a glance at his retired boss. Clive caught the old-fashioned look, one of disapproval and a hint of surprise. It was clear Chakra had expected better of him.

'And you must be Mr Quinn?' Chakra nodded, his eyes scanning the heaps of papers on the office floor. He held up his identity card. 'DS McClaren.'

Pember seemed to bristle.

'And this is DC Paulton. So, Mr Quinn, I hear you're a private investigator and new in town. Let's hope this isn't a taste of things to come. Shall we start with your security camera recordings?'

It wasn't how Clive would have started, but he swallowed the comment on the tip of his tongue and kept his face neutral as they clustered in front of the monitor on the desk. Pember played the security camera recordings. To begin with, he whipped through the previous nine hours at speed. Then more slowly, he concentrated on the time frames just before 01:08 am when the image on camera 1 blacked out, but the timer had kept going.

'So, at 01:08 am, on camera 1, night vision setting, someone with a dark-coloured backpack, wearing a black hoody, black tracksuit bottoms, trainers with white flashes across the sides, climbs the stairs,' Chakra said, his commentary flowing at the pedestrian pace of the slowed, jumpy images on the screen, 'Hmm, he–'

'Or she.'

'Yes, thank you, Paulton. *They*...medium height, slim build...keep their face looking down, away from the camera.' Chakra leaned in closer, 'Now they reach up with one arm. Look, the hand is dark…they're wearing gloves but there's a glint…it's…a spray can. And the other hand, also gloved…is cupped to the face and–'

'It goes black. They've bloody sprayed paint on my camera.'

'And then…five seconds later, camera 2 goes black,' Chakra murmured.

'And then camera 3. Bastards!' Pember shouted.

'They were wearing gloves, so I don't think we'll get any fingerprints. So, no reason to bring the SOCO team in but…'

'They? You think there was more than one?'

'No, Mr Quinn. It's a *they* – meaning one person but gender as yet unspecified. And we don't know what time *they* left because there isn't a working security camera on the entrance to this building.'

'We're in central Bury. There'll be security cameras dotted around outside, Chakra.'

'Yes sir. But for now, we'll take your security recording.'

'It's cloud backup every 24 hours,' Pember muttered.

Chakra nodded. 'So still on the hard drive. I'll need your machine or the original file.'

Muscles on Pember's face tightened as he clenched his jaw and slipped a new USB stick into the recorder. 'I'll make a duplicate.' Clive tried to catch his eye, but Pem was having none of it. He seemed white-hot angry. *Hell, surely Pember knows this is how the police behave? It wasn't personal.*

'Hmm. What do you keep in this office, Mr Quinn? Is anything missing?' Chakra asked.

Clive waited for Pember to answer and when he didn't,

shot his old DS a give-me-strength look. But of course, Chakra wasn't his DS anymore. The goal posts had moved, and the game had changed. He was on Pember's side now. But in that moment, Clive felt he understood Chakra better than he did his old friend and his interest in the Royal Doulton.

Chakra picked up a wadge of photos showing Royal Doulton marks. The kind of thing stamped on the bottom of Toby and character jugs and mugs. 'Are you a collector, Mr Quinn?'

'He must be, or a dealer, sir. There's lots of price guides here. But why would you need to know so much about fakes, forgeries, and reproductions, Mr Quinn?' DC Paulton asked, pronouncing the words slowly, as he read out the headings on his handful of papers.

'Or Europol?' Chakra added as he read what was written on the back of a photo. He rubbed his lip before continuing, 'Which reminds me, sir. I've turned up some more contacts for you relating to the SCUBA diving death. Drop by the station, lunchtime.' He had directed his words at Clive, but now addressed Pember, 'You still haven't said, Mr Quinn. Is anything missing?'

They waited. Clive caught Pember's warning glance to keep his mouth shut.

'No, nothing missing,' Pember said. 'This was a trespass while I was absent from the property. No one threatened me. There's no need to take it further.'

'But there's been an illegal entry and I see some minor damage. This isn't the work of a random intruder, Mr Quinn. Your property has been searched. Are you sure there's nothing more you want to tell me?'

'There's nothing more to tell, DS McClaren. Please, I

want you to leave, now.'

'Hmm, you may not have been the only property broken into round here, nor the only office in this building. I'll take the security recording on the stick.' Chakra held out his hand.

Pember hesitated and then handed him the new USB stick.

'Thanks, Mr Quinn. If you change your mind, here's my card. If we find a match on our records for the person on your stairs, I'll get back to you.' Chakra took one last look around the room, nodded and left. DC Paulton followed close on his heels.

Clive felt too stunned to say anything and stood staring at Pember. He waited until the heavy tread of the detectives' feet had died away down the staircase.

'What do you mean, nothing was taken? What about your Royal Doulton mugs? Don't D'Artagnan, Porthos, Aramis and Athos count?'

'Yes. And they're *character jugs*.'

'Okay, but why didn't you say they'd been stolen?'

'They're not worth more than a few hundred pounds and I don't want McClaren and Poulton crawling all over my office. And haven't you learned anything? A *Toby* jug has the character's whole body on it. A *character* jug only has the head, sometimes shoulders. And, what's more, *jugs* have pouring lips and spouts such as the corner of a hat. *Mugs* don't.'

His friend was trying to distract him with technicalities, and Clive wasn't going to fall for it. 'If this was only about your four musketeers, why turn your office upside down? The jugs were sitting in plain view on the top of your filing cabinets. What else were they looking for, Pember?'

A feeling of hurt seeped into Clive's frustration. This was turning into issues about trust. 'You can trust me, Pem,' he blurted.

'I work on a need-to-know basis. It's not about trust, it's about keeping the people around me safe.'

'But you're not in the military police now. Isn't it about time you consigned what happened in the past to the past? We're not in Ireland, Bosnia, Kosovo, Afghanistan, Iraq, or wherever you've done tours of duty. This is me, Clive, a Norwich boy, and we're both in Suffolk.'

'Yeah, then check out the headlines in late 2018. Spanish and Bulgarian police smashed organised crime gangs trafficking looted and forged cultural artifacts across Europe. You think they weren't the only outfits? You think it isn't still going on? Some of those artifacts were pottery and ceramics. We're talking valuable items.'

'But not your character jugs?'

'Mine were Dad's. He thought the world of them.'

'Right, they had history, your past. But somehow, you're tangled up in all this, aren't you? Why didn't you just say when the box with D'Artagnan was delivered? Hell, was there more to that character jug?'

'I don't bloody know.'

'And Paul & Veronica Smith, are they part of this?'

'No. Paul's a nasty conman who wouldn't know the base from the spout of a Toby jug. He'll be after Veronica's inheritance from Brafman. That's his level.'

Clive nodded. 'You know, I'm going to take a walk and clear my head. It's a lot to take in.'

***

Clive hurried down the stairs and out into Hatter Street. He wanted some fresh air. He needed space to think, and he suspected Pember had calls to make. Private ones. The very thought tempted him to creep back and spy on his friend, but something warned him against it. If the problem between them was about trust, then getting caught in the act of eavesdropping might break their friendship forever. He wasn't cross enough to take that risk, at least, not yet. There had only ever been space for one of them to get very angry and today, once again, it was Pember. Frustrated, Clive broke into a brisk walk.

Along the street, a delivery van door slammed. The sudden sound caught him mid-step. It pulled him up sharp on the curb and he paused, automatically looking for traffic. But he didn't register anything. Instead, his mind filled with an image flashed from his memory. Chakra had rubbed his lip!

Was the tell-tale sign linked to Europol or more contacts relating to the SCUBA diving death? Either way, Clive wanted to know, and Langton Place wasn't going to lead him to Chakra and the Raingate Police Station. He changed direction and headed down the gentle slope of Churchgate Street to Crown Street with its view of the Cathedral and Norman Tower.

His fast pace helped him to think. It cleared his mind of extraneous noise, the kind of thought-clutter that blurred detail. His friend was mixed up in something bigger than tracking two-timing spouses. The signs pointed to a larger stage; the world of pottery and ceramics. *Hell, how am I going to play it if Chakra tells me Pember is the criminal, and the stage is Europe and beyond?*

'Stick to facts. No pre-judging, no presumptions,' he told himself. But the pit of his stomach lurched at the prospect, and his sense of humour failed when he remembered Toby jugs had the full torso, and character jugs & mugs only had the head and sometimes the shoulders. *Is the theft a coded threat? A hint of what's in store for Pember?* No one had said these people were nice.

By the time Clive reached the security camera and door admission buzzer at the entrance to the police station, his emotions were buckled down and his professional persona back in control.

'Good morning.' He flashed a smile at the duty uniform behind the main desk. 'DS McLaren is expecting me. First floor. I know the way.' He walked on.

'Morning, sir. The DS said he'd come down for you.'

Clive pretended not to hear and continued towards the stairs, aware that the duty uniform had picked up the phone and was making a call. By the time he reached the top step his harassed former DS was already in the first-floor corridor, one arm partially in his grey jacket, the other searching for the second sleave. Clive stood and waited, his sixth sense telling him to stay silent.

'My new boss, DI Cedar's here,' Chakra whispered as he reached him. 'Come on. Let's go for a coffee.' He led the way down the stairs and out through the main entrance. They walked fast. The uneven pavements were soon left behind as they took a shortcut through the Cathedral grounds, and slipped into the Cathedral Refectory, known as the Pilgrims' Kitchen. Its large counter was laden with cakes and scones, ready and fresh for the day. A welcoming smell of coffee filled the air. The large space was airy, calming and, more importantly, at this time on a Thursday morning, almost devoid of customers.

Clive glanced up at the massive, wooden beams spanning the ceiling, all painted white. Large windows along one wall gave views of green lawn and a box-shaped marquee, a legacy of outdoor-eating popularised by COVID and smokers. However, as there were only a couple of other customers drinking coffee in the main refectory, he opted for the comfort of inside.

Leaving Chakra to buy the coffees, he headed to a secluded corner and drew back one of the ex-chapel chairs to give himself more space at the table. Its legs grated on the solid, parquet flooring. He hadn't wanted to draw attention to himself. He sat down.

So, Chakra doesn't want his boss to know he's talking to me. Interesting. His thoughts were soon interrupted when Chakra set a couple of coffee cups on the table. 'Thanks,' Clive murmured.

'The coffee's good here.'

'I know, Chakra. It's only been a couple of months since I retired.'

'Yeah well, I wanted somewhere quiet.' He checked his watch, 'We've an hour before the late morning and lunchtime punters hit the place.'

'And no one from the station is likely to drop in, right?' He'd stopped short of naming DI Cedar, but the way Chakra quickly looked away told him he was spot on target. He sipped his coffee and waited for Chakra to speak.

'Okay, I wanted to tell you Pember Quinn is a person of interest,' Chakra finally blurted.

'Oh, yes?'

'I checked with the CPS after you visited yesterday. I spoke to one of my contacts there. Narrowed it to Pember Quinn's name and Norwich, pending and past prosecutions, or him being on a witness list.'

'I thought the Crown Prosecution Service's database was…' He pulled a face.

'Yeah, but they're getting better, at least with the recent stuff.'

'And?'

'He was a witness for the prosecution in a case last November against a Willy Hindle–'

'Is that a real name?'

Chakra shrugged. 'He's a small-time thief and drug dealer, and it was a name the county-line kids could remember.'

'This was all in Norwich?'

'Mostly, except it turned out Willy wasn't quite so small time, or rather he branched out a bit.'

'Meaning?' Clive sipped his coffee.

'He scouted some of the kids for the local paedo ring.'

'And then blackmailed the paedos?'

'No. A local gang network took it on. By chance, Pember had a client who'd had some silver stolen. Willy was the main suspect and Pember'd been following him, hoping to trace his fences and then the silver. He just happened to also get the names and addresses of some of the drug dealers, paedos and gang members along the way.'

'So why aren't the CPS going after the big guns?'

'They are, but they wanted to secure Willy's conviction first. If he sings, then both Willy's testimony and Pember's information will nail the rest of them.'

'So, is Pember in witness protection?'

'Not exactly. They helped him move but…he hasn't changed his ID. You see, only the CPS know how much Pember has on the gang. Dates, times…he was logging it for expenses. Pember reckoned he'd be safer if the gang think it's Willy who's grassing them up in return for early release and a protection deal...which I believe he is.'

'Hmm, it explains a lot. And Europol? What's that about, Chakra?'

'I don't know. I was hoping you'd know.'

Clive frowned into his coffee. *Should I say about the missing Doulton character jugs?*

'What's the matter? What are you thinking, sir?'

'Nothing.' He'd forgotten Chakra could read him and raised his guard. 'I suppose I was wondering if you can ever know someone as well as you think you do.'

'Is that a hint for me to pursue the Europol / Interpol line?'

'Weren't you going to anyway?'

'It hadn't crossed my mind until this morning. But seeing all those papers about ceramic marks...I hadn't got him down as someone interested in fine arts.'

Clive nodded. He wasn't going to mention all the tours of duty in Europe and beyond. He reckoned it could have altered anyone's tastes.

'Hey, while I remember. The name of the pathologist and the biochemist on the toxicology reports for your SCUBA diving death - you'll know them from before you retired. No staff changes there.'

'Good.' He sighed. These were names he had already.

'The tox results, gas chromatography results, and post-mortem CT body scan were sent to the diving investigators as well as the coroner – they have their own experts, but we've duplicates of the results. All the victim's SCUBA diving gear was bagged up for the investigators to check. I've written down a name and number for you, someone you could try contacting.' Chakra rummaged in his breast pocket for a business card.

'Thanks. Any further names for me?'

'Sorry, I haven't had time. Pember was more of a priority.'

'Okay, but have you collected Morton Alconbury's phone yet?'

'Paulton's contacted his wife. When she drops it in for us, he'll take a statement about the threats and the dead hare on her husband's windscreen.'

'Good. Learn his lesson by revisiting his oversights?'

'Yeah, something like that. Right, I've got to go now.' He downed the rest of his coffee in a couple of gulps. 'Good to talk to you, sir.' He stood, nodded to Clive, and headed out through the arched doorway.

Clive watched him leave. It was like old times, a relaxed report on progress with his next in command. He'd always tried to make it more of a flow of ideas on how to progress the investigation than a battle of egos. For a moment Clive wanted to turn back the clock. Then his cynicism resurfaced as he remembered the double standards of some of his colleagues, the pressures amid the mind-numbing bureaucracy and paperwork, the unrealistic demands, and the hours worked but not logged.

Brrring! His mobile burst into life. He pulled it from his pocket. *Caller ID - Chrissie.*

'Hi,' he said, pleased for the distraction.

'Sorry to bother you–'

'I was only finishing a coffee. Anything up?'

'No. I'm booking a service for my car.'

An image of her yellow TR7 flashed though his mind.

'Can you give me a lift to the workshop from the garage next Thursday morning? Jason can drop me back to pick it up after work.'

Clive hesitated as he placed Jason, Chrissie's carpentry employee, from the myriad of names swirling in his head. 'Y-yes, that should be okay.'

'Ah thanks.' Her tone sharpened, 'You sounded...are you sure?'

He knew the signs. She was curious and she'd wheedle it out of him in the end. He sighed. 'I've just met up with Chakra,' he explained.

'How is he?' Her interest was obvious.

'He seemed fine.'

'Good. He hasn't persuaded you to go back, has he?'

'No, no. Nothing like that. He was giving me the low-down on why Pem left Norwich. Seems he got mixed up with some very unpleasant people.'

'Really? I told you it'd either be his temper or a woman. Is he in a lot of trouble?'

'Maybe. The thing is, Pember won't talk to me about it.'

'Don't sound so hurt. He's probably embarrassed. Un-less...is he trying to protect you?'

The idea of Pember staying silent to protect him didn't cut. Information on a need-to-know basis is what he'd said. *No, this is about trust, or rather a lack of it.* He kept his voice even, 'Hmm, and since when has ignorance been a protection?'

'It is if there are people out there wanting to extract it from you, Clive.'

'Huh!'

'And anyway, he knows you. You always get involved when your friends are in trouble.'

Clive didn't answer.

'Oh no. You've already got involved?'

'What? No, not directly. But I want to know what's going on. Just like you want to know what's going on.'

Her voice lightened, 'Are you calling me nosey?'

'It would be an understatement,' he laughed.

'Well, stay out of it. Please, I couldn't bear it if something happened to you. Just concentrate on the SCUBA diving case. It sounds safer, unless of course, you get tempted to take up diving. Bye now.'

He smiled and finished his coffee. It was so like Chrissie to give sound advice, often driven by her own agenda. Usually it was curiosity, but he guessed today's concern for his safety was coloured by Bill, her dead husband. He'd died back in 2008, a couple of years before Clive had met her. It turned out Bill had been allergic to latex. Very allergic. And the anaphylactic shock that killed him had been more dramatic and as fatal as a lightning strike. Clive knew that just because Chrissie didn't talk about it, didn't mean it wasn't floating in her subconscious. There were bound to be emotional scars.

He reckoned it was the same with Pember, and for himself, in fact anyone who'd lived a life. Past experiences and hurt either floated or sank in the subconscious. 'The problem,' Clive muttered, 'is that Pember's keep bobbing on the surface. Damned icebergs for the rest of us.'

'Can I take these cups?'

'What? Oh yes. Sorry, I was miles away.' Clive smiled vaguely as the young server stacked the dirty crockery onto a tray. It was time to turn his attention back to the SCUBA diving investigation. He sighed and rang the number Chakra had given him.

***

Pember's agitation had peaked by the time the police left his ransacked office. The half hour or so he'd spent with Clive after this calmed him a little, but when Clive announced he needed to get out and clear his head, Pember cast a glance heavenwards as he left. It was just like Clive to need a walk to process his thoughts. *How would that have worked in the army out in Iraq? Bloody snipers would have picked him off! This* - he glared at the loose heaps of papers and files on the floor – *could be about any manner of things*. His mind swirled with paranoia and his right ear hissed intrusively. He closed his eyes, breathed slowly, and counted to ten. At least he could think more clearly now that he didn't have to keep up his guard in front of Clive. His friend was too sharp to be fobbed off easily. It was unfortunate he'd had to throw him a few crumbs about Spanish and Bulgarian police, and the gangs trafficking cultural artifacts across Europe.

So, is the gang in Norwich behind this? Or is a resurgent crime syndicate dealing in looted relics, forgeries, and works of art putting a shot across my bows? And there's always the unlikely Paul Smith. But more to the point, have they got what they're looking for?

'At least I've got a tracker on Paul's car now.' He'd eventually found the Honda Jazz hybrid parked several roads away from number 17, Idris Brafman's old home.

Oh Jeeez! Has the intruder bugged my office?

He made a quick tour of the room with his bugging sensor – no listening devices or hidden cameras detected. Next, he stood in front of the filing cabinet closest to the door and frowned. Drawers had either been wrenched fully open, or hustled off their sliders and stops, and cast onto the floor.

113

He lifted out the remaining drawers and turned his attention to the inside of the filing cabinet and the metal support rails, guides, and sliders for the wheel-shaped rollers.

The hissing geared up as his fingers brushed along the drawer support and sliders for the third drawer down. *Is it loose? Has the intruder found the small memory stick concealed inside it?* His first impression was that it looked okay, but he'd need a Phillips head screwdriver to check for sure.

A few minutes later he'd removed some Phillips head screws and detached the metal drawer support. His adrenaline surged. His heartbeats thumped across the hissing as he turned the support over. A mini-USB pen drive glinted from its hiding place in the metal. He could have sworn it winked at him and slowly he smiled back. *Those bastards haven't won. It'll take a damned sight more to get the better of Staff Sergeant Quinn. Ha!*

The relief was almost overwhelming. If he'd learnt one thing in the military police, it was that a ransacker did just that; searched destructively. Every book would be swept off a shelf. There was no time or inclination to examine each one in turn. Likewise, a filing cabinet might be thrown over and drawers wrenched out. But ransackers rarely carried Phillips head screwdrivers, and rarely dismantled a metal carcass. Their philosophy on fire a bullet or drill out a rivet? Simple, fire a bullet. Better still, empty a whole magazine of bullets.

Bzzt! Bzzt! His phone vibrated in his pocket. It was still on silent mode from his night's work putting a tracker on Paul Smith's car.

There was no *Caller ID*. Elation flipped to a wrench in his stomach. *Is this a follow-up call from the intruder?*

'Yeah?' he breathed.

'Hi Pember. Jerome from the CPS speaking.'

'Ah.' He would have thanked God, but he'd lost him somewhere along the way. 'What's up? Is it court-time soon?'

'It might have been, but Willy Hindle was found dead in his cell last night.'

'Shite!'

'He'd been moved to a more secure wing for his own safety.'

'Right, so what happened?'

'The Kanes must have got to him. He was found hanging.'

'Bloody hell. Was it suicide?'

'No, his hands were tied. They hadn't even tried to make it look like suicide.'

Pember didn't say anything.

'You still there, Pember? Is it okay to talk?'

'Yeah. My office was done over in the early hours this morning. Hindle's murder might explain why.'

'Anything taken?'

'Nothing you'd be interested in. You've got my notes and log. You've got all you need to bring your case against the Kanes. You're still bringing it, I presume?'

'Yes.'

'So, were you calling to check on me?'

'I was calling to keep you informed.'

'Are you sure you weren't checking to see if…' He let the word fade away.

'You haven't kept anything back, duplicate files, that kind of thing? Safer if you haven't. I mean safer for you.'

'You have everything. How much do they know about

me?'

'Nothing. Well, only in relation to putting Hindle away.'

'And the break-in here?'

'How'd I know? But keep your head down.'

'You mean disappear?'

'No, not yet. They'll expect the case to be dropped, and...'

'And what?'

'The Kanes'll be distracted. The police will be investigating them for Hindle's murder. Don't draw attention to yourself. I'll call when I've an update.'

Jerome ended the call before Pember could ask more.

He sank to the floor and sat with his head cradled in his hands. He didn't need to ask what the Kanes would do. If they were behind the break-in, they already suspected he was involved and were checking him out. And if the case still went ahead, they'd put two and two together, figure Pember was a witness and come for him.

Why Jerome's question about duplicate files?

'Oh no,' Pember groaned. 'What if Jerome's on their payroll?'

Pember felt as if time was accelerating. If he was to stay ahead of its consequences, then he'd better move fast. Bloody fast.

His RMP training slotted into gear. *Focus. Keep a clear objective. Make every action count.*

The trouble was, he had too many objectives. He needed to timeline and prioritise. Staying alive was number one, but it depended on keeping the mini-USB pen drive out of the wrong hands. *Will they search my office again? Is the filing cabinet drawer-slider support still a secure hiding place?* He couldn't take the risk. He slipped it into a zipped pocket in the biker trousers he still wore from yesterday.

And objective two? Clear up the mess. Get the files back in their hanging folders and into the filing cabinets. If he left it to Clive, his old friend was bound to look through the papers to sort them correctly. It would be a level of prying Pember could do without.

'Right,' he muttered and bundled each mound of paper into the hanging folders.

Finally, objective three. Take what was essential and get out. And see if he could get the CCTV cameras cleaned up on the way.

Knock, knock!

The sound was muted, soft, but it hit him like a soft-nosed bullet. He stood and gently swayed, the sisal matting clear of paper, the filing cabinets closed on the chaos inside the drawers.

'Yes?' he said, more a hiss than a command.

The door opened slowly. Dove stood at the threshold; her gaze directed at the floor.

'Hello, good morning. I mean it's not a good morning for you. I-I'm sorry for your trouble, Mr Quinn. Please don't worry, I won't come in.'

'Yes?' he repeated, his tone sharp. It was a question, not an invitation to enter. He was relieved it was only her, but he was damned if he'd show it.

'Sorry, Mr Quinn, but the landlady, Ms Webbington... She sent me to ask if any rooms need to be cleaned after the break-in.'

'How'd you know about the break in?'

'Ms Webbington said when she rang. I came straight away. You can ask her.'

'You came in specially? For me? Because no other

rooms were broken into?'

Dove frowned. 'No, Mr Quinn. I came because Ms Webbington rang me.'

'Of course. The police will have wanted the CCTV footage. I expect Ms Webbington wasn't too happy when she had to say her CCTV cameras are dummies. It'll probably null n'void the insurance cover.'

'Null and void the cover, Mr Quinn?'

'Slang, Dove.'

'Do you mean invalidate the cover, Mr Quinn?'

He was surprised she spoke so precisely. *Hell, is she–*

'Are you ex-embassy staff, Dove?'

'It is something I prefer not to talk about, Mr Quinn.'

So, the answer's yes.

'Here I am the cleaner,' she added, 'Dove.'

'Then you can at least tell me if any of the other offices were broken into last night or the early hours of this morning?'

'I wouldn't know, Mr Quinn. Ms Waddington - she only said I was to clean your offices.' She fixed him with sad eyes for a moment, dropped her gaze and added, 'In the mornings I have four offices to clean. Three on the ground floor and one on the first. They weren't broken into. I didn't come up here.' She flicked a glance at him, then studied the sisal matting.

He understood the body language.

'That isn't quite true, is it, Dove?'

She shifted her weight from one foot to the other.

'You came up to check if there was a binbag of rubbish for you. I didn't say I wanted you to collect any for me, but you weren't going to risk getting it wrong. So, just in case there was rubbish to collect, you came up. What did you see, Dove?'

'I-I didn't walk on the landing, I smelled the paint, saw the open door, and…no garbage bags so, I went back down the stairs.'

He waited. He knew his silence was enough to tease more from her.

'If I don't see, I don't know anything, Mr Quinn. And it's safest that way. You've guessed I'm a refugee. I don't want trouble with the police, Mr Quinn. It would look bad to the authorities.'

'But what if I'd been lying on the floor stabbed and bleeding?'

'I called your name. You didn't answer. If you were there and silent I was too late.'

'And that's it?'

'I'm pleased you aren't stabbed or dead, Mr Quinn.'

'Well, thank you Dove.'

She smiled.

'One more thing, do you have any white spirit or paint remover?'

'I'll bring some up for you, Mr Quinn. And…it was Kabul.'

He nodded. 'I guessed Afghanistan. Look, I may be away for a few days.'

'Yes. Please stay alive, Mr Quinn.'

***

When Pember hurried down the stairs a pang of regret caught him by surprise. He hadn't expected to be on the run and under cover so soon. Instead, he'd hoped the PIA in Bury would be a new beginning and put distance between the Kanes and gangland retribution.

Re-connecting with Clive had been a bonus, but he hadn't been prepared for the avalanche of childhood memories to stoke his competitiveness and paranoia. No one else knew him as well as Clive, and he wasn't used to having someone around who could read him like a book and decipher his reactions in the way newer colleagues and friends couldn't. It implied he was predictable. It was a chink in his survival armour. He reckoned no one, including Clive, would be expecting him to disappear.

***

Clive strode from the Pilgrims' Kitchen. By chance, Dr Ariana Landry had been in her office when he phoned after his coffee with Chakra. He'd introduced himself and explained why he'd called.

'It's no trouble. In fact, it'll make a break from ploughing through endless reports and admin. So, Chakra McLaren suggested you ring me.' she'd said.

'Yes. He was my DS before I retired. I'm sorry if I'm stopping you get on with all you diving reports.'

'Goodness no. I only referee health and fitness forms filled in by recreational divers. It's usually straightforward and they don't take much of my time. It doesn't interfere with my hospital work. I'm a chest physician, Chakra must have told you. And...after respiratory medicine, diving is my passion. It's how I keep my sanity.'

He'd chuckled. 'I keep mine by walking.'

'Well diving's not for everyone. Luckily, you've caught me on my admin morning. I will have cleared most of it by twelve thirty. Phone me again then, and I'll try to answer your diving questions, okay?'

'Yes, twelve thirty, sharp.'

She'd ended the call. He hadn't had time to ask where she was based, which hospital and respiratory unit, and how she knew Chakra. All he had was her mobile number, so not even an area code. He couldn't quite form a mental picture of her. The Chakra question was the type of thing Chrissie would have asked. Pure curiosity on her part but to Clive's way of thinking, the answer would have explained connections, and connections were how he processed and remembered information.

He slowed his pace. Yes, walking had saved his sanity, even when he was a kid. The walk home from school was when he'd re-tuned his focus from absorbing information to processing it. Walking, and then running; it had been a natural progression. Diving hadn't been an option back then, but he believed if there'd been a diving club and Pember had wanted to join it as a teenager, then he'd have tagged along as well. Except he doubted Pember would have wanted to. He liked the rush of adrenalin. Something speed and motorbikes gave him. It matched his personality.

Clive recognised, as he headed back to Hatter Street, that their friendship was the meeting of chalk and cheese, and later, the intersection of hiking and biking. There was also something intangible in the essence gelling their friendship. Clive had never considered it fragile, but now he was starting to re-evaluate. Something had changed Pember. The suspicion and secrets were becoming dominant. There were too many icebergs for Clive to avoid.

As he climbed the stairs, he wondered if Pember would still be in his office but was surprised and quietly relieved to find the office tidy and Pember gone.

'It must be his army training. Tidiness equates to order and an organised mind,' he muttered. 'And don't leave any-

121

thing behind for the enemy.' *Do I count as enemy, Pember Quinn? Is that why you wouldn't tell me about the Norwich case and the offer of witness protection?*

Exasperation and hurt flashed through Clive. 'How dare you keep me in the dark?' Well, he wasn't going to play the part of some squaddie taking orders or worse still, the enemy. He was an ex-detective inspector, a professional and a friend. He'd do what he was good at. He'd investigate what he'd set out to investigate, but he'd also get to the bottom of whatever it was that had twisted the fun and good humour out of his friend.

Irritation competed with frustration as he chose randomly and pulled open one of the filling cabinet drawers. Pember must have worked fast to find homes for all the piles of paper. *Did he call in the cleaner to help? No, he's too paranoid.* Clive figured it was more likely down to his military efficiency.

'So, what to search for?' He chose randomly.

A hanging folder contained sheets of paper on the topic of gold sovereigns. Curious, he leafed through it, wondering why Pember kept a chart compiled in 1999 of the value of gold coins relative to their age and rarity. And then it dawned on him, 'Of course. 1999; the year Pem's dad died while he was in Kosovo.'

A newspaper cutting confirmed his guess. *Lucky Find*, the headline announced. *Grieving Wife Strikes Gold. When brokenhearted widow, Lizzy Quinn, discovered a gold sovereign in the pocket of her recently deceased husband's suit*...and so the article ran on.

'Lizzy Quinn? So, Pem's mum found a gold sovereign in MJ's old suit.' Pem's dad was known by his initials. A memory floated back. The old man had kept an antique coin scale on his mantlepiece. Clive remembered being intrigued by the coin-shaped pans on a rocker bar with a counterbalancing brass weight. Each pan had a slit in it. But MJ had refused to explain how it worked.

'If you can't work it out, you don't deserve to know,' MJ had barked at him. And that had summed Pem's dad up. Unapproachable and secretive, a man of modest means who liked puzzles and didn't waste his time on words or children. It was why Pem had spent so much of his time out of the house.

Clive turned his attention to the next drawer down. It contained files on porcelain and ceramic marks. *Is there anything related to Spanish and Bulgarian police and trafficking cultural artifacts?* Pember had hinted there might be. Clive sensed it would be complicated and decided it could wait.

The drawer below was filled with old newspaper cuttings and magazine articles. They had been replaced randomly. Clive guessed Pember must have scooped them from the floor without sorting them, although their random nature could have been a ploy to throw Clive, or anyone else who looked, off the trail.

He checked his wristwatch. The morning had flown, and it was time to call Dr Landry again. He closed the filing cabinet drawer and settled at the desk. Comfortable in Pember's office chair, he logged into the computer, opened the Alconbury file, and made the call.

'Hi, you phoned back,' she said, answering his call.

He couldn't decide if she sounded surprised or pleased. 'Yes, of course,' he murmured.

'So, tell me. What do you want to know about diving?'

'Well, first can you explain what immersion pulmonary

oedema is and if it's the same as drowning?'

'*Pulmonary* is anything pertaining to the lungs, and *oedema* means fluid build-up in tissue. So, *pulmonary oedema* is fluid build-up in lung tissue.'

'Like inhaling water and then drowning?'

'No. *Immersion pulmonary oedema*, or rather IPO, is different. The fluid swamping the lungs has come from inside your own body. It hasn't been inhaled.'

'Okay, how does it come about?'

'That's the *immersion* bit, *immersion* in water. Put simply, it's triggered by swimming or diving, and more common in cold water.'

'Right. So, would a SCUBA diver in one of our local chalk quarries get IPO because the water's cold?' He remembered the chill striking through his fingers when he'd dipped them in the chalk-quarry water.

'Yes, it's possible. The water can be very cold in this country. That's why our SCUBA divers wear dry suits with warm clothes underneath.'

'So why, hypothetically speaking, if there are two divers diving in the same cold water in the same chalk quarry at the same time...does only one of them get IPO?'

'Because there's more at play than the temperature of the water. Both the cold and the pressure of the water drive blood and tissue fluid from the swimmer's extremities into the swimmer's central blood vessels and lungs. It can swamp the lungs.'

'It still doesn't explain why one of the divers is okay and one isn't.'

'One of them might have had heart or blood pressure problems.

'And that's it?'

'Not entirely. Divers are advised not to drink any fluid for a few hours before a dive. One of them might've ignored the advice.'

'But a younger, fitter diver with a strong heart is still unlikely to get into trouble?'

Clive couldn't say that one diver, Phil Barner, was aged 30 and the other, Morton Alconbury, was aged 52. Dr Landry had said when he'd first phoned her that she wouldn't answer about specific people, nor give her expert opinion as to the cause of the diving accident in question.

She spoke slowly, 'A young, fit diver can still get into trouble because of lack of oxygen, overhydration, diving position and an unsuspected, underlying, heart condition.'

She fell silent for a few moments, as if she was thinking, before adding, 'Of course SCUBA divers are taught to watch out for the early signs of IPO. They know to abort the dive and head for the surface.'

'So, what are the signs?'

'You get a tickle in your throat, an urge to cough, and it's harder to breathe because your lungs get stiff with the extra fluid. Your brain can't get enough oxygen, and carbon dioxide builds up. You can't think straight, and you can't get yourself to the surface. So, you die.'

'Which is why you dive with a buddy. Someone to help you get to the surface?'

'Yes. Did your hypothetical diver have a buddy?'

'Yes, and he was the younger one, the one who survived.'

'So, tell me, why did these divers want to dive in the quarry?'

'The younger one dived it with a buddy last September and knew there was a van at the bottom. He went back this

March with a different diving buddy, and this new one gets IPO and dies.'

'I know this is only hypothetical, but have you spoken to the earlier diving buddy? It might be interesting to get their account of the first dive.'

'They've moved away. I'll have to track him down.'

'How very inconvenient.'

'Or you could say convenient.'

'Oh dear, now you're sounding like a policeman.'

Clive couldn't help smiling. 'They did a whole-body CT scan as part of the post-mortem.'

'Probably looking for decompression sickness. That's bubbles of gas in the body. How deep was the dive?'

'Hmm, it was,' he tried to remember Chakra's words, '*a 25 metre, no stop dive.*'

'So, the divers wouldn't have needed to decompress.'

'But there must have been bubbles because the pathologist's report said something about gas sampling.'

'When the body starts decomposing, it makes hydrogen sulphide and methane gas bubbles. That's what he'll have meant.'

'And talking gases, carbon monoxide poisoning?'

'A blood test will have excluded it. Do you know, I think you're getting me to talk specifics about your case.'

'No, not at all. But can I ask how you come to know Chakra?'

Her tone changed, more chatty, less respiratory physician, 'He and my brother have been friends for years. A shared passion for flying model aircraft.'

'Really?'

'I call it toys for boys. We used to live near a model flying club. That's back when I was a kid. We lived in Hertfordshire. I'm not a Suffolk girl you know.'

'Well, I knew Chakra was originally from Hertfordshire, but an interest in model aircraft? I'd never have guessed.'

'Chakra doesn't have time for it now, but as teenagers they both spent most weekends on it.'

'And your brother? Does he still fly model aircraft?'

'Not so much. It's drones now. He flies them, designs them. They're his passion and his business.'

A thought struck Clive. 'Do the police use his drones?'

'I wouldn't know.'

'Don't tell me. You don't like to talk specifics with him?'

They both laughed.

'He's based in Hertfordshire, but he travels all over. Look I must go now, but if you've more questions about diving, call me again sometime.'

'Yes, I will. And thank you, Dr Landry.' He ended the call, closed his eyes, and concentrated for a moment. Nothing she'd said conflicted with the pathologist's conclusion. The cause of Morton Alconbury's death had been fatal IPO.

***

Clive sat in Pember's office chair and let everything Dr Landry had said gel in his mind. It was the interlude between absorbing information and processing it. The transition stage. Normally, he'd have gone for a brisk walk to set his analytic mind into motion, but he rather enjoyed sitting in Pember's chair. It was like being the boss again, and back with his team before he retired. He relished the feeling for a few seconds before drawing the keyboard closer and typing notes into the Alconbury file.

He logged the duration of his call with Dr Landry and

the cause of death as IPO but added the questions - *what triggered the IPO? Why a second dive in the quarry?* And a to do list - *interview Phil Barner. Locate and interview the first diving buddy.*

It struck Clive that investigating the Alconbury case was like working alone. It felt relaxed.

If only Pember would lighten up, tell him more, share the bad things from his past, and allow Clive to assess dangers for himself. Clive wrestled with his conscience. The honest thing to do was to call Pember and tell him straight. Tell him he was having difficulties working with this secretive Pember. There had to be more sharing, more honesty, and trust between them.

He pressed Pember's automatic dial number and waited.

Number unavailable - phone not connected flashed across his mobile's display.

'What? Is Pember playing with me?' He pressed automatic dial again. The same *Number unavailable - phone not connected* came up.

For a moment Clive teetered on the edge of a void. Pember had evaporated. Vanished into thin air. The shock stabbed, and then Clive recovered.

This is so like Pember. Just as I decide to have a serious talk with him, he goes off grid, unless…

Fired with anxiety, Clive sprang from Pember's office chair and hurried onto the landing.

'Pember!' he shouted as he hammered on the locked door to the second office, 'Are you in there? Open the damned door.'

He was met with silence. *Should I break it down?* He was frustrated enough to smash the panels with some well-placed kicks, but something held him back. He'd seen

Pember make a copy of the CCTV recording and hand it to Chakra. He glanced up at the cameras. It was as he'd guessed. His partner had acted with predictable paranoia. The casings were still splattered with paint, but the lenses were smeary clean.

'Of course,' Clive muttered. There was no way Pember would have left without setting the cameras to record again. Fear would have driven him, although the quality of the view through those part-cleaned lenses might be questionable.

He dashed back into the main office, logged into the security programme and displayed the current view from the CCTV cameras. It was poor, very poor; what he imagined near blindness would be like. Only the camera aimed at the head of the stairs had enough light and focus to capture anything vaguely discernible. He scrolled the time back to 10:30am and ran the recording. The screen view resembled fog but at 10:45am something dark showed on the stairs for two frames and then was gone.

'Is it Pember doing a runner?' he breathed.

It's what he'd do if he feared for his life. He'd take what he needed, turn off his mobile, and disappear. And if the image of a shadowy blob moving down the stairs meant Pember hadn't collapsed in the locked office next door, then Clive was pleased.

'I bet he's taken his gun with him.'

The whispered thought chilled. And then another thought dawned. 'Seems I'll have to run things here by myself.'

Clive re-evaluated the situation, and like a boss, let his brain do the searching. Pember may well have turned his phone off to stop his GPS signal being traced. But he'd still need the apps on his phone for the car trackers and viewing the office security CCTV recordings. So, while Pember was watching the Smiths, then Clive figured Pember wouldn't be too far away. It meant if Clive wanted to stay close to Pember he too needed to keep an eye on the Smiths.

But there was someone else of interest to Pember. Matt Finch. He was meant to be dropping by the office in the afternoon. Clive pressed his fingers to his temples. If he assumed Pember had remembered, and wanted to stay clear of the office, he reckoned Pember would arrange to see Matt in Stowmarket. He didn't put it past Pember to cut his old friend out of the meeting.

He needed to text Matt. His fingers flew. *Hi Matt. Change of plan - meeting this pm moved to your place, Stowmarket.* He fired off the message.

'Right, I better get out to Stowmarket fast.' And like a boss he apportioned his time, 'I'll call Phil Barner, our heroic diving buddy, from my car. He's next on my interview list.'

He turned his attention back to the Alconbury file, found Gillaine Alconbury's list of contacts for her husband's friends and relatives, and keyed Phil Barner's mobile number into his phone's directory.

Ten minutes later Clive was in his black Lexus and easing through the traffic on Southgate Street as it fed onto a landscaped roundabout. Some more queueing frustration, and soon he was on the A14 and heading to Stowmarket.

He planned as he drove. *Which angle will work best with Phil Barner? What kind of man is he?* So far, he was a bit of a mystery hero. No one had made direct comments about his personality, not even Ann from the quarry or, indeed, Gillaine Alconbury. She'd only talked about him being mad about diving, having started when he was a kid, his parents' yacht, and family money.

He changed lanes on the dual carriageway. 'Beige,' he breathed. Phil Barner was the equivalent to beige; nothing to like or dislike, someone who blended in. One thing was sure. Clive couldn't flash a police ID and launch into questions. He guessed it would take a gentler touch. *What the hell would Pember's approach be?*

Tumble Weed Drive appeared deserted. Clive drove its length. Matt's mercury-coloured Vespa, with its custom yellow and black trim, and Pember's Yamaha Tracer were nowhere to be seen. Clive guessed he was too early and headed back into the maze of Flower Estate roads. He parked where he had a good view of any vehicles turning into Tumble Weed Drive. There was time to make his call while he waited.

'Right, Phil Barner, let's see what you have to say.' He pressed the automatic dial.

Four ring tones, and the call was answered. 'Hi, Barner speaking.'

'Hello, I'm–'

'I'm sorry but I don't recognise your number. I should tell you now. I report scammers and cold callers.'

'Good, then you won't need to report this call,' Clive countered smoothly. It wasn't the start he'd hoped for. 'I'd like to ask you a few questions about SCUBA diving.'

'Are you a reporter?'

'No, I'm interested in SCUBA diving.'

'Sorry but I've had reporters on my tail recently. How'd you get my number?'

Clive decided to bend the truth. 'My partner, Chrissie, knows Gillaine Alconbury.' Strictly speaking, he should have said Chrissie knew *of* Gillaine.

'Gillaine? Did you just say Gillaine Alconbury?'

'Yes, and according to Gillaine, you're one of the most experienced divers in Suffolk. Gillaine recommend I speak to you.'

'So, you've spoken to her?'

'Yes.'

'I'm sorry, but who did you say you are?'

'Clive Merry. I work from offices in Hatter Street, Bury St Edmunds. We're thinking of sponsoring some kids as part of a personal development and confidence-building programme. We want to get more young people interested in the health of East Anglian coastal and inland waters. It struck me that diving was a brilliant way of engaging and connecting young people with our water-based environmental issues...our future.' He was throwing out ideas, hoping Barner would identify with one of them.

'Go on, I'm listening. Sponsor these kids to do what, exactly?'

'It's more of a feasibility study at this stage.'

'Like SCUBA-diving taster-sessions in a swimming pool and then paying diving-club membership for the kids interested in taking it further?'

'I was thinking more of practical stuff in the field.'

'Like what?'

'Well, I'm a walker, and walkers have litter-picking campaigns. So, why not set up de-littering dives? There's so much rubbish in our rivers and lakes.'

'De-littering dives? For beginner and novice divers? You're crazy!'

'Why crazy?'

'It's dangerous. The silt and mud would be disturbed,

the water impossible to see through. That's assuming they hadn't already got trapped in weed. Then there'd be currents and tides to contend with. And the water's freezing cold here.'

'So, what do you suggest?'

'Are you sure you've spoken to Gillaine?'

'Yes, why?'

'She of all people should be safety conscious about diving. Her husband died recently.'

'Chrissie said something about a heart attack. Really tragic. Did you know him?'

'Yeah.' It was the first trace of an American accent.

'Ah, I'm sorry. How did you know him?'

'Through SCUBA diving. But you weren't calling about Morton Alconbury. So, have you contacted any of the local diving clubs? Asked about subsidising some youngsters' memberships?'

'Not yet. I reckoned I'd talk to you first.' It was time to try a different approach. 'Look, if the truth be known, I think Chrissie's the one interested in SCUBA diving. She's been told she should learn to SCUBA dive before throwing money at the project, but I've said why? You don't have to be an artist to be a patron of the arts.'

'Hmm.'

'That's why she asked me to…'

'To what?'

'Put out some feelers. A diving club might say *yes* just to boost membership revenue. But you've been straight with me about the danger of litter-collecting dives. I don't suppose you'd…' Clive let his words drift. He'd always found silence more eloquent than a clumsy request.

'What? Talk to Chrissie?'

133

'Really? You'd talk to Chrissie? That'd be fantastic.'

He could almost hear the man working through what he'd just stumbled into offering. But it needed cementing and Clive slipped in fast. 'I can't believe how helpful you're being.'

'Okay, okay. Why don't you both drop round? Just for half an hour, tomorrow afternoon, four o'clock?'

'So helpful,' Clive breathed, and scribbled the address as Barner gave the details.

Clive ended the call and sat for a moment. *What exactly have I achieved?* He'd made contact and got the man's home address without having to run back to his old DS and the witness statement; it had to be a start. He'd also put Chrissie in the frame. His excuse? Well, he'd guessed Phil Barner might be a bit of a charmer with the ladies. After all, he'd told Ann there was nothing of interest in her quarry and then returned wanting to dive it again. Ann hadn't questioned it because...he'd charmed her?

But Chrissie wasn't Ann. When she wanted to know something, she honed her curiosity with the single minded-ness of a heat-seeking missile. He should know, he'd lived with her long enough. Intuitively he sensed Phil Barner might be less evasive and hostile with a woman asking questions. All Clive had to do was persuade Chrissie.

He checked the time on his car dashboard. 14:37

***

Pember rode from Hatter Street. He had to get away from the office and clear of the Kanes' reach. He headed east towards Stowmarket and Matt. Once he'd joined the A14, his Yamaha Tracer hummed as he flew like the wind. The backpack nestled between his shoulders and close against his spine. It gave snug reassurance. And like a passenger, it rode pillion as the bike ate the miles.

His thoughts lined up. At least the Kanes were East Anglian gangsters with straightforward objectives. They were lethal but manageable, unlike the terrorists and international gangs he'd experienced in the past.

An idea dawned. *What if the gift followed by the theft of the Doulton character jugs wasn't about the Kanes but a different message? One I've misread.* Paranoia told him it was the Kanes, or an agent on their payroll. But *shouldn't I check it with...CB?*

He swung off the dual carriageway. *Is it chance or destiny that I'm exiting on the Woolpit junction again?* It was the same one he'd used while tracking the black Lexus on Clive's challenge.

He swirled through it and raced onto the A1088 and north towards Thetford Forest. Except he wasn't heading for the forest itself, but Euston, a picturesque village nestling close by. It was rich with trees, almost part of the forest.

He could have kicked himself. This was a trip he should have made a couple of days ago. He should have responded after the D'Artagnan character jug was delivered. But he hadn't. He thought he'd buried his role fighting the trade in conflict antiquities, or more figuratively, blood antiquities. And when Flossy struck once again, all the old anger surged out, and with it the paranoia. He hadn't been in the right frame of mind to get involved. But now, when he looked at it after a burn-up on his Yamaha, his unfettered eyes saw beyond the mess of the break-in and read the message behind the missing character jugs.

It was from CB, a person who demanded his attention. Someone who liked to keep their messages coded and hadn't responded well to having their first message of a gift ignored. And CB's anonymity included an isolated, traditional, flint cottage at the end of a quiet track near Euston.

In the past, Pember had approached the cottage from the direction of Norwich, and the years had given him a familiarity with it, such that he figured he could have singled out the track simply by the scent of the pines and the feel of the rutted, sandy soil beneath his tyres. But today he was riding from the south, and he felt a mounting tension as he closed in on the cottage.

He hadn't warned CB of his imminent arrival. He reckoned he'd be picked up by the surveillance cameras surrounding the cottage. There was one hidden in the birdbox on the large oak at the gate, one in the seat of the disused swing slung high on the branch of a mature silver birch, and one in a garden gnome flanking the birdbath. He knew there'd be more cameras in the trellis on the side of a flintstone wall and in the recesses of the wooden porch. His RMP training noted the lack of a letterbox breaching the front door. He guessed the glossy black paintwork disguised the reinforced metal of the door and its frame. He was about to enter a discreet fortress.

He parked his motorbike in front of the porch and stowed his helmet. He didn't bother to knock; he knew it would only be a matter of seconds before the front door opened with a swoosh and she stood in the doorway.

'Hi. You're late.' The timbre of her voice matched her sun-damaged skin, but the style of her language was younger, sharp, of the moment.

'Late, ma'am? Sorry, I mean Ms Cranberry.'

'You're not in the RMP now.'

'No, CB.'

She inclined her head. He read it as acknowledgement of her preferred manner of address and an invitation to step into the hallway. She stood aside to let him pass.

'Why didn't you come when I sent D'Artagnan? You must have understood my invitation.'

'You mean your summons.'

She closed and bolted the front door. 'You ignored me.'

He felt the sting in her tone. 'No. Something else grabbed my attention.'

'Like what?' She stood, facing him.

Damn Flossy, he thought and bit back a string of curses. 'D'Artagnan could have come from another source and with a different meaning.'

'I don't see how. When you didn't respond, I was forced to activate a more direct approach to get your attention.'

'You mean the break-in and theft? It narrowed the field.'

'Good, so are you onboard?'

'Maybe.'

'That, I guess, is a *yes* from you.' A curt nod and fleeting frown sharpened her face before she smiled. 'So, coffee? Let's talk in the kitchen.'

Pember followed as CB led the way. She was heavily built, but neat with her hair swept up into a loose bun and she walked with her back held straight. He was torn between his RMP-instilled deference for a former senior officer, and irritation triggered by the assumption he was available at the drop of a hat. Or in this case, the disappearance of a set of Doulton character jugs and his office being turned over.

The kitchen spanned most of the rear of the cottage. He noted the old flintstone wall. It lacked a plaster skim and was finished with a simple whitewash. Kitchen cabinets lined the other walls. The contrast was chic and momentarily stole his attention from the 15mm-thick, toughened-glass windows and reinforced kitchen door leading to a neat lawn.

'I want the Doulton jugs back,' he said. 'They were my dad's.'

'All in good time.' She flicked on the sink's waste disposal unit. The motor churned, almost drowning her words as she said, 'As you know, ISIS has reared its head and taken control of the illegal excavation sites in Syria. This time it's a shipment of two Sumerian temple plaques. The laundering trail passed through Switzerland, then Holland.'

'*Two* Sumerian plaques. And from Syria? Not from the Sumerian city-sites in central and southern Iraq? You know the plaques'll be incredibly rare.'

'2,400BC years rare. And worth millions to the right buyers. They could be fakes.'

It was too much, trying to hear her against the droning motor. His right ear hissed and he needed to work through the implications behind her words. 'Do you really think your kitchen is bugged? Please!' He tapped his ear.

'Old habits. It's sensitive information.' She shrugged and turned off the disposal unit. 'Still drink espresso?' she asked and loaded the coffee maker with a pod.

He nodded. 'So where do I come into it?'

'There's a key player in Suffolk. We're not sure who, but we've picked up activity in what we think is a sleeper cell.'

'What kind of activity?'

'Coded messages, mostly, for the last couple of months. But they tie in with the movement of the temple plaques.'

'And the sleeper cell?'

'That's where you come in.'

'How?'

'We're not sure. Our information is patchy. You're good at shaking trees to see what falls out, and until we know more, that's your approach.'

'But what about more intel on the sleeper cell? And if you're tracking the temple plaques, why not bloody seize them when they enter the country?'

She smiled. 'You always were predicably direct. But the stakes are high. We want the plaques, and we also want the network behind them.'

She flicked on a tap, and cold water jetted at main's pressure into the sink. She reached for a jug.

'Something more sensitive you wanted to say?' he asked, raising his voice.

'No.' She adjusted the flow and held the jug under the tap. 'I need to fill the coffee machine.'

'Pity. I was hoping for more on the sleeper cell.' He marshalled his thoughts while she poured water into the reservoir. 'Do you think I'm wearing a wire?'

'You? Probably not.'

'Yeah, your people made sure of that when they turned my place over.'

She smiled. 'Hmm, delicate equipment. You know I don't take unnecessary risks.'

'Do you also know the bloody Kane gang are after me?'

'They're Norwich based.'

'So? Are they branching into artefacts now?'

'Not that I've heard.'

'Good. So, they're only into sex, drugs, extortion, and revenge? That makes me feel one hell of a lot better.'

'Don't be such a drama queen.'

When Pember left the cottage, he was filled with foreboding. Putting himself out there and shaking trees was akin to pinning a target on his chest and then waiting to see who came for him first. He was already in the Kanes' sights. *Do I really want a sleeper cell with terrorist affiliations after me as well?* But he was certain of one thing. He'd need some insurance, the kind of life insurance that held sway with the Kanes. His fingers brushed against the fabric of his biker trousers, and automatically he patted the zipped pocket. The mini-USB pen drive was safe for the moment.

He rode along the rutted track, all the while toying with the idea of turning back and leaving the pen drive with CB. But he knew lines of communication with her were tenuous, and he couldn't be sure she wouldn't use it as a handle to make him do her bidding.

He joined tarmacked road and headed towards Stowmarket and Matt.

***

Clive gathered his thoughts. His call to Phil Barner hadn't taken long, and as he sat and pondered over their conversation, the time readout on his car dashboard relentlessly moved forward minute by minute. Soon it would be 14:45. *Surely Matt should have come home by now after teaching at the academy?* Clive speed-dialled Matt; no answer.

A throaty, 4-stroke burbling caught his attention. The sound grew louder as a figure in a black biker jacket coasted into view on a mercury-coloured Vespa scooter. It was Matt. Hardly the silhouette of an Isle of Man TT rider, but reassuring, none the less.

Matt didn't appear to see him and turned at a steady

speed into Tumble Weed Drive. Clive killed the urge to drive after him. He figured if Pember turned up, it would be best if the Lexus was out of sight in case Pember was frightened away. That's if he was still trying to stay off Clive's grid. Happy to walk, he got out of his car and made the last few hundred yards on foot.

By the time he reached the bungalow, the Vespa was parked close to its side wall, and there was no sign of Matt. Clive approached the front door, its neglected paintwork warning off any would-be doorstep hawkers. He glanced up at the security camera hiding in the eaves.

'C'mon, Matt,' he breathed though an exaggerated smile. 'Just open the door, will you?'

A heavy footfall loomed, the latch turned, and a moment later Matt stood in the open doorway. 'Hiya, Clive.'

'Hi. Have you seen Pember?'

'Nah, he ain't here yet. Why?'

'It's complicated.' He followed Matt through the gloom of the hallway and into the living-room office with the beached-whale sofa. 'Have you got anything more on Paul Smith, or the list of names we gave you?'

'I checked the Land Registry, like you said, for Idris Brafman's house and it ain't his name on it. It's Veronica Brafman - since 2021.'

'2021? That's interesting. Veronica Brafman? I guess we know her as Veronica Smith. Anything on Paul Smith?'

'D'you mean when Paul Smith were Dave Jones and broke his restrainin' order in 2018?'

'Yes. Something else happened in 2018 that Pember may have been mixed up in. It's a long shot, but maybe there's a connection.'

Mat gaped at Clive. 'What you on about?'

'In 2018 Bulgarian and Spanish police smashed organised crime gangs trafficking looted and forged cultural artifacts across Europe. I saw newspaper cuttings about it in Pem's office. I can't believe it's a coincidence. He must have been involved.'

'Killer app! What did them cuttin's say?'

'Ah, I didn't have time to read them.' Clive felt stupid and inadequate, like a junior detective on a first investigation, but countered, 'I assumed you'd be able to find it all in the online versions. I didn't want to be restricted by what Pem chose to keep as cutouts.'

Matt nodded. 'That kinda stuff'll be in the nationals.' He settled at his desk and computers. It didn't take long before headlines and articles from 2018 about the illicit trafficking of looted artefacts filled his screen. 'What am I lookin' for? Some kinda mention of a Dave Jones or Paul Smith?'

'I don't know, Matt. Hey, I tell you what; why don't I skim through it while you see if you can find more about the restraining order?'

'Sure. But I'll need money up front. That kinda stuff don't come free on the dark net. It's *divl diggin'* and the *divl's* got a collection plate.'

Clive smiled at Matt's Suffolk lingo and nodded. Information cost money. Even a formal request through legal channels incurred a fee. They'd touched on the subject last time. He guessed the *divl's* payment wouldn't be in anything so easy as folding money. *Hell, I've only been at this private investigation malarkey for less than a week, and already I'm thinking Bitcoins and darknet shortcuts. What's happened to me?*

He dipped into his wallet and extracted a couple of twenty-pound notes. 'This is all I've got and I've no idea how much it converts to in Bitcoins,' he muttered, tapping the depths of his pragmatism. It was a relief to immerse himself in the newspaper articles as he scrolled through headlines and read columns of copy while next to him, Matt worked on the second keyboard and screen.

'That'll be Pember,' Matt said, breaking Clive's concentration as outside an 847cc, 3-cylinder engine chortled deeply and then cut out abruptly.

'What?'

'It's Pember's bike.' Matt stood up and lumbered past the giant sofa and into the hall.

Moments later Clive heard the front door swoosh open, and the latch click as it closed.

'Hi, what've I missed?' Pember said as he followed Matt back into the living room.

Clive twisted in his chair and watched his friend cross the room. Something about his face had changed; it was impossible to read any emotion in his eyes. They seemed lifeless. Clive's stomach sank. Something very bad must have happened. He reckoned he was catching a glimpse of his partner in tour-of-duty mode.

'You turned your mobile off, Pem.'

'Yeah. Too bloody right I did.'

'I was worried for you.'

'Well, I don't want to make it too easy for the Kanes, now do I?'

'Sure. But you're not with the RMP in some lawless territory. This is Suffolk, remember?' Clive turned his attention back to his screen, conscious that Pember was looking on. 'You dropped a few hints, and I couldn't help noticing your newspaper cuttings.'

'Ever the great detective.' This time Pember's tone was

flat, more observational than derogatory.

'You keep saying that, but no one needs to be a great detective to get the gist of this.'

'What you on about?' Matt asked and slumped into his office chair.

'I've read this lot, and identifying illegal artefacts for sale is done by anoraks. Not sophisticated tracking.'

'Train spotters? Birders?'

'No, forget the anoraks, Matt. I meant experts in niche fields.' He glanced at Pember and knew by the frown he was on the right track. 'So, how does it work, Pem? You watch the online auction sites for rare artifacts without provenance, or anything so rare it couldn't possibly be for sale on a non-specialist site? The kind of relic museums or wealthy collectors want?' He paused, waiting for a reaction.

Pember stared at the screen.

'Do you watch out for rare pieces that are so valuable they should be handled by major auction houses, but aren't? Sellers who can't authenticate a valuable artifact, or its origin and don't offer some kind of insurance against it being a fake. I'm on the right track, aren't I, Pem?'

The tight-lipped silence gave him his answer.

'But you aren't a curator at the British Museum, nor any museum for that matter. You aren't an expert, although you're interested in porcelain and ceramics. Your RMP tours of duty took you close to source regions. I'd guess you were once familiar with some of the archaeological sites. You've no doubt helped to investigate looting at illegal diggings, tracked ISIS or other terrorist groups overseeing the excavation and plundering of cultural artefacts.'

'Are you or ain't you sayin' Pember's one of them anoraks?'

Clive thought for a moment. 'Well, maybe not a British Museum level of expert anorak but good enough to…' He gasped as the full weight of the idea struck him.

'Run out of steam, have you? Flight of fancy crash landed, has it?' Pember's tone was measured.

'No. I think you're a frontman with expertise. You're the plausible interface with a dodgy seller. You're the one who bids for the suspect artefacts. Yes, of course you are. You'll have the right expert contacts. You've knowledge and muscle. You're the perfect combo.'

'Botics! You sayin' Pember collects looted relics?'

'No, Matt. But I think he's part of a team that runs them down. He won't be working alone. Am I right, Pem?'

Pember shrugged. 'Dad got me interested. He's the one who…' The words died.

'Fake gold sovereigns?' Clive murmured as he cobbled together childhood memories. 'Your dad was on the lookout for fakes. It all makes perfect sense.'

'So, Clive. Are you sayin' Pember were involved in the 2018 heist?'

'Pem was smashing it, Matt, not committing it.'

'And you're also sayin' in 2018 Dave Jones', aka Paul Smith's, restrainin' order were against Pember? Is that what you're sayin', Clive?'

'What? A restraining order against me? You bloody fool, Matt.'

'Ah; the old Pember's back!' Clive tried to hide his smile.

'Yeah, but frag n'burn. Would you clock it if it were one of your older cases?'

'I'd still bloody remember, Matt.'

'Okay, Pem. Calm down. Anything back yet from the

divl's search, Matt?'

They all turned their attention to Matt's screen.

'Yeah, killer app! A court list for Ipswich County Court, May 2018. We got court number, case number, defendant. Yeah, see. *Defendant* – Dave Jones.'

'Who was the restraining order protecting?'

'It don't say Clive but at least I got summut to work on now. Hey Pember, will them Kanes be after all of us or just you?'

'Just me unless you're connected with the Norwich drugs and extortion ring. Now, what about the other names on your list?'

'You're still holding back, Pem,' Clive murmured.

'Oh yeah? Like on what?'

'You haven't said if you're currently targeting a specific item. Nor how you go about the bidding…like do you need backup? Do you want us to place bids for you?'

'Oh sure. Like Matt even knows what a Sumerian temple plaque is.'

'What? I got Asterix comic-strip books. Gauls an' Romans sloggin' it out in 50 BC. See, I know what a Menhir is, coz Obelix carries them giant stones round on his back.'

Pember closed his eyes. 'So, the sum of your knowledge is Asterix, and Obelix the Bronze Age superhero. Give me strength!'

'Is something still rattling you, Pem?'

'Yeah, like a break-in this morning wasn't enough?'

'I mean since we spoke this morning.'

'I've been told to shake the trees and see what falls out.'

'Told? Who tells you? Who wants you to paint a target on your back and see what happens?'

'But ain't you already a target? For Paul Smith and them

Kanes?'

'You're going to need backup,' Clive breathed, his mind alive with several threads. *Should I offer my friend a safe bed in Woolpit? Will I simply be inviting danger closer to my own door? And what the hell will Chrissie say? The Kanes are bad enough, but at least they're homegrown. The trade in ancient artefacts from ISIS war zones could crank up the threat to finger-scorching levels.*

***

Still in Matt's living-room office, Pember caught the frown Clive shot at Matt. It was an unspoken message. *What the hell are the pair cooking up?* He glanced at the screen in front of Clive as Matt reached across and angled it to get a better view. The newspaper headlines and columns had vanished and instead pictures and articles touching on Sumerian temple plaques filled every square centimetre.

'Hey! I thought I just told you to bloody stay out of it.'

'But I like searchin',' Matt said as different selling sites flashed across his own screen. 'Mais would like them hieroglyphics on them cuneiform tablets. Hey, fancy a cylinder seal? Ancient Mesopotamian writin' would look kinda cool on a tee-shirt.'

Pember gasped. 'What the...?' He'd spotted it immediately. A piece of stone from the edge of a plaque. 'That one.' He pointed at the image; all caution cast adrift. 'It reminds me of another Sumerian temple plaque.' He wasn't going to say it was the one with links to a particular gang operating from Turkey in 2018. *Hell, I've already said too much.*

'Anything to do with the old newspaper cuttings or is it what you're looking for now?' Clive asked.

Damn, should have kept my mouth shut. Clive was far too quick. And as for CB, he knew she'd drop him if it leaked he'd shared this.

Clive seemed to read his turmoil. 'It's okay, Pem. You need us. Get used to the idea. Anyway, who would we tell? Your secret's safe.'

Matt enlarged the image to fill half the screen. 'It don't look much.'

The enlarged image drew Pember closer. 'If it's genuine it'll be shallow carving on sandstone.'

'Pixels! Some joker's taken a shot at it. Look, a spammin' great bullet got it on one edge! Too right it's a *conflict antiquity.*'

Pember struggled to keep his tone even, 'No Matt. It's meant to have a hole. A central one. It dates from when it was made. It's how it was fixed to the temple wall. The plaque's been broken.'

'So, frag n'burn. Most of it's missin'!'

'Yeah, it's a piece of a plaque. More difficult to tell if it's fake than if you've got the whole thing to examine.' He ran through a check list, barely breathing the words as he scanned its surface, 'Torso of a man, face carved in profile, smooth scalp, large nose, no beard, bare chest, layered-leaf skirt, and some hieroglyphics. Hmm, I'm no expert but they look early.'

'Early? What looks early?' Clive's words broke his train of thought.

'The hieroglyphics They're earlier than on the cylinder seal Matt was eying up. His were Assyrian cuneiform style, dating from 600 BC. It means this plaque is much older. More like 2,000 years older.'

'Okay, but is it what you were told to watch for?'

Clive's question felt direct, like a bullet straight on target. It jolted him into a response. 'It could be, except I don't think it's from Syria. So, either the Syrian tag is to throw punters off the trail or it's a fake.'

'Does it look like a fake?'

'Not on first glance, but I reckon it's from Iraq.'

'Phishin' hell, the blurb about it says Syria. It were found with some coins. You sure you ain't a closet anorak?'

'No. Now who's the bloody seller, Matt?'

'Okay, okay. It's a coin collector's site. Private dealer, based in East Anglia. It don't give a name, just an email address. *Seller can supply provenance details.*' Matt clicked and scrolled, his fingers flying across his keyboard as he typed in more searches.

'Tell me about the coins, Matt.'

'Gold coins. Roman.'

'What? Even I know Roman coins weren't around 2,500 years BC. This doesn't make sense,' Clive said.

'It's meant to be bloody obvious if even you know it, Clive.'

'Like red-flaggin' it?'

'Yeah, Matt.'

'Is…is it to draw attention to the plaque or the coins?' Clive asked.

Unease gripped Pember. His right ear whistled. It was almost as if the whole posting was aimed at him. 'I reckon it's a trap and it's intended for me.'

Pember's head whirled with the realisation. Paranoia pulled at the facts like gravity, drawing them in to make an uncomfortable ball in his stomach. Matt's living-room office had already felt warm but now the air was stale and suffocating. He focused on steady breathing and counting to ten.

'Trust you, Pem. You've got every sociopath in East Anglia gunning for you. How do you do it?'

Pem bit back the tetchy curse on the tip of his tongue.

'But the thing is,' Clive continued, addressing the screen on Matt's desk, 'the threat from the Kanes is business. It's how they work. You're a witness, and they want to take you out. And Paul Smith...he'll be an opportunist, ready to kill for the highest bidder. But this trade in looted, cultural artefacts feels different. More personal.'

'Yeah, but them conflict antiquity looters don't know you got us with you.'

'Well, that makes me feel a damned sight better, Matt.'

'Ta.'

Pember looked heavenwards. *The Asterix & Obelix fan can't even catch my sarcasm. How can he be any help in this?*

'He's right, Pem. No one'll know it's Matt answering the ad, or guess he's linked to you. And he's able to stay anonymous on the net better than you.'

'Jeeez, if it had to be anyone, I'd rather it was you, Clive.'

He was rewarded with a smile that reached Clive's eyes. 'It's easier for them to guess it could be me. After all, we go back a long way.'

'D'you want me to ask about them coins or the plaque...or both?'

What? Pember thought. *He's a computer geek. No understanding of what he's up against. He'll just blunder in. He's even built like a hippo.* Pember swallowed his bile as the words *gun fodder* and an idea sprang to mind.

'Okay, I'll be straight with you. I was informed there

were two very ancient, looted, Sumerian plaques coming onto the market. So, start with the coins. If you mess up, all's not lost. Opening by wanting both this plaque and the gold might make them think you could be me. I've a history with gold sovereigns as well.'

Clive butted in, 'How long has the ad been posted?'

'Since yesterday.'

'Good. Being too keen draws attention. At some point Matt will have to send an email pretending to be you, Pem.'

'What?' The tinnitus surged.

'Calm down, Pem. You know you can't connect with a terrorist on the agency email or your personal one. It's too dangerous. I guess you'll use the *divl's* Onion, or a VPN and fake name, right Matt?'

'Yeah, but I ain't composin'. If Pember writes them, I'll send them. Deal?' Matt spun his office chair round to face Pember.

'Okay, but if this one's from you, you'll need to use the right jargon. From 100BC to 500AD, a Roman gold coin was called an aureus.' He took a long, slow breath, collected his thoughts, and dictated while Matt typed:

Dear seller, I am interested in your advertisement for what I assume are Roman aureus coins. I collect early examples. Please send more details.

Also, are the coins for sale as a separate lot or jointly with the Sumerian temple plaque?

Regards, Oliver Blix

'Frag n'burn. I like me name.'

'Yeah well, it's politer than some that sprang to mind!' He caught Matt's frown and added, 'Only joking. The full *Obelix* is too obvious.'

Pember needed fresh air before he suffocated. He rubbed

his face. 'Look, I've got to go. I need space to think.' He didn't bother to add *and figure what to put on the next email*. Instead, he forced a smile. 'And it's okay, Clive. I'll beg a bed when I need one, but for now I reckon I'll be safe. Anyway, I want to get a full face shot of Veronica.'

What he really wanted was to be alone.

Outside Matt's bungalow on the Flower Estate, Pember's pulse throbbed high into his throat while his paranoia hit the Richter scale. He'd managed to keep a cap on it in front of Matt and Clive, but there were limits before he wouldn't be able to cope with his ear as well. He was close to being knocked sideways by it all.

Clive had made a valid point; the ad fitted Pember's area of expertise too well. It felt like a trap designed for him, and him alone. Setting a professional assassin on his trail was bad enough. This felt bloody eerie.

Pember zipped up his biker jacket and donned his helmet. He took long, slow breaths. There wasn't time to let his mind wander. He had to stay focused on the plan. Veronica…*who was she really?*

He checked the tracker app on his mobile. The white Fiat Panda was stationary on a slip road leading into Bury St Edmunds from the A14. He guessed the traffic would be snarled up in Bury's five o'clock rush hour, but if he could burn up the A14 and cut through the queueing traffic on his bike, then he might be in time to get a face shot of Veronica as she arrived home. And Paul Smith? His Honda Jazz was parked in Bury, a couple of roads away from No. 17, formerly Idris Brafman's home. Pember sighed. At least Paul Smith wasn't sitting on his tail with an assassin's bullet aimed at his chest.

He unlocked his bike, flipped down his visor, pulled on

his gloves, and rode away.

By the time Pember climbed the two flights of stairs to his office, he'd sent new face shots of Veronica Smith to Matt, and Hatter Street was bathed in evening darkness.

***

When Clive walked back to his Lexus, early evening shrouded the Flower Estate in murky darkness. A single streetlight shone a few yards beyond his car and cast shadows along its side, like mood-lighting in a B movie. It had been a long session at Matt's. Too long. He felt drained.

'Oh no,' he sighed as he started his car. He'd forgotten about Chrissie! And now he was going to be late. Her TR7 was being serviced, and he'd agreed to help with drop off and pick up. *But hell...* He tapped his forehead. *Am I losing my mind? She phoned this morning, and the TR7's service is next Thursday. Is it still only today?* It had been one hell-of-a long one.

But Chrissie was on his mind as he headed back to Woolpit. He called her on his car's hands-free. She answered almost immediately.

'Everything okay?'

'I don't know. I've had an intense afternoon with Pem and Matt.'

'That doesn't sound good.' Her voice sounded casual, and he waited a moment for her curiosity to kick up a gear. It might distract her from any I-thought-I'd-see-more-of-you-now-you're-retired type of comments.

'Pem has fingers in lots of pies and they're all turning sour at the same time.'

'Pem's a catalyst. Things happen round him.'

It wasn't the response he'd expected. But then she'd always seen straight to the heart of things. Either that or she'd think outside the box and shoot off on a tangent. He wondered how she did it.

'Are you still there, Clive?'

'Yes, I was thinking how right you are about Pem. Look, I'm going to need your help on something.'

'Really?'

'How's your SCUBA diving knowledge right now? You may need to mug up on it for tomorrow.'

FRIDAY

Pember had spent Thursday night in his Hatter Street office-cum-storeroom. He figured he'd be okay for the night if he kept his SIG Sauer close and his wits about him. But sleep came slowly and sparsely.

By Friday morning he'd concealed the memory stick back in its hiding place in the filing cabinet, but he felt jaded and only half-ready to take on the day. He sat at his desk with both elbows on its surface and cupped his forehead in his hands. His ear hissed gently. It was time to update his plan. First, call Matt.

'Any news from our trader?' he asked, cutting preliminary niceties.

'No bites yet, mate.'

'Any ID on Veronica's photo I sent yesterday evening?'

'No. It were late by the time I loaded it. And the *divl*'s net's been spammin' slow.'

'Okay.' He swore under his breath, 'let me know as soon as you get anything.'

'Yeah, sure. I'm workin' Balcon & Mora today. Damon don't like me lookin' at nonwork stuff, not when it's on his time. I could stop at your office on me way home?'

'Hmm, maybe better to see you at your place.'

'What? Balcon & Mora?'

Pember swallowed his spike of irritation. 'No, Matt. Your place, Tumble Weed Drive.' He ended the call. Now for the next item on the plan; another shot of espresso.

While he sipped the black coffee, he recalled Clive saying that Idris Brafman might be the key to unlocking the Paul and Veronica Smith mystery. And so, while he kept an

155

eye on his tracking app, he scoured the social media sites for anything that might shed light on Brafman.

But there was little to find. It appeared Idris had cut a lonely figure. The man had been seventy-six when he died of COVID in January, and most of what had been written about him had appeared in his death announcement and short obituary in the local Bury press. 'At least I've a photo of Idris,' Pember sighed. It was the one he'd gleaned 3 days earlier from the *Pipl* site and added to the agency's Paul Smith file. 'Jeeez!' *Was it only 3 days ago?*

There was a funeral director's contact number for anyone wanting to leave a donation to a charity for rehoming ex-racehorses, and the time, place, and date for the service at the crematorium. According to the obituary, Idris had been born in Lavenham, a village in Suffolk, and had spent most of his adult life in Bury St Edmunds. The only next of kin named in the obituary's will-be-sadly-missed-by paragraph was his great-niece, Veronica.

'So, a Suffolk boy from cradle to grave and not much else to bloody go on. Ha, and if that idiot Matt has bothered to search, this'll be about all he's found as well.'

Brring! Brring!

He snatched his phone off the desk. 'Yes, Clive?'

'Hi, Pem. I'm not getting any answer from Matt. Any email back for Oliver Blix yet?'

'No. He says he's working at Balcon & Mora today.'

'That'll be why he didn't pick up. You okay?'

'Why shouldn't I be?' Then he relented, 'Yeah, no intruders last night. I'm looking into Idris Brafman.'

'Right. So, did he have a wife, or husband or kids?'

'No. His obituary says he was single and a loving great-uncle. How's the SCUBA diving case going?'

'Okay, and thanks for the hint to keep my nose out of your case!'

Pember caught Clive's chuckle as he rang off. It touched a chord deep inside. Matt's voice seemed to chant in his head, 'Yeah, but them conflict antiquity looters don't know you got us with you.' Pember was transported back to the RMP. In a flash he was the Staff Sergeant trying to communicate with one of the Privates. It felt like trying to walk through quicksand. It was weird, almost part of a patchy dream. He shook his head, blinked, and he was back in Hatter Street.

Without really thinking, he keyed in the number for the funeral director.

'Good morning. Jones Funeral Directors. How may I help?'

'Right, yes…I-I'm sorry to trouble you but I've only just learned that a friend of mine, Idris Brafman, died this January.'

'Our condolences.'

'Thanks. It's a bit of a shock. I understand you arranged the funeral. I-I wondered, sometimes there's a video made for people who can't attend the ceremony.'

'Yes, but anything like that would be with the relatives by now. You'd need to ask them. Is there something more I can help you with, Mr…? I'm sorry, I didn't catch your name.'

'Mr Quinn. Yes, there was one more thing. The funeral notice said no floral displays. Instead, donations to an ex-racehorse rehoming charity. It said the funeral directors were collecting the donations. Would you be able to tell me the name of the charity so I can donate directly? I'd like to pay my respects. It's what Idris would've wanted.'

'Just a moment, let me check our records.'

Pember stifled a yawn and sipped more coffee. A few minutes waiting, and he was rewarded with the contact details of an ex-racehorse sanctuary near Newmarket.

He ended the call, but his thoughts sped on. *Didn't Veronica shed her tracker in the Newmarket racecourse carpark? Was Newmarket a coincidence or a significant thread?*

Something flickered on the CCTV monitor. Pember's stomach tightened. A familiar figure came into clearer view. He breathed a quiet, 'Phe-e-e-w.' But he was curious.

A soft knock at the door cut short further speculation.

'Yes? Come in, Dove,' he called across the room.

The door opened slowly. She wore her signature slim-cut trousers under a knee-length pinafore-style overall. Her headscarf lightly framed her face and fell in elegant folds onto her shoulders. She seemed to hesitate before stepping into the room.

'Mr Quinn?' Her tone was confident but reserved, part statement, part question.

'Good morning, Dove.' He smiled. 'I said I'd be away for a few days…but here I am, back again.'

'Yes, I see. Are you safe now?'

'I don't know. The people who were behind this.' He waved his hand to encompass the office. 'Let's just say, I think they'll leave me alone now.'

'The police have them?'

'No.'

'But you have neutralised them?'

'Not exactly. I believe it was a warning.'

'But if they decide to come back, it will be worse for you, Mr Quinn. In Kabul the second visit was always worse.'

'If I get another visit, Dove, it will be from different people. A different agenda. They'll kill me.'

'Kill you on their first visit? Mr Quinn. It sounds very bad for you.'

'Yes. Very bad, Dove. So, if you see anyone hanging around, or asking about me, or any packages left for me, please tell me.'

'How will I know who is dangerous, Mr Quinn?'

'I'll print photos for you of my main suspects. But I think, if you've lived in Kabul, you'll sense it.' He watched her drop her gaze to the sisal flooring. 'You can sense fear and lies,' he added.

'Yes, and treachery.' She inclined her head in a kind of acknowledgement and farewell. She left, moving as silently as she had entered.

Pember absorbed her sense of calm. He felt an automatic bond, perhaps she felt it too. He guessed it was their past but separate experiences in war-torn, near-eastern countries. *But why did she come to my room?*

He rang the landlady.

'Ms Webbington?' he asked when she eventually answered.

'Yes?'

'Pember Quinn here. New tenant for the two offices, top floor on Hatter Street. It's about yesterday's break-in.'

'Ah yes, in the early hours of Thursday morning. It's with the police now. We've never had anything like this before. Do you need any extra office cleaning?'

He smiled. She'd played straight into his hand. 'Well, no. The cleaner's done an excellent job already. What was her name? Dove...or Thrush or...?'

'Dove. It's an initiative for Afghan Refugees. It's been very successful.'

He closed his eyes. He could relax, the cleaner wasn't part of an elaborate plan to spy on him. 'Good. When will this building have functioning CCTV security cameras?'

'It's in hand. You have your own contents insurance, I assume.' Her voice turned frosty.

'Yes, of course,' he purred. 'But I don't like being broken into.'

'None of us do, Mr Quinn. Did you leave your office unlocked?'

'No, I did not.' He bit back the string of expletives on the tip of his tongue.

'Good. Well. It's been nice talking to you.' The line went dead.

'Cow,' he muttered.

***

Just before four o'clock on Friday afternoon, Clive drove with Chrissie into Cavendish, a picturesque village in the west of the county. They were heading to Phil Barner's home, and Chrissie sat with an introductory SCUBA diving manual open on her lap.

Ping!

A little spark of excitement caught Clive's breath. 'I hope that's from Matt. I've been waiting all day to hear from him. Can you check my mobile?' He glanced at it recharging in the central console.

The previous evening, Clive had briefly explained the illegal trade in conflict antiquities to Chrissie, along with the very real threat to Pember's life from the Norwich gangland scene, as well as the international antiquity rings. She'd appeared a little subdued since then.

She reached for his mobile.

'I hope to God he hasn't forwarded the actual email from the seller. It could be laced with trackers and malware. I told you Pem gave Matt the alias Oliver Blix, short for Obelix?'

'Hmm,' she sighed as she looked at his phone's screen, alight with a message banner.

'Well?'

'Without your face or fingerprint, I've only the first ten words to go on, and it's Matt saying *nothing back for Oliver Blix yet.*'

'Damn! It doesn't feel right.'

'It feels like a poker game.'

'Since when did you know so much about poker?' He slowed as Cavendish village green came into view, sweeping up a grassy slope to the Five Bells pub. He turned onto Peacocks Road along the edge of the green and drove past the war memorial. Pink cottages with thatched roofs hid the church, until seventy-five yards on it sprang into view. It was historic, imposing and dressed with flint.

'Wow,' she said. 'Despite the grey flint, it's soft on the eye, like they've used a sandy limewash in the mortar.'

They followed the road past wooden-framed houses, then newer, more recent builds, until they were free of the main village. The land rose gently. Hedges and ditches gave way to views across acres of rolling fields, green with young wheat and barley. The afternoon light had begun to fade.

'I bet they get amazing sunsets up here,' Chrissie said.

'If that's a hint about finding Phil Barner's place before it gets dark, I think we're here.' He slowed to a halt and

161

eyed a gravel track off to the right. The wooden, five-bar gate at its entrance stood open.

'Phil said something about a gate. And there's the name of the house. Shearwater.'

The track was short and curved sharply, opening into a shingled area with a long, brick outhouse on one side and a modest-sized, Edwardian house another fifty yards ahead. A young man, a couple of inches short of six feet, strode from the outhouse. He had short blond hair and looked athletic. *No wonder the ladies like him*, Clive thought and smiled.

'He's younger than I expected,' Chrissie murmured as they parked alongside the outhouse.

'He's thirty, according to the details on his police statement. Remember, we don't know anything about the accident.'

'Hi,' she said as she got out of the car.

'Hey there. I'm Phil. And you're Chrissie…and Clive, right?' The Americanisms in his accent were subtle.

'Hello. Thanks for inviting us.' Clive hoped he didn't sound plummy and clipped. *Relax. Fall into character*, he told himself. 'Chrissie's so excited to be talking to you,' he said.

'I'm a total novice,' she said raising her SCUBA diving book in one hand, 'but I've nailed some names like: diving regulator, buoyancy compensator, and air compressor. Oh yes, and you call flippers *fins*. Right?'

She's doing her dumb blonde act, Clive thought. A single glance was enough to tell him Phil had dropped his guard. Even the way he said, 'So, do you want to talk about SCUBA diving or promoting it?' had lost the suspicion and defensiveness he'd adopted during Clive's phone call.

'Both,' Chrissie answered breathily, 'but first tell me why and how you got into diving.'

'I was born in San Francisco, but I've not been back in years.' He flashed a smile. 'My parents owned a yacht. As a kid growing up, I was always swimming, surfing, and snorkelling. It was a natural progression to SCUBA diving.'

'So, it's about opportunity?' Clive said.

'Yeah, and the right equipment.'

'Hmm, so I've read.' Chrissie tapped the SCUBA diving manual.

'I'll show you. My outhouse makes a good storeroom, It's this way.'

'Really? That'd be great.'

Clive didn't know how she managed to sound so excited, and settled for a nod and smile as Phil led the way.

'Wow, it's like the Tardis in here. It's bigger than it seems from the outside.' Her voice was steeped in awe as they stepped through the open doorway.

Clive glanced round. It struck him as tidy and airy.

'I keep all my diving things at this end.' Phil opened a large, walk-in, metal locker with hanging space for several diving suits, and shelving for diving masks, mouth pieces, tubing with valves and gauges, a weight belt, gloves, boots, hoods, and fins.

'It's air conditioned. I've installed a heat exchanger. The unit's on the outside wall of the storehouse and an indoor unit is up there.' He pointed at a box with louvers along its base and fixed to the locker wall.

'Of course, the kit needs somewhere to dry.'

'Oh, don't be so practical Clive.'

'If you join a diving club for lessons, you can hire their equipment by the hour. They're responsible for that side of things.'

She picked up some tubing with valves and gauges attached. 'How's it maintained. How d'you know it's working okay?'

'You're holding a first stage pressure regulator. It controls the pressure of the air coming from the air tanks. Before you get in the water, you check it's working okay by setting the gauges and test-breathing through the mask or mouthpiece.'

'And I'd be diving with an instructor?'

'Sure, and later a diving buddy. Diving's great for training youngsters to take responsibility for themselves and others.'

'So, are you a member of a diving club, Phil? Is that how to find a buddy?'

'Yeah, Chrissie. But diving's a small world. You soon get to know the local divers...at least the serious ones. You can team up with them.'

'Would you recommend your diving club?'

'Yeah, sure, Chrissie. It's the Clare SCUBA Diving Club.'

'But...' Clive knew he'd voiced doubts about impartiality. It was the reason he'd given Phil for phoning him. 'There's one in Bury St Edmunds and Ipswich as well, isn't there, Phil?'

'Yeah sure, and they're kinda bigger.' Phil cut further questions by leading them out of the locker.

'I think I saw air cylinders near your workbench. You call them tanks, right?' Chrissie said, following him.

A pair of air cylinders were supported in wheelable standing-racks and stood close to a work bench, its surface clean and bare. Clive pictured a diver's wet or dry suit laid out on it, like a post-mortem table. He blinked away the image.

'Ah, this is interesting.' Clive focused on what he figured was some kind of air compressor, its workings resting on a baseplate in an open metal frame. The ends of the frame were made of tubular metal, as if for ease of lifting or pulling. It sat on the floor next to the cylinders. 'Is it a compressor for filling your diving tanks?' he asked and stepped closer. Something caught his eye. He crouched to get a better view. An A5, notebook-sized logbook had been slipped into the space between the tubular metal frame and the side casing of a large fan, integral to the compressor.

'Yeah, it's the dive compressor from my parents' yacht. It's over twenty years' old, but it still works great.'

'Does it run on an electric motor?' Chrissie asked, deflecting Phil's attention briefly from Clive.

Now was Clive's moment. He began to stand up, leaning in against the compressor, one hand dangling low.

'No, it's a 2-stroke petrol, about 3.5 cubic feet per minute.' The American drawl was more pronounced.

Clive's fingers brushed the log. He gripped its upper edge.

'The petrol tank's at the top.' Phil looked in Clive's direction and pointed.

'Right.' Clive let go of the log and straightened his legs to stand. *Did he see my light-fingered attempt?* His pulse raced.

'And the gas in the cylinders is air?' Chrissie asked without missing a beat.

'Well yeah. It's nothing special. Just fresh air. The motor gets hot and of course, there's heat generated when air is compressed. It's kept cool by the big fan on the side of the frame. The air is passed through those column filters. One contains activated charcoal. It'll catch volatile organic compounds and minute particles, like pollens. And that's a condensing tower for the water vapour.'

'Water? From compressing the air?' Clive kept his voice steady and smiled.

'Yeah, Clive.'

'But it's down on the ground. How's that fresh air?' Chrissie's voice rose, as if this was a concept she finally understood.

'Sure. The machine's heavy. So, it stays on the floor. But there's a long hose with filters, attached to the air intake. I put the hose outside in the fresh air.'

'Through this window?' She walked past the end of the workbench and peered through the window.

'Honestly, Chrissie. You'd have to go outside to tell if the air's fresh,' Clive laughed.

She nodded. 'So, what do you drive, Phil? I don't know if all the diving gear would fit in my TR7.'

'A Range Rover.'

'The blue one parked down there by the side of the house?' She frowned.

'Don't worry, Chrissie. It'll all fit in my Lexus.'

'Hmm.' Chrissie took several paces and stood next to him, her back to the workbench and facing Phil. Casually, she put the diving manual down behind her and folded her arms. 'It strikes me…learning to SCUBA dive is elitist and privileged. Because, as far as kids are concerned, it's down to their family, opportunity, and money.'

'That's why I advised your sponsorship should be free, diving-club memberships,' Phil drawled.

'Hmm, would the theory and technical stuff be beyond

some of the kids?'

'It could be.' Clive shrugged.

'So, maybe only snorkelling for the younger kids?' Chrissie added.

Clive put an arm round her back. 'Just because you find the technical side a bit daunting, doesn't mean all the youngsters will. So, Phil; do you recommend the larger diving clubs when they're starting out?'

'Yeah. It's more fun if you're learning with lots of others your age.'

Clive nodded, 'Yes, I think I get it now. Well, thank you for giving us so much of your time.' Clive kept his arm around Chrissie's back and began to move towards the door. She fell into step beside him, no irritation in her body language. He guessed she'd realised he was blocking Phil's view of the abandoned diving manual.

Phil smiled and led the way out through the storeroom to the Lexus.

'Oh no!' Chrissie said as she put her hand on the passenger door handle. 'I've left my SCUBA diving manual on the workbench.'

'Don't worry, I'll get it. Honestly, Chrissie, if your head wasn't attached…' Clive turned and strode back into the storehouse.

'I'm sorry, Phil but did you say your car…' Chrissie's voice faded into the background, as Clive homed in on the log. He crouched low and prized it from the compressor. Lines of neat writing ran across each pair of pages opened flat. Dates and place were recorded in the single margin. Columns for dive time, air consumption, weights, temperature, depth… He flicked back to September and found the disused, chalk quarry dive. In a flash his mobile was in his hand. *Click! Click! Click!* He'd got what he'd come for. Three more seconds and the log was back in its place, his phone returned to his pocket, and the abandoned manual on the workbench safe in his hand.

He rushed back to the doorway, slowed to a saunter, and called, 'I've found It!'

'That was fun,' Chrissie said as they drove away.

A mix of excitement and adrenalin ebbed through Clive's body, so very different to an average day when he was a DI. 'We got it! We got the first diving buddy's name!' He was too busy driving and digesting it all to say more, and Chrissie barely spoke. He imagined she'd be coming down from the thrill of the subterfuge.

At home at last and standing in their snug kitchen, he felt elated, like a kid getting away with a prank.

'The last of the Sauvignon, or a cold lager to celebrate?' Chrissie asked and peered into the fridge.

He settled for a bottle of lager while Chrissie poured herself a glass of the white wine.

'C'mon, I've got to have a proper look at the shots I took–'

'With my help. We make a good team.'

He kissed her and led the way to the sitting room, swigged lager from the bottle and sank onto the modest sofa. 'You know, this whole business feels like the shapes on this rug.' He cast a glance at the geometrically patterned rug of burgundies, midnight blue, and beige. 'None of the shapes make sense on their own. They're just crazy. But if you piece them together it makes–'

'A stunning rug,' she said and sat down beside him.

He pulled his mobile from his pocket. 'Of course, the rug takes my eye from the lines between the floorboards.'

'Maybe it's what this is about? Maybe it's meant to be a distraction?'

'Oh Chrissie, just stop talking in riddles and concentrate on the log.'

'Yes, but just think about what there *wasn't* in Phil's walk-in locker.'

'What are you talking about?'

'There was a load of technology, even a diver's watch-style computer. But there wasn't an underwater camera. People take selfies when they eat a piece of cake. Don't you think one of the divers might have worn or carried an underwater camera? After all, it was a dive to explore a submerged van, right?'

'Yes…no, I don't know. It was poor visibility. They'd have needed powerful lights for photos. Diving in a quarry isn't like diving the Great Barrier Reef. Now c'mon, let's have a look at the log.'

'There was a diving lamp in the storeroom. I don't know how powerful it was, but they'd have had to take it with them.'

Clive frowned. *What's she trying to say?* He shook his head and opened his photos. He held his phone so she could see as well and slowly scrolled through the shots of the logbook. First, he focused on the September 2021 dive and read aloud: 'Dive buddy: Brian Milledge. *15 minutes* to reach and find van at 25 metres, *10 minutes* at 25 metres exploring the van, *2 minutes 30 secs* to ascend to surface. Total dive time: *27 minutes 30 secs*.

'2022, March 21st dive. Dive buddy: Morton Alconbury. *15 minutes* to reach and find the van at 25 metres, *8 minutes* at 25 metres exploring the van, *2 minutes* pulling buddy out of van and cutting free of rope-entanglement, *2 minutes 30 secs* to ascend to the surface. Total dive time: *27 minutes 30 secs.*'

'Well, it doesn't move things on much,' Chrissie sighed.

'It will when I set Matt onto finding Brian Milledge's contact details.'

'Hmm, any updates on the Oliver Blix email?'

'No. Thanks for the reminder. I'll give Matt a call.'

***

It was five-thirty on Friday afternoon. *Ping!*

'About freaking time,' Pember snorted and opened Matt's text message.

I'm home. Where R U? Bring pizza – pepperoni.

'What?' Pember's irritation skyrocketed. 'I'm not a pizza delivery!' He tapped in *Any news?* and zapped off the text. *Kinda complicated*, came the reply. *I'm on my way,* he shot back.

Pember threw on his biker jacket, grabbed his helmet, and hurried down the two flights of stairs. Outside on Hatter Street, he slowed to walking pace. No point in drawing attention to himself. A couple of minutes later, he unpadlocked his Yamaha Tracer.

The ride to Stowmarket didn't take him long. He cut between lanes of queueing cars as he negotiated Bury's rush hour traffic. He swung onto the slip road and cut along the A14. He glided past fields of wheat and barley, still young, green, and patchworking with eye-watering shocks of yellow-flowering rapeseed. His bike gave him height, and in places, a view across hedges to the horizon. Speed made him feel weightless and detached from the road, almost flying. Calm permeated his mind and body. He checked his wing mirrors without emotion. No one was following him.

He took a zigzag route from the A14 into Stowmarket and the Flower Estate.

'Didn't they do pepperoni?' Matt asked when he opened the door.

'No. My panniers won't take a 14inch pizza.'

Matt nodded.

Pember looked heavenwards. The sarcasm must have passed over Matt's head again. *What a dolt.*

'I got summut interestin' for you,' Matt said, leading the way into the living-room office.

'The trader's emailed you back?'

'Nah, not yet. But Veronica Smith's mug shot…'

'Go on.'

'Well, it spammin' matches a Kristina Svoboda, a Czech from the Czech Republic.'

'What?'

'Yeah. You sure it were Veronica Smith you photographed?'

Pember thought his head might explode. 'Yes, of course I'm sure. Show me this Kristina Svoboda,' he said with a tight jaw.

'That's her.' Matt pointed at a full-face shot, the one Pember had taken of Veronica, late the previous afternoon. It stared from one of Matt's computer screens. Next to it was the shot of a younger face, a teenager with curly hair, lighter and shorter than Veronica's dark, shoulder-length locks. The proportions of the face, cheekbones, and nose matched Veronica's, but the complexion was fresher, more youthful. There was no mistaking, it was a younger version of her. The tentative smile hovering on the lips decided it.

'What the hell?'

'Yeah, seems she were into petty crime. No record of

her on the net after 2010. Guess she bunked out of the Czech Republic, changed her name, grew her hair and dyed it.'

'Hah! Then meets Paul Smith somewhere along the line and now passes herself off as Veronica Smith, and Idris's great-niece.'

'Yeah 'cept that's complicated.'

'Why?'

'I done a bit of family history on them Brafmans, and I found Idris's great-niece. She were called Veronica Brafman. It said Lavenham, Suffolk on her birth certificate. Trouble is, she's dead. Died, 1993, aged one.'

'What!'

'Yeah, it's DOSin' true.'

'So, Idris had a great-niece called Veronica Brafman?'

'Yeah, 'cept she's dead.'

Pember sat down heavily at the computer desk. 'So, Kristina Svoboda took the child's identity?'

'Yeah, Trojan, ain't it? Some faker used a copy of the birth certificate for her to get a passport, and fake ID. And from the passport, then a photo drivin' license. Yeah, there's a drivin' license out there with Veronica Smith's photo on it but sayin' it's Veronica Brafman.'

'But what about the rest of the Brafman family? They must know Veronica Brafman can't be who she says she is. She died twenty-nine years ago.'

'Yeah, but now Idris is dead, there ain't no relatives left to say it.'

'Jeeez! Idris must have known she couldn't be his great-niece when she visited him. That's why he had to die.' Pember let the thought percolate. *Hell, if it's true, then it was pure, premeditated evil. But clever. Someone went to one hell of a lot of trouble to research and plan it and get the false ID. Was Number 17 worth so much effort?*

He glanced at Matt who had settled at the computer desk and seemed absorbed with opening messages.

'Something from the trader?'

'Nah. Summut from Clive.'

Disappointment, then paranoia flickered deep in Pember's brain. 'Which case?'

'I reckon the divin' death case. Clive's sent a name to trace. A Brian Milledge. Bloke dived the chalk quarry September 2021 with Phil Barner. He were okay after the dive, then moved out the area, don't know where. Clive wants to ask him what they found at the bottom of the quarry.'

Beep-itty-beep! Beep-itty-beep beep!

Matt fumbled his mobile out of his jeans. 'Yeah?' he answered. 'Nah, nothin' yet. Hey, can you bring pizza? Pepperoni.'…'Yeah, Pember's here.'…'Yeah, course, everyone likes pepperoni.'…'Nah, Mais is out with her mate, Sandy.'…'Ta.'

'Is Clive bringing pizza?'

'Yeah. He knows I work better when I ain't hungry.'

Pember closed his eyes and counted slowly.

'You starvin' too?'

'No. Now is there anything else you've found? Bring me up to speed.'

'Yeah. Dave Jones, aka Paul Smith.'

'Go on.'

'The restrainin' order breach weren't against a woman.'

'What? Are you saying the slime ball *wasn't* harassing a woman or hounding a kid?'

Matt shrugged. 'I'm sayin' the restrainin' order were protectin' a bloke. I'm still drillin' down, but d'you reckon

173

it could be Idris Brafman?'

'Timeline, give me the timeline,' Pember barked.

'2018; breach of restrainin' order. Paul were callin' himself Dave Jones back then. Also, it were the year of smashin' the international smugglin' ring.'

Pember frowned. 'Next date?'

'August 2021. Number 17 were changed from Idris Brafman's name on them deeds to Veronica Brafman's name.'

'Go on.'

'Idris dies of COVID January this year, 2022.'

'Yeah, Matt. But before he dies, Veronica and Paul spend Christmas 2021 with Idris. The Omicron variant was around, and Idris was an antivaxxer. As it turned out, it was one hell of a toxic Christmas for Idris.'

'Killer app! Opportunity and motive?'

'Yeah, or deadly coincidence.' Pember smiled at Matt and meant it. Slowly, it began to dawn on him that, when he cut out his own sarcastic remarks, as he had with Matt since stepping inside the living room, he felt calmer, less irritable. He smiled again, more deliberately. 'Can you open the selling site. I want to take another look at the advert.'

Matt opened the coin collectors' site on the second screen. Over the next half hour, Pember used the second keyboard to scroll through the for-sale posts and other platforms selling antiquities. The more he searched, the more he appreciated how the Sumerian plaque's true rarity had been effectively and cleverly hidden by attributing it to the wrong country and age, and by placing the sale notice on a single site with limited traffic. But according to CB, there should be two Sumerian plaques coming onto the market, and he'd only found one.

He closed his eyes and rubbed his temples. At least this one was still for sale as a single lot with the decoy Roman gold coins, and they hadn't scared the seller away with the Oliver Blix email.

'It's one hell of a sly hook for collectors with two areas of expertise,' he muttered. Matt seemed too busy with his own searches and screen to hear him.

'Hey, pizza!' Matt pointed at the security monitor and stood slowly as, outside, Clive grinned up at the front door camera. He lumbered off to let him in.

Without a second thought, Pember leaned across to look at Matt's screen. He had split the view to display several web pages at the same time. 'Yeah, it's where I'd have started a search as well.' Pember sighed and nodded briefly as he glanced across the Electoral Register site and the Driver and Vehicle Licensing Agency site. He reckoned Matt must have found a contact phone number or address for Brian Milledge by now. Aromas of tomato, mozzarella and pepperoni wafted in.

'Do you want it in the kitchen?' Clive asked from somewhere out in the hallway.

Pember hadn't thought he felt hungry, but the smell of freshly baked pizza in warm, cardboard packaging was irresistible. His empty stomach gurgled. He hoped Clive had got enough pizza.

'You should have brought Chrissie,' Matt said as he led the way back into the living room and directed Clive to lay the pizza boxes on the marine monster sofa.

'No, I want to keep Chrissie out of this. Blood antiquities are too dangerous. It's one thing to come along with me to see Phil Barner and pretend she wants to learn about SCUBA diving, but international gangs and terrorists? It's beyond risky.'

'What? You've involved her in one of my cases?'

'Oh hi, Pem. Good to see you too. Matt, can you get some plates and a knife from the kitchen?'

Pember drew a breath ready to object to Chrissie being involved, but his body language was somehow being ignored. Matt hadn't even picked up his outraged tone. He waited until Matt had left the room. But before he could say anything, Clive spoke.

'I needed Chrissie's help. In fact, I wouldn't have been able to get Brian Milledge's name without her. She's good at distracting people.'

'But–'

'Look, Pem, be reasonable. You assigned me the case. It's complex, specialist stuff.' He paused as Matt returned, armed with a knife and plates. 'Now eat some pizza. There's olives and artichoke on a section of one of them.'

'Really? Artichokes?' Pember had forgotten how Clive had always read the signs he was hungry. 'How did you know artichokes were my favourite?'

'You said years ago. And food was always a distraction when you were getting tetchy.'

'Really?' A gust of pepperoni hit his nose as Matt opened the pizza boxes. The good humour of it all caught him.

'Ever the great detective,' Clive and Pember said together, and laughed.

'Well, *I'm* stickin' to pepperoni,' Matt said and helped himself to a large slice.

The whole exchange had gone over Matt's head, but Pember bit back the sarcastic comment and concentrated on the artichokes.

It didn't take long to bring Clive up to speed regarding Kristina Svoboda and the restraining order. Again, Matt suggested, 'What if it were Idris Brafman needin' protectin'?'

Clive looked thoughtful. 'It sounds like identity theft, fraud, and obtaining property with menaces. Something the police should be involved in,' he said.

Pember sighed. 'Yeah, it'd get the bloody Smiths off my back with something else to focus on. Except I figure there's more to it than stealing a house. I think there's a Newmarket connection.'

'What? Bettin' on them races?' Matt said, scraping congealed mozzarella off the inside of a pizza box. 'But what we gonna do about Oliver Blix and me email?'

'It's up to Pem. Do you want the seller to think it's the relentless Pember Quinn, the expert who's helped to catch blood antiquity traders in the recent past?'

'Why the spam'd he stick his neck out like that?'

'Because, Matt, if this is a trap to catch Pem, then they need to know it's him they're snaring.'

'But if they ain't springin' a trap, and they realise it's Pember Quinn, they'll run a mile, right?'

'Yup, got it in one, Matt.' Pember almost added a slow hand clap, but smiled instead.

'So, what we doin'?'

'We make a plan, Matt, and keep our options open. We send another email showing interest in the combined lot, start negotiating a price, and ask to see more provenance.' Pember hoped he radiated the confident authority of a patrol briefing. It was a professional skill he'd acquired, and it wasn't the moment to lose his touch.

'Do we sign it Oliver Blix?' Clive asked.

Pember thought for a moment. 'No, it'll have to be a new name. I can give hints later that it's me if I need to.' His gaze fell on the open pizza boxes, smeared with drips of tomato, and pepperoni oil, and blotched with cooked mozzarella. 'I could be Artichoke.'

'Yeah, or Yum!' Matt grinned. 'I spammin' prefer Yum. What you say, Clive?'

'Let's get it written. Okay, Pem?'

It took a few drafts, but twenty minutes later Matt launched an untraceable email with Pem's fake name to the seller through a Virtual Private Network.

Dear seller, I am interested in the items you have for sale, namely the Sumerian plaque with relief carving and the Roman coins. I am willing to pay a good price, but I would like more information regarding provenance, and more photos of the plaque before committing to a price.

Regards, Arthur Yum

'Arthur Yum,' Clive said, seemingly letting the name roll on his tongue.

'Yeah well, Artichoke sounds a bit like Arthur,' Pember muttered, then laughed. It felt good to be working in a unit again. His unit.

SATURDAY

'Ah, you're in here,' Chrissie said and smiled from the doorway into their snug living room. 'I woke up and you'd gone.'

'Hmm, it was a bad night. Horrible dreams. I couldn't drop off again, so I came downstairs, made a mug of tea, and mentally tossed and turned on the sofa. I didn't want to disturb you.' Clive rested his head against the firebrick-red, corduroy cushions.

'You should have woken me up. I wouldn't have minded. It's Saturday. I could've caught up with a lie-in.'

'Well, as it is, you've already had one,'Clive chuckled.

'Hmm,' she checked her watch, 'it's nine o-clock. I need tea. Another mug for you?' She padded away in slippers and wrap and disappeared into the kitchen. 'Have you had breakfast? I'm making toast,' she called.

'Two slices, please.' He hoped she'd heard him and yawned. He'd spent half the night digesting all that Pember and Matt had discovered. *How much do I tell her*?

The smell of hot toast wafted into the living room, heralding Chrissie's return with a tray. She set it down on the coffee table and unloaded plates, tea, toast, butter, and marmalade.

'Okay, tell me about your bad dream, and where Matt found Brian Milledge. Hey, and shift your legs. Make some space.' She play-swept his legs off the sofa as he swung them to the ground, then kissed him.

'In my dream I was wearing the complete SCUBA diving kit.'

'Definitely a nightmare,' she said and settled next to

him.

'I was at the bottom of the chalk quarry pool. I couldn't find my way up.'

'That's terrifying. Could you breathe? Could you work the equipment?'

'I was breathing okay, but I wanted to shout. I couldn't make any sound through my diving mask.' He didn't add that she was down there with him, and he was shouting to tell her they had to get to the surface. But it was dark. They couldn't find their way.

'Well, there's no mystery where your nightmare came from,' she said in a matter-of-fact voice and hugged him. 'And Brian Milledge?'

'He wasn't down there with me.'

'No, I meant where did Matt find him? You said when you got back that Matt had a number for him. It's pretty much all you said.'

'I was exhausted. Yes, he's living in Cambridge. But the thing is, Cambridge isn't far. I'd have expected Phil Barner to know.'

'Unless he didn't want Phil to find him.'

'Woah, now that's a bit of a stretch Chrissie. More likely Phil just didn't want to tell anyone. Didn't want Brian getting involved in the accident inquiry. The less said about the chalk pit, the better.'

She shrugged. 'Are you going to call Brian Milledge?'

'Yes, this morning. I know it's a Saturday, but I'd like to catch him before he goes out.' He watched Chrissie sip her tea. He recognised the distant look, the conspiratorial pucker of her forehead. *Uh oh. She's been scheming.* 'What? Go on, tell me.' He sighed.

'I've some questions I think you should ask him. I mean

in your own way and only if you want to. But after you left yesterday evening to see Matt and Pember, I went through the dive in my mind and with the manual. It turned up some things we haven't asked about, so I'll get my list and...well, see what you think.'

'That's great, Chrissie. But first I'll finish my toast and take a shower. It'll help me feel sharper when I make the call.' He let a breath escape slowly.

It could be worse. She could have contacted her friend Sarah, and the pair of them signed up for diving lessons with Phil Barner's diving club.

Half an hour later, Clive sat on the sofa in dark chinos and sweatshirt. His notes and Chrissie's list lay on the coffee table in front of him. Chrissie had settled in the armchair, and he'd put his phone on speaker so she could hear. The little flutter in his stomach told him this was important. For a moment he was back in the police. He pressed automatic dial. The tension racked up with each ringtone. Eight...nine...ten...elev–'

'Hello.'

'Ah good morning. My name is Clive Merry from the Hatter Street Agency in Bury St Edmunds. Am I speaking to Brian Milledge?'

'Who's calling? What's this about?'

'It's about the disused chalk pit, out Nettlestead way. I believe you've dived it.'

'Where did you get my name from? How'd you know I'd dived it?'

'The SCUBA diving community is relatively small, Mr Milledge. I think your name was from the farmer landowner. I've been asked to take a look. Do you have a moment to talk to me about it?' He wondered if he should say who

he'd been asked by, but sensed he'd get a more open response if he kept it vague.

'I don't know. I'm just a bit surprised someone's called
out of the blue like this.'

'Well, not entirely out of the blue. I don't' know if
you've heard, but there was a fatality there about six weeks
ago, the 21st of March. A SCUBA diver lost his life.'

'What? Was it Phil Barner?'

'I'm not at liberty to divulge the name, but I can tell you
it wasn't a Phil Barner.'

'Oh good. He was my diving buddy when I dived it in
September, last year. I'll have to look at my dive log to be
certain of the details. It's with my diving kit. I won't be a
moment. Hold on.'

'Thank you.' Clive glanced at Chrissie and gave a
thumbs up.

A couple of minutes later, Brian Milledge was back on
the phone, 'Hi, the log brings it back. It took about fifteen
minutes to reach and find the van at twenty-five metres. It
was one of those old Commer Express delivery vans from
the 1950s. The driver and passenger door windows were
open, and the two back doors were wide ajar, so you could
see inside. There was a lot of rope and wire floating in and
around it. I guess it was an old electrician's van. The visibility was poor, and once we'd disturbed the bottom, the
chalk silt swirled around and turned the water into something resembling cream of mushroom soup. So, it was too
dangerous to get close or go inside the van.'

Chrissie tapped one of the questions and frowned. Clive
shook his head and mouthed, *he's in full flow.*

'It was obvious there was nothing of interest, no bodies,
nothing shocking. In fact, as far as we could tell, it was

empty. We circled it and came up,' Brian continued. 'Yes, ten minutes down there and then a two minute and thirty seconds ascent to the surface. Total dive time: *27 minutes 30 secs*,' he said, as if reading from his log.

'Had you planned to go back and take a second look?' Clive asked.

'No, there was no reason. And anyway, it was blooming dangerous with all those ropes and wire floating around. Easy to get tangled in.'

'Did you take lanterns or torches?'

'Yes, of course. We wouldn't have seen a thing without them.' His irritation was obvious.

'And a camera?'

'You are joking. If we were serious about taking shots or filming down there, we'd have needed a separate person simply to manage the camera. Fully waterproof camera casings are bulky. Remember, the diver would be wearing gloves and needs both hands to hold it and work the control buttons.

'So, three divers?'

'Four, if you wanted descent footage. A cameraman needs a buddy and someone to carry powerful lights. But the more divers down there, the greater the chances of disturbing the silt…that would be the end of filming or stills.'

'But if you'd found something down there, wouldn't you have wanted to take a photo?'

'Only if we could bring it up with us. Then we'd have taken a picture, once we were back on dry land, with our phones.'

'But if you thought there was something down there too large to bring up, and you were going back to dive the quarry again?'

'There wasn't anything like that down there, and going back would have been dangerous.'

'So, are you surprised that Phil Barner went back to dive the chalk quarry again this year?'

'What? But that's crazy. Hey, didn't you say he was okay? Was it his diving buddy who died?'

'Yes.'

'Oh no, that's awful. But Phil would have warned his buddy about the ropes and wire, and not to swim too close or enter the van.'

'Hmm. It seems clear, from what you've told me, that the owners need to know their quarry isn't safe for diving down to twenty-five metres.'

When Brian didn't say anything, Clive added, 'Would you mind making a statement for the coroner's hearing? An account of your dive and what you found, just as you told me, but not all the camera stuff you explained. It's simply to get an idea of the conditions down there.'

'Yes, of course.'

'Thank you. I'll ask someone to contact you for a statement. It'll be the accident investigators, or the widow's solicitors, or possibly the police. And please don't go talking about this. Keep it to yourself, okay?'

After Clive had ended the call, he glanced at Chrissie. 'What? Did I miss out anything?'

'Nothing. You got him talking quite openly.'

'People react differently when you aren't a policeman.'

'Hmm…the bit he said about the number of divers needed if there's to be camera work. Do you think that's why Phil Barner said there'd be a third diver coming. The fictional third diver to pad out his claim there was something of interest down there?'

'It could be. But that reminds me. There's something I didn't think to ask Morton Alconbury's widow.'

He pressed the automatic dial, impatient with himself while he waited for her to answer.

'Hello. Mrs Alconbury. Clive Merry speaking from the Hatter Street Agency.'

'You do know this is a Saturday morning, Mr Merry,' she answered, rolling her Rs low in her mouth.

'Yes, my apologies, but I won't keep you long. There's a question I forgot to ask when we last spoke.'

'On Tuesday when you came to interview me.'

'Yes, and since then you've handed in your husband's phone to the police.'

'I have, but as you know, Mr Merry, I don't hold much hope with their ability to trace the threatening calls and messages. Now, what was your question?'

'Did your husband have a diving camera? Did he take it with him to the chalk pit, and do you still have it?'

'That sounds like three questions.'

'Yes, three questions, but one theme.'

'Okay, let me think...he had a waterproof diving case for a neat Olympus camera. He used to keep it with his diving kit. He didn't take many shots under the water; I think it was only waterproof to a few metres. Mostly he used it without its case as a standard camera. He said he got better photos with his Olympus than his phone, *and* they weren't automatically stored on the cloud or filling his phone's memory.'

'That makes sense.' At least it did to Clive, now that he'd heard Brian Milledge's words on diving cameras at twenty-five metres.

'The investigators took all the equipment he had with

him when he…' Mrs Alconbury's voice broke.

'I don't remember seeing a camera or its diving case on the inventory of items taken,' Clive murmured.

'No. But he would have taken it with him that day.'

'Okay. Can you check if it's somewhere at home with you? And let me know either way, please?'

'Sure. Do you think it's important?'

'I don't know, Mrs Alconbury. You've got my number. As I said, let me know either way.' He ended the call.

Clive needed a few minutes to collect his thoughts. All he was getting was circumstantial evidence; nothing solid, and nothing resembling proof. Morton Alconbury could have been led to his death by Phil Barner, but without hard evidence, conjecture was meaningless. He glanced at Chrissie to see how she was reacting. She seemed to have her faraway look.

'What are you thinking, Chrissie?'

'I'm remembering what you always say to me. Motive and opportunity, they're key. And the question you always ask. What are the chances of things being random coincidences?'

She's right. It's okay for an amateur to go on a flight of fancy, but not for a professional, a former DI. He sighed, checked his phone for any messages from Pember or Matt, and rested his head back on the sofa. His eyelids felt heavy, his mind drifted.

It was half an hour before Mrs Alconbury phoned, jolting Clive back from his nap.

'Mr Merry, I've searched through Morton's things, and everywhere he might have left his camera, including his car,' she said, cutting straight to the point, 'and I can't find his Olympus or its diving case.'

'Do you remember him saying he'd lost or mislaid it?'

'No.'

'Can you recall when or where he last used it?'

'It was his camera, Mr Merry, not mine. He didn't tell me every time he took a photo. Hmm, let me think…yes, he used it when we went mud larking, New Year's Day.' Her voice broke. 'Do you really need to ask all this?'

'I'm sorry. So, assuming he hadn't lost it after that, it's likely he'd take it with him to the chalk pit dive. It wasn't left in his car, it wasn't amongst the impounded items, so we need to check if it was dropped somewhere around the dive site.'

'*We*, Mr Merry?'

He was tempted to ask if she was offering to help but thought better of it. 'The Hatter Street PI Agency, Mrs Alconbury.' He ended the call, just as Chrissie put her head round the doorway.

'I thought I heard you talking. I leave you to have a snooze and–'

'Mrs Alconbury called to say she can't find her husband's camera or its diving case.'

'Wow! So, what happens now?'

'We look for it around the chalk pit.'

'We? Does that mean you need my help, sorry, I mean I can come as well?'

'Both,' he laughed. 'Ann, the good lady of the farmhouse at the entrance to the pit, knows me as an official she showed round to check the gate locks, fencing, and warning signs to keep people out. If I say I've come back to look for a camera with a diving case, it'll break my cover. She won't let me in.'

'You could say it was yours, and you've lost it.'

'But she'll have seen me use my phone as a camera.'

'Hmm, you could have had a camera in your pocket as well for official shots?'

He thought for a moment, 'I'll phone the farm, ask if they've found it and say I'm walking in the area with you. Makes sense to drop by to pick it up or look for it.'

'Perfect. You're a natural liar.'

***

Pember lay on the floor on the inflatable mattress, both arms free of his down sleeping bag. He massaged his temples. His Hatter Street pad, aka his storeroom-cum-second office, had taken on the appearance of a recycling tip; one degree worse than a junk den. He gazed up at its ceiling. Daylight filtered through the window, heralding the start of Saturday. The stacks of boxes, piles of files, and heaps of biking gear and clothes broke his view across the sisal flooring to the neutral, paint-wash walls. He was hemmed in. A shield of camouflage. 'Don't militarise it, Pember. It is what it is. A mess,' he sighed, as indeed was his life.

He'd left Matt and Tumble Weed Drive at the same time as Clive the previous evening. It struck him as being the first time they'd left anywhere together since Clive had climbed the two flights of stairs to his Hatter Street office and stepped back into his life again. That had been on Monday, five days ago 'Hah, my ride out to Woolpit doesn't count. I was bloody tailing him. Yeah, and walking to and from the White Heart pub might, except Chrissie was there as well, so, it doesn't qualify.' He smiled. He didn't want to admit it, but it was okay, now he was getting used to hooking up with Clive after all these years.

While Flossy gently hissed in his right ear, Pember

thought about the seller on the coin collectors' site. CB had said there were two ancient Sumerian temple plaques coming on the market, but Pember had only found one. The more he thought about it the more it made sense. Two incredibly rare Sumerian plaques for sale at the same time would attract attention. A beginner's mistake. These sellers were clever. The second Sumerian plaque wouldn't appear until the first had been sold. He needed to contact CB and find out if the first one would be enough to lead her team to track or seize the second one and the network. *Why the hell didn't I ask her that question when I visited her?* A sudden flash of irritation fizzed, sent his pulse rushing, but for once failed to ignite. Flossy whistled smoothly, barely ruffled. 'It's okay, just make a plan,' he told himself.

It didn't take long to throw on his clothes. He could mingle later with the Saturday crush visiting the Bury St Edmunds Leisure Centre and slip into the changing rooms for a shower. Until then, a flannel wash at the sink would have to do.

He hurried along the top floor landing and unlocked his main office door. It only took a moment to reload his coffee machine. Soon the room filled with the aroma of double-shot espresso, and he sat at his desk and downed his meds. His next task took longer. He logged into his computer and installed the same encrypted, secure VPN that Matt used, and linked the installed app on his phone.

'Okay, Matt Finch, now you've no excuse not to keep me bloody informed if the seller replies. From here on in, you forward all the communications to me.' He emailed Matt via the VPN to that effect.

He wasn't entirely sure how CB would react to the next part of his plan, but he needed her direction. Again, his irritation sparked but didn't catch. Instead, he concentrated on tapping her restricted number onto his phone's keypad. It was secure while it was in his head. He couldn't imagine anyone wanting to hack into his mind. After all, it was a mess. He waited, listening to the ringtone.

'Hello?' The voice was sharp, alert, feminine, obviously CB.

'Hi. I've a query about the wine order for Arthur Yum, and if I don't occasionally use your number I'll forget it,' he said happy to play it light when he was at a distance.

'Then I'd better see you at the vineyard.'

'Thirty-five minutes?'

'Forty, if you want the name on it. And in the shadow of the tower.' She ended the call.

He knew she meant a particular water tower and vineyard; a place they'd met from time to time over the years. She chose it when she didn't want him visiting her home, he assumed to keep the members of her team separate and anonymous. It might be safer and more secure for them all. But it didn't stop him being curious about the other operatives. It had taken a couple of warnings to stop him asking questions. He reckoned it was probably why he still worked for her.

When he pounded down the two flights of stairs from his office wearing his motorbike gear, he half expected to pass Dove somewhere on the way. And then he remembered it was Saturday, she'd have finished cleaning and left by now. He felt stupid. 'Sharpen up, Quinn.'

With his own words ringing in his ears, he rode his Yamaha Tracer like the wind along the main roads northeast of Bury. He was heading towards Ixworth and the Wyken Vineyard, and he dipped and cornered like a bird on

thermals as he rode the contours of the slowly rolling countryside. He cut onto small lanes, the corners becoming
tighter and the hedges higher as he homed into Stowlangtoft, a village recorded in the Domesday Book of 1086. He
sensed the history as he rode past the red-brick, early 17th
century alms houses. He slowed to almost walking pace and
swung off the main street onto Kiln Lane. He rode on, the
lane crossing old parkland of a country estate, with large,
mature oaks, beeches, and conifers dotted near hedge lines
and in the distance. 'Almost there, stay sharp,' he breathed
as he passed a sign to the Dark Horse Inn, totally hidden
from view from the lane.

The water tower stood about twenty yards from the lane,
starkly visible and seemingly easily accessible. It reached
towards the sky from its empty compound and low perimeter fence. The ground was partially concreted, but shrub-
sized weeds had fought their way to guard the tower's base.
Brush-like trees cocooned its northern aspect. And somewhere, out of sight behind the tall hedges and trees, a vineyard spread down a gentle, south-facing slope.

Pember slowed to a halt at the entrance to the water
tower's compound. He guessed CB would approach from
Euston, the opposite direction to him, and he sat astride his
bike and waited. Five minutes later, true to expectation, a
burgundy-coloured, hybrid Volvo appeared along the
straight section of lane. CB was instantly recognisable, her
hair swept into a loose bun on the top of her head, making
her taller behind the steering wheel. It struck Pember that
her bun doubled as an officer's peaked cap. He resisted an
urge to smile at the association, or to salute and waited for
her to pull into the side of the lane in front of him. She nodded a greeting. He knew the format. It was an invitation to

sit in her car.

'Thank you for meeting me,' he said once he'd settled with his helmet on his knee in the front passenger seat. He tried to appear relaxed.

'This works quite well. It's halfway between my place in the forest and Bury St Edmunds.'

'Seven miles.'

'What's the news?' She held her back stiffly as she turned a little to face him.

'I've located an ad for a Sumerian temple plaque. It must be one of the two we're after because its flat style of carving and hieroglyphics obviously place it as originating from Iraq. But confusingly, the ad says Syria. And it's 2000 years older than the ad implies when it says there's a Roman gold aureus collection apparently found with it, and also for sale.'

She nodded. 'So, the provenance is deliberately wrong on two counts. Go on.'

'The ad was placed on an obscure site with limited traffic. A coin collectors' site.'

'It's sounding even more likely it's one of them.'

'I've expressed an interest and I'm waiting for a response. I need to know if you want me to ask what else the dealer may have and hint about the second plaque? It could frighten them away. Can we assume he or she has the second Sumerian temple plaque?'

'Hmm.' Her sun-damaged skin lent itself to a deep frown.

He waited a few seconds. 'Well?'

'I might need to take advice on this one, but gut feeling…don't broach a second plaque with the dealer.'

'Okay. How do I pay? Have you brought a card?'

'Yes, the usual arrangements. It will work with your phone app. And there's a tracker on the card.'

'Good.' He knew the card would be fronting a sham account.

'Ask to see the artefact before paying,' she added.

'Of course. I've bloody done this before.'

'I know. Go to the seller's location of choice. He or she won't come to you in case it's a trap. But activate the tracker. We'll be following.' She slipped a debit card out of her pocket and handed it to him. 'There's a genuine balance of one hundred pounds, so you can make the test electronic transfer to them.'

He read the name on the card, '*Arthur Yum.*'

'A slight departure from your usual repertoire,' she said.

'Yeah, I get a feeling the seller is fishing for me. It feels personal, so I've gone for a more cosmopolitan name. Less obviously me.'

'Hmm, let's hope they decide to sell this one to Arthur Yum because they think Pember Quinn will bite on their hook for the next one.'

'Yeah, let's hope. I'll keep you updated with any developments.' He didn't wait to be dismissed but opened the passenger door and got out of the car. He raised his arm in a loose goodbye as she drove past him in the direction of Stowlangtoft.

He gazed up at the water tower and imagined the thousands of gallons stored above him. The scale was humbling. Jeeez, he felt vulnerable.

Brring! Brring! He pulled his mobile from his pocket. *Caller ID - Clive.*

'Hi, what's up?' he asked, leaning against the low perimeter fence.

'Some developments. Seems Morton Alconbury had a camera with a diving case, and there's no record of the investigators taking it. His wife can't find it at home. She insists he'll have taken it with him to the chalk pit dive.'

'Is that it?'

There was a pause before Clive answered, his tone measured and controlled, 'Why would I have news about the seller before you, Pem?'

'Sorry, I'm a bit...I've been busy too.'

'Okay. I've also spoken to Brian Milledge, the first diving buddy. There's nothing of value at the bottom. In fact, it's a death trap with old rope and wire floating around an empty Commer van. I think Phil Barner set it up to be an accident.'

'Do you think the camera's at the bottom with the van?'

'If it is, we'll never find it. No, Chrissie and I'll do a search around the edge of the water and where Morton Alconbury parked his car.'

Pember's irritation sparked and fired, 'Since when has Chrissie been on the books of the Hatter Street PI Agency?'

'Well, do you want to come and help instead? *Needle in a haystack*, comes to mind.'

'I...' He counted slowly under his breath.

'Yeah, I thought not. I know you're worried but lighten up, Pem. Working together is supposed to be fun. Hey, we're having lunch at the Hollow Duke. You're welcome to join us. One-thirtyish. Then we'll drive to the chalk pit.'

'Really? I'm invited?' His surprise slipped out before he could bite it back. It was hardly the rejoinder of a tough Staff Sergeant. 'Sharpen up, Quinn,' he muttered.

'Did I just hear you offer to help?'

'Yeah. I guess I'm hungry, and when was I ever good at

just sitting around?'

'Great. You'll be safe there from the Kane gang killers.'

'Not down market enough for them, then?'

'The pub's great. The chalk pit is super secluded.'

'Ah.' Pember laughed. 'Hey, I meant to tell you I installed the VPN Matt used to contact the seller. I've got it on my computer and phone now.'

'Well, that makes it easier. You're not cutting Matt out, are you?'

'Not bloody likely! He's another layer of protection. He's to forward any communication to me via the VPN. See you in thirty!' Pember ended the call. Something felt better inside his head. He wasn't sure what or why.

***

Clive and Chrissie led the way in the black Lexus. Pember followed close behind on his motor bike. For the first time in forty-eight hours, he forgot about assassins' bullets and almost felt content, his stomach now filled with the Hollow Duke's signature steak and ale pie. The route to the disused chalk pit twisted and turned as the country lanes led them further and further from the pub. The terrain rose in a low, hilly ridge of chalk and limestone, while out of view on the far side of the ridge, the River Gipping snaked across gravel beds hemmed in by the railway line and the A14.

They turned into the entrance to the farm courtyard. Clive had called ahead from the pub, to warn Ann that he was coming to search for his camera with a couple of friends. Pember had been sitting opposite Clive when he phoned, and he'd been reminded how smooth and relaxed Clive could sound when he was spinning a yarn. If anything, he'd become more plausible with the years. It was impressive and Pember wondered if one had to be relaxed and at peace with oneself to convey such a convincing storyline. And of course, Clive was, and it showed. It had always been like this. They might be chalk and cheese, but some of it used to rub off on Pember.

They had barely parked up before Ann opened the front door and strolled out of the old farmhouse to meet them. To Pember she looked large shouldered, buxom, and smiling; pleased to see Clive.

'Sorry to trouble you again, but it's such a magical place. I needed an excuse to come back again,' he laughed. Pember could see Clive had made a connection with her. It seemed so effortless.

'I'll unlock the gate for you,' she said, 'I hope you find your camera.'

'Well, Chrissie and my old friend, Pember are here to help me.'

Ann led the way with Clive. Pember and Chrissie fell in-to step behind them. It was an easy walk, the track turning towards the hillside as it sloped downwards from the farm buildings. Trees had sprung up on the thin soil covering the limestone and chalk. A fence ran down the hillside, as if corralling the stunted silver birches, ash, and elm. Shrubby hawthorn and rough grass had sprung up under the canopy of budding leaves. A gate blocked the track, and a notice was nailed to it saying *DANGER PRIVATE KEEP OUT* in bold lettering. A large chain and padlock reinforced the message.

'Okay, I'll leave you here,' Ann said as she unpadlocked the gate.

'We'll let you know how we get on.' Clive smiled, add-ing, 'And thank you.'

They waited until Ann had left them before anyone spoke. Pember simply stood and soaked in the atmosphere and silence. It felt tranquil. 'I can think of worse places to die,' he murmured.

'No one's dying here today,' Clive said in a matter-of-fact tone. 'Look, I think this'll work best if you get a feel for the lay of the land first. So, this,' he swept his hand in a panoramic movement, 'is bowl shaped and we're coming into it near its base. The sides of it are the old quarry face and it rises above us with the hillside. Down there is a pit.'

'And is that the bit that's twenty-five metres deep and full of water?' Chrissie asked.

'Yes. So, if I lead the way to where they dived, we'll walk past lots of tracks from the rescue vehicles and where the divers parked.'

'And then fan out searching back from the water's edge?' Pember asked.

'Yes, because I don't think the camera will be on ground higher than where Morton Alconbury parked his car.'

'You mean, where the tyre tracks are?'

'Yes, Chrissie.'

'It sounds like a plan. I don't know about anyone else, but I'm going to find a long stick to poke around with in the grass,' Pember said and started to hunt for something suitable as Clive led the way to the water's edge.

'Should have brought the walking poles,' Chrissie murmured.

The leafy bowl felt enchanted, but Pember found the quarry pool and its dark surface ominous. He couldn't imagine anyone wanting to submerge themself in its icy depths. But Morton Alconbury had, and he'd died. Knowing it made the air around Pember seem heavy with sadness. And chilly. He shivered.

They fanned out. Chrissie in the middle, Clive to her left, and Pember to her right. Pember imagined Clive would have done this kind of thing in the past. Although he reckoned ground searches were more the remit of junior constables and volunteers than DIs. But it wasn't new for Pember. His experiences had been soaked with personal risk. Everywhere he'd walked in Iraq had held danger, but once off the beaten track, there was always the chance of a landmine. 'And bloody IEDs,' he breathed.

Pember zoned in and concentrated on the task. He trod precisely, his steps unhurried, his actions deliberate. All he saw was below the tip of his stick as he moved it back and forth in measured, slow movements a couple of inches above the ground. Blades of grass, nettle leaves, and straggling brambles were coaxed and persuaded to one side. Time had no meaning as he worked. He saw chalky stones, gritty soil...

'Yes! Eureka!' Chrissie shrieked on his left side.

A flash. A bang...Pember flung his arms up, covered his eyes and his face. Private Mendoza landed against him, unbalancing, and knocking him down. The lad's foot and half his lower leg were missing. Greasy microdroplets, fine dust, the smell of explosive, ears ringing, and someone screaming.

'Tourniquet. Make a tourniquet,' Pember breathed fast.

'Hey, Pember! Are you okay?' It was Chrissie's voice.

A hand on his neck, fingers lightly on his carotid. A more familiar voice muttered, 'He's okay, he's got a good pulse. What happened?'

'He curled up and fell backwards. He said *make a tourniquet.*'

'After you screamed?'

'I didn't scream. I yelled. Look! I've found the camera.'

'Really? Well done! Let me see.'

Pember let the voices wash over him. He focused on his breathing by counting and slowing the rate. He moved his hands from his face, felt grass against his cheek and scratchy brambles against his wrist. The air was deathly still. Could he taste moisture in it? Gradually it dawned; this wasn't dusty Iraq. The ground was too cold and damp, and it smelled like the temperate parts of the world. He opened his eyes.

'That's good, you're back with us,' Chrissie said. 'What happened? Did you faint?'

'Was it your ear?' Clive butted in.

Pember rolled onto his back, straightened his legs, and gazed up at the sky, grey-blue above branches with leafy buds. It took him a moment to find the word. 'Landmine.'

'Landmine? Did you just have...was it a flashback? I asked Clive if you got them. PTSD, that's what I said, didn't I, Clive?'

'Yes, but you could have told me, Pem.'

'I don't like talking about it. I had counselling to help with Flossy. That was enough.'

'Flossy?'

'It's Pem's ear problem, Chrissie.'

'And the PTSD?'

Pember's thoughts had scrambled with the flashback, but slowly he marshalled them. 'The counsellor wanted to talk PTS and anger. I said no, and that all of us get flash-backs. It's...just a question of degree. And you can't wipe out memory; it's always lurking in there waiting for the right trigger. When I'm angry, I don't get flashbacks. I use my anger.'

'But it's not so easy to let go of,' Chrissie finished for him.

'You should have said, Pem. What are you so angry about? Your Dad? Your ear? Your service years? What?'

'The landmines, the snipers, the indiscriminate nature of it all. Yeah, I'd say it was the *why*. Like, why did Private Mendoza have to lose half his leg? Why him? And why on my patrol?'

'Fate. Bad luck. A bit of both,' Chrissie said, and shook her head.

'I don't accept that. It makes me angry even suggesting I should.'

'Are you happy when you're angry?' Chrissie asked.

It was a simple question and one that Pember hadn't thought about. 'There isn't room for anything else when I'm angry.'

'Is that why you're always snapping and snarling, trying to pick a fight? Well, I'll tell you something Pem. Your brain isn't so sharp when you're flooding it with anger. I'd rather you curled into a ball every so often than bite my head off.'

Pember sat up slowly.

'I'm sorry, but you're hearing it straight, Pem.' Chrissie grimaced; it was her I'm-only-adding-up-the-numbers-like-an-accountant look.

'What is this? Are you two bloody ganging up on me?'

'Slow down. And don't kick off, Pem. I'm saying I'd like to work with the other, nicer Pember. The one I re-member. So, stop getting angry with me, like you have this past week.' Clive's eyes bored into him.

Something snapped into place in Pember's brain. He

knew he'd pushed himself and everyone around him too hard, but he wasn't used to backing down and he wasn't a bully. 'I'm sorry. It's how I am.' He caught the glance between Clive and Chrissie.

'You've always fired off easily. That's you, Pem. Just direct your anger at the bad guys. You know who they are,' Clive said.

'And how about getting help with your anger management and PTS,' Chrissie added. 'Think of it as an investment.'

'Hey, is that the diving camera?' Pember said, catching sight of something colourful and plastic in her hand, and sidestepping her suggestion. 'Where was it?'

'Amongst the nettles over there, between those two boulders.' She pointed.

'Let me see it.' Clive took the camera carefully, turning it over and inspecting it before opening the water-tight case and pressing the *on* button. 'Ah, low battery but it's still working. I can scroll back over the last few shots.' He sat down next to Pember.

Chrissie crouched to get a view. 'Isn't that outside Phil Barner's storehouse? Whose car is it?'

'Morton's, Phil's…I don't know, Chrissie. There's several shots of it. Hey, this one's of inside the storehouse. There's the air compressor.'

'Is it being used? There's the air inlet hose. Hey, is it feeding through the window?'

'I don't know. Oh…low battery warning light. Better turn the camera off. At least we know it's okay.'

'You can look at the photos on its SDHC card,' Pember said.

'That's its Secure Digital High Capacity card, Chrissie.'

'You sound like Matt, Clive. It's a memory card, Chrissie,' Pember sighed.

Ping! Ping! Two message alerts cut through the still air. Pember dragged his phone from his pocket.

'Is that–'

'Yeah, Clive. One from Matt, and one from the seller.' He held the phone so that Clive could see the screen as well.

'What is it?' Chrissie asked peering over his shoulder.

'Matt 's forwarded the reply from the seller.' Pember opened Matt's email. It'd be quicker than opening the original on his phone's VPN. He frowned as he read, *Dear Mr Arthur Yum. You are the second customer interested in my sale items. I am trusting perhaps you want it more than my first customer. If you agree to pay more than my first customer, you will be the owner. Yours cordially. Van d'Ore*

'Arthur Yum? Who's he?'

'Me, Chrissie.'

'Do you think the other customer is Oliver Blix?' Clive asked. 'Remember, Oliver Blix is Matt, Chrissie.'

'I don't know, he could be. But I'll ask to see the plaque and coins before shelling out more.'

'But it's extortion. This Van d'Ore is…well unless it's an auction site, this is like forced gazumping. Can't you report him to the selling site?'

'No, Chrissie. I'd lose the sale and he'd bloody disappear.'

'Pem's right, Chrissie. This is…' Clive glanced at Pember, who half nodded.

'Yeah okay, Clive. It's easier if I tell her. This is about dodgy goods from dodgy sellers. I'm trying to bring down an illegal importing ring. It's what I do. Now keep it to yourself, Chrissie.'

'I thought you ran a PI agency.'

'He does that as well. Well, not quite so well, if you see what I mean.' Clive laughed, and Pember found himself grinning.

Nice play on words he thought and remembered the old times. 'Right, I'm going to call Matt.' It only took a few moments before Matt answered.

'Hiya, Pember. Spammin' cool you got the same VPN.'

'Yeah. It made sense.'

'But frag n'burn, the plan worked. The seller's emailed back!'

'It's only stage one. Look, I want you to email the seller back now, okay?'

'But the email only came through just now. I ain't been pixellin' around and sittin' on it.'

'Good. Put your mobile on record so you get all this. I want you to write, *Hello Mr Van d'Ore.*' He'd been thinking about it for hours. The words just flowed, *'I like to see items first. If looking okay, then I consider bidding against the other customer. Regards, Arthur Yum.*' He realised Clive was mouthing something at him. 'What?' Then he caught the gist of what Clive was trying to say. 'Another thing, Matt. Have you, sorry, has *Oliver Blix* heard back from the seller yet?'

'Nah. Do you want me to send it again?'

Pember saw an exaggerated nod from Clive, and answered, 'Yeah, okay but not at the same time as the one from me.'

'You mean Arthur Yum?'

'Yeah, of course I mean Arthur Yum. I'm not using my real name, am I?' He sensed rather than saw a frown from

Chrissie, and added, 'So, yes, another one from Oliver Blix. That's you. Make sure you're recording this.'

It had been on his mind since Thursday. Again, the words flowed, '*Dear seller. You may not have received my email, so I am sending it again. Please, I am interested in your advertisement for what I assume are Roman aureus coins - I collect early examples. Please send more details. Also, you haven't let me know yet if the coins are for sale as a separate deal or jointly with the Sumerian temple plaque. Regards, Oliver Blix.* Okay, got that, Matt?'

'The style is kinda different.'

'On ruddy purpose. They're different people. They're–'

'Chalk n'cheese?'

'Yeah, something like that.' Pember ended the call and sighed. 'Will Matt manage it, d'you think?' He was surprised it was Chrissie who answered.

'Yes, of course. Matt will do exactly what you've asked him to do. Although, it might be an idea if we dropped in on him on the way home. We could look at the SDHC card on his system.' She smiled. 'And yes, the pair of you, I work with HMRC. So, I'm used to picking up on acronyms as well. Maybe we should make a copy before you hand it over to Mrs Alconbury?'

'And the coroner or police,' Clive murmured.

Pember stood up wearily. On a whim, he checked his tracking app. 'Shite, Veronica Smith is driving round Newmarket.'

'Are you going to check on her? See what the attraction is in Newmarket? I haven't had a chance to talk to Chakra about the Smiths, so the police haven't taken the case over yet. Chrissie and I can do the drop in on Matt?'

'Thanks, Clive.'

Pember tailed Clive's black Lexus out of the farm courtyard and onto the lanes leading from the chalk pit towards Stowmarket. He raised his hand in a loose salute as he peeled away from Clive and followed a more direct route to join the A14 and head to Newmarket. As always, the ride and speed of his Tracer took possession of his mind and body, releasing it from the buzz of problems and transporting him into a state of weightless composure. He hadn't expected to enjoy an afternoon spent searching for a camera in a diving case, but the trees and foliage sheltering the quarry-like chalk pit had felt safe from snipers. Despite the constant awareness of Morton Alconbury's death, the place had seemed strangely calming. He wondered if the soothing effect was simply the steak and ale pie satiating him. Or perhaps it was spending time with Clive and Chrissie and focusing on a shared purpose. He reckoned it was more likely from feeling part of a team, like being back in the RMP and working with his unit. And then he remembered the flashback. It was something he'd tried to suppress, a nightmare he'd tried to leave in Iraq.

He forced his mind back to the task in hand. He watched the position of Veronica's car trackers on his phone, clasped in a special holder close to his bike's instrument displays. But the size of the screen, scale of the road map, and transmitted vibration made it difficult to see the details. He needed to slow down and look for longer than millisecond glances if he wanted to work out the intricacies of Veronica's route. He dropped his speed.

Her car had headed northwest out of Newmarket, passing under the A14 dual carriageway to Exning, a small village barely a quarter of a mile from the town. He sped to the A14 exit for Exning and instead of riding into Newmarket, coasted north of the dual carriageway and turned into Windmill Hill, a minor road taking him directly to Exning.

'Oh hell!' *Veronica 's turned into Windmill Hill. She's driving towards me. She'll be on me in a moment!*

The road was straight, had one long bend and no obvious escape. To the sides, tamed, grass verges offered no cover and beyond, walls, fences and hedges were continuous with gates and houses. He saw a display of bright green vehicles off to one side of the road. His brain computed the shapes. Tractors? He was passing a retailer for tractors and heavy agricultural equipment. It was now or never. He swerved sharp left and pulled up close to the display, just as the white Panda drove past on the road. He waited astride his bike and watched her brake at the T junction, the one he'd turned onto Windmill Hill from. She drove north and out of his direct view. But it was easy to see her progress as her trackers moved on his screen in the direction of Snailwell, a small village one and a half miles away.

For the next hour or so, she drove slowly round and between the local villages, stopping for five or ten minutes at a time, and then moving on. He followed the trackers, never far behind, but keeping out of her eyeline. It took him a while to figure out what she was doing, but eventually he tumbled it. She was stopping near studs and stables; anywhere she might get a sighting of racing or ex-racing horses. She was obviously looking for access over fences or through gates, or views across fields or exercise paddocks, but seemingly always without involving an owner. Then using a camera and long lenses, she took photographs of the horses.

He managed to get a quick shot of her with his phone,

her attention on something through a five-bar gate and her camera with long lens held to one eye.

'What the hell's her game?' he asked himself. 'Is she working for a horse magazine and wants pretty pictures? Or am I watching horse identity theft?' It wasn't the kind of thing he'd encountered in Norwich. Of course, betting syndicate scams and Ponzi schemes weren't confined to horseracing, and he felt reasonably at home with that kind of fraud. *But actual physical racehorses? Scams around the animals themselves?* Horses were outside his comfort zone, and like SCUBA diving, a specialist area.

Veronica appeared to be working her way eastwards and back towards the A14 to Bury St Edmunds. He guessed she'd be heading home and made a snap decision not to follow her onto the dual carriageway. While he was close to Newmarket, it made better sense to retrace the route she'd taken before he'd picked up her tail on Windmill Hill. He reckoned it would be more efficient than riding back another time. So, he re-ran her car tracker recording on his mobile and rode back into Newmarket. It didn't take him long to check each place she'd stopped. And sure enough, as with north of Newmarket, she'd obviously been checking out every stud and stables she passed. He made a note of the names.

By the time Pember was ready to ride back to Bury St Edmunds, he felt exhausted. Automatically he looked at his tracker app in real time to be sure Veronica's car was back home. Yes, it was. But only one of her trackers was transmitting. *Hmm, but wasn't that why I put on more than one? A spare?*

And Paul's car? He checked the Honda Jazz Hybrid's whereabouts on his tracker app again. And yes, it was where it had been for the past couple of days. *Good. Except...*

Foreboding tingled in the back of Pember's neck. Every time he'd looked at the app over the past couple of days, Paul's car hadn't moved. Its stationary position had been reassuring. Now it felt wrong. *What if Paul removed the tracker and left it hidden where his car had been parked? Paul could be out tailing me at this very moment.* 'It makes me bloody vulnerable,' he muttered.

Pember instantly geared into shaking-off anyone tailing him. He stamped down to low gear, accelerated hard. and turned a sharp right. Then he waited out of sight to see if a car or motorbike followed him. When neither Paul's car nor anything suspicious appeared after several minutes, he took a zigzag route following B roads and lanes back to Bury St Edmunds. He headed to where the tracker he'd put on Paul's car was still indicating its position, somewhere a few roads away from No. 17.

He dismounted and walked along the row of cars parked the length of the residential road. Paul's Honda Jazz had vanished. Pember's guts twisted and his ear hissed. He held his phone in front of him, viewing the screen as he pinpointed the tracker's exact location. It was fixed to the metal bars on a gutter drain close to the curb. He removed it and turned it off. But of course, it was predictable. He was bound to come and check the stationary tracker.

'Damn, damn, damn.' He felt stupid. *Have I walked into a trap?* He spun around, scanning his surroundings. There were no CCTV cameras on the houses close by or hidden in the sycamore tree a few yards away. No one lurked like an assassin waiting to kill him. There was nothing obvious, but it didn't mean he was going to hang around.

He hurried to his bike, flipped his visor down and sped away. Again, he made sharp turns and waited out of sight in case he had a tail. But no one followed. He made his way back to Hatter Street and his second-floor offices.

It was only while he sat at his desk, sipped a double espresso, and gazed at the empty space on the filing cabinets where his musketeer jugs had stood, that a thought dawned. None of the addresses he'd noted down or ridden past that day had been the racehorse sanctuary or centre for re-homing ex-racehorses, the beneficiary of donations instead of flowers from Idris Brafman's funeral. *Hell, is that an elaborate scam too?*

He glanced at his tracking app on his computer screen. There was only one tracker transmitting and it was close to the exit from the A14 for Risby and Barrow, villages to the north and south of the dual carriageway, about three miles east of Bury St Edmunds. The tracker was stationary, he assumed on Veronica's car.

'What the hell's it doing there?' he hissed and ran the monitor recording back. Fifteen minutes earlier the monitor was clearly transmitting on Veronica's Panda parked outside No 17 in Bury St Edmunds. And then it simply stopped transmitting.

He ran the recording back further and saw the moment he'd taken Paul's car tracker from the drain cover and turned it off.

'Oh n-o-o,' he moaned as paranoia gripped him. 'What the hell's going on? It's like someone's playing with my mind.' His tinnitus responded with a more strident hiss.

***

Clive exchanged a brief glance with Chrissie. They were in Matt's living-room office in the bungalow on Tumble Weed Drive. Chrissie sat at the table desk, a computer screen ahead of her, while to one side, Matt sat and worked on his main computer, typing commands on the second keyboard and clicking with his mouse.

Clive stood, moving between them both and watching the two screens. He was horrified when an image from Morton Alconbury's photocard flashed onto Chrissie's screen.

'Am I looking at a dead hare?' Chrissie asked.

Matt leaned across. 'Bloggin' hell, yeah. And lyin' on a car windscreen. Why's he got it on his divin' SDHC card?'

'I'd guess, Matt, he had his diving camera in his car, along with his diving gear. His wife told me he took it on all his dives,' Clive said calmly. But he felt anything but calm. He was looking at evidence. The camera and its memory card needed to be handed to the police or dive specialists investigating the alleged threats and fatal accident. And soon, before any legal team cried 'tampering' and 'inadmissible evidence'. But could he bypass the widow and hand it directly to the police? *Mrs Alconbury will expect me to hand it over to her. What if she chooses not to pass it on to the police?*

Until that moment Clive hadn't thought twice about looking at the memory card. He'd been carried by the momentum of his investigation. But he'd forgotten things had changed for him. He was no longer a police officer. *Have I broken rules by looking at the photos without permission? Am I skating outside the law or on its blurry margins?* He didn't know if he should confide in the widow and tell her he'd looked at the images. *Would she be right to consider his actions unprofessional?*

'What are you thinking?' Chrissie asked, now facing him and obviously catching his frown.

'I'm just not sure if…well, I've always tried to do things by the book.'

'What's up?' Matt asked.

'I'm not certain we should be looking at the memory card like this.'

'Yeah, well, technically it ain't Alconbury's SDHC card we're lookin' at. It's a copy I made. See, no one'll know it's been copied. It's already back in his camera.'

'But…'

'Widgettin' hell, Clive. There weren't no password protection for it. I ain't unlocked or broken into anythin'. You said the camera were lost, discarded at the chalk pit. So, it weren't a theft, least not in my book. It were fair game.'

'Stop, stop,' Chrissie moaned. 'Surely, it's about what type of digital material you're looking at and what you do with it. If you feel bad about it, delete the copy, Clive. All I know is this is too much for me. If I keep my eyes on that poor creature any longer, I won't be able to get it out of my head.'

'Yes, of course. Would tea or coffee help?' Clive caught her withering, glance. 'I mean, assuming there's tea and coffee in the kitchen and you go and make it?'

'You mean distract myself? I think after this afternoon I deserve something a little stronger than a mug of tea.'

'There's lager in the fridge. Yeah, but careful coz stuff falls out the door when you open it.'

'Thanks, Matt.' Chrissie sighed and headed to the kitchen, leaving her place at the computer desk free for Clive. He sat down, let his conscience tussle with Matt telling him he couldn't get caught, and opened the next photograph. It was a different angle of the same dead hare. He clicked on the photograph's information and ignored the details about size and pixels, but noted the time and date it had been taken. 'I guess it's the day Morton Alconbury found it on his windscreen. Hmm, his wife's right. It was about two weeks before he died.'

'What's right?' Matt asked. He looked distracted by emails on his screen.

Clive didn't answer but opened the next sequence of photos, finding his moral compass less jittery with the mundaneness of each image he viewed. He checked the date and time. They'd been taken two weeks later, on the morning of the fatal dive. The time order suggested Alconbury's first photograph was inside Phil's storehouse and showed his tank attached to the diving air compressor and the air inlet hose running to the window. Clive assumed it had been taken while his tank was being filled. Five minutes later, the next shots were outside the storehouse and were of a blue Range Rover, its bonnet up with views of the engine, and the vehicle's front, rear, and sides. Clive studied each one slowly.

'How does this strike you?' he asked Chrissie when she returned from the kitchen with a single can of cold lager.

She looked over his shoulder at the screen. 'Hey, we got a glimpse of those this afternoon, but the camera's battery was starting to fail. They're the kind of photo you'd take of someone's new car or a car you're interested in owning or lusting after. Like if you were a Range Rover enthusiast. Why?'

'Because it isn't a new car. And it isn't a classic. It's ten years old, judging by the 2012 registration number. I wondered if there was something wrong with it, and that's why the bonnet's up. Or maybe Alconbury was a Range Rover buff and just wanted to see the engine?'

'I don't understand what you're getting at, Clive.' She pulled the tab on the can.

'It could be relevant if they had the engine running.' He opened another photo, 'In this shot you can see what I think might be the air inlet hose for the diving compressor. Look there on the ground near the car's exhaust closest to the storeroom window.'

'Ah ha, it's got twin exhausts. They're not easy to see.' She sipped some lager from the can.

'You don't usually drink lager,' Clive frowned.

'I don't see a dead hare on a windscreen every day, either.' She touched his shoulder. 'Okay. Let's think. If you enlarged the image enough, we might be able to see fumes or drips of condensation from the exhaust pipes. That'd tell you if the engine had just been started. Is it a diesel?'

Clive was dubious but scrolled up the magnification and focused on each of the exhausts in turn. 'Hey, you may be right Chrissie. It looks fuzzy at the outlets. Forensics would be able to tell the difference between steamy fumes and poor definition or focus.'

Matt seemed to become aware of them frowning at the screen and leaned across to see what they were looking at. 'What you got there?' he asked.

'A can of lager,' Chrissie answered.

'Yeah…no, I mean what's on the screen?'

'It's a magnified car exhaust tip. But whose car is it?' Clive said, voicing his thoughts as he opened a search for the DVLA website and logged in using his not-yet-cancelled police access. 'And the car reg is…?'

213

Matt reached across, clicked back onto the photo and reduced the magnification. 'It's pixelin' simple when you know how,' he said and read out the registration on the Range Rover's number plate.

'Thanks.' Seconds later, the website responded. *Land Rover Range Rover, Diesel, Blue, Automatic, Euro 5, First registered 2012, Registered Keeper – Phillip Barner.* 'Yes, it belongs to Phil,' Clive said, feeling slightly more pragmatic about the tactics open to a PI.

'I still don't get the significance.' Chrissie swigged more lager.

'Ah, but you would if you'd spent half an hour on the phone with Ariana Landry, like I have. She's a chest physician and the sister of one of Chakra's oldest friends,' he added catching Chrissie's blank expression, 'She knows about SCUBA diving. The question is...could where the inlet tube is on the photo have made a difference to the air quality in Alconbury's diving tank? Could it have increased his chances of fatal immersion pulmonary oedema?'

'Well, don't hackin' look at me. How'd I know?'

'Nor me,' Chrissie added. 'Hey, when are you expecting Maisie'll be home, Matt?'

'Around now, any time after six o'clock. But...'

Clive smiled at him and remembered it was Saturday. He'd been so focused on the SCUBA diving case, he'd forgotten other people had a life. And Chrissie, a wine-or-ginger-beer kind of a girl, was drinking lager from a can. It wasn't a good sign. 'Hmm, you're right. It's Saturday night. I guess it can wait until tomorrow before I tell Mrs Alconbury we've found her husband's camera. We all need a break.' But his conscience had decided that if Mrs Alconbury handed in the diving camera to the investigators or the police, then he'd tell Matt to delete the copy they'd made.

'Yeah, and the Smiths? What's your police bloke Chakra say? What's his take on 'em?'

'I'll call him about them, tomorrow. I'd got the impression Pember wanted a day or two to check out the Newmarket connection.'

'Frag, I hope Pember's still watchin' his back. I keep checkin' me emails.'

'And?' Clive raised his eyebrows.

'Nothin' yet.'

'Keep checking.'

***

Pember sat at his desk, his elbows on its surface and his head cradled in his hands. It was his equivalent to curling into a foetal ball. He would have rocked back and forth as well, but he wasn't going to risk setting Flossy off. Someone was playing with him and his trackers. It had to be one of the Smiths...or perhaps both. *But why?* And with the *why* came another wave of paranoia. 'Don't stop at the Smiths, Pember. It's more like the whole bloody world's after you,' he groaned, remembering the Kanes and the rogue antiquity importers. Now would be the moment to unleash some anger and counter his paranoia, but Clive and Chrissie's stern words still rang in his ears from the afternoon.

'Count and breathe slowly,' he told himself, 'Think and use your brain to fix this. Drop the rage.' He looked at the monitor, taking his time to work out exactly where Veronica's white Panda appeared to be stationary. He made a plan. First, check Veronica's car. Then decide what to do next.

He downed the dregs of his espresso, zipped up his biker

jacket and headed out of his office and down to his bike on Hatter Street.

He fixed his phone in its holder and burnt up the A14, knowing the speed would focus his mind and steady his nerves. He kept an eye on the tracker as he flew off at the Saxham Business Park exit, then over the dual carriageway, north towards Risby. But before he had travelled many yards, he cut onto the Newmarket Road running parallel to the A14.

Scrubby bushes shielded him from the traffic whooshing past on the dual carriageway close by. He slowed, watching the tracker signal on his phone's screen. He traced the roads towards the stationary signal, somewhere off to his right. He found a tiny lane, single-car width. A high overgrown hedge intruded on one side, while a tamed hedge blocked a clear view of sugar beet fields on the other. He headed along it, closing in on his target. *Surely the Panda must be coming into sight by now...unless it's a trick to lead me to an isolated place and kill me?* 'Yeah, it's remote and secluded, all right,' he muttered.

His pulse thumped through the hissing in his right ear. He kicked down to second gear and coasted. The signal intensified. It was close, off to his right. A sudden break in the hedge revealed a wide, ungated, field entrance and the start to a broad, muddy track. It was signposted with a notice saying *Footpath* pointing straight across the field. A white Panda was parked in the field on the other side of the hedge, close to the beginning of the footpath.

He drifted to a halt, wary of the mud and leaving tyre tracks. He figured keeping his bike on the road and exploring on foot would leave less evidence of his visit. So, he eased the bike forwards before dismounting on the opposite side of the road ten yards on.

The stillness was unnerving as he took disposable plastic gloves and shoe covers from his pannier and unclipped his phone. He walked back, keeping to the road. It was as if the car had been parked in a hurry. Its angle jarred with the right-angles of the straight hedge line, road, and footpath. All its doors were closed, but he needed to get closer to check if anyone was inside.

He donned the gloves and shower cap-style shoe covers and padded across the ruts and mud leading from the road into the field and start of the footpath. He trod carefully, looking in all directions for signs of anyone watching him. Initial glances at the car told him there was a figure sitting in the driver's seat leaning forward, head against the steering wheel. He approached on one side from behind with caution and made sure to keep in the driver's wing-mirror blind spot. But the figure didn't move. It was motionless as if asleep or...*or what? Dead?* But Pember had seen so many dead bodies, the possibility was bound to suggest itself. The sense of unnatural stillness, posture, and position was usually the giveaway, and this driver was, dare he think it, *dead* still. Pember steeled himself.

But the figure didn't have Veronica's dark, shoulder-length, curly hair. The head seemed more streamlined and, as on a mannequin, bald. *Is it Paul Smith?* He'd worn a wig when he'd visited Pember in the Hatter Street office the previous Monday, six days ago.

Pember was drawn closer. A rapid check told him the rear and front passenger seats were empty. He ducked down, removed the tracker from under the chassis, switched it off and bagged it. The signal stopped abruptly on his phone's screen. He made a quick search for the second but non-transmitting tracker and found it on the chassis towards the rear of the car. He removed it as well and put it to join the first in the plastic bag in his pocket. Strange, he thought, how it had already been switched off. *Has it been left for forensics to find and incriminate me?*

He turned his attention to the body in the driver's seat. He'd felt no emotion while he'd thought it was Paul Smith. Now, on his second more exacting look, a wave of sadness engulfed him. There was no mistake. This was Veronica. The attractive, slightly sassy Veronica aka Kristina Svoboda from the Czech Republic. Her head was wrapped tight in plastic clingfilm. Her hair was pressed to the contours of the back of her skull, giving it the mannequin look. One arm hung down next to the steering wheel. The bare skin of her forearm and hand was mottled. It told him it had been hanging there a while. His guts twisted. Veronica was hours dead.

He slipped into RMP professional mode. He noted that the camera and long lens she'd been wielding earlier in the afternoon weren't in the car. He wondered if his phone's own GPS tracking would show him to be innocent of her killing or put him in the frame for her murder. He retraced his footsteps back to the tarmac road and carefully removed his disposable shoe covers. He took care not to step in any mud shed from them and picked his way along the lane back to his bike. He'd throw them in a bin, miles away. He rode a circuitous route into Risby, all the while fighting with his conscience. *Should I phone the police and report the dead body, or get the hell away from this place and lie low?*

'Clive'll know what to do. Jeeez, it'll be his old DS dealing with this,' he groaned.

The phone call was brief, and Clive was economical with his words.

'I'm in the car driving back from Matt's with Chrissie. I'll meet you in Hatter Street ASAP. Oh, and Chrissie refuses to be dropped off at home on the way.'

**

By the time Clive and Chrissie climbed the two flights of stairs to the Hatter Street PIA office, Pember had had a chance to ride back and park his bike, sit at his desk, count, and breathe slowly.

'Hi, Pem.'

Pember caught the concern in Clive's voice as he walked into the room.

'Hi,' Chrissie echoed as she followed Clive in and glanced around the room before sitting on a conference chair. 'I hope you don't mind but it was quicker if Clive drove straight here.'

He didn't bother to ask what difference it would make if he did mind. Instead, he nodded and concentrated on controlling his paranoia and compartmentalising his anger.

'Okay then, Pem. We're going to have to call the police and notify them of the car and body inside. The longer we leave it, the more suspicious your involvement will look.'

'But they'll pin it on me anyway.'

'They'll try to.'

'Why?' Chrissie asked, looking at Clive. She sounded genuinely puzzled.

'It happens. Remember that "losing the evidence" case I uncovered, about six months before I retired?'

Pember had no idea what he was referring to but guessed Clive hadn't filled her in about the Smiths. Part of him was grateful for his discretion. But it didn't stop Pember hovering on the edge of irritation, knowing he'd have to give some kind of explanation.

He took a deep breath and tried to keep his tone measured, 'They'll try and pin it on me because her bloody husband asked me to put a tracker on the car she drives. So, after we left the chalk pit, I followed her. It's why I know she drove round the Newmarket area taking photos of horses at studs and stables. All her car movements are on the tracker programme on my computer and my phone app. I was probably within one or two hundred yards when she was murdered. Of course, it freaking puts me in the bloody frame. They'll love pinning it on me.' His heartbeat thumped in his ears.

'Ah.' Chrissie grimaced.

'And the proof she was taking photos will be on her camera. But of course, her camera 's gone from her bloody car.'

'How'd you know?' Chrissie sounded sharp.

'Because I went to see why the car was stationary somewhere off the A14, just after six o'clock. That's how I know she's in the car and bloody dead. That's when I removed the two trackers I'd put on it.' As if to emphasize the point he put the plastic bag with the two trackers on the desk. 'And here's the tracker from Paul Smith's car. I retrieved it from a drain cover at five-twenty-five this afternoon.' He dropped a second plastic bag next to the first. He glared at Clive, daring him to say it didn't look bleak for him.

'It sounds like someone's doing a good job of framing you, Pem. Or at the very least, discrediting you as a witness. Come on, ring Chakra. I know he's straight. Let's hope he's on duty.'

'But–'

'It's your best chance. If you want the police to believe you, they'll need to hear the whole of it from you and at the start of their investigation. Otherwise, it won't make sense to them. And remember, trackers and your phone's GPS don't lie. It's proving who or what was moving the trackers that could be difficult.'

'Yes, so why remove them?' Chrissie murmured.

Her question pulled Pember up short. In the heat of the moment his only thought had been to remove all connections between him, the car and Veronica Smith. He hadn't even considered the trackers could work as an alibi.

'No, Pember. Don't even think about returning to the scene and putting them back,' Clive said, as if reading his thoughts.

'Oh no, I've been a bloody fool,' he groaned.

'Here, give me your phone.' Clive held out his hand for Pember's mobile, tapped in a number, waited for it to be answered and said, 'Hi, Chakra. Sorry to mess up your Saturday evening, but Pember has discovered a body to report.' He handed the phone back to Pember.

'Umm, yeah, hi, DS McLaren. I want to report a dead body.' His stomach was in knots.

***

Clive listened while Pember gave Chakra the car's make, registration number, and the location where it was parked at the edge of a field between Risby and the A14. Admittedly, Clive was only hearing one side of the conversation, but what he was party to sounded professional and unruffled. He hoped Pember didn't launch into explanations. That kind of thing could end up messy, but for the moment it appeared he was letting Chakra take the lead and simply answering questions.

'Good, so you'll send out a patrol car?'…'No, I haven't touched the body,' his voice cracked. 'It's obvious she's dead.'…'Yes, you can contact me on this number.'…'At the Hatter Street office. I'll be here for a while.'…'Yes, the one you visited on Thursday morning.'…'Thank you. I'll wait to hear from you.' Pember ended the call.

'Well done, Pem. You held that together well.' Clive shot his old friend a look of genuine respect. The stress had already etched shadows on Pember's face, adding extra contours under his eyes and across his cheeks, the old scar under his chin an extra shadow.

'Right, we have a breathing space,' Clive said, voicing his thoughts. 'Let's use it wisely.'

'What d'you mean? Use it for what?' Chrissie piped in.

'The filing cabinets in here were ransacked in the break in, early hours of Thursday. I know how the police think.'

'You're talking in riddles, Clive. What do you mean?'

'He means, Chrissie…hell, you were bloody one of them until only eight weeks ago.'

'Okay, Pem. The point is, Chakra will assume there's information held here, and the hoods were after it on Thursday's break in. He'll want to get his hands on whatever it is because he'll think it could be relevant to this woman's death.'

'Are you saying we need to empty the filing cabinets?' Chrissie looked shocked.

'I don't know. Do we, Pem?'

'No. Old client files are in a secure storage facility elsewhere. These filing cabinets contain professional licenses and insurance, training updates, auction catalogues, newspaper cuttings, and articles about porcelain and coins. Current clients' files are mainly digital, and password protected. They're on this computer and cloud storage. It has a secure boot.'

'Secure boot?'

'Yeah, Chrissie, a security feature. It stops unauthorised access to my computer before the operating system loads.' Pember indicated the computer on his desk. He sounded calmer while he focused on the technical things.

'And current clients' paper documents?' she added.

'Scanned but the originals are in hanging files, second drawer, third cabinet.'

'So, no need to wipe your computer or ditch your phone,' Chrissie said with a weak smile.

'What? Wipe his computer and ditch his phone?' Clive almost exploded. 'That would be stupid. Not only would it look suspicious, it would *be* suspicious. What the hell have you got yourself, no, *all of us* into, Pem?'

'It's not everyone. It's only me.'

'You think? Are you so sure?' Clive figured the Kanes would have police on their payroll with influence beyond Norwich. *If they were framing Pember, why stop there?* He reckoned it was a fair bet they'd try to fit him up as well. His world reeled. But this wasn't the moment to lose his cool. He needed to keep Pember rational and on track. They both depended on it.

'Okay. Don't get cross, Pember, but is there anything here you don't want found or seized?

'The material about the Kanes is saved on an encrypted, password protected pen drive. It's hidden. And anyway, the CPS has the evidence as well. I've cloned my phone's SIM card. My emails are safe. I use encrypted Virtual Protected Networks for anything sensitive. That way the sender and recipient are concealed. It's more private than WhatsApp.'

'Good. And any links to the illegal trade in cultural artefacts they could pin on you?'

'There's nothing here.' Pem seemed to give his head a shake as if coming out of a bad dream. 'They'll want what I've got on Paul Smith and his wife. That's okay, I've copies. And I guess they'll want my CCTV and the tracker recordings...' His words drifted as he caught Clive's withering look. 'You think they could lose the recordings; lose my alibi?'

Clive nodded.

'Okay, I'll copy them now.'

While Pember slipped a USB stick into his desk computer, Chrissie leaned across to Clive. 'What about his gun?' she whispered.

Oh God, the gun Clive's inner voice moaned. He closed his eyes for a few seconds and composed himself. 'That's next,' he whispered. It felt like a while, but it was less than fifteen minutes before Pember looked up.

'It's copied, now.'

'Good. And the SIG Sauer?'

'Jeeez, it's still in my backpack. Hell, the CCTV'll pick up if any of us leave. I suppose I could–'

'No. Don't turn it off. Any break in the recordings will tell them we might've moved a load of stuff out of here.'

'So, what do you suggest?

'Hide it where you know it won't be found.'

***

Pember had been waiting for the call, but when it came, the

224

sudden, strident ringtone as good as winded him. He dared not snatch his mobile from his desk. He had to control his breathing first. And besides, a hasty pick up would only make him appear anxious, needy…guilty. He let a couple more ringtones shrill while he pushed the pizza delivery box to one side. 'Hello. Pember Quinn, Hatter Street PIA,' he answered.

'Hi, this is DS Chakra McLaren. We spoke earlier this evening.'

'Yes, I've been expecting a call.'

'I'd like to ask you some questions. Over the phone will do for now, but I'll need you to come to the station tomorrow, and we'll want a statement from you.'

'Okay.' He glanced around his office. Clive and Chrissie had left. He was on his own, vulnerable in the face of a hostile police investigation, and momentarily surprised to miss Clive's reassuring presence.

'What time was it when you saw the car in the field and went to check it out?'

Pember glanced at a notepad with the times he'd copied from the tracker recordings 'Just after six o'clock. Five minutes after, to be precise.'

'And you called me at around six-thirty from your Hatter Street office. Why didn't you call straight away when you found the car and dead body? Why wait twenty-five minutes and drive back to Bury St Edmunds, Mr Quinn?'

He wanted to say *I didn't think you'd believe me*. Instead, he opted for, 'I was on my motorbike. It's a complicated story. I didn't know how to explain it and…I panicked.'

'You don't strike me as a person who panics, Mr Quinn. Please explain why you waited so long before calling it in.'

'You see, the body…I thought it might be my client, and it freaked me out. I was so shocked I wanted to get the hell away from there as fast as I could. So, I did. As soon as I'd calmed down, I called Clive. After that I called you from Hatter Street. I guess you'll find it all took twenty-five minutes.'

'What's the name of this dead client?'

'Paul Smith. But then I thought it might be his wife.'

'Why?'

'Because it's his car but she tends to drive it.'

'Go on.'

'At first, I thought the car was empty, like it had been abandoned or dumped there. So, I went to check it out. But when I got closer, I saw the driver was slumped onto the steering wheel. I couldn't tell which of them it was from the back of their head. Not when wrapped so tight in layers of plastic cling film. The shape of a head, yes. But without visible features, no. And I wasn't going to open the car door to see more.'

'Will there be any of your DNA inside the car, Mr Quinn?'

The question felt like a trap, but he didn't dare hesitate. 'No.'

'How did you know the car was there? What made you go to check it out?'

'Because six days ago, Paul Smith instructed me to put a tracker on one of his cars, the Fiat Panda his wife drove, that's the car I found in the field today.'

'Go on.'

'The first tracker came off after a day or so. It turned out she'd removed it, all part of a trick to ask me to protect her rather than track her.'

'And why would she want you to do that, Mr Quinn?'

'She said her husband was trying to kill her.'

'And you believed her?'

'I didn't know what to believe. I advised her to go to the police, but she didn't want to. She knew I'd replace the lost tracker. But this time, I put two trackers on her car and one on his to be sure she'd be safe. I said it was complicated.'

'It also sounds very irregular. We'll need to see the recordings, Mr Quinn.'

'Of course. So, have you...do you know who it is?'

'We're waiting for formal identification. Ten o'clock tomorrow morning, Mr Quinn. Raingate station. Don't be late.'

SUNDAY

Clive felt unsettled when he awoke on Sunday morning. He'd slept fitfully, tormented by the nightmare of a never-ending race to reach the evidence room. Groups of SCUBA divers had blocked his path as he sprinted between the Raingate Police Station and the Bury St Edmunds Police Investigation Unit. And of course, because it was a dream, he had taken a route through the abbey grounds and No Man's Meadows, then cut along a footpath beside the River Lark, complete with a white-knuckle road-crossing beyond the Rugby Football Grounds.

He didn't need Chrissie to interpret any of it for him. His dreams were born of his fear of dishonest police. *What if evidence is deliberately mislaid again, this time in Pember's case?* At least he'd managed to coach Pember, or more accurately, as much as Pember would allow. It was a case of Pember being open, honest, and careful with some of the details, and stressing the importance of getting his story straight from the beginning. He'd done the best he could for his old friend. Now he'd leave it to Pember. But he still felt anxious.

'Does PIA client confidentiality work like it does in accountancy?' Chrissie had asked as they'd driven home. 'In my job there's a duty to report client fraud to HM Revenue & Customs. So, when there's a dead body involved, where do you stand?'

'How do you mean?'

'Can Pember break client confidentiality when the police come asking questions about his client?'

'You mean before Paul Smith's been arrested or

charged? Probably not, but if the client has misled and lied to you, as Paul has, then I reckon it invalidates some aspects of the client-PIA contract, particularly if the police are accusing Pember and he gives information to defend himself,' Clive had said, once again feeling uncomfortable with the blurry lines for codes of practice for a PI.

'Hmm, it's like that in accountancy as well.'

He'd let the subject drop, but it had planted a seed that sprouted into troubled dreams.

He turned over again and wrestled with an empty edge of the duvet cover, the duvet inside having slipped sideways and centred itself over Chrissie. Restless and unable to settle, he reached for his mobile phone on the bedside table. He checked the time. 06:30. Not as early as he'd expected but still early for a Sunday morning. *Were there any messages or emails from Matt or Pember?* He checked. There was nothing. Relief was quickly followed by concern. *Did it imply all was well or catastrophically wrong?*

'You've been tossing and turning for hours,' Chrissie sighed. 'Are you okay?'

'Sorry, didn't mean to disturb you. Bad dreams.'

'Poor you. What about?'

He didn't answer.

'Is it about the case? You don't have to do it, you know. You're meant to have retired from this kind of thing.' She yawned.

She was right, of course. He could walk away from it. Except his case, the SCUBA diving death, was intriguing and to be honest, he was enjoying the challenge. He suspected Chrissie was enjoying it too. The stress and anxiety were coming from Pember's cases, not his. But it had always been like this with Pember, the difference being that when he was younger, it had seemed like an adventure. It was as Chrissie had said a few days earlier, *Pember's a catalyst. Things happen around him.* Unfortunately, they weren't always good.

'I thought you said Pember was being set up,' her voice drifted sleepily beside him, as if she was omnipresent.

'Hmm. Do you think I should walk away from it all?'

'I don't know. What if whoever is setting Pember up expects you to walk away?'

It was an angle he hadn't considered, but the more he thought about it the more it seemed plausible. *Is a secret force trying to manipulate me and best guess my next move?* He frowned. 'Bluff, double bluff and counter bluff? You mean they want me to walk away?'

'Hmm, maybe, or something like that.' It was obvious she was dozing off.

But Clive was now wide awake. His mind geared into the day, with questions of loyalty to an old friend jostling with the instinct of self-preservation. *How will this unseen hand setting Pember up expect me to behave?* He figured an early morning run would help him to think it through and plan the return of the diving camera.

***

Clive phoned Mrs Alconbury as early as seemed acceptable for a Sunday morning.

'Bring the camera straight over,' she'd said, sounding her Canadian Rs in the floor of her mouth. So, Clive had driven to her home in Great Bricett by ten o'clock. He guessed she'd been waiting for him because he'd barely rung the bell before she opened the front door.

She nodded in response to his *Good Morning* and led

him through the hallway and into the lounge. The large French windows were open, and a mild breeze gently worried the curtains, drawn back but unsecured by ties.

'Is this a breakthrough, Mr Merry?' she asked.

'I don't know. But it may count as evidence,' he said handing her the diving-camera case and camera.

'Have you looked at the photos?'

'I checked the camera was working, if that's what you mean. It's been out in the open for six weeks. I know it's supposed to be waterproof, but that's assuming the case was closed properly. Anyway, it turned on okay, which is good. But it's reading low battery.'

'But are there any quarry dive photos? Come on, you must've looked.'

'Yes, I did. But there were none of the dive site. I reckon the shots taken that day were at Phil Barner's place on the morning of the dive.'

'Really? At Phil's place? How can you tell?'

'I drove over to Cavendish to visit him a couple of days ago. I recognised it on the photos.'

'So, I'm paying you to drive all over Suffolk, am I?'

'Mr Barner was very defensive and suspicious when I called him. So, I changed tack and arranged to visit him on the pretext of finding out more about SCUBA diving in general.'

'At my expense. I hope it was worth it.'

'Yes, it's what made me wonder if your husband had a diving camera. It's why I searched for it and why you're holding it in your hand right now.' He didn't see the point in mincing his words with this woman, even if she had lost her husband recently. He wasn't going let her assume she knew how to oversee an investigation. 'So, to look at the photos, you'll need to recharge the camera or slip the memory card into your computer.'

'Let's do it.'

He frowned, momentarily confused.

'I'll get my laptop.' She smiled, almost excited.

While she was out of the room, he took a closer look around the lounge. He was struck by how few ornaments and photos graced the surfaces. She'd told him on his previous visit that she'd met Morton Alconbury about ten years ago, around the time his first wife died in a car accident in Canada. If there'd been any children from his first marriage, they certainly weren't represented in any photos on show. Only the obligatory, happy couple shot of the current Mrs Alconbury, her arm around Morton and Niagara Falls in the background.

A gentle gust lifted the edge of the curtain and pulled Clive's attention outside. He was drawn onto the decking by the weathered, stone sea creature close to water spouting into the ornamental pool. He didn't know much about stone carvings, but the naivety of this one was compelling. *Didn't she say something about putting her mudlarking finds in the pool?* He narrowed his gaze and focused into the water. But the ripple-effect from the fountain made it impossible to see clearly. He crouched and looked again, ready to dip his hand into the water.

'What are you doing?' Her voice was sharp. Accusing.

'I was looking at your pond. I remember you said you put the clay pipes you'd found in here. I wondered what they looked like.' He ignored her frown and focused closer to the bottom. 'Ah, I think I can see one. Can I pick it out?'

'If you must.'

He pulled up his sleeve and dipped his forearm into the

cold water. His fingers brushed down past decorative pondweed confined in a planter and onto the bowl of the pipe. It was smaller and slimmer than he expected. He drove his fingers under the pipe, disturbing gravel covering the bottom of the pond and clouding the water. Chilling water rose above his elbow. He winced and grabbed the pipe. 'Got it!' he said and lifted it out. 'Wow, that was colder than I expected. And it's smaller than I imagined.'

She smiled and nodded. 'Tobacco was expensive. So, you'd only need a small amount to fill the bowl of that pipe. The stem's the most fragile part. Unusual to survive intact like that.'

'Can I take a photo of it?' he asked, turning it over in his hands.

She laughed. 'If you like.'

He set it carefully on the wooden guard rail and pulled his mobile from his pocket. He made a play of crouching and taking shots of it from different angles, making sure to get the weathered, stone sea creature into the frame. He hoped he'd disguised his real interest. 'Shall I put it back?' he asked when he'd finished.

'No, leave it.' Again, the sudden sharpness in her tone.

'Okay, well if you've got your laptop, let's have a look at the photocard.' He kept his stance casual as he slipped his phone back into his pocket.

She had already set her laptop on a glass-topped table behind the sofa. She drew up a chair, he guessed one from a set of dining chairs kept elsewhere, took the photocard out of the camera, and slid it into her laptop's portal There was only the one chair, and it was clear she expected him to stand.

'Let's see what we've got,' she said as the images covered the screen like a wall of tiles. She homed in immediately on the shots of a dead hare on a car windscreen.

'Uuugh. I didn't know he'd taken photos.'

'Well, it backs up your claim that Morton was being threatened. You should hand it to the police.'

She scrolled to the photos taken on March 21st, 2022.

'That's the inlet pipe to the diving compressor,' Clive said, pointing at the tube in the photo. 'See how close it is to the Range Rover's exhaust? If the engine was running, then the air in your husband's tank might have been defective.'

'What? Oh, my poor darling. That would have been bad. I knew something wasn't right. I've said all along.' She looked at the floor, her eyes a little watery, as if struggling to control her emotion.

Clive decided it was time for practicalities. 'Have you instructed a solicitor to present the information to the coroner at the hearing?'

'No. I mean yeah, our solicitor is already involved because of Morton's will and probate. There's a misunderstanding with the inland revenue. So sure, I guess Gotten & Ghorton might as well do the coroner's hearing thing too. I'll call them.'

'Good. And tell them I'll be contacting them. I'd like them to take a sworn affidavit from Brian Milledge, Phil Barner's diving buddy from the first time he dived the quarry pool. Brian has agreed to make a statement about the conditions, visibility, and there being little of interest to warrant the second dive.'

'What? Why haven't you told me this before?'

'I only spoke to him yesterday and finding the camera…'

'Okay, suppose I should say *good work*, Mr Merry.'

'Thank you. But we can't risk the photos of the air inlet pipe not being sent to the specialist investigators.'

'You think the police will block the investigation?'

'Not on purpose, but I know how they work. The shots of the dead hare are on the same photocard as shots of the air-compressor hose taking air from close to the car exhaust. Will they recognise what it is? Or its effect on the air quality in the tanks? Will they take the time to separate and select the relevant photos to send to the different investigators on the case? He shook his head. 'I'm sorry, it's not high enough profile.'

'So, what do we do?'

'We get the solicitors to send the photos to the specialist dive investigators. Which means you need to copy or move them onto a stick.'

'I can do better. I'll send the photocard to Gotten & Ghorton, and *they* can send the dead hare shots to the police and the morning-of-the-dive shots to the special investigators. What d'you say?'

'I'd say it's a great idea. But before you give them the photocard, please look through all the photos to check there are no surprises.'

'Like what?'

He softened his tone. 'It wasn't your camera. Until you look, you won't know what or who your husband photographed.'

'What are you insinuating?'

'Nothing. But as a rule, it's best if you check through before you hand over.'

'Have you looked at all the photos?'

'No, which is why you should.'

He jotted down the Gotten & Ghorton contact details and left her to her thoughts.

***

At 10:20 on Sunday morning, Pember sat at a table in an interview room in the Raingate police station. He had arrived at precisely ten o'clock, as Chakra had requested, and had waited, knowing he was being watched on the CCTV surveillance. He checked the time again on his mobile. Four more minutes had crawled by. He scrolled through his messages and emails breathing slowly and maintaining his relaxed composure as his right ear gently hissed. *Making an interviewee wait was the oldest trick in the book.* He added counting to his measured breaths. But somewhere beneath his façade, an inner voice kept asking why the police felt the need to make him wait.

Ping! A text alert punctured the silence. He stopped counting and opened the VPN email forwarded by Matt.

Dear Mr Arthur Yum. If you want to view the items, then be at Unit 4 on the Purple Blue Business Estate, Framlingham at 1:30pm today, May 1st. Yours cordially, Van d'Ore.

'Jeeez,' he breathed.

A second email popped onto the VPN site. It felt more like a punch to the solar plexus than a civil communication.

Dear Oliver Blix. Thank you for your interest. Your persistence suggests you are a most serious collector. If you want to view the Roman aureus coins and Sumerian temple plaque, then be at Unit 4 on the Purple Blue Business Estate, Framlingham. 1:30pm today, May 1st. Yours cordially, Van d'Ore. And the forwarding remark from Matt - *What the blog Almighty do I do now?*

Pember put his phone into silent mode, slipped it into

his pocket, closed his eyes, and tried to collect his thoughts. The door swooshed open, and DS Chakra McLaren walked in followed by DC Paulton holding a folder.

'Are we keeping you up?' Chakra said, adding, 'You've met DC Paulton already. Thursday, I seem to remember.'

'Yes, good morning.' Pember nodded to the DC, then turned his attention back to Chakra. 'I like to be punctual. You said to be here at ten o'clock.'

'Yes, sorry to keep you waiting, but there've been some developments.'

'Oh yeah? And what would those developments be?'

'Well, Mr Quinn. I think I'll be the one asking the questions, this morning.' He pulled back one of the chairs on the other side of the bare table and sat down, quickly followed by DC Paulton.

'Okay, let's start by asking if you know who these people are,' Chakra said as the DC opened the folder and slid a photo of a woman with dark, curly, shoulder-length hair onto the table.'

'It's Veronica Smith, Mr Smith's wife. It's the same shot her husband gave me. Did he give you this one?'

'Okay, and this person?' Paulton slid another photo onto the table. This time of a man with a fine-boned face, close-set eyes, and sharp features. His hair was thick and dark, verging on black.'

'It's Paul Smith. He visited my Hatter Street office on Monday, six days ago. Clive Merry will attest to it. I remember wondering if he wore a wig. He asked the Hatter Street PIA to put a tracker on one of his cars, the one his wife drove.'

'Okay, and when did you first meet Veronica Smith?'

'I first laid eyes on her on Tuesday, when I put the

tracker on the Fiat Panda she was driving. I first spoke to her when the car tracker came off on Wednesday in the racecourse and National Stud carpark in Newmarket. It's when she told me her husband, Mr Smith, was trying to kill her.'

'Ah, but here we have a problem, Mr Quinn. You see, Mrs Smith apparently told her husband that *you* were trying to kill her.'

Pember had been expecting something like this. He'd even planned for it. Clive's voice echoed in his head and through his tinnitus, *don't lose your temper, Pem*. He chose his words carefully. 'So, am I to understand that Mrs Smith was the victim in the car, not Paul Smith?'

Chakra nodded.

'What possible reason could I have to kill her?'

'It's what we wondered as well, Mr Quinn. But here's the thing. Her husband thinks she'd discovered you were selling fake, Royal Doulton, character jugs. He said Dick Turpin with his horse, Black Bess as the jug handle. You were targeting the racehorse community in the area. He thinks she faced you with it and you killed her.'

'What?' Pember thought his head might explode. *Of course! Paul Smith must've seen my character jugs when he came to my office on Monday. Opportunistic bastard!*

'We can see you have a short fuse and a temper, Mr Quinn. Who knows what you might do in a fit of rage?'

Pember thrust himself into warzone, iron self-control. 'Do you have a single shred of evidence to support any of this…this crazy theory?'

'We've plenty of circumstantial evidence, like your interest in fake and forged artifacts. And of course, we have Mrs Smith's fake, Royal Doulton, Dick Turpin character jug you sold her.' Chakra rubbed his lip.

'What?'

'So, we would like your fingerprints and we will need to hold you longer for questioning.'

'Are you charging me?'

'Not yet, Mr Quinn. At this stage we are arresting you and transferring you to the Police Investigation Unit for further questioning. Read him his rights, Poulton. Then get him over to the unit. No, on second thoughts, the search warrant is about to come through, take him via his Hatter Street office.' Chakra smiled at Pember. 'As a special favour to Clive Merry, you can open your office for us on the way. It'll save us having to break the door and any locks.'

***

Clive avoided the B roads and took a leisurely Sunday morning route, heading home along a network of lanes from Great Bricett. He drove slowly, his mind on his visit with Mrs Alconbury. An uncharitable suspicion took shape as he wondered about the weathered, stone sea creature. He decided he'd ask Pember to look at his photo, and Matt to search it through his dark net sources.

Brrring! Brrring! The ringtones broke his train of thought. Matt? He let it ring a couple more times as he anticipated another disjointed conversation, faltering on Matt's literal interpretation of a single word. Clive had learned to ignore Matt's mildly autistic traits and focus on what drove him to behave the way he did. It was fair to say Clive still didn't understand how Matt could appear more comfortable when he was pretending to be a different person than when being himself.

'Hello, Matt. What's up?'

'I've emailed Pember, but he ain't got back to me, and we're runnin' outa time.'

'Why did you email Pember and what do you mean, running out of time?'

'It ain't just me runnin' outa time, it's Pember as well. And why ain't he answerin'?'

'Is this…have you heard back from the seller? Mr Van d'Ore?'

'Yeah, how'd you know?'

'It was a guess. What did Van d'Ore say?'

'He spammin' said I were to go to Unit 4, on the Purple Blue Business Estate in Framlingham. I can view them gold Roman coins at 1:30pm today.'

'Right. And Pember?'

'Same thing. He can view them plaques, same place, same time as me.'

'Only one plaque, I think.'

'Yeah, okay. But you got where I'm headin'?'

'Yes, it's kicking off at 1:30 this afternoon. And it's Framlingham. Leave Pember to me. Right, dress like a coin collector, mug up on Roman gold coins and get there on your Vesper. But don't go in alone. Wait for Pember. And remember, you haven't met him before. You don't know him. You are Oliver Blix. Got it?' He ended the call, surprised by the kick of adrenaline firing his pulse. The excitement felt far more visceral than at the start of a police sting.

'So, it's started,' he breathed as he slowed to turn at a road junction. 'Trust Pem to be the one causing the stress.' He tapped his car's automatic dial system and listened to the call tones. No answer from Pem. He figured Chakra would be formally interviewing him today. *But where? The*

Hatter Street office, the Raingate Station, or the Bury St Edmunds Investigation Centre?

***

DS Chakra McLaren and DC Paulton sat opposite Pember in the interview room at the Raingate station and waited for him to say something more.

Pember recognised their stance for what it was; a ploy to make him trap himself with careless words. He sat quietly and waited.

His mobile vibrated in silent mode in his pocket. He kept his expression steady. He couldn't risk drawing their attention to his phone, not even with a blink, in case they took it from him. He had just over two and a half hours left before the viewing in Framlingham. The communiqué had to be about it. Sweat began to break on his temple.

'Okay,' he said, putting his elbows on the table and cupping his head in his hands. His palms moistened with sweat, but nothing ran down his face. He hoped he'd hidden the product of his acute anxiety. 'If we're going via the Hatter Street office, I'll be able to pick up my meds,' he breathed.

'Good,' Chakra said. 'Then I'll see you down at the investigation unit. Over to you now Poulton.'

'Yes, stay here, Mr Quinn. I'll send a constable to wait with you while we organise a car.'

The minutes stretched as Pember waited to be taken to his Hatter Street office. In his mind a giant digital clock counted down the seconds to the meeting at 1:30pm. Tensions within him tightened and released like a clock spring, and all the while his right ear whistled and his stomach churned. It was almost eleven o'clock. Only two and a half hours left. He swung between desperation and the iron self-control of his RMP training. He had been taught: *if you're taken as a prisoner, don't give your captors an excuse to beat you up. Beatings rupture organs, fracture bones, smash teeth, and injure brains. If you don't die, you survive but with permanent damage. So, appear polite and stay passive.* However, it went against the grain. Pember's grain. Of course, the police in Bury St Edmunds were unlikely to beat him up, but he wasn't going to risk it. He psyched himself to appear submissive on the transfer to the investigation unit but ready to grab the first opportunity to escape.

His RMP training had also taught him to plan an exit strategy before entering a danger zone, and the Raingate police station interview room counted as a danger zone. He'd left his trusty Yamaha Tracer parked out of sight in the private hospital grounds earlier that morning, before walking along Prussia Lane and cutting across to the Raingate Police Station for the ten o'clock interview. He'd nicked the idea from Clive. Pember reckoned that if the location was the deciding factor on Tuesday, when Clive had challenged Pember to follow his car, then why not again today? It seemed a lifetime ago.

'Right, Mr Quinn, the car's ready now. If you would like to come with me?'

'Yeah, sure.' He stood slowly, smiled, and followed the constable out of the interview room and along a corridor with rooms on both sides.

'We'll be leaving by the back entrance, this way. Follow me.'

They were already on the ground floor, and he felt the chill of cool air as the constable turned and took his arm before they approached the open door. The hold on his arm tightened as they stepped outside. A quick scan of the area told him they had entered a tarmacked inner courtyard, hemmed in by single-storey buildings. He glimpsed a rear wall spanning behind and police vehicles parked nearby. The exit appeared to be between the buildings on one side.

Appear submissive, his inner voice whispered as he matched the constable's stride. He was being guided towards a marked police car. The driver waited behind the wheel, while a second policeman got out and opened the rear, near-side door for Pember.

It was now or never. Pember imagined a starter pistol about to be fired as the constable's grip loosened on his arm, and a hand, palm flat, was placed against his upper back.

Now! The pistol fired in his head. In a flash he ducked and stepped back, swivelled, and dashed round the rear of the car. The exit beckoned ahead. He launched into a trajectory towards it. A policeman ran, lunged at him from behind, missed and sprawled on the ground. Another tried to block him in front. Pember dodged and leapt into a striding sprint. His quads burned. His toes propelled him forwards. He accelerated and ignored the pain. He bent his elbows, swung his arms, gained more pace. He cleared the inner courtyard exit.

Behind him there were shouts, car doors slammed, and an engine revved, a police siren shrieked. The commotion spurred him on.

He crossed the police station outer carpark, burst onto Raingate Street and dodged between cars, his footwork worthy of a boxer. He fled down Prussia Lane, an alley with high, red-brick walls hemming it in. His feet pounded and echoed as he headed on. He cut across a busy residential street with timber-framed houses, colourful in Suffolk pink and sandy limewash, and followed a short length of road which funnelled into Westgate Street. Each breath burned as he tore on. *Less than a hundred-and-fifty yards to go, only one more bend.* He spotted the entrance into the walled, private hospital grounds. He was through in a flash and collapsed out of sight behind some bushes and shrubs. He reckoned he'd barely run a quarter of a mile. It had taken under four minutes. His lungs hurt. He thought he might vomit.

Panting, he pulled his mobile from his pocket. He could barely focus as Clive's missed call banner popped onto his screen for a few seconds. He pressed automatic dial to return the call. It was 11:10 on his phone's readout.

Clive answered almost immediately. 'Hi? What the hell's going on. Where are you Pem?'

'The police,' he gasped, 'they're arresting me.' He took more breaths. 'I legged it before they took my phone.'

'What? You bloody fool, Pember!'

'I've an appointment with the seller!' He paused and coughed, 'Ask Matt. He'll explain. Where are you?'

'In my car. On my way to Hatter Street.'

'Turn round. It'll be swarming with police.' He continued more slowly, 'I'll meet you at the windmill outside Framlingham, Saxstead Green.'

'When?'

'Twelve o'clock.'

'Are you okay?'

'I'll have to be. I'm in the best place if I'm not. You should know.' He coughed on a broken laugh and ended the call.

Pember knew he didn't have long before the police came looking for him. He imagined they'd fan out from the

Raingate Police station, combing every conceivable hiding place, checking the traffic camera footage, and sending a squad car to his Hatter Street office. So far, he'd barely put a quarter of a mile between himself and the Raingate station. He'd done it in four minutes. So, he figured he had five minutes before the police drew closer and searched the private hospital grounds The thought sent his pulse into rapid fire.

'Okay, Pember, make every action count,' he whispered. Police sirens wailed in the distance.

He closed his eyes for a moment and put his phone in his pocket. Now he needed to connect with his bike. He slipped between the bushes, crossed an edge of mown grass between flower beds and headed to a groundsman's shed near some service buildings. His Yamaha Tracer was parked out of sight close by. He opened a pannier, donned a black motorcycle jacket with red shoulder flashes, swung a pack across his back, and pulled on his helmet from the top box. In the blink of an eye, he'd attached a false number-plate, flipped down his visor, started the bike and gently cruised to the hospital grounds' exit. He hung back until a bolus of traffic roared past, then, without any flashy moves, he slid in behind the cars and away amongst them through the next junction. He resisted showy cuts between traffic lanes and thundering above the speed limit. He rode it like a safe and unremarkable biker.

The Sunday traffic thinned out as Pember headed north-east of the A14. He pulled off the road, took his phone from his pocket and tapped in CB's restricted number.

She answered almost immediately. 'Yes?'

'There's a viewing. Today. 1:30pm. Others have been invited.'

'So, it's going to be competitive bidding. You've got your card?'

'Yeah, but I figure several items may be up for auction. When will your people make their move?'

'Where's the location?'

'Framlingham. Purple Blue Business estate. Unit 4.'

'Framlingham? You haven't given us much time.'

'It wasn't up to me. I only heard an hour ago. Unfortunately, I was with the police, so I was…forced to leave in a hurry. They're after me for a murder I haven't committed.'

'You mean you're on the run again. You always complicate everything, Pember.'

He ignored her reference to his capture and escape from European artefact traffickers in 2018. Instead, he hissed, 'Yeah, and you still haven't said if your people will be there.'

'It depends on the audience. It could be awkward if my team reveals itself.'

'But you'll be watching?' He tried to quell his rising frustration.

'Yes. Be careful, and good luck.'

'Thanks.' He ended the call. He wasn't quite sure what he was thanking her for. He opened his sat nav, and with the map clearly visible, slipped his mobile into the bike's display holder, flipped down his visor and eased back onto the road.

The ride soothed him. Part of his mind focused on the route while his body meshed with the bike's motion and balance. He cut along lanes between hedges hemming fields rich with rapeseed and ripening wheat and barley. His thoughts separated from his emotion. It helped him to feel above it all and distanced, as if looking down at a chart. At first the terrain was flat, but as he joined the A1120 beyond Stowupland, the pace quickened, and he flew up and down low hills, and inclines where the slowly flowing River Deben had followed the contours and cut into the landscape. A sense of calm took charge. He was in command. The mission was active.

He made good time, cruising into Saxstead Green at about ten minutes before midday. He had followed the A1120 as it swept round a generous bend, the view of a large triangular green on one side and off to the other, the white sails and clapperboard body of the old windmill. He spotted the short entrance track to the local Mill Hostelry and drifted along it and into its carpark, shielded by leafy shrubs and trees. He dismounted and positioned himself to observe unseen, the road and windmill entrance. It was the perfect spot to think through the next part of his plan.

***

Clive took a few moments to process what Pember had said. He was approaching Bury St Edmunds, and the words *turn round. It'll be swarming with police* echoed in his head.

The Blackthorpe junction, the last exit on the A14 before Bury, was only a few hundred yards away. He pictured the scene in the Hatter Street office, with the busy chaos of the police boxing up Pember's computer and paper files. Clive knew if he was there, he wouldn't be able to alter anything. In fact, he was more likely to end up getting arrested himself. For once, Pember was right. He needed to turn round.

He took the exit slipway, followed the road under the A14 dual carriageway and rejoined it, this time heading east, back towards Stowmarket and Ipswich. He reassessed the situation as he drove. Pember still had his phone and his liberty. That is, if one considered being on the run as liberty. But now he was being pursued by the police as well as the Norwich gangs. Clive checked the time. It read 11:15 on his dashboard. He had 45 minutes to get to the windmill; time enough for a five-minute stop at Woolpit to pick up some kit in case the rendezvous with the artefact seller turned ugly for Pember.

By the time he pulled in and parked in front of No.3 Albert Cottages, Clive had made a mental list of what he needed. He dashed from his car, only to be met by a barrage of questions from Chrissie, who was in the kitchen and busy loading the washing machine with an armful of dirty laundry.

'You mean Pember's now a fugitive?'

'Yes. It's the only way he'll get to the meeting with the Sumerian plaque seller for 1:30 this afternoon.'

'And Matt? When you phoned on your way back from Mrs Alconbury, you said he was going to be there as well?'

'Yes.'

'Really? Because the more I thought about it, the more I couldn't decide if I'd misheard you, or you'd lost your mind. Have you forgotten these people are thugs, maybe killers? Pember's ex-RMP. He can take his gun. What chance does Matt have if things turn nasty?'

'Okay, let me think it through, but right now I need to be there for Pember and Matt, and with some basic kit. I don't have time for a debate.'

'I'm not happy about this, Clive.'

'I told you. I don't have time. I've made up my mind.' He watched her frown.

'Right, Clive, if you won't listen to any sense, and you're determined to be reckless, then your backpack is on the shelf above your walking boots. The binoculars, space blanket and first aid kit will still be in it.'

'I'll also need kitchen scissors, rope, masking tape, a box of matches, a packet of biscuits, a bottle of water, pencil and paper...the usual survival stuff. I could be hanging round for a while doing surveillance, or I might have to go in. Can you please throw those things together while I put my toolbox in the car?'

'Really? You want me to help you in this madness? Do you at least still have your police body armour?'

He nodded. 'Yes, the bulletproof body armour vest is something I managed to forget to hand in.'

'Good. So, where's the rendezvous? And don't shake your head. If it all goes badly wrong, I have a right to know where to start looking for you. And I won't help you get your kit together unless you tell me.'

'Nothing's going to go wrong. Promise to stay out of it, or I won't tell you where it is.'

'Okay, I promise.'

He caught the way she'd answered too quickly and looked down. She was lying. He knew it. 'Okay, it's an industrial unit at Great Saxstead.' He'd always found part truths without details rolled off the tongue easily and were far more believable than complete lies.

'An industrial unit? In Great Saxstead? It's a tiny village.'

'Yes, and why not? It's...some farm has diversified. They're the ones with the all the land these days.'

'Hmm, better take the telescopic ladder with you. Never know, you might need to look through a window or climb onto a flat roof.'

'What? I thought you were against this?'

'I am. But I'm also practical.'

'Hmm, more like it's the kind of thing you'd like to be doing!'

Within the allotted five minutes, his car was packed and ready to leave with enough equipment for a camping trip without a tent or sleeping bag. *Some camping trip* he thought, but as he drove, he couldn't help mulling over Chrissie's reaction. She was right, he'd forgotten to worry about Matt. And just because Matt idolised the comic-strip characters from his youth, it didn't mean he could fit convincingly into the skin of the imaginary Oliver Blix, a sham collector of Roman coins. He hoped the seller would simply see Matt as a strange individual, impossible to pigeonhole into a character type, and not a threat or time waster.

Clive knew he was responsible for Matt's involvement. If the meeting went wrong, the consequences could be dire. The looming reality hit Clive hard while his Lexus ate the miles, and he headed from Woolpit onto the A1120 and to Saxstead Green.

Brrring! Brrring! Still feeling unsettled, Clive answered the call as he swept round the bend between the triangular green and the windmill.

'I'm in the pub car park. Far side of the green from where you are now.'

Clive couldn't help but smile. 'Thanks, Pem.' *At least Pem had been trained to look after himself.*

***

'So, how do you want to play this?' Pember asked, leaning against the trunk of a mature horse chestnut in the pub car park. He didn't turn to greet Clive, but instead gazed across the green, his thoughts on an ethereal level. He felt calm and separated from any emotion. The team was starting to gather, and he recalled the camaraderie of an active service unit. He slipped into the role. 'Thanks for coming, Clive.'

'Well, I wasn't going to leave you to mess this up on your own, was I? But the clock's ticking. We need to reccy Unit 4 and...about Matt. D'you think I should be Oliver Blix instead?'

'What? Jeeez, no. That's a bad idea. You don't know the first thing about gold coins. You wouldn't recognise an aureus if it hit you in the bloody face.'

'That's a bit harsh, considering you're the idiot who got us into this.'

Pember ignored the *idiot*. 'Look, I've been thinking about the reccy. The sellers may recognise me or my bike from past encounters or intel. I've got a false plate on my Tracer today, but they certainly won't be expecting your Lexus.'

'Okay, we reccy in the Lexus. Have you looked at Purple Blue on Google earth yet?'

'Yeah. It's on my phone. Here...' Pember opened the app and held it so that both he and Clive could see the screen. He waited a few moments before giving his take on the business estate layout. 'Lots of trees. One entrance, it doubles as the exit and feeds onto a network of lanes north of Framlingham College and the Castle.'

'This unit here looks different,' Clive added. He pointed at a structure with a darker roof and squarer outline.'

'Could be an older barn converted into a business unit.'

'Right, we've a rough ground plan of the estate.'

Pember followed Clive to the sleek black Lexus parked

near the exit from the car park. 'Can it run silently? Just on battery?' Pember asked as got into the car.

'No, just electric motors to assist the petrol engine. Makes it economical.'

'Ha; the three-year-old hybrid! Bet it sounds like a swarm of bees when you floor it.'

They followed the B road through what seemed to be more of a hamlet than a village. The massively wide, grass verges made Pember wonder if it had once been common grazing land, or a cattle droving route onto the green. Framlingham was three miles away, and they drove past endless fields before newbuild and then 1950s estates, then older residential houses clustering around the old town. The centre was ancient and hilly, with Tudor and wood-framed houses crowding the narrow streets. They avoided the signposts to the Castle and followed a minor road tracing north between the college and a large fishing lake created for the castle in the 14th century.

Soon they were into a network of narrow lanes. 'There! A sign to the right. *Purple Blue Business Estate*,' Pember said, breaking the silence.

'The trees have grown a bit since Google Earth's aerial views,' Clive's voice drifted as he turned into a smoothly tarmacked entrance. A cluster of trees and rough undergrowth merged with a hedge on one side.

The unmanicured appearance made Pember wonder if the trees were the survivors of what had once been a small wood. 'Good, those are the metal-clad units we saw. Hey, and beyond the trees there's the larger square building,' Pember said. He scanned the area as Clive cruised round. The grid layout of units and service roads matched the aerial shots. The familiarity boosted his confidence. 'Okay,

Unit 4 is the square one closest to the trees. Probably why they chose it. Look, a notice: *BDI - Asian and Oriental carpet cleaning & repairs*. Bet it's a front.'

'Hmm, let's get out of here,' Clive muttered and eased the Lexus onto the exit road.

'Where are you going to watch from?'

'I reckon somewhere up there,' Clive said as he drove past a turning to one side of the cluster of trees, rough undergrowth, and hedge. I'll run you back to your bike, then I'll take up position here. Okay, Pem?'

'Yeah. And thanks, Clive. Call if you need to warn me of anything. Let my phone ring for about three seconds, then cut the call and repeat for a further 3 seconds.'

They drove back in silence.

***

Clive glanced into his rear-view mirror. For a moment he watched Pember walk towards the Yamaha Tracer in the Mill Hostelry's carpark. A kernel of excitement fired adrenaline and gripped his guts. This was the start, the beginning of the op. 'Good luck, Pem. And don't mess up,' he whispered as he slipped back onto the road to Framlingham. He wanted to arrive at the Purple Blue Business Estate before Pember. It would give him time to get into position.

***

Pember walked through the Mill Hostelry's carpark to his bike. He took five, slow, deep breaths and cleared his mind of extraneous thoughts. He switched his phone into silent vibrating mode and slipped it inside his innermost breast pocket where he could feel it next to the payment card with its tracker. He zipped up his jacket, pulled on his gauntlets, started the Tracer, and gently eased out of the car park. He had about twenty-five minutes before the 1:30pm meeting. He flipped down his visor. The mission had begun in earnest.

He rode with care, retracing the route he'd taken with Clive to the Purple Blue estate. This time there was no Lexus cabin to protect him; he was exposed to the elements. Instinctively, he connected with his surroundings, switching into the hyper-awareness essential for the active part of the mission. He felt the road surface through the bike's suspension and tyres. The breeze ruffled his neck where the top of his jacket was open a little. He lived the steepness of the town's slopes and sensed its history. He glanced back at the stone battlements of Framlingham Castle, built on its hill, and experienced the taste of awe and the weight of time. Throughout it all, his right ear gently hissed.

The wooded area on one side of the Purple Blue entrance appeared a little wilder than he remembered, and the green leaves more vibrant to his ultra-vigilant brain. *Good, more cover for surveillance*, he thought. He already knew which building was Unit 4, but he dared not ride straight to *BDI - Asian & Oriental carpet cleaning & repairs*. It was better to act like a first-time visitor and ride around the circuit of service roads and follow the numbers, counting back from Unit 12.

The business estate struck him as Sunday quiet, although active – verging on busy in one or two of the units, with muffled sounds of machinery escaping through van entrances, their roller doors part-raised. He took in more details as he cruised past a classic car, repair shop specialising in old Rovers, the cars parked on a forecourt. He noted a joinery outlet, and then a carpentry firm making bespoke kitchen units, and a metal worker and welder. An outfitter of old, metal shipping-containers occupied a stretch of space on the perimeter, and a customised motorbike outlet was housed in the unit on the unwooded side of the entrance to the estate. A handful of cars and vehicles were parked in a designated, communal parking area fed by the service road, conveniently opposite Unit 4. Pember headed to it, parked his bike, stowed his helmet, and checked the time. He had eight minutes before the 1:30pm meeting. *Where the hell is Matt?* He glanced to his left, focusing beyond the trees, coarse grass, and brambles. *Is Clive in position yet?*

The sound of a 4-stroke bike engine drifted on the air. Pember waited, willing it to get louder and materialise into Matt on his Vespa. Sure enough, the engine dropped its pitch as a rounded figure swept through the entrance on a scooter the colour of mercury with yellow and black trims.

'What the hell's he doing?' Pember hissed under his breath, as Matt turned into the forecourt of the customised bike company. He swallowed the urge to yell or wave at Matt. *It should be obvious Shout Your Own Style isn't in Unit 4. He must have seen Unit 12 clearly displayed on the sign outside.*

Conscious that he might be being watched by the artefact sellers, Pember ignored the customised bike forecourt, and without breaking his step, strolled to the *Asian & Oriental Carpet Cleaning & Repairs,* its name displayed alongside the sign, *Unit 4.* The double front doors and shuttered van-loading entrance were closed. It seemed lifeless, shut for business. He looked up at its front wall. An old barn's structural supporting posts and more recent RSJs were obvious between the sections of modern brick infill. It struck him as naked, missing an outer skin and displaying the secret of its past, open-sided construction. A small window, set close to the corrugated metal roofline, stared out above the entrance. He guessed there must be a second or mezzanine floor. Two security cameras near the roofline covered the front entrance. Yes, they were wired in. No chance of blocking those with a Wi-Fi blocker.

He pressed the entrance buzzer, stepped back from the door, and casting a half-glance over his shoulder, saw Matt look in his direction. It was enough. He knew Matt had seen and recognised him.

Pember waited and listened. There were no sounds from inside the building. Frustration threatened and he pressed the buzzer again and for longer. This time he caught the sound of a door opening and closing deeper within. A few moments later, he heard the latch to the double doors being turned. One of the doors swished open. A man in dark glasses and wearing a fedora hat, stood in the doorway. He wore a tan-coloured linen robe, fitted like a shirt across the shoulders and chest, then flowing down to his ankles. The neckline was collarless, the top two buttons unfastened. Pember was familiar with the *thobe*, a common style of dress worn by men in Iraq and other middle eastern countries, but there was nothing modest about this one. It was too tight to disguise the man's shoulders and chest, seemingly bulging with muscles. The soft felt hat with the medium brim and a crease through the crown looked incongruous, almost jaunty. His body said bouncer. The fedora and dark glasses said gangster.

Pember heard, more than saw, Matt approaching from the sidewalk along the verge of the service road. 'Hiya! Wait for me,' Matt called a little breathily, as if he'd been hurrying from *Shout Your Own Style*. 'I'm s'posed to be meetin' someone in there.'

It wasn't clear which of them Matt was addressing. Pember kept his back to Matt's lumbering approach and ignored him. The man in the doorway adjusted his gaze from Pember onto Matt, as if fixing him in the crosswire-aim of his dark glasses.

'Yeah, Mr Van d'Ore,' Matt puffed, 'he's the bloke I'm meetin'. 1:30, mate.'

'What?' Pember said, in character and playing his role. 'But I have an appointment with Mr Van d'Ore at 1:30.' He frowned at Matt, who was now standing next to him.

'Welcome. It seems you both have appointments with Mr Van d'Ore. Your names, please?' The man's tone was bass, his words delivered slowly, as if hinting at the power in his body's muscle mass.

Mixed messages, Pember thought. *Is his game to keep the other side guessing? Well, two can play at that.* But before he could answer, Matt jumped in with, 'The name's Oliver Blix, mate.'

'And I am Arthur Yum.'

The man inclined his head. 'Please, this way.' He stood back from the door, inviting them to step inside.

'You ain't said who you are?'

'My name is not important, Mr Oliver Blix. It is Van d'Ore you have come to see.'

They stepped inside, Pember leading the way through what felt like a ceilinged lobby into a large airy space extending to steel roof beams above. It was dominated by an enormous table with a traditional Turkish rug laid out on its surface. Stainless steel sinks and drainers stood against one wall, domestic-sized cylinder vacuums with flexible hoses stood close by. A bank of hand-held rechargeables and a selection of end attachments were stored on shelves. The scent of wool hung in the air and coloured skeins of woollen yarn filled a large cabinet. Drying lamps were corralled in one corner, but a few had escaped and stood close to the large table along with spotlights and large magnifying lenses on mobile stands. Racks were loaded with rolled carpets and rugs, neatly wrapped in plastic and with their name tags hanging free. There appeared to be no one in the unit. Pember noted a door at the rear of the building labelled *washroom* and a fire exit on a side wall.

'So, where's Mr Van d'Ore?' Matt asked.

'Up in the office.' The Fedora closed the double door and slipped the latch. 'But first I must ask you to take off your bulky jackets and leave them down here before we go upstairs.' He indicated the wooden stairs leading up to a mezzanine floor above the lobby at the front of the building.

It wasn't what Pember had expected. 'I'll need to bring my card and phone with me. They're in my pocket,' he said removing them before taking off his leather biker jacket and placing it on the large table.

Matt followed Pember's lead, shrugging his off as well.

Is he serious, Pember wondered as he gazed at Matt's T-shirt, coloured black with *CAFFÈ NERO* emblazoned across the front and back in white lettering. Oliver Blix was supposed to be a collector of Roman gold aureus coins, not a coffeeshop aficionado.

Matt smoothed his T-shirt over his ample belly and smiled. 'He were one of them aureus emperors. 64 AD, mate.'

'So, Nero liked a good cup of coffee as well as minting

gold coins, did he?' Pember murmured, not sure if Arthur Yum should smile or look heavenwards.

'Nah, you got that wrong, mate. Earliest I read 'bout coffee were some Ethiopian goatherd goin' under the moniker of Kaldi. His goats started eatin' them berries in 850 AD. That's when coffee started.' Matt stood, eyes glazed for a moment, as if reading the text from his memory. 'The emperor Nero would'a been pushin' up daisies by then.'

'Please follow me,' the Fedora said, cutting short further discussion.

This time Matt walked behind the Fedora, and Pember brought up the rear. He wanted to turn on the stairs and look down to get an aerial view of the workshop, understand the layout, see the blind spots and hiding places. He settled for a quick glance back. A shadow moved and was gone. *Was it a trick of the light?* The flicker had been near the washroom door. Too fleeting to analyse. *And CCTV cameras?* He hadn't seen any inside yet, but there'd been two outside, trained on the front entrance.

***

Clive parked his car down the turning immediately to one side of the wild area of trees bordering the Purple Blue Business Estate. He zipped up his dark green anorak, slung his backpack over his shoulders, hung his binoculars from his neck, and negotiated the remains of a broken fence. He was shaded and screened by the mature trees as he picked his way through rough grass and between brambles, bushy hawthorn, and birch saplings. He headed towards the outline of the square barn, Unit 4.

He moved slowly, stooping a little. His ears were alert to the faintest sound, his eyes raking the scene for any sign of the artefact sellers. The trees thinned out as he got closer to the barn. A service road skimmed past its front forecourt before entering the communal car park. He heard Pember's Tracer 900 GT and stood hidden behind a tree as Pember rode past. He listened to the distant engine as it toured the estate. Shielded by a bush, he examined the outside of the barn through his binoculars. The side wall facing him was a patchwork of old brick and breeze block infill. He noted a fire exit door towards the rear of the building.

He skirted round to view the rear of the barn. It was a complete wall of brick. No doors, no windows, only an eight-inch, grilled, fan vent about seven feet from the ground. Moving slowly and still shielded by the trees, he gazed along the barn's wall closest to the Purple Blue entrance road to the estate. Again, just a sea of brick and breeze block infill.

Clive circled back through the trees and hid closer to the car park. He had a view of Unit 4's front doors and shuttered van entrance, and Pember parking his bike. Clive lined up his binoculars. He spotted security cameras just below the roof line and overlooking the main entrance doors. They were the only ones he'd seen so far. He reckoned he was out of their field.

Minutes later, Matt's Vespa chortled into the estate and parked on a neighbouring unit's forecourt. *Smart move*, Clive thought. He crept a little closer to get a better view of the unit's double-door entrance. Was someone watching from the small window high above the double doors? It was difficult to get a clear view of the face behind the glass. A large man wearing a fedora hat, dark glasses, and a brown linen robe stood in the doorway.

Clive reached for his phone and took shots of the Fedora, and Pember and Matt entering the building.

Wham! The blow landed hard between Clive's shoulder blades. His body crumpled forwards. His face struck the ground. Everything went black.

***

The Fedora knocked on the office door and entered without waiting. Matt and Pember followed. The office was small and crowded with filing cabinets. A man who sat behind a desk stood up to greet them. He was of an athletic build, about five-feet ten-inches tall, but slimmer and smaller than the muscle-bound Fedora. He wore a medical grade face mask.

'Hi. I'm Van d'Ore. Thanks for coming today. It's an unusual location, but I see it as a special place to view artefacts. We're amongst,' he waved his hands expansively, 'all these wonderful traditional rugs and carpets. It is so kind of Ahmed to let us use his premises today.' He nodded to the Fedora.

'Cool,' Matt said.

Pember smiled a greeting and took in Van d'Ore's casual jeans and sweatshirt, topped with a trucker's cap. His speaking style seemed more fluid than his email style.

'Good afternoon, I'm Arthur Yum. I can wear a face mask as well if it makes you feel more comfortable?'

'No need. My own mask should be sufficient.'

'Good, so let's get straight down to business.' Pember looked at him more closely. The trucker's cap covered Van d'Ore's hair, and the peak shaded his forehead. The face mask concealed most of his face apart from his eyes and eyebrows. *Hmm...tanned, but fair skinned, judging by his hands and sun-bleached eyebrows. Difficult to guess his age, but probably youngish. Is he Dutch? A COVID anti-vaxxer?*

'Well, I ain't wearin' a mask. I'm here to look a Julius Caesar aureus straight in the eye. 8.18 grams of pure gold. Yeah, from somewhere round 50 BC. I said in me email I were interested in early examples.' Matt shifted from one foot to the other.

'Of course, but the advertisement was deliberately vague. It said a collection of gold Roman coins found with part of a Sumerian temple plaque from Syria. Specific emperors weren't mentioned, Mr Oliver Blix.'

'But it did say the seller can provide provenance.' Pember smiled the eager, impatient smile of a serious collector. 'I believe that would be you, Mr Van d'Ore? Can we see the plaque and coins please, and hear more about them? I-I'm really very excited.'

'Of course. Please sit down.' Van d'Ore indicated two chairs and signalled to the Fedora to bring the artefacts. It took a few minutes before a tray on a stand was set between the chairs. A linen cloth had been thrown over the tray and Van d'Ore waited until the Fedora had stepped away before saying, 'Are you ready gentlemen?'

'Cool,' Matt breathed.

Van d'Ore removed the cloth with a sudden flourish. It reminded Pember of a conjuring trick. All attention was on the tray, but Pember caught the sideways movement of the Fedora. He positioned himself directly behind Pember and stood very close, breathing through his mouth, his breath almost palpable on the back of Pember's neck. Something was wrong.

Pember kept his voice even. 'You're only showing us the coins. What about the Sumerian plaque?'

'I thought we'd start with the coins, and then Mr Oliver Blix can leave. He emailed me previously to say he wasn't interested in the plaque. So, if you want to bid against Mr Oliver Blix for the coins, now is your opportunity.'

'Okay, yes.'

'Yeah, great.' Matt grinned. 'What you askin' for 'em?'

Six coins, one glinting gold and contrasting with five duller ones, were arranged in a row. Each coin was just under 2 cm in diameter.

'I thought we'd start at five hundred pounds,' Van d'Ore said.

'Yeah, but them dull ones ain't gold.' Matt shot the words at him.

'No, they're silver. A Roman denarius tarnishes over time. As I'm sure you know, at the time of Julius Caesar twenty-five denarii would have contained the equivalent weight in silver to the gold in one aureus.'

'Yeah, 'cept from where I'm sittin' the head on the aureus don't look like Caesar. And I've read, the weight of silver in them denarii went down coz over time less valuable metal got used in them. So, I'm guessin' them five denarii ain't even worth a hundred quid for the lot of them!'

The Fedora stepped nearer to Matt.

'Perhaps *you*'d like to take a closer look?' Van d'Ore purred at Pember.

'Yes, please.' Pember picked up the gold coin. Its edges were smooth and a veiled head depicting the Roman goddess Vesta, along with letters, and a ringed border of dots were stamped on the gold. The reverse had what were probably some priestly objects, more letters, and the ringed border of dots. 'He's right. This isn't Caesar's head. But the letters say C· Caesar.'

'Here, use the digital scales.' Van d'Ore placed something the size of a mobile phone on the tray.

'Thanks.' Pember smiled at Van d'Ore while his mind whirred through the possibilities. He placed his lucky marble, ten grams of childhood memory, on the scales and watched the digital readout settle at ten grams precisely. 'Scale seems accurate,' he said and placed the aureus on the scale. He nodded. 'Yeah, close enough to eight grams.'

Was he looking at an incredibly rare Julius Caesar aureus from the Gallic campaign? *Or is it a clever mock up and fake?* 'I wasn't aware Julius Caesar had conquered Syria, and certainly not while he was alive. So, under the circumstances, I'll give you three-hundred and seventy-five pounds for the weight of gold in the aureus and round my offer up to four hundred for all six coins.' There, he'd as good as said the provenance was wrong, or more accurately, missing. It was code that he'd guessed the coins were fake or from an improper source, and the price would have to be lower for that very reason.

'And what about the Sumerian plaque? Are you going to offer a laughably low amount for that as well?'

'No, Mr d'Ore. But I would have to see it first.'

'And you, Mr Oliver Blix. Are you going to better Mr Yum's bid of four hundred pounds for the coins? Or is this the moment you leave us?'

'I already said me best bid'd be one hundred.' Matt paused, as if expecting Van d'Ore to relent and say he could have them all for a hundred. Silence stretched five or six seconds. He stood up. 'I'll collect me jacket and see m'self out, okay?' Matt headed for the office door.

Pember watched from the corner of his eye, willing him not to look back. *Just go.* But the telepathy failed before he'd refocused on the tray. Matt shot a how'd-I-do glance directly at him. Pember saw Van d'Ore catch it. *Jeeez. The game's up.*

'Mr Yum, please wait here with Ahmed while I see Mr Oliver Blix out of the building.'

***

Pember couldn't help but hear Matt's ponderous footfall on the stairs down to the carpet workshop below. Van d'Ore nodded to the Fedora and followed. Pember listened for his tread on the steps. There was nothing. *Is the man light on his feet or is he waiting outside the office door?* It was unsettling. He glanced at the Fedora. They were alone together in the office. *Was the nod a signal for the Fedora to threaten, question and then dispatch him?* Pember knew he had to engage with the man, and fast.

'So, please may I see the Sumerian plaque?' He didn't like to call the man Ahmed, as he hadn't been invited to use the man's given name, in fact, quite the opposite. Ahmed had withheld it earlier. Pember smiled instead.

'Of course. It's why you are here.' The Fedora inclined his head slowly, stepped back and brought a second tray on a stand from behind some boxes. He set it down in front of Pember's chair. Once again, a linen cloth covered the tray.

'May I?'

'Of course,' the Fedora said with a graciousness that belied his body-builder's physique.

'But Mr Van d'Ore isn't here.'

'He has something to take care of. He may be a few minutes. I am to host your viewing.'

'Oh? Okay.' Pember lifted an edge of the linen and turned it back. He gasped. His mind in that moment com-

265

pletely absorbed by the sight of the plaque. 'May I?' he asked but didn't wait for permission. He ran his finger over the pale stone. It was a corner segment of what had once been a rectangular plaque. 'Here,' he murmured, 'the central hole would have been here.' He let his finger rest against the remnant of a curved edge, once at the centre of the plaque. The surface was shallow carved with a relief depicting a banquet scene. A figure, his head and face shown in profile, sat bare chested in a fronded robe. Pember let his eyes feast on the stone as he took in the upper right corner segment and pictured the rest of it.

'Are you satisfied with what you see, Mr Yum? I am instructed to ask if you have any questions.'

'I'd like to know its provenance…where it comes from and its age.'

'I believe a private collector in Turkey. But Mr Van d'Ore will be able to tell you more. He will return shortly.'

*****

Clive opened his eyes. *Where am I?* Cold struck up from the ground chilling his face and body. He caught the smell of soil and grass and tried to raise his head. A foot pressed into his back. His binoculars dug into his breastbone. He attempted to move his arms. He couldn't. His wrists were secured behind his back.

'What's going on?' he groaned confused, disorientated.

A booted foot slipped under his chest and rolled him onto his back. He saw grey sky, leafy branches, and a face staring down at him from about five feet. Memory flooded back.

'Quiet. If you make a sound, you're dead.' A pair of granite eyes fixed on him, expressionless, dispassionate, the look of a man who killed. He wore a black sweatshirt and slate walking trousers. 'I ask the questions.' He squatted, a sudden athletic move landing hard with one knee on Clive's chest. Now closer, he pressed a gun with a silencer into Clive's cheek. He held his position as if maximizing the pain. 'Who the hell are you? What are you doing here?'

'Pember's an old friend. I'm watching his back,' Clive wheezed.

'Your name?' He jabbed the silencer further into Clive's cheek.

'I ca…can't shp…shpeak.'

The man lessened the gun-tip pressure a fraction.

'I'm Cl…' *Will I be safer if I don't use my name?* 'I-I'm Cliff. I'm an old friend.' He noted the lack of a tattoo on the man's hand or peeping up from the man's neckline. The face – three-day stubble, no identifying marks. He guessed ex-military. It was a gamble. 'Are you CB's man?' he croaked.

'What d'you know about CB, Cliff?'

'It's why Pem's here today.' He used his shortened name, a sign to anyone in the team that he knew him well.

'What d'you know about CB?' The knee pressed harder into his chest, crushing his bound hands into his back.

'Agh! Nothing. What's the time?'

'How long have you been friends? When and where did you meet…Pem?'

'Been friends since we were kids in Norwich, same school. Is this about…Toby jugs?'

'I ask the questions.' The knee pressed harder again.

'Agh!'

'Why were you taking photos?' The cold eyes flicked away for a moment.

Clive guessed something didn't make sense or confused the man. 'To prove I was watching,' Clive croaked.

'So, you're being paid to watch. Who's paying?'

'Pember. And you? Are you CB's man?'

'I'm with a branch of the Art & Antiquities Unit.' The man frowned and seemed to hesitate, 'So, yeah, CB.'

'Sounds like we're on the same side.'

'Huh?'

'We're watching Pem's back.'

The man's eyes didn't soften, but he took his knee off Clive's chest and stepped back. 'Sit up.'

Clive's wrists hurt like hell. They were bound behind his back. Not easy to sit up. He focused, tensed his intercostals, and psyched himself into action. One heaving, chest-lifting movement with his abdominals, and he sat up. 'Ugh! How long've you been watching Unit 4?' he asked.

'Long enough to see Pember and another man going in at one-thirty.' The man's tone had lost its edge. Clive took it as a sign they were temporary brothers-in-arms, bound by a common purpose.

'Did you need to deck me?'

The man inclined his head, acknowledging the knockout blow. 'I could've broken your neck?'

'Oh thanks. What's the time?'

'It's two o'clock.'

'What? It's been half an hour. Have either of them come out yet? Look, I'm no use like this. Untie me, for God's sake.'

The man still held the gun pointed at Clive's head, but with a sudden twist of his other wrist, a blade glinted. He stepped behind Clive's back, and in one swift move, bent and cut the cable tie binding his wrists.

'Thanks.' Clive rubbed his wrists and worked his shoulders. 'Now my phone, please. I need to check if Pem's sent me a distress signal.'

The man sheathed the blade and pulled Clive's phone from a pocket. 'Here, take it, but I'll put a bullet through your head if you play any tricks.' He squatted behind Clive, the silencer cold against the base of his skull.

Clive's fingers felt like large, tingly sausages, fuzzy and clumsy from the cable tie ligature. He fumbled as he checked his mobile for missed calls, all in silent mode. There hadn't been a let-it-ring-for-3-seconds, end-the-call-and-repeat-for-three-seconds call from anyone.

'Well?' the man asked behind him, his breath mildly warm against Clive's neck.

'No, there's nothing. Pem's okay.' He hoped he sounded cool, but relief threatened to send a vein of emotion through his words. He lifted his binoculars and trained them on the small window above the double doors. 'You haven't told me your name? What do I call you?'

***

Pember continued to gaze at the Sumerian plaque, as if in rapt awe. In truth, he felt overwhelmed by the audacity of the deception. The plaque was over four thousand years old, at least a couple of thousand years older than Van d'Ore had said in the advertisement. He knew from the style of the shallow-carved relief that it was early Sumerian. There wasn't a beard on the almost flat, facial profile. The forehead and nose formed one sweeping line, the ear was large and out of proportion, all indications to its age and origin. The character of the symbols was in keeping with the style of the relief. It all pointed to it coming from an ancient Su-

269

merian kingdom now in modern Iraq, not modern Syria. And if the haul of gold Roman coins was supposed to authenticate the age of the plaque, how could it when it was carved thousands of years before any Roman set foot in the area, if they ever set foot there at all?

This artefact was incredibly rare and had been looted or stolen from a collection. It had passed across borders and continents to obfuscate its illegal provenance and make it saleable on an open market. It had been kept out of the spotlight by pricing it below its real value. And of course, its sale would discreetly fill the coffers of smugglers and terrorists.

'Ah, Mr Yum. You feast your eyes on our small antiquity from Syria.'

'What?' Pember said, dragging his thoughts from the plaque and only now aware that Van d'Ore had returned to the office.

'Our Sumerian temple plaque. Are you interested? Do you wish to buy it?'

'Yes.' He nodded, conscious that more eloquence might give away his expert knowledge and hint his disapproval. *Play it simple, don't make Van d'Ore suspicious*, he told himself.

'Do you have any questions, or has Ahmed told you all you need to know?'

Is Van d'Ore intimating the plaque's hot status? 'It came from a private collector in Turkey, I understand?' Pember said softly.

'Yes. Now, shall we get down to business? Sixteen-hundred pounds is my price.'

'I'm giving four hundred for the coins…will you take less for the plaque?'

'No. Please don't insult me, Mr Yum. I want two thousand pounds; four hundred for the coins and sixteen hundred for the plaque. Nothing less.'

Pember nodded. Van d'Ore smiled. It would have appeared suspicious if Pember hadn't tried a gentle haggle and he nodded again as he got out the special debit card from CB.

'May I?' Van d'Ore held out his hand for the card. 'I'd like to check the payment links are working. So, first a test run. I'll take…how much do you say, Mr Yum?'

'For a trial? Fifty pounds, and I'll hold onto my card thank you.'

'Hmm, no. I think one hundred would be better.'

'Oka-a-y.' *Jeez, it had been a gamble, but predictable and just within CB's traceable money limit*. He watched stony-faced as Van d'Ore produced a card reader and set it up ready for the amount. *A card reader? Is this a trap? A test of my naivety or experience?*

'The money'll reach you faster, if I pay your account directly with my debit card phone app.' Pember spoke hesitantly, not sure if Arthur Yum would suggest this.

Van d'Ore fixed him with a cold stare. The silence felt charged, close, like the air before a thunderstorm. 'Yes, of course, Mr Yum. I'll be able to see on my phone when it arrives in my account. You've done this kind of thing before, haven't you?'

'I'm a simple collector. But it's worked for me in the past when I've paid on collection. And as for today? I didn't know how much cash to carry. So, I haven't. Now,' he logged into his phone, 'let me open the app… Okay, the account I'm paying, please?'

The room seemed airless. Ahmed stepped nearer. Pember kept him in his peripheral vision and tapped in Van d'Ore's account details as they were given. It took less than a minute to complete the payment. Van d'Ore's eyes remained fixed on his phone's screen. The seconds passed slowly as they waited for the money to appear in Van d'Ore's account.

'Would you like a tour of the carpet restoration workshop, Mr Yum?' Ahmed asked, breaking the silence.

'What, now?' Pember frowned.

'You might prefer to wait here. Enjoy a coffee while you make the second payment and Ahmed packs up the plaque and coins for you?' Van d'Ore said without moving his eyes from his phone.

The office grew more claustrophobic. Pember's right ear hissed. He felt hot. *Let the payment go through*, he inwardly pleaded.

'We're good. One hundred pounds successfully transferred from your account into mine.' Van d'Ore looked up from his phone. 'Okay, now pay the balance of nineteen hundred pounds. Would you like coffee while Ahmed packs the plaque and coins?'

For Pember it was a leap of faith. He had to trust CB's people and hope to God the balance would be enough. 'No coffee, thank you. Just pack the items for me, please.' He counted slowly and re-opened his debit card app.

'This time the account details will be…' Van d'Ore smiled and reeled off details for a different account.

Pember's stomach lurched. This wasn't the plan. CB hadn't warned what would happen if he tried to pay more than one hundred pounds and to more than one account. He guessed the payment would fail, a ploy to stop him stealing the money. Feeling sick to the gills, he nodded and as slowly as he dared, entered nineteen hundred pounds and the new account details.

'I won't complete the payment until I have the plaque and coins. I'm sure you understand,' he said and smiled at Van d'Ore. He steeled himself to radiate confidence. It was his only gambit short of grabbing the antiquities from the trays and dodging past Van d'Ore and Ahmed in a suicide dash to the office door.

'Yes, of course,' Van d'Ore murmured. 'Ahmed, please get them ready for Mr Yum.'

Pember was torn. *Do I complete the mission or run while Ahmed's distracted?* He sat still and planned his route to the office door while he weighed up the odds of success.

***

'What do I call you?' Clive repeated.

'Hawk. See anything through those binoculars, Cliff?'

'No one's at the window. But the cameras'll pick us up if we approach the front doors.'

'I can block them if they're on Wi-Fi. Here, let me see if they're wired in or not.' He held out his hand for the binoculars.

Clive hesitated and then reasoned if Hawk had wanted to steal them, he could have taken them when he floored him. 'You brought a Wi-Fi blocker but no field glasses?' He shook his head and handed them over. 'Well?' he asked after a couple of minutes.

'No evidence of wiring.' Hawk slipped the binoculars around his neck and pulled something the size of a 250gm pack of butter from a cargo pocket in his walking trousers. Clive left him to fiddle with its screen and controls while he stared at Unit 4.

'Right, I'm set up now.'

'Good. So, first you jam the cameras. We get to the front door. Pick the lock or…'

'No. You ring the bell, Cliff. I'll stay out of sight against the front wall. Someone opens the door. You go in, I slip in behind you and immobilise them.'

Images flashed through Clive's mind…a gun with a silencer pressed into his cheek, the flash of a steel blade, the granite eyes, the look of a man who killed. 'How many smugglers do you reckon are inside?' he asked.

'One, maybe two.'

'No, Hawk. There are at least two, maybe three,' Clive said, remembering the face at the window. 'And Pember and the other man are also in there. Four or five people. What if bullets start flying around? I won't take part in a gun fight or killing anyone.' *Why did I leave my bulletproof vest in the car?* He could have kicked himself for being so stupid.

'I could've killed you, but I immobilised you. And you? Unless you've got hidden fighting skills, I doubt you could kill even if you tried. I've already checked you for weapons. A Swiss army knife, and kitchen scissors in your backpack. It's pathetic. You aren't going to kill anyone. Whatever I do will be in self-defence.'

Clive tapped his pockets. His penknife was missing. *Is CB's man ex-SAS or an assassin? But then, Pember is one of CB's men and Pember keeps a gun. This is getting ugly. I have to call Chakra.* 'Okay, I'll sweep round to the right and approach as if I've come from the car park.'

Hawk nodded, crouched low and swept off to the left.

Without Hawk breathing down his neck, Clive moved quickly. Within seconds, he was to the right of one of the cars in the carpark and out of Hawk's eyeline. He pulled his phone from his pocket and speed dialled Chakra.

'Yes?'

'Clive, here,' he whispered. 'I've only a few seconds. Pember is in Unit 4, Purple Blue Business Park, Framlingham. He's being held by a gang dealing in looted and stolen artefacts from the Middle East. They're armed.' He ended the call. Next, he put Pember on speed dial. Hand now in pocket, he let it ring for three seconds. He killed the call and repeated the warning as he walked towards the double doors of Unit 4.

He gazed upwards. *What?* From this angle and up close he saw a wire to one of the CCTV cameras. *Hawk lied to me.* He made to turn on his heel.

'Agh!' His world turned green, then black.

***

The Fedora set two boxes on the tray in front of Pember, one small, one larger.

'You can complete the payment now,' Van d'Ore said.

'Certainly. But you'll understand if I look in the boxes first.' Pember leaned forwards and lifted the lid on the small box and then the larger one. The artefacts were in clear view inside. 'Good, everything seems in order.' Pember stacked the boxes and tapped *confirm payment*. His phone vibrated in his hand, stopped, and vibrated again. *What the hell?* His stomach flipped.

'Everything okay?' Van d'Ore asked.

'Of course.' He kept his tone light but Van d'Ore's eyes were no longer on him. They were fixed on the desk monitor. The CCTV must have caught something interesting. Pember slipped his phone into his pocket. The Fedora moved to see the monitor and in doing so, cleared a straighter path for Pember out of the office.

Pember saw his chance, grabbed the boxes, and sprang to the door. He wrenched it open. He glimpsed the panoramic view of the workshop floor. Stairs led down from the mezzanine landing. He grasped the rail and thrust himself to the top step. Running, jumping…down the stairs he flew.

The Fedora was on his tail, closing fast. Pember, now with both feet on ground level, bolted for the main entrance. One of the front double doors opened. A familiar figure with a green anorak pulled over his head crumpled in the doorway and onto the floor. A man dressed in black and slate-grey hurdled over him and ran at Pember.

Pember accelerated. He dodged and weaved. The man's fist connected with his chin. Stars…darkness.

**

Pember sat on the concrete floor. He was propped against the carpet repair table. His arms were behind him and around one of the table legs, his wrists bound together with a cable tie. His jaw throbbed. His ear hissed. His shoulders burned, and cold struck up from the ground. *Did the main payment fail? What is Van d'Ore going to do to me?*

He scanned around. *Is it Clive?* He was similarly tied to the diagonally opposite table leg. His green anorak had been pulled up around his head. *Oh Jeeez, what have they done to him?*

And the artefacts? He remembered hugging the boxes close as he ran. Pember cast around. There was no trace of them. *Van d'Ore must have taken them back!* The mission was a disaster. *And Matt? Has CB had time to send anyone? Will they know to raise the alarm?* The questions burned in Pember's brain. He forced himself to focus, to think in the way he'd been trained. He relived the initial minutes after Matt left the office. He'd heard him stomp down the stairs. But he hadn't heard Matt's Vespa start and drive away. *Would I have been able to even hear it from inside?*

The office door opened. Pember looked up. Van d'Ore stood above on the mezzanine landing and locked eyes with Pember. He walked down the stairs, his tread slow and silent. The Fedora followed.

In a blink, Pember re-lived his leaping dash for freedom. Once again, he saw the workshop from the stairs. There'd been a carpet spread on the table when they'd arrived. But when he'd hurtled down the stairs it had gone. He focused hard. *What exactly did I see?* He concentrated again. *No, the carpet hasn't gone. It's been rolled up and it's lying at one end of the table. Oh no, what's Van d'Ore done to Matt? Is he...could he be inside the carpet?*

Pember twisted his neck to look up at the table. The carpet lay in a bulky roll and in touching distance, if his hands had been free.

'You might well look worried, Mr Yum. Except, I figure you aren't Mr Yum.' Van d'Ore, now at the bottom step, spoke slowly, his voice cut like a flint.

'What? Of course I'm Arthur Yum.'

'Stop lying!' A man dressed like an off-duty commando in black and slate-grey stepped from the shadows of the lobby. 'Your mate over there called you Pember or rather, Pem.'

Hearing his shortened name was a shock. A betrayal. He winced. 'He's not my mate. Not everyone uses their first given name,' Pember countered.

'You're not Mr Arthur *Pember* Yum. We know your face. We've had dealings with you before. This was our trap, and you sure walked into it.' Van d'Ore advanced and stood directly in front of him.

'I've never seen you before, Mr d'Ore.'

'But my associates have seen you, recognised your face. Does 2018 mean anything to you?'

'No. Should it?'

Van d'Ore pointed at Clive. 'Your friend here–'

'He said his name was Cliff when I caught him sneaking around outside,' the man in black and slate-grey said, taking a step closer, 'and *Cliff* said something about CB.'

'What?'

'Cliff, thought I was CB's man out there.'

'CB's man? Who's CB?' Pember asked.

'Stop this farce, Mr Yum. We're wasting time. We need to decide if Oliver Blix is one of CB's men. The look he gave when he left the office, tells me he's working with you.' Van d'Ore glanced first at the Fedora and then at the man in black and slate grey. 'What do you say?'

'Cliff has to be one of CB's men.' The Fedora spoke softly. 'What else could he be? And as for Oliver Blix. He was playing the foil to drive the price down. Does it matter if he's with CB or not? He's seen and heard too much. He is a risk to us. He must be silenced.'

'Cliff hasn't the mettle to be with CB. He's an amateur. I took him out with one hand…twice. Yum and Oliver Blix will be with CB. But…yeah, maybe it's safer to throw Cliff in as well. Make it a round three. He's already seen too much. CB must think us very important to send three operatives.'

'Well, you should know.' Van d'Ore shot a knowing

look at the man dressed in black and slate grey.

What the hell? Pember blinked. *Is the off-duty commando the sellers' double agent spying in CB's camp?*

'One thing's for sure, Mr Arthur *Pember* Yum. You're going to pay with your life for your part in 2018,' Van d'Ore said.

'They're *all* going to die for his part in in 2018,' the Fedora echoed. 'It's how it should end for them.'

'What?' Pember felt nauseated.

'Ahmed, Hawk, get the van. Wrap Cliff and Mr Arthur Pember Yum in carpets. Don't waste expensive ones on them. And take Oliver Blix away with them in the van …tonight.'

Pember started rubbing the cable tie locking mechanism against the sharp edge of the table leg.

***

Clive's world was shrouded in darkness. Voices and words around him, at first disconnected, almost strung themselves into sentences as they drifted into his consciousness.

'For sure…Arthur Pember Yum… Pay with your life… Your part in 2018.'

Clive opened his eyes and blinked. Still darkness. Something covered his face and head. He frowned, and his eyebrows brushed against it. He breathed out through his mouth and sensed it lift a fraction from his lips and cheeks. He stuck his tongue out and felt, no tasted…fabric. And the smell. *Is it my anorak?* He opened his eyes but all he saw was darkness. He tried to move his arms, but they were bound behind his back and this time a stake. *Where am I?* He made to speak and move his legs, but the voice struck up again.

'Ahmed, Hawk, get the van…' He caught the words. 'Wrap Cliff…in carpets…' Now the words had weight and meaning.

Clive froze. He knew the voice. He'd heard it only two days ago. Nothing made sense. Except now he knew there were at least three smugglers in Unit 4. Someone called Ahmed, Hawk from outside, and the voice of a man he'd met on Friday. He felt woozy, sleepy…best stay silent until he'd worked out what was going on.

***

'Argh…cyber hell!' Matt's muffled groan was followed by grunts and puffs.

Matt? He's alive! Relief and pleasure flooded through Pember. The sounds were close. They came from above and behind him. He pictured Matt regaining consciousness, opening his eyes inside a roll of carpet. *The one resting on this end of the table.* He imagined Matt's confusion. The half-light. His panic, his struggle against unyielding layers of carpet tight around his waist. But at least he had a belly on him, the largest circumference of his body and the diameter of the carpet roll. *He's the shape of a spinning top*, Pember thought. It meant Matt's legs by comparison were relatively spindly. He had space around them to move his feet and knees. And from the open head end, air could reach him. He'd be able to breathe. He'd be okay for a while.

Pember glanced around. All clear. For the moment the smugglers were up in the office again, the door ajar. Pember had been counting. He reckoned Ahmed stepped out onto the staging to check on them every fifteen minutes. Pember figured they had about twelve minutes before the next visual check.

'Keep your voice down, Oliver Blix. Are you okay? They rolled you up in a carpet,' Pember hissed.

'What? Then fraggin' unroll me!'

'I can't. You're on the repair table. I'm on the floor, tied to one of its bloody legs.'

'Just get me out of here.' Matt's voice rose.

'Quiet! We're being watched, guarded. Now do what I say. Take five slow breaths and calm down.' He waited almost a minute, 'Now tell me, are your hands or feet tied?'

'What? Oh yeah, me hands...pixel! Yeah...they're trapped behind me back.'

'Feet?'

'I can't see 'em.'

Pember swallowed hard. 'Can you move your feet and ankles independently of each other?' He listened to some rustles and grunts. 'Well?'

'They ain't tied.'

'Good, you can unroll the carpet and free yourself.'

'Ugh... phu... huh!'

'No. Not now. Ahmed checks us every fifteen minutes. You'll need the full fifteen. I'll tell you when it's safe to try.' Pember thought for a few moments. 'Did Van d'Ore knock you out?'

'S'pose he must've. Spammin' malware! Yeah, he were right behind me. Somethin' held over me mouth... Somethin' I breathed. I reckon he drugged me.'

'Keep calm. Five slow breaths. You'll be okay.'

'Yeah. But what 'bout Clive? Can he save us?'

'Don't break our cover. We don't know Clive. Remember? And no, he can't. He's tied to one of the other legs of the repair table. His head's been wrapped in his anorak. Now, take five slow breaths.'

'What?'

'Shhh. Ahmed's coming out to check on us.'

Pember bowed his head and closed his eyes. The cable tie still bound his wrists. He needed time to think, and plan, and keep rubbing its lock mechanism against the sharp edges of the table leg. *Matt is alive. What state is Clive in?*

***

Clive's shoulders ached, his wrists smarted, but he'd heard his friends' voices. Matt and Pember were alive.

Relief stoked the memory of what he'd heard through his semi-consciousness. It returned with the power of an avalanche, striking, pitching, knocking the wind out of him. He took deep breaths. The full depth of the information sank in. *So, Matt's been knocked out by Van d'Ore, his hands are bound behind him, and he's rolled in a carpet on a repair table.* Van d'Ore's words, the voice he recognised, echoed in his mind. *Wrap Cliff...* It felt ominous.

And Pember said he was tied to a table leg. In a flash he pictured the 3D layout. The post hard against his back must be a table leg. Pember was tied to another leg, same table, and up above them on the tabletop was a roll of carpet with Matt inside it. But the flash giving him the 3D layout also evoked an image of Matt, his sedentary lifestyle, and bulky figure. There was no way Matt had the core strength to twist himself into a rolling motion without leverage or a slope.

Clive moved his legs very slowly and gently. No pain, no restriction. If Pember's ankles also hadn't been tied, then maybe... An idea took root.

'Everyone quiet,' Pember hissed. 'Ahmed's doing his rounds.'

***

'All clear,' Pember hissed. 'Ahmed's back in the office again.'

He let his thoughts run. Things were looking bad for them. He was the only one who could see what was going on. *How can I conceive a plan or follow it through while two of my team are effectively blindfolded and one of them's also unconscious...or worse?*

'Anyone got any ideas?' he whispered.

'Yeah, I have,' Clive murmured.

Pember barely believed his ears. 'Are you...okay? 'He twisted to look at Clive. Relief and pleasure surged through him.

'I'm...yeah, I'm okay, but there's something over my head. I can't see.'

'It's your anorak. How long've you been awake?'

'I don't know. I've been drifting in and out. Look, I-I think I know one of the voices...but it doesn't make any sense.'

'Doesn't make sense? Is your head okay? Move your right foot for yes and the left for no.'

Clive moved his right foot.

'Good.'

'Pem, am I tied to the leg next to, or opposite to you?'

'Same table. Opposite leg.'

'Under or against the table?'

'Against.'

'And Matt's rolled up onto your end?'

'Yeah.'

'Then he has to *un*roll towards my end.'

'Yeah.'

'He won't manage it unless it's down a slope.'

'Bugger.'

'If you swivel round so you're sitting under the table, can you stand up, so your back is against the underside of the tabletop? When you straighten your legs fully, you'll lift your corner of the table.'

'And Matt unrolls towards the other end. Matt! Did you catch any of that?' Pember asked in a hissy whisper.

'I thought I were Oliver Blix. What 'bout me cover?'

'Yes, yes, Oliver Blix. Did you get that?'

'Yeah, mate. I mean, Mr Yum.'

In Pember's stressed head, Matt became the raw recruit. For a few seconds, his ear squealed. He began to sweat and hyperventilate. A flashback threatened. He had to get a grip on himself and fast, before he slipped into the abyss. 'Oka-ay,' he whispered, dragging out the word to slow his breathing. *Now count...or talk*. 'Oka-ay,' he whispered again. 'So-o, when you feel me lift this end of the table, you unroll yourself down the slope.'

'Epibotics!'

'Ye-a-h, Something like that.' His tinnitus quietened to a hiss. He hadn't plunged into the flashback. *Just keep my thoughts here, don't drift back, plan an escape*, he told himself. But it was still only half a plan. They all had their hands tied. He rubbed at the cable tie lock again.

'They've used a cable tie on your wrists, Clive. The table legs are four-by-fours, so, there'll be a sharp edge if you rub the cable's locking mechanism against it.' Being wordy helped.

'Hey! Quiet down there!'

Clive moved his right foot.

Pember froze. Ahmed stepped out onto the mezzanine staging and slowly walked down the stairs.

'I heard you talking, Mr Arthur Pember Yum. Have your friends woken up?' Ahmed moved with the grace of a heavyweight boxer and kicked Clive's leg. The counterpart to a vicious jab. 'Hmm, not a sound from Cliff. He's still out of it. So, you must've been talking to Oliver Blix, wrapped up like a sweet here.'

He moved round to Pember, made to kick him, seemed to think better of it and peered into the open end of the carpet roll on the table above Pember's head. Seconds passed. With his eyes still on the gloom inside the roll, Ahmed brought the flat of his hand down on the table with a sudden, resounding *SMACK*. It could have been gunfire.

'Agh!' Matt shrieked.

'So, Mr Oliver Blix, you are awake. What were you saying to your friend sitting on the floor here? Were you plotting an escape?' He swung his arm down and smashed the palm of his hand across Pember's face. It was technically a slap but delivered with the force of a punch.

'*Ugh!*' Pember tried to hide his pain and surprise, but he'd met the likes of Ahmed before. Inscrutable, with extreme views on punishment and retribution. There'd be a deep vein of theological certainty and criminality firing the blood lust. *Keep him talking* Pember thought. 'What are you going to do with us?'

'Mr d'Ore calls it disposal. I think of it as reprisal.'

'But why? What for?'

'With Mr d'Ore it's about the money. For me and my friends, it's about 2018 and those who died.'

'I had nothing to do with you or your friends and whoever died.'

'You and your people must take responsibility for it!'

'What's going on down there? Are you having trouble

285

with them, Ahmed?' Van d'Ore stood in the office doorway.

'I heard them talking, so I came to check on them,' Ahmed answered without turning to look up at Van d'Ore
above.

'Getting restless, are they? Well, the van will be here
soon. Hawk, stay with our guests until their transport arrives.'

***

Clive pressed with all his might and rubbed the cable tie
locking mechanism up and down against his table leg. He
forced the side of the small, plastic, box-shaped lock hard
against the corner edge. The plastic caught and dragged
across the semi sharp angle. He had to distort, squash, or
damage the lock so that the flexible flap inside couldn't
catch on the ratchets. Each up and down movement pulled
and twisted the tie bruising and biting into his wrists. He
had to believe he could release the ratchet locking mechanism. In a few seconds Hawk would be at the bottom of the
stairs, too close to miss any suspicious movement.

*What chance do I have of getting out of here if my hands
are still tied?* It was now or never. He made one last gut-
busting effort as the footsteps grew louder. He pressed 'til
his muscles might rupture and pulled 'til his lungs might
burst. Something yielded. Abruptly the tension released.
The constricting burn on his skin eased. His wrists parted.
He'd broken the ratchet's grip on the tie.

'Okay, Cliff. Let's check on you, shall we?' Hawk said
softly and squatted down to Clive's level.

***

It happened fast.

Pember's cable tie lock broke and his hands came free. He watched Hawk, a large knife in his hand, drop to a squat in front of Clive. Hawk held the tip of the blade to Clive's head, wrapped inside the anorak. It looked murderous.

In one, lithe, swivelling move, Pember turned onto his knees and under the table. 'Now Oliver Blix!' he yelled and stood, pushing up his end of the tabletop with his shoulders and back. Their biker jackets slithered off the table.

'Yiaow!' Matt yodelled as the carpet began to unroll. It gained speed, turning faster, bowling him down the table to Clive's corner. Hawk stood up from his squatting position. Clive clawed the anorak down from his face and sprang forward, driving his shoulder into Hawk's legs and groin. Out of the carpet Matt rolled, a fifteen-stone skittle, un-hampered, free, released like a bowler's spin ball off the edge of the table.

Matt skimmed over Clive's back and thudded into Hawk's chest. They flew a few feet, propelled by Matt's momentum and Clive's shoulder in Hawk's groin. They pounded onto the floor.

'Ugh!' Air escaped from Hawk's mouth as he cushioned Matt's landing. Neither of them moved. Clive wrestled free from the body heap and twisted anorak. He scrambled to his feet. 'Matt are you okay?' he hissed.

Pember let the table down with a crash, and still crouch-ing, dashed from under it. He grabbed the nearest biker jacket. He reckoned its armour and strong fabric would be a lifesaver in a knife attack. From the corner of his eye, he saw Van d'Ore and Ahmed running out of the office.

'Hawk's out of it,' Clive yelled as he made a rapid

search of Hawk's pockets and grabbed the throwing blade from his grip.

'Quick! Get out of here NOW!' Pember shouted. He grabbed Matt by the elbow and heaved.

'Frag n'burn,' Matt groaned as he struggled and failed to stand.

'Head for the fire exit. Hey, get Hawk's phone, Clive!'

'Wait, this'll make it easier.' Clive swung round and sliced through the cable tie binding Matt's wrists. 'The police'll be here soon, it'll be okay, Pem.'

'What? You told the police? You bastard!' His oldest friend had double-crossed him. Anger exploded. Adrenaline surged. The red mist took hold. He'd save this raw recruit. He'd failed to in Iraq, but he'd bloody well succeed in Framlingham, Suffolk. He yanked Matt onto his feet.

Van d'Ore and Ahmed were already down the stairs from the mezzanine floor. Van d'Ore had fanned out to the right. Ahmed hurried to the left sidewall, the one with the fire exit towards the rear of the building.

With a howling shriek, deep in red mist, Pember pulled Matt's arm, towing and tugging as he tore towards the fire exit. Ahmed broke into a run. He was gaining on them despite the long thobe. Pember side-stepped the corralled heating lamps. The jacket protected his free hand as he smashed aside a tall, workbench stool. He sent it spinning on its casters. It careered across Ahmed's path and broke his stride. Pember accelerated. Matt stumbled, now a deadweight dragging on his arm. Pember jerked him up with super-human strength. The door loomed closer, its push-bar, release handle an arm-stretch away. Pember lunged. The bunched-up jacket extended his reach. Ahmed dived at him and collided with Matt. It broke Pember's grip. He was free of the deadweight. Onward momentum propelled Pember into the push-bar. The fire exit door flew open. He catapulted out. Behind him Matt and Ahmed writhed in a heap.

Beyond the rear of the building, Pember glimpsed policemen, partly hidden by the trees. A second glance behind caught Clive leaping over Matt's legs, Van d'Ore in pursuit.

It was a no-brainer. Pember scrambled to his feet and bolted into the undergrowth and trees straight ahead, still holding the biker jacket.

***

Clive ran for his life. Ahead of him, a man in a shirt-like robe floored Matt. The fire door swung open and Pember hurled himself through to the world outside. The man lay on Matt, his arms locked around his chest. Matt thrashed, and flailed, and kicked the air.

'Oh FOAD. You DOS-in' hack!' Matt yelled.

Clive couldn't stop. He leapt over the milieu of legs and skidded to the open doorway. Panting, he turned to face Van d'Ore. He stood, Hawk's throwing knife in his hand and glared at Van d'Ore.

'You? Clive Merry?' Van d'Ore shouted and slowed to a stop. 'What the hell are you doing here?' He made to step round the body heap.

'Stop! Stay where you are, Barner,' Clive barked. 'I've got a knife. I'll use it if you come closer.'

'Oh yeah, Clive? Or you'll do what? Hawk said you aren't a killer. Pathetic, yeah, he called you pathetic.' Van d'Ore took a step closer.

'Stop right there. I didn't get time to tell Hawk I'm an ace at throwing knives. He's the one out cold now. I'm the

289

one with his knife.'

Van d'Ore stood his ground. 'Tell me. Why are you here?'

Clive saw his eyes flick away and focus into the distance, as if he'd seen something through the open fire door. It was the oldest trick in the book, and he wasn't going to fall for it and take his eyes off Van d'Ore. 'No, Phil Barner. You tell me why you're here. How deep are you in?'

Van d'Ore, still looking past Clive's shoulder, opened his mouth to speak and then closed it again without saying a word.

'That old ruse won't work on me,' Clive said softly.

'Armed Police! Down on the ground, arms out straight in front of you! On the ground, NOW!' The voice was loud, the tone rough and harsh. It intimidated, shocked, terrified.

BOOM! A mini explosive blew the locks at the main entrance doors.

Van d'Ore dropped to his knees, lay flat on the ground, and stretched out his arms.

Two policeman grabbed Clive from behind, bending his arms hard behind him. 'Drop the knife,' one of them shouted and forced him to the ground.

Armed police in bulletproof jackets and visored helmets streamed in through the main entrance.

'Thank God. Chakra got my message,' Clive breathed.

'Quiet!' a policeman yelled.

***

Pember kept running. There wasn't time to look back. He needed to put as much distance as he could between himself and the police. He heard the BOOM of the mini explosive, knew the Armed Response Unit vans and police cars would be crowding the carpark where he'd parked his Yamaha Tracer. *How the hell am I going to escape without my bike?*

He still held the bunched-up denim jacket he'd scooped from the workroom floor. *Of course, Matt's biking jacket.* He stopped and slipped it on for size. It was overgenerous in girth and short in the body for him, but otherwise, not a bad fit. And easier to wear than carry. Besides, if he discarded it now, the police would find it when they searched for him. *Best not leave pointers for them.*

He tapped the pockets. He was in luck. The Vespa keys! He could borrow Matt's scooter, parked on the forecourt of *Shout Your Own Style* Unit 12. He pictured the estate's ground plan. He reckoned he could get to the scooter if he stayed hidden by the trees. He'd head beyond the carpark to the units at the back of the estate. The rear service road would bring him round past the shipping containers to the front service road and to *Shout Your Own Style* from the far direction. He'd slip away on Matt's Vespa and into the network of neighbouring lanes. It was a plan. Something to stop him thinking about Matt and the artefacts left behind. And as for Clive, he was the Judas in the team and no better than Hawk.

Pember moved with stealth and at speed. He kept low, skirting the periphery, hurrying past the units on the rear service road. He spotted a narrow animal track between a couple of them. *If I can ride the scooter along it...?* He cut on between the shipping containers. From there he sneaked onto the *Shout Your Style* forecourt, unlocked Matt's Vespa, and slipped the keys into the ignition. The main entrance road would be swarming with police. He knew he couldn't escape by outrunning them through the main exit.

He pushed the scooter off its stand and wheeled it to between the containers. It burst into life with the first press of the starter. He quietened back the revs, and sitting on the scooter, eased away from the containers. He coasted back to the rear service road. He pulled off the tarmac and carefully followed the rough animal track threading between two of the units. It felt like forever, but eventually he reached a gap in the perimeter fence. There was a footpath tracing the edge of the field beyond. With a foot on the ground, and a bit of a push, he was through the gap in the fence. The earth was rutty, but he rode with care and joined the footpath. After two-hundred yards, he reached one of the lanes criss-crossing the countryside beyond the estate. He had escaped. What's more, he had a pair of wheels and was wearing Matt's biker jacket and helmet from the Vespa's top box.

Pember considered his options. *Should I keep running?* He didn't know, but he guessed a life on the run would be safer and longer if he had some insurance. It would mean returning to Hatter Street and his office to retrieve the pen drive from its hiding place in the filing cabinet, and his SIG Sauer wrapped in oil cloth under some tiles on the roof.

He headed for Bury St Edmunds but with every mile he rode, his heart grew heavier. He should have been riding to the Midlands and away from East Anglia and the reach of the Kanes, or to Europe and putting the Channel between him and the long arm of the UK police. But he knew better than to over-analyse. It would lead to indecision, delay, and capture. He rode on and kept his mind focused on the road.

He parked the Vespa on a residential street, away from security and traffic cameras. More importantly it was on the opposite side of town to the Raingate Police Station. He hurried across the Parkway dual carriageway, through the Buttermarket, and to Hatter Street. He turned the collar of

Matt's denim jacket up high and tucked his chin down low inside. It was quiet in the town, late on a Sunday afternoon, and he slipped unseen through the front door and into the lobby area.

'Psst!' The sound was soft, the voice familiar.

'Dove?' he whispered.

'Mr Quinn! What are you doing here?' She stood in the shadows, close to the bottom of the staircase. A pink head-scarf was draped loosely over her head and wrapped freely onto her shoulders.

'It's Sunday, Dove. What are you doing here?'

She held an aluminium pipe with a vacuum cleaner head, the hosing trailing to the body of the machine behind her. It was plugged in but not switched on. 'The Police have searched your offices. They've taken…'

'My computer? My files?'

'Yes, and now the stairs need cleaning.'

'Did they take furniture…my filing cabinets?'

'No, Mr Quinn. They say you killed a woman. They caught you, and you ran away.'

'I haven't killed a woman. I've been set up. Framed.'

She nodded slowly. 'You seem like a good man, but…'

'But what?'

'Good men can do bad things.'

'I didn't kill the woman. I found her, but she was al-ready dead. Please believe me.'

'They've stuck tape across your office doors. *Police Keep Out* tape. They'll know if you enter your rooms, Mr Quinn. They'll know you've come back here.'

'But–'

'Your face…have the police beaten you?'

'No, but some bad men tried to kill me.'

She frowned. 'Your face is hurt. People will see it. But…no one will look in my cupboard. You'll be safe until the morning.' She opened the door to the space behind the stairs. It was the storage area for her cleaning materials and equipment, and the way through to a back door.

'Are you going to lock me in while you call the police?'

'No, Mr Quinn. I have an electric kettle. I will make a cup of tea.'

He smiled. 'Thank you, Dove. But I can't stay. I must leave as soon as it's dark.'

'I will clean the stairs quickly, then I will make tea.'

He lay on the floor in the store area while the vacuum cleaner hummed up the stairs. He let his mind go blank, breathed slowly, and tried to think through a plan. If the police hadn't taken the filing cabinets, then the pen drive would still be safe in its hiding place. There was no need for him to get into his rooms. Fifteen minutes later, Dove opened the door and packed away the vacuum cleaner.

'Now, Mr Quinn, I will make tea.' She switched on the kettle. 'Why do the police frame you?' she asked when the tea was made, and he sat sipping the soothing brew.

'No, it's a gang in Norwich. They're trying to set me up and discredit me. I'm a key witness against them. The case comes to court soon.'

'So, the gang framed you, Mr Quinn. Do they control the policemen?'

'I don't know.'

'When I worked in the Consul Offices, I had to know who I can trust. Who do you trust, Mr Quinn?'

'Hah! I thought my oldest friend. But he betrayed me.'

'But when? And why?'

'Today.'

She sipped her tea silently, as if waiting for him to say more.

'Okay, if you must know, he said he'd look out for me, and then tipped off the police. They knew where I was, and they came to arrest me. I'd be behind bars by now if I hadn't run. I should've realised he'd double cross me. He was a policeman himself.'

'We all must know who we can trust, Mr Quinn. Even your oldest friend knows. If some of your police are owned by this gang, then maybe he told a policeman who is clean.'

'Hah!'

'And why? Why did he double cross you. Has the gang also paid him?'

'No, of course not.' Pember surprised himself with the speed and certainty of his answer. But she was right. He hadn't asked himself why Clive had behaved like a Judas. 'We were both in danger. He wanted to save his own skin. I was there, I was collateral,' he murmured, voicing his thoughts.

'Were you in danger from the gang when the police came? Were they the bad men who beat you?'

'Yeah, they were going to kill us both and the raw recruit.'

'And a raw recruit? But only you escaped from these bad men and the police, and now you are on the run. Who will help you now?'

He didn't answer. He knew CB's team had been infiltrated. Nowhere was safe.

'The tall man who works with you here, is he the Judas friend?'

'How did you guess? Is it that obvious? You know he called the police after the break in?'

'Somebody had to. But he doesn't look at you like a be-trayer would. His eyes don't tell that story. If he isn't with the gang and he knows which policeman to trust…then *you* can trust that policeman too. If you didn't kill the woman, the good policeman he believes in will find the real evidence. You will be cleared. You keep your life. Believe me, when you are forced to leave your home and country, you lose part of yourself. It is difficult to settle, to be you…*really* you again.'

'You think I should turn myself in?'

'I can't tell you what to do. It is not my place.'

'But you think I should trust this Judas friend.'

'What you say about your friend does not sound like what you call a Judas. If you respect your friend's decision on who to trust, then you should turn yourself in to the po-liceman *he* trusts. If you want to be a witness and take down the gang, then you must clear your name.'

Pember nodded slowly. 'It sounds risky.'

'Going on the run is risky. I'll make another cup of tea for you, but then I must go home. Let yourself out when you are ready. Mr Quinn, you're a good man. You will do the right thing.'

***

Clive sat with a blanket around his shoulders in the Bury St Edmunds Police Investigation Centre. The modern, red-brick building was situated on River Lane, close to the Rougham Road and A14 junction, on the east side of the town. He had been examined by the police surgeon, his clothes bagged for forensics, and Chakra had finished inter-viewing him. It only remained for him to give his statement and for Chrissie to arrive with some fresh clothes and take him home.

'Are you being absolutely straight with me when you say you have no idea where Pember Quinn is?' Chakra asked. Clive thought his old colleague looked weary, worn down by the complexity of it all.

'He can't have gone far. You said his Yamaha Tracer was still in the carpark. And the dogs tracked him to…you said, across the forecourts of most of the units but no further?'

'If he contacts you, can I trust you to let me know?'

'Only if you promise to deal with him yourself and don't hand him to your heavies.' Privately, Clive doubted Pember would contact him. Hadn't his last words been on the lines of *traitor* and *bastard*?

Chakra nodded. 'And you're absolutely certain the man calling himself Van d'Ore also goes under the name of Phil Barner, the surviving diver in the fatal accident at the chalk quarry?'

'Yes, I think he trades in antiquities and artefacts, and I guess from today they aren't always legal. He's ruthless. He was going to get his henchmen to kill us. It'll all be about money. Will you be able to hold him?'

'He'll be charged with abduction, assault, and unlawful imprisonment. It's enough to be getting on with. The Art & Antiquities Unit are interviewing him and Ahmed.'

'Ha, Phil aka Van d'Ore is the only one who *didn't* hit or kick me. Did Hawk come round eventually?'

'Hmm…we had to release him.'

'What?'

'We still have an interest in him. But it seems he's with the Art & Antiquities Unit. Their people collected him.'

'What? But he was one of the smugglers and sellers.

He's their spy. He's–'

'He's not the only one of you connected to the Arts & Antiquities Unit. They wanted to interview Pember as well, but we don't have him. They certainly wanted the artefacts he was supposedly buying, but they'll have to wait for them. At least until we've completed the forensics and photographing them. And they've only given me an hour or so longer with Van d'Ore. Then they're moving him to an investigation centre in the Metropolitan catchment.'

There was a knock, and a policeman poked his head round the door. 'Mrs Jax is in reception for Mr Merry, here. Do you want me to show her in?' Clive imagined the words were code for *I can't stop her. She's very insistent.*

Chrissie arrived with a flurry of questions and a carrier bag of clothes.

'Clive!' she said rushing to him. She flung her arms around him and kissed him. 'Thank God you're all right. I've been so worried. I won't say I told you so, but…' She turned to Chakra, 'I said they'd be thugs. I told him not to go. But he wouldn't listen. He even refused to tell me where the meeting was. If I'd known…'

'Do you have my number, Mrs Jax?'

She shook her head. 'No.'

'If you see Pember Quinn or he contacts you, ring me.' He handed her a card with his number.

'Is he still missing? And Matt? Is he okay? He's not answering his phone.'

'Mr Finch is with the police surgeon and forensics. He's having a full toxicology and forensics screen.'

Clive caught her frown. It was time to explain, 'Matt was drugged and rolled up in a carpet. No, no; it's fine. I mean it isn't fine, but he's okay. The police need evidence to link him and the carpet.'

'What? They think he's lying?'

'No, Mrs Jax, we believe him. It's just that we need hard evidence to nail these smugglers in court.' Chakra's weary tone made it clear this was the end of the matter. No more questions would be answered. 'So, if you'll come with me, Mrs Jax, I'll take you back to the waiting area while Clive makes his statement.'

**

Pember decided the idea of handing himself over to the police might not be such a crazy plan after all. But only if he could trust their integrity. He figured he had some protection in the copies he'd made of his own CCTV and car-tracking records. So, if he was going to hand himself in, he might as well do it now rather than wait until the morning. It might even gain him some brownie points. But first he had to make a call to smooth the path and maximise his chances.

He watched Dove rustle up another mug of tea. She'd be leaving in a moment to go home. 'Dove, would you do one more thing for me?' he asked.

She looked at him, her face expressionless, calm.

'Please could you lend me your phone? I've lost mine. The smugglers, the men who tied me up took it. I need to call...'

'Someone you trust?'

'Yeah.' He considered his options. Firstly, there was Clive, but Pember wasn't ready to talk to Clive yet and anyway, the smugglers would have taken his phone. Then there was Chakra, admittedly a policeman, but one he could speak to directly, and Clive trusted him. Last on his list was

CB. He took orders from her. *But do I trust her? Could she have set me up as the fall guy for Hawk's infiltration into the smugglers?* Cold logic and military training told him to choose CB, a former superior officer. But something didn't feel right.

Dove's words came back to him. She had touched on something deeper. She'd spoken from experience and her heart. Trust wasn't based on logic alone. Loyalties and gut instinct came into it as well.

'Yeah,' he said. His pulse thumped in his ear; his tinnitus squealed. 'I'll call DS Chakra McLaren, the policeman my friend trusts.'

'No, Mr Quinn!'

'What? You don't think I can trust him?'

'No, Mr Quinn. You can't use my phone to call the police. They will trace the call back to me. I will be incriminated, accused. I could be deported. You ask too much.'

'Okay, okay. You call Chakra McLaren and report me. Tell him you came upon me here. It's true. Tell him you've persuaded me to hand myself in. It's what happened. No one's lying.'

She nodded slowly. 'Do you have the number?'

***

It had taken Clive another twenty minutes to complete his statement. When he walked from the interview suites to meet Chrissie in reception, he heard the heavy tread of a quartet of policemen and recognised a distant voice. *Pember?* The last time he'd seen him, Pember was hare-tailing it out of the fire exit. Clive hurried towards reception, hoping to catch sight of him, but the footsteps had disappeared.

'Did you see Pember?' he asked Chrissie.

'I caught a fleeting glimpse. He looked tired and I think I saw a red mark across his cheek. Do you think he's okay?'

'I don't know.' But Clive guessed things might go badly for his old friend. Being set up and framed was disorientating, frightening, and enough to make anyone question their sanity. He imagined Pember would react with anger. Things had never gone well when he lost his temper. Always the short fuse.

'You look worried,' Chrissie whispered and kissed him.

'Then I must be. Come on, let's go home.' He slipped an arm around her waist.

***

Pember had calmed a little by the time he'd seen the police surgeon and been swabbed and photographed for forensics. He sat waiting in the interview room, with its two-way mirror, CCTV camera, recording equipment, table, and utilitarian chairs. He knew they were trying to unnerve him and felt vindicated for requesting legal representation.

Fifteen minutes passed before Chakra entered with a young detective constable.

'Good evening, Mr Quinn. This is DC Advent. While we're waiting for your legal representative, I'd like to ask you about an incident this afternoon at the Purple Blue Business Estate near Framlingham. You, along with two other people, were assaulted and unlawfully imprisoned. You aren't a suspect...more of a victim. So, please will you tell us what happened? We'll need a statement.'

'Hmm...okay,' Pember said slowly. At least he had witnesses who could say he'd been the victim of the smugglers, not a perpetrator.

'So, why did you visit Unit 4 on the Purple Blue Business Estate and what happened there this afternoon?'

Pember ran through the bare bones of the afternoon, being careful to obfuscate his link with CB, and by extension, the Arts & Antiquities Unit.

When he'd finished speaking, Chakra frowned, put his elbows on the table separating them, and clasping his hands together, said, 'I'm puzzled, Mr Quinn. Why haven't you mentioned the Arts & Antiquities Unit? They've taken a keen interest in you and this incident. In fact, they've asked to interview you.'

'Really?' Pember was surprised. Hawk must've spoken to CB, because he hadn't.

'I know you're interested in gold sovereigns, porcelain, and the international smuggling rings of 2018.'

Pember raised his eyebrows.

'Mr Quinn, most of the contents of your filling cabinets were strewn on the floor when I attended your office break-in, only Thursday morning.'

'Ha, I knew you'd been bloody snooping. You won't have had time yet to go through all you took from my office today! Oh, and copies of my CCTV and car tracker files are with my solicitor. Insurance in case you lose them.' Pember's voice rose as anger threatened to take hold.

Chakra stood slowly. 'Right Mr Quinn, shall we stop there for the moment? I'll leave you with DC Advent. He'll take your statement about this afternoon's incident.'

DC Advent was fast and efficient, and Pember kept his statement clear-cut, avoiding unnecessary detail. But once the DC had left the interview room, Pember was plunged into the waiting game again.

He was irritated, but reckoned it was what the police intended. *Have they forgotten I was in the RMP? Ha, the psy-*

chological aspects of interrogation! He concentrated on clearing the noise in his head and quelling his anger.

Swoosh, the door opened and in filed Chakra, DC Advent, and a young man who looked little older than a child. He was dressed in smart jeans and a collarless linen shirt. 'Your legal representative is here,' Chakra announced.

'Hi, I'm Dennison Lowse. I'm your legal on tonight's rota.' He smiled, as if to lighten the seriousness of the situation and revealed a full railroad of orthodontic, silver wires running between tension plates stuck to his front teeth.

'Hi,' Pember said, weariness descending.

'Right, let's get on with this, can we?' They all took their seats at the table. Chakra opened a folder. DC Advent read Pember his rights and informed him the interview was being recorded. He switched on the recording equipment and said the names of all present, the time and date.

'Mr Quinn,' Chakra opened, 'how well do you know Paul Smith?'

'I never met him before Monday, six days ago.'

'Tell me what you know about him.'

Pember tried not to frown, but the question seemed less a trick and more genuinely wanting to know. 'Ah, you've discovered Paul Smith isn't his real name, haven't you?'

'I'll ask the questions, Mr Quinn.'

'Okay, he told me his real name was Idris Brafman and he was the registered owner of a white Fiat Panda hatchback, the car his wife Veronica Smith drove. But you'll know this by now.'

Chakra nodded slowly.

'And you'll have discovered that Idris Brafman was a seventy-six-year-old man and died in January, this year.'

'Yes, we'd got that far, Mr Quinn.'

'And I guess you've taken Paul Smith's fingerprints to exclude him from the other prints on the car. Have you found a match for his prints on your database?'

'As I said, I'll ask the questions.' There was something about the way Chakra looked away.

Ha, Pember thought, *the jokers haven't taken his dabs yet*. 'Has Paul Smith disappeared? Done a runner?' he asked on impulse.

Chakra didn't answer. Instead, he said, 'You put a tracker on his car, Mr Quinn. Can you tell me it's make and number?'

Pember toyed with being unhelpful, caught the glint in Chakra's eyes and decided to appear reasonable, cooperative. 'I put a tracker on the car he was driving...a Honda Jazz hybrid. Grey. But he took it off and left it on a drain cover. The registration number'll be on my tracker app.'

He looked at Dennison Lowse, 'Is it correct that the police can use leads I give, but illegal data sources, or information obtained illegally...like my tracker on Paul Smith's car, may be inadmissible in court?'

'There is a difference between using information to investigate a suspect or a crime, and what is admissible as evidence in court,' the young solicitor said.

'Okay, I'll tell you what I've learned about Paul Smith.' He glanced at the solicitor who shrugged. 'Paul Smith,' he continued, 'has used previous aliases - Dave Jones, John Williams, and James Brown. He may have used more. As Dave Jones, he breached a restraining order in 2018. It may have been against Idris Brafman, but your team will be able to legally access the records. I'm just giving you a pointer.'

'And why would Idris Brafman need the protection of a restraining order? It's a little farfetched,' Chakra said.

'I don't know. Ask Clive about who holds the deeds to Idris' house. And his funeral donations were for a racehorse sanctuary in Newmarket, which I don't think exists. That's pretty much all I know about him. Oh, and he'll be *sadly missed* by his great-niece Veronica Smith, née Brafman. Except Veronica Brafman died as a baby in 1993.'

Chakra frowned. 'You seem to know a lot about Paul Smith, someone you say you only met for the first time six days ago. It sounds like your association goes back further.'

Pember had been expecting this. 'No, I've been based in Norwich for years. I've been in Bury for less than a couple of weeks. As you know, I'm…well, I'm a witness in a case coming up against the Kanes, a Norwich gang. The other witness died unexpectedly in jail this week. Convenient for the Kanes, wouldn't you say?'

'Just answer my question.'

'Paul Smith is based around here. Our paths never crossed until he contacted me. I met him for the first time on Monday.'

'I reckon he contacted you because he already knew you,' Chakra said and slowly nodded his head.

'He couldn't have. We'd never met before. But the Kanes will have been looking for someone like him. A contract killer without known links to Norwich. You see, because of what he's done to implicate me in Veronica's murder…if I go down for it, then I won't be a credible witness against the Kanes, will I, Mr Lowse?'

'Possibly not.' The young solicitor shook his head.

'Why not just kill you?' DC Advent asked.

'While in jail? Implicating me is cleverer. It keeps the Kanes out of it. Killing Veronica Smith and framing me discredits me as a witness and gets me banged up in jail, but

Paul Smith also gets rid of Veronica.'

'Why? What's Paul Smith's motive for killing his wife?' Chakra asked.

'A falling out among thieves.'

'Falling out over what, Mr Quinn?'

'You'd have to ask Paul Smith, but I doubt you'd get a straight answer. I even wonder if he knows his wife's real identity. You'll be able to find it if you contact the Czech Republic National Law Enforcement Agency. She has a criminal record there. Her mug shot is on their records.'

'Do you investigate all your clients this thoroughly, Mr Quinn?' Chakra asked.

'If their stories don't add up. Have you found Veronica Smith's camera yet? I've a shot of her taking photographs with it around Newmarket yesterday, mid-afternoon. It's on my phone…but you've got my phone.'

Chakra exchanged a resigned look with the DC and nodded.

'Interview with Pember Quinn is being terminated at,' he checked the time, 'nineteen hundred hours.' He switched off the recording.

'Are you charging Mr Quinn, or will you be releasing him?' Dennison Lowse asked.

'I'll hold him a little longer. He can sample one of our cells overnight, while we check his prints against the car.'

THURSDAY
ONE WEEK LATER

It was early Thursday afternoon when Clive got a call from Chrissie. As planned the previous week, she'd left her TR7 at the garage for a service first thing that morning. He'd driven behind her to the drop off and then given her a lift to her carpentry workshop at the old barn near the Wattisham Airfield.

'They've found why my car is overheating,' she said.

He guessed from her tone she was calling to share the pain of bad news. 'What did they find?' An image of the 1981 yellow car flashed through his mind.

'The cooling lines inside the radiator have blocked. They thought it might be the thermostat, but no, nothing as straightforward.'

'Is it the original radiator?'

'Yes. So, either they source a replacement or re-core my old one.'

'Ouch, it sounds expensive.' He tried to sound sympathetic, but really, what did she expect from a forty-plus-year-old car? 'How long will it take?'

'It'll be faster if they replace it. I suppose…maybe sometime next week. Can you pick me up from work, please?'

'Yes, of course. I've something to check with Matt, so I'm at Utterly Academy 'til well after three o'clock. Is four at the workshop okay for you? I'm meeting Chakra around five.'

'Yes, you said about Chakra this morning. If it's in Bury, can I come too? I've something I want to talk to him about.'

Clive tried to keep the frown out of his voice, 'Yes, sure.' He was too curious to say no.

'Jason is using the van at the moment, otherwise I could have driven myself home.'

'But you'll be able to use it next week?'

'Yes, I expect so.'

'But not today. Okay, see you at four. Bye.' He smiled, but he couldn't help thinking how Jason using the carpentry workshop van was suspiciously convenient as an excuse for her to go with him to see Chakra.

***

Chakra slipped onto the backseat and closed the Lexus door almost silently.

'Why all the secrecy?' Clive asked, gazing across the carpark. There was a large garden centre a stone's throw away, barely fifty yards from the Bury St Edmunds Investigation Centre along the main road. He twisted his neck to look at Chakra, as if to drive home his question.

'Things are getting sensitive.' He nodded and smiled at Chrissie in the front passenger seat. 'Hello, Mrs Jax. I wasn't expecting you to be here.'

'I know, but I've something for you about another case and I don't want any hint of it being traced back to me.'

Clive felt confused, hurt. *Why couldn't she have given it to me to pass on? Doesn't she trust me to be discreet?*

Chakra must have read his face. 'Yeah, you can stop worrying. Pember Quinn is in the clear.'

'Thank God,' he breathed. 'I knew you'd got Paul Smith. It was on the local news on Tuesday.'

'More importantly we got the Honda Jazz he was driving. Tyre marks at the scene and soil in the tread and on the bodywork...preliminary checks can link the car to the field where Veronica Smith was found.'

'Anything else to place him there?' Clive asked. 'Soil could be circumstantial.'

'The clingfilm, as Pember Quinn called it, constricting Veronica Smith's face turns out to be pallet stretch wrap.'

'How does that...what's the significance?' Chrissie asked.

'It's made of polythene, not low-density polyethylene. So, it's stronger. It has different properties to your kitchen clingfilm. Far more suitable to wrap tightly around your victim's head. And, *if* it comes on an extended core there's something to hold like a handle when you unroll it. That's how he'd have pulled it tight and stretched it over irregular surfaces. It'll grip everything as you wind it round.'

'Like his wife's face, neck and chin,' Chrissie whispered.

'Did she put up a fight?'

'Yes, sir...I mean, Clive. There were traces of blood under her fingernails. We're waiting for DNA.'

'What if Paul Smith says they were into S & M the night before? With his background, a jury would likely believe him.' Clive tried to keep the scorn out of his voice.

'We found a fresh scratch on his neck. He must have pulled hard to control her. Any straining and he might have bled. Traces on the stretch wrap are all we need to nail him. We're waiting on the lab to check for any.'

'But there has to be a purchase or manufacturer's trail on the stretch wrap,' Chrissie said.

'We've found rolls of it at their house. Probably from when they moved in. It looks similar, complete with extended cores. The lab techs are checking it.'

'Their house? You've checked the land registry. Poor old Idris Brafman. Did you find a Dick Turpin, Doulton Character Jug?'

'No, and no evidence of Pember selling them one. Paul Smith accused him, and I only said we had it to rattle Pember. Okay, I've told you my news. What've you got for me?'

Chrissie glanced at Clive. 'You go first,' he said.

'Morton Alconbury, the man who died on the dive with Phil Barner,' she said, a little breathlessly.

'Phil Barner, aka Van d'Ore?' Chakra asked.

'Yes. I think you should request information from HMRC about Morton Alconbury. They're investigating his finances. Probate is held up because of it. And it struck me that what they're investigating might have had a connection with Phil Barner and could have been a motive for…Phil silencing Morton.'

'I'm sorry, Mrs Jax. But the diving accident is with the coroner.'

Her cheeks flushed.

'I think she's saying, Chakra, a police request now would get the HMRC information in time for the coroner's inquest. And it is legal evidence if it's come via your request.'

Clive caught Chrissie's barely perceptible nod. He smiled and forged on, 'Which brings me to what I wanted to tell you. I spent some time this afternoon with my IT expert Matt.'

'Matt Finch? Aka Oliver Blix? How is he now?'

'He's pretty good. Remarkably unphased by being drugged and rolled in a carpet.'

'Yes,' Chrissie chipped in, 'on Monday he said something about having felt like Rug Raider, a comic-strip hero of disguise and surprise. But he's always been into comic-strip heroes. It's his way of coping. He sounded good when I rang him yesterday, thank God. Didn't say anything about Rug Raider, seemed more worried about getting his scooter back.'

'Same as this afternoon. He didn't want to talk about being rolled in a rug. Remembers it but seemed more upset by Pember borrowing his scooter.'

'Hmm, I asked him if he wanted us to charge Mr Quinn with theft. But as Mr Quinn had told us where he'd left it, and we'd recovered it undamaged, Mr Finch said no, because he wanted it back ASAP.'

'What? You'd have kept it as evidence?'

'It's okay, Chrissie. It's…it's just police process.'

'Right, sir. What were you going to tell me?'

'There's an ancient, stone, water serpent figure in the Alconburys' ornamental garden pond. I showed Matt a photo and he's identified it as a likely match to an ancient artefact stolen from a Greek collection in Athens. The figure is from the Mycenaean era, that's over three thousand years old. It's thought to have originated in Hydra.'

'Hydra?' Chrissie looked surprised.

'Yes, they've lots of freshwater springs. Back then it was a watering point for boats.'

'It sounds priceless,' Chrissie murmured. 'I wonder what it was valued at in his assets, or even if at all. It smacks of Phil Barner supplying it.'

'I think the Arts & Antiquities Unit are best to follow up on it. I'll pass it to them. Okay? Oh, and while I remember, after your tipoff, Clive, we sent all of Phil Barner's diving equipment, including his air compressor, to the insurance company's dive specialist investigator. They'll report to the coroner. Mrs Alconbury's solicitor has contacted the specialist. She's paying for some extra tests.'

'You seized it when you searched his property last week?'

'Don't remind me. We'd already arrested Phil Barner before the Arts & Antiquities Unit arrived and took him away. We had the paperwork for a search warrant but...they led the search of his property. One of my constables managed to be present. What are they looking for in the dive compressor?'

'Particulate matter from a diesel car exhaust, as suggested by those photos of the air inlet hose. And...don't let anyone know the tipoff about Mrs Alconbury's Mycenaean artefact water feature came from me.'

'No problem, you're one of my sources now!'

He began to open the car door.

'Thanks, Chakra.'

'It's okay sir, I haven't done anything except follow the evidence.'

'No, you've done a lot more than that. I've always believed Pember couldn't have done it, but it's good to have proof.'

'Are you dropping the charges?' Chrissie asked.

'Don't worry, he'll be out with you soon.'

THURSDAY
A FURTHER WEEK LATER

Another week had passed and Clive and Pember were in the Hatter Street office setting up a new, desktop monitor and computer.

'It's good to be back,' Pember said and grinned at his old friend. He was on a high. The pendulum had swung back from the low of his arrest for murder. 'Has Chakra got to the bottom of Veronica Smith taking photos in Newmarket?'

'Some kind of Ponzi scheme selling shares in fake racehorses, I heard.' Clive said and frowned at a USB port and connector.

'I knew she was up to no bloody good. Hey, good news. Mrs Alconbury paid her account.'

'Great! She phoned to tell me the dive compressor's been examined. They found microscopic soot particles with...' Clive scrolled through his phone. 'Yes, PAHs. That's polycyclic aromatic hydrocarbons. It's consistent with the compressor inlet hose being close to the diesel car exhaust, so less oxygen in the air. She's asking for another post-mortem to re-examine the lungs and look for PAHs.'

'So, you were right! Phil Barner *was* bloody trying to kill Morton Alconbury! Don't you just love this job?'

'Yeah sure, Pem.' He sighed. 'But there's something I need to know if I'm going to stick around.'

'What d'you mean, *if* you're going to stick around? Are you leaving?' He felt a sudden chasm open in front of him. He hadn't expected Clive to hint about leaving, or an overture to saying goodbye. Not today, and certainly not after all they'd been through in the past two and a half weeks. It almost winded him.

Clive sounded serious, 'Is there anything else I need to know, Pem? More skeletons in the cupboard? Are there things you should tell me? More secrets from your past coming back to bite you…like the ones you've already sprung on me?'

'No. No bloody way,' Pember said and meant it.

'Look, I must be able to trust you. It's a two-way thing if we're going to be working together as partners in a PIA. You of all people should understand. After all, you've a problem trusting people.'

'I've told you everything. No more secrets' His right ear started to hiss. *Did the SIG Sauer P226 count?*

'And what about CB? Is that still a secret? Still off-limits?'

'To the rest of the world…but not you.' He frowned and pretended to fiddle with the monitor.

It had been painful for Pember when he was told that Hawk had been placed to infiltrate the smuggling ring. 'Why the hell didn't you tell me before the mission?' he'd asked when the Arts & Antiquities Unit collected him for debriefing after Chakra dropped the murder charges. CB had been there for one of the sessions.

'Think of our work like espionage,' CB had said. 'We don't want our players to know the complete picture. It's for their own safety. They can't give away information they don't have. Remember, we're dealing with international terrorists. They're sociopaths, lawless, ruthless.'

'But you didn't trust me, did you?' he'd breathed.

'I trusted you to do the right thing. And you did. I've always trusted you to do the right thing. Access to information is different. You should understand that. You served in the RMP.'

He pulled himself back to the here and now, and the office. 'Look Clive, for the record, I trust you and, yeah, I know what it's like when people don't tell you things.'

'Oh yes?'

'Yeah, like CB's still as secretive as hell.'

'And Matt and his scooter? Are you going to tell me how you're going to square that with him?'

'Ah…that's going to cost me–'

Brring Brring! The desk phone burst into life. Pember picked up. 'Hello. Hatter Street Private Investigation Agency. How can I help?'

'Is that the one in Hatter Street, Bury St Edmunds?'

'Yes. How can I help you?'

'I'm phoning from Cable and Crank, solicitors in Diss. You've been recommended by some colleagues regarding your work related to a recent SCUBA diving accident investigation.'

'We're not specialist diving investigators.'

'I know, but by all accounts, you are reliable investigators, reasonably priced, and you get results. We may have a case for you.'

Pember pressed *speaker* mode. 'Go on.'

'We have a client who's been contacted by a hitherto unknown relative who says they have claims to pieces of our client's jewellery. Are you interested?'

Pember looked at Clive.

Clive nodded.

'Yeah. Tell us more.'

The End

Also by Pauline Manders

The Utterly Crime Series

PAULINE MANDERS

Pauline Manders was born in London and trained as a doctor at University College Hospital, London. Having gained her surgical qualifications, she moved with her husband and young family to East Anglia, where she worked in the NHS as an ENT Consultant Surgeon for over 25 years. She used her maiden name throughout her medical career and retired from medicine in 2010.

Retirement has given her time to write crime fiction, become an active member of a local carpentry group, and share her husband's interest in classic cars. She lives deep in the Suffolk countryside.

ACKNOWLEDGMENTS

My thanks to: Beth Wood for her positive advice, support and encouragement; Pat McHugh, my mentor and hard-working editor with a keen sense of humour, mastery of atmosphere and grasp of characters; David Withnall for his proof-reading skills; A J Deane for his editing help; the Royal Military Police Museum and Richard Callaghan for their advice and information; various SCUBA divers who didn't wish to be mentioned – you know who you are, thank you for your advice about equipment and diving; the Write Now! Bury writers' group for their support; my husband and family, on both sides of the Atlantic, for their love and support.

Printed in Great Britain
by Amazon

43073017R00178